W9-CAT-418

PHILIPPA

Books by Bertrice Small

The Kadin
Love Wild and Fair
Adora
Unconquered
Beloved
Enchantress Mine
Blaze Wyndham
The Spitfire
A Moment in Time
To Love Again
Love, Remember Me
The Love Slave
Hellion
Betrayed
Deceived
The Innocent
A Memory of Love
The Dutchess
The Dragon Lord's Daughters
Private Pleasures

THE O'MALLEY SAGA

Skye O'Malley
All the Sweet Tomorrows
A Love for All Time
This Heart of Mine
Lost Love Found
Wild Jasmine

SKYE'S LEGACY

Darling Jasmine
Bedazzled
Beseiged
Intrigued
Just Beyond Tomorrow
Vixens

THE FRIARSGATE INHERITANCE
Rosamund
Until You
Philippa

ANTHOLOGIES

Captivated
Fascinated
Delighted
I Love Rogues

BERTRICE SMALL

PHILIPPA

NEW AMERICAN LIBRARY

New American Library
Published by New American Library, a division of
Penguin Group (USA) Inc., 375 Hudson Street,
New York, New York 10014, USA
Penguin Group (Canada), 10 Alcorn Avenue, Toronto,
Ontario, Canada M4V 3B2 (a division of Pearson Penguin Canada Inc.)
Penguin Books Ltd, 80 Strand, London WC2R 0RL, England
Penguin Ireland, 25 St. Stephen's Green, Dublin 2,
Ireland (a division of Penguin Books Ltd)
Penguin Group (Australia), 250 Camberwell Road, Camberwell, Victoria 3124,
Australia (a division of Pearson Australia Group Pty Ltd)
Penguin Books India Pvt Ltd, 11 Community Centre, Panchsheel Park,
New Delhi - 110 017, India
Penguin Group (NZ), Cnr Airborne and Rosedale Roads, Albany,
Auckland 1310, New Zealand (a division of Pearson New Zealand Ltd)
Penguin Books (South Africa) (Pty) Ltd, 24 Sturdee Avenue,
Rosebank, Johannesburg 2196, South Africa

Penguin Books Ltd, Registered Offices:
80 Strand, London WC2R 0RL, England

First published by New American Library,
a division of Penguin Group (USA) Inc.

First Printing, October 2004
10 9 8 7 6 5 4 3 2 1

Copyright © Bertrice Small, 2004
All rights reserved

 REGISTERED TRADEMARK—MARCA REGISTRADA

LIBRARY OF CONGRESS CATALOGING-IN-PUBLICATION DATA:

Small, Bertrice.
  Philippa / Bertrice Small.
    p. cm.
  ISBN 0-451-21299-1 (trade pbk.)
  1. Great Britain—History—Henry VIII, 1509–1547—Fiction. 2. Great Britain—Court and courtiers—Fiction.
  3. Attempted assassination—Fiction. I. Title.
  PS3569.M28P48 2004
  813'.54—dc22

                          2004009315

Set in Goudy
Designed by Leonard Telesca

Printed in the United States of America

Without limiting the rights under copyright reserved above, no part of this publication may be reproduced, stored in or introduced into a retrieval system, or transmitted, in any form, or by any means (electronic, mechanical, photocopying, recording, or otherwise), without the prior written permission of both the copyright owner and the above publisher of this book.

PUBLISHER'S NOTE
This is a work of fiction. Names, characters, places, and incidents either are the product of the author's imagination or are used fictitiously, and any resemblance to actual persons, living or dead, business establishments, events, or locales is entirely coincidental.

The scanning, uploading, and distribution of this book via the Internet or via any other means without the permission of the publisher is illegal and punishable by law. Please purchase only authorized electronic editions, and do not participate in or encourage electronic piracy of copyrighted materials. Your support of the author's rights is appreciated.

For my beloved husband, George,
from his adoring wife.
An eternity isn't time enough. . . .

Prologue

Spring 1519

"*I* cannot marry you," Giles FitzHugh said bluntly to Philippa Meredith, whose pretty jaw dropped open in surprise with his statement.

It was May, and the court was at Greenwich. The trees were full with new green growth, and the scent of early flowers was intoxicating. Beyond the royal gardens the river Thames flowed smoothly like a rippling satin ribbon beneath the sparkling sun as it made its way down to the sea. It was a place for romance, not rejection.

At first Philippa thought her heart had stopped at his words. But no. It yet beat. She closed her mouth, and tried to wrap her mind about what he had just said. Her temples throbbed. "You have fallen in love with someone else?" she finally managed to say.

"No," he answered her simply.

"Then why?" Philippa cried. "Our families have always planned that we wed, Giles, and I have just turned fifteen. I am ready to be a wife."

"There was never any formal betrothal between us, Philippa," he answered her calmly. "Your own mother preferred it that way, my dear." At nineteen Giles FitzHugh was tall and stocky. Like his elder brother he had their father's sandy hair and their mother's mild blue eyes.

"But everyone knew we were to marry one day," Philippa Meredith persisted stubbornly. She could not believe Giles was behaving in such a caddish way. "If it is not another woman, then what is it that takes you from me?" she demanded. Should she be angry with him? Oh yes! She should be very angry.

"God," he replied piously, crossing himself.

"What?" She could not have heard aright. She was definitely confused now. Was this not the same Giles FitzHugh who used to avoid the morning mass more often than not when he was in service to the king as a page? And he usually escaped punishment by offering the most creative excuses for his absences. She laughed aloud. "You jest, of course," she told him.

Giles shook his head. "I wish to take holy orders, Philippa," he told her. "I am going to be a priest. I studied in Rome with the king's cousin, Reginald Pole. I did not go there with such a vocation in mind. It just happened. I have no other explanation, but I have decided it is what I want, my dear. Far more than I want marriage to a woman."

"How long have you known this?" Philippa queried him. She couldn't believe what he was saying. It was ridiculous! Absurd! Giles? Her Giles a priest! No!

"I went to Europe to study, Philippa. First Paris, and then Rome. I wanted my fill of literature and histories. I meant to study, drink, and wench freely like all the other young men with me, and before me. And I certainly did in Paris," he chuckled, grinning, and breaking her heart with a glimpse of the old Giles she had fallen in love with so long ago. "But then I came to Rome," he continued. "And something happened to me there in that ancient city." He looked into her hazel eyes, attempting to explain it to her.

"What happened, Giles?" she inquired softly. "Tell me what happened in Rome."

"It began with the city itself," he said slowly. "It is so old, so holy. The sounds of the sung mass fills the air. The light is golden, and sanctity permeates the very air that one breathes. Rome is so beautiful it hurts your heart, Philippa. I do not know how I knew, but suddenly I did know that I was meant to remain there. To serve God with every fiber of my being. So I ceased my frivolity, and began a more serious concentration of the vocation to which I had been called. God does choose those whom he wants to serve him, my dear. I only returned home to tell you this myself, and to receive my parents' blessing. They were as surprised by my decision as are you, but they do understand. In fact, seeing my devotion to holy Mother Church, they are overjoyed."

"Well, I do not understand!" Philippa snapped, her anger fully surfaced. "You would choose a life of celibacy, toiling in some miserable church or dusty archives, rather than marry me? An heiress with her own estates? You are a second son, Giles! A match between us served both our families well. You would have had Friarsgate, and I should have taken a step up the social ladder in return. I have loved you since I was ten. And now you tell me that you do not love me?" Tears were beginning to slip down her face.

"It is not that I do not love you, Philippa. You were the most enchanting child, and you have grown into a beautiful young girl. But I do not love you as a husband should love a wife, and I love God more," he answered her with cruel honesty. "We met but briefly when you first came to court. Then you returned to your Friarsgate, and when you came back to court to serve the queen I had already gone abroad. You do not really love me. You love the dream you created, and you will get over it, I promise you," he told her, his voice a bit more tender now.

"I shall love you until I die!" Philippa declared. "I cannot believe that you do not want me. That you would chose the life you claim to want over a wife and your own lands! It cannot be!"

"Philippa, I do not want your lands. It is too northerly a place for me. Before I came to court I grew up in the Marcher country to the south. I do not think I could have survived in your harsh clime, so far from my family. The north is not known for its hospitable climate, my dear."

"Will you not be miserable in Rome?" she countered. "It is much farther away from your family than Cumbria is. You may never see your family again unless you come back to England." She wiped away the tears that were staining her pretty face.

He smiled gently. "I shall be ordained in Rome when I return. I have been promised a post in the Vatican serving the Holy Father himself. It seems I have a small talent for finance that will be of service to the church. But wherever I am sent, I shall be at home, and I shall be content to be in the service of my God." He took her hand up in his, and kissed it. "Will you not wish me well, Philippa?" The blue eyes surveyed her quietly. There was no feeling in them for her at all except perhaps pity.

She snatched her hand from his, and then she slapped him with it as hard as she could. "No, Giles, I will not wish you well! You have ruined my life. I hate you! I will never forgive you for this wretched perfidy!"

"Philippa, please, I beg of you, try to understand," he said to her, rubbing his cheek where her hand had made such ferocious contact with the smooth sensitive flesh.

"No! Do you not understand what you have done to me, Giles? I came to court to serve the queen with the understanding, formal or not, that we would one day be wed. Now you say we will not. How could you do this to me? I am fifteen, and ready to marry. Yet what kind of a match can I make now, cast off by a man who prefers God to a flesh and blood wife? I shall be the laughingstock of the court. The witty jest of many a drollery until some other fool is exposed to the court's humor, and heaven only knows when that will be. If you had spoken to me a few days ago I could have been titled the April's fool! You say when you came to Rome you knew that the religious life was what you wanted. Why did you not then write your father, or if not at first, at least a year ago? My mother would have been free then to seek another match for me. Have you any idea how long it takes to make the right match between families like ours? Neither of us possesses a great name, Giles. You have been incredibly selfish in your own desires. Nay, I do not understand, nor will I wish you good fortune. I am not a saint, Giles FitzHugh, although it is obvious that you aspire to be one."

He drew himself up proudly, saying stiffly as he did so, "I am sorry that you will not be happy for me, Philippa. Nonetheless I will forgive you your childish disappointment. And I will always remember you fondly, and pray for you."

"Go to hell!" Philippa spat angrily. Then giving him a hard shove that sent him sprawling backwards into a bed of fragrant Damascene roses, she whirled around, storming furiously towards Greenwich Palace, her auburn head held high. She had begun to cry again, but he neither saw nor heard her sorrow as he struggled to extricate himself from the thorny briars, swearing softly under his breath, for the rosebushes exacted a fearsome and bloody toll on his ungloved hands.

He would have never suspected that the little wench had such a nasty temper, Giles thought, finally pulling free. God had surely saved him from an unpleasant termagant in Philippa Meredith. Well, the worst was over. He could return to Rome with all due haste. Despite her unpleasant and unladylike behavior he really would pray for Philippa Meredith's happiness. After all, if God had a plan for Giles FitzHugh, he certainly had something in mind for Philippa Meredith.

Chapter 1

"Why did you not tell me?" Philippa Meredith demanded of Cecily FitzHugh. "I do not think I have ever been so sad and angry in all of my life. We are best friends, Cecily. How could you keep this from me? I do not know if I can ever forgive you."

Cecily's blue-gray eyes overflowed with tears at Philippa's words. "I didn't know," she sobbed piteously. "It is as big a surprise to me as it is to you. I only learned of my brother's decision this afternoon as Giles was speaking to you. My father said they kept it from me because they knew I would tell you, and it wasn't up to us to speak with you. It was Giles's responsibility. I think my brother is horrid, Philippa! We were to be sisters, and now you will marry someone else."

"Who?" Philippa sniffed. "I am not noble, and while I am considered an heiress, my estates are in the north. Giles's selfishness has probably rendered me impossible to marry off. Look how long it took your parents to find you a proper bridegroom. And soon you will be married, Cecily, while I shall wither away." She sighed dramatically. "If your brother has decided to devote his life to God, then perhaps it is a sign that I should too. My great-uncle Richard Bolton is the prior of St. Cuthbert's, near Carlisle. He will know of a convent I may enter."

Cecily burst out laughing. "You? A nun? Oh, no, dearest Philippa, not you. You have too great a love of all things worldly to be a nun.

You would have to give up all the possessions you so love, like beautiful clothing, jewelry, and good food. You would have to be obedient. Poverty, chastity and obedience are the rules in any convent. You could never be poor, docile or biddable, Philippa." Cecily's blue eyes danced with merriment.

"I could too!" Philippa insisted. "My great-aunt Julia is a nun, and my father's sisters."

Cecily laughed all the harder.

"Well, what else is there for me now that your brother has rejected me?" Philippa demanded of her best friend.

"Your family will find you another husband," Cecily said practically.

"I don't want another husband!" Philippa cried. "I want Giles! I love him, and I shall never love another. Besides, who would want to exile themselves to the north where my estates are located? Even Giles said the thought of having to live at Friarsgate made him miserable. Why my mother fought so hard to retain it I will never know. I don't want to live there either. It is much too far from the court."

"You are only saying that because you are disappointed in my brother," Cecily said. Then she changed the subject. "My father has written to your mother telling her of Giles's decision. The messenger will leave for the north in the morning. Do you want to send a letter to your mother with him?"

"Aye, I do," Philippa said. She arose from where they had been sitting together in the queen's antechamber. "I will ask the queen's permission to go and write it now." Without a backward glance to her friend Philippa moved serenely across the room. At fifteen she very much resembled her mother at that age, with her slender carriage and her auburn hair, but her eyes were not Rosamund's. Philippa had her father's changeable hazel green eyes.

Approaching the queen, she curtseyed and waited for permission to speak. It was given almost immediately. "What is it, my child?" Queen Katherine asked, smiling.

"Your highness has undoubtedly heard of my misfortune by now," Philippa began.

The queen nodded. "I am sorry, Philippa Meredith," she said.

Philippa bit her lip, for she suddenly found herself near tears again. She swallowed hard, and then forced herself to continue. "Lord FitzHugh is sending a message north on the morrow. I should like the courier to also carry a letter from me to my mother. With your highness's permission I will withdraw to write it." She curtsied again, giving the queen a weak smile.

"You have our permission, my child," the queen said. "And you will give your mother our kind regards, and say that if we may be of help to her in seeking a new match for you we shall be glad to come to her aid, but I remember your mama likes to do everything on her own." Queen Katherine smiled with fond remembrance.

"Thank you, your highness." Philippa curtseyed once more, and backed away. She slipped from the queen's rooms, hurrying to the maidens' dormitory where she might be alone with her troubled thoughts as she wrote to Rosamund. But the girl Philippa liked least among the maids was there preening as she prepared to join the queen's ladies.

"Ohh, poor Philippa!" she cried with false concern as she saw her enter the chamber. "I understand you have been jilted by the earl of Renfrew's son. What a pity."

Philippa's eyes narrowed. "I do not need your concern, Millicent Langholme, and besides it is none of your business."

"Your mother will have some difficulty finding you a decent husband now, and especially as your estates are so far north," Millicent murmured. "Did I hear aright? Giles FitzHugh is to become a priest? I wouldn't have thought it of him. He must have wanted to get out of marrying you quite badly to do that," she tittered. Then she smoothed her velvet skirts, and adjusted her gabled headdress.

Philippa had never wanted to hit someone so much in all of her life, but her situation was bad enough without deliberately bringing disgrace upon her family by assaulting another of the queen's maids. "I have no doubt that Giles's vocation is an honest one." She found herself defending him although what she really wanted to do was pound the wretch who had deserted her with both of her fists. Then she said, "You had best hurry, Millicent. The queen was looking for you."

Seeing she could not bait Philippa into bad behavior, Millicent Langholme hurried off without another word. Philippa opened the chest that held her possessions, and drew out her writing box. Opening it she sat down on her bed to write, and when she had finished Philippa gave the sealed letter to a page who saw it was dispatched with the earl of Renfrew's messenger, who rode north the following day.

Reading her daughter's missive some days later Rosamund gave a little shriek. "Give me Lord FitzHugh's letter, Maybel. Quickly! Just when I thought all was well, it would appear we have difficulties again."

"What is the matter?" Maybel handed the younger woman the packet from Lord FitzHugh. "What does the earl say?"

"A moment," Rosamund replied, holding up a delicate hand. "God's foot and damnation!" Her eyes quickly scanned the parchment, and then she set it aside. "Giles FitzHugh has decided to enter the priesthood. There will be no betrothal between him and Philippa. The wretch! Well, I never liked him that much anyway."

Maybel gave a little shriek of outrage.

"The earl apologizes," Rosamund continued, "and says he still thinks of Philippa as a daughter, and always will. He offers to aid me in finding another husband for Philippa. I must send to Otterly for Tom. Even though he has been away from the court for several years he will still be wiser than I in this matter. Poor Philippa! Her heart was so set on that boy."

"A priest," Maybel lamented. "That fine young man! 'Tis a pity, and now our lass left bereft at her age. That selfish lad might have told her sooner, I say."

Rosamund laughed. "So do I," she agreed. Then she picked up her daughter's letter again, and began to read it completely, shaking her head as she did so. When she had finished she set it aside with the other. "Philippa says there is nothing for her but to become a nun. She asks that I consult with my uncle Richard as to a good convent."

"Stuff and nonsense!" Maybel said. "The lass is overwrought, although who could blame her under the circumstances. However, I do not see Mistress Philippa taking holy orders at all, no matter what she says."

Rosamund laughed again. "Neither do I, Maybel. My daughter has too great a love of all things fine to give them up. Tell Edmund to send to Otterly for Tom today. And see that the earl's messenger is properly cared for, Maybel."

"As if you should have to tell me such a thing," Maybel muttered as she made her way from the hall to find her husband. Thank God Rosamund was sending for her older cousin to help in the matter. Tom Bolton would know just what to do, unlike Rosamund's husband who would simply lose his temper.

Thomas Bolton, Lord Cambridge arrived from his estates at Otterly two days later.

"What is the emergency that I have been summoned to come with such haste?" he asked his cousin. "The children are alright, aren't they? And where is that reckless Scots husband of yours, cousin?"

"Logan is at Claven's Carn seeing to a strengthening of the defenses. The border has been unruly ever since Queen Margaret was driven from Scotland," Rosamund replied. "The children are fine. It is Philippa with whom we have difficulty, Tom. I need your advice and counsel badly. Giles FitzHugh is entering the priesthood."

"Jesu and all the beautiful angels in heaven!" Thomas Bolton swore. "And now our lass is left high and dry, having just turned fifteen, without prospects. 'Tis a caddish thing to do. Surely the lad might have given us more warning. These churchmen are so thoughtless. All that seems to concern them is God, and amassing great wealth."

"Uncle Richard should not like to hear you saying such a thing," Rosamund laughed. Then she grew more somber. "What am I to do, Tom? Oh, I know, another husband must be found for my daughter, but how will I go about that? We had an earl's son for Philippa. How will we do as well again? And to make matters worse my daughter is threatening to take the veil!"

Thomas Bolton burst out laughing, and he laughed until the tears rolled down his face, staining his elegant velvet doublet. "Philippa? A nun?" He laughed some more even as he brushed away the evidence of his humor. "Philippa has too great a love for the good life and for beautiful things to allow her disappointment to drive her to a convent," Lord Cambridge finally said. "Of all your daughters, dearest cousin, Philippa was always my best pupil. Her knowledge of gemstones astounds even me, and the finely woven woolen underskirts she wears in the winter must always each be protected by a layer of silk lest her fragile skin be chafed. The rough linen robes of a holy woman would certainly not do for our Philippa. Well, dear girl, there is nothing for it. She must come home until the ignominious fate Giles FitzHugh has left her to can be forgotten. Send a message back to court to that effect, directed to the queen. Certainly Katherine will understand, and be gracious enough to welcome Philippa back to her service at some later date. In the meantime I must think on possible matches for our lass. She is ripe for marriage now, but if we allow too much time to pass her chances will be gone."

Rosamund nodded. "I agree. Of course when Logan learns of Philippa's predicament he will begin suggesting all the sons of the men he knows."

"No Scot will do for Philippa," Tom Bolton said, shaking his head.

"She is too in love with her life at the court of King Henry, and more English surely than you are, cousin."

"I know," Rosamund agreed, "but you will have to help me with my husband, cousin. You know how obdurate Logan can get when he sets his mind on something."

"The trick, dear girl," Lord Cambridge answered her, "is not to let it get that far with your bold Scot." He chuckled. "Do not fear. I know how to handle Logan Hepburn."

"Indeed you do," Rosamund laughed, "and Logan would be most annoyed if he realized it, Tom."

"Well, I shall certainly not tell him," Tom Bolton said with a wink. "In the meantime what does the queen say, other than she will make an attempt to find another husband for Philippa? This is not something I would choose to leave in her hands, cousin."

"I agree." Rosamund nodded. "However, if we call Philippa home now I fear it will make her plight more difficult to solve, Tom. Unless the queen sends her home let us leave her where she is. She is no longer a child, and she must learn to handle the difficulties that life will hand her. This is not the last serious disappointment she will face, and the lady of Friarsgate must be strong to hold this land."

Lord Cambridge sighed. "The court is a very different world from our world," he reminded Rosamund. "I have come to realize that I should rather face the bitterest of cold winters in Cumbria than the court. I am astounded that I survived it all. Still, if you think it best we leave her there for now I will bow to your motherly instincts."

Rosamund laughed at him. "Oh, Tom, do not tell me you have come to love Otterly after all these years. And the quiet life as well?"

"Well," he huffed, "I am not as young as I once was, cousin."

Rosamund laughed again. "Nonsense," she said. "I am quite certain that Banon keeps you on your toes. She has always been a lively lass."

"Your middle daughter is a delightful girl," he replied. "She has brought life into the house since she came to live with me last year. I was frankly astounded when she asked to come, dear Rosamund. But as Banon has so wisely observed, if she is to be the mistress of Otterly one day she must know all about it, and its workings. A most clever lass. We shall have to find a man worthy of her one day."

"But first we must consider Philippa's vicissitudes," Rosamund reminded him. "We are agreed then? She will remain at court in the queen's service unless Katherine sends her home. And I will thank the queen for her offer, but assure her that Philippa's family can handle the matter of finding another husband for her. One to whom the queen and the king will, of course, give their blessing."

Thomas Bolton smiled archly. "You have not lost your touch, dear girl," he told her. "Yes, write the queen just that. It is perfect. And tell Philippa when you write to her that I send her my love. Now, cousin, having settled your problems I find I am ravenous. What have you to feed me? And do not drag out a pot of rabbit stew. I want beef!"

Rosamund smiled fondly at him. "And you shall have it, dearest Tom," she said, but her mind was already considering what wisdom she would impart to her daughter when she wrote to her. It was difficult to know whether to be soft or hard with her eldest daughter. Too much sympathy was every bit as bad as not enough. It would not be easy.

And Philippa Meredith, reading her mother's missive some days later, was neither moved to tears nor comforted by her mother's words. Indeed she flung the parchment aside in a fit of pique. "Bah! Friarsgate! Always Friarsgate!" she said, irritated.

"What does your mother say?" Cecily FitzHugh ventured nervously.

"She offers me ridiculous advice! Disappointment, she says, is very much a part of life, and I must learn to accept it. A nunnery is not the answer to my problems. Well, did I say it was, Cecily? I am hardly the type to enter a convent."

"But just a few weeks ago you said you were going to take the veil," Cecily replied. "You mentioned relations who were nuns. Of course we all thought it highly amusing. You are hardly the type to be a nun, dearest."

"So!" Philippa snapped. "You and the others are laughing at me behind my back. And I thought you were my best friend!"

"I am your best friend," Cecily cried, "but you have been so filled with histrionics, and we all knew you were not going to become a nun. It is funny to even consider it. Now, what else does your mother say?"

"That they will find me another husband. One who will appreciate me and help me to prudently manage Friarsgate. Oh, God! I don't want Friarsgate, Cecily. I don't ever again want to live in Cumbria! I want to remain here at court. It is the center of the very universe. I shall die if I am forced back north. I am not my mother!" She sighed dramatically. "Oh, Cecily! Do you remember the first Christmas we had at court as the queen's maids of honor?"

"Of course I do," Cecily responded. "They called it the Christmas of the Three Queens. Queen Katherine, Queen Margaret, and her sister, Mary, who had been queen of France until she was widowed. They hadn't all been together in years, and it was so wonderful. Every day offered us a new excitement."

"And Cardinal Wolsey had to give Queen Margaret two hundred pounds so she might purchase her New Year's gifts. The poor lady had virtually nothing, having fled Scotland after the lords there overturned King James's will and made the duke of Albany the little king's guardian. She should never have remarried, and especially to the earl of Angus."

"But she was in love with him," Cecily said. "And he is very handsome."

"She lusted after him," Philippa said. "She was a queen dowager, Ceci, and she threw her power and authority away just so she might be swived by a younger man. The other earls, the other lords, did not want the Douglases running Scotland. That is why they chose a new regent for little King James."

"But John Stewart is French-born," Cecily said. "I don't think he had ever set foot in Scotland before he was sent for to come and be the king's regent. And he is the king's heir, you know. I can understand why Queen Margaret was frightened."

"Yet his reputation is one of great loyalty and integrity," Philippa answered.

"Twelfth Night!" Cecily said, changing the subject. "Remember that first Twelfth Night? Was it not wonderful?" Cecily looked dreamy-eyed with her remembrance.

"How could anyone forget it?" Philippa responded. "The entertainment was titled "The Garden of Esperance," and there was an entire artificial garden set upon this enormous pageant cart. The ladies and gentlemen taking part danced within that garden before it was hauled off. I remember how our little baby princess Mary clapped her hands in glee."

"How sad there are no other princes and princesses," Cecily murmured softly. "Despite our good queen's faithfulness, her many pilgrimages to Our Lady of Walsingham, her charitable works, there is no other child of her body."

"She is too old," Philippa replied as low. "She has aged even in the three years we have been here. She becomes more religious by the day, and withdraws early now from the court revels. The king's eye has begun to wander. Do you not see it?"

"But she has never shirked her royal duties," Cecily noted. "And she and the king have always had much in common. They still hunt together, and he goes every day after the midday meal to visit her in her apartments."

"But he comes always with courtiers," Philippa said. "They are rarely alone now. How does a man make a son when he hardly ever visits his wife? The king complains much, but does little to change the situation."

"Hush!" Cecily cautioned Philippa.

"Have you noticed how he has begun to look at Mistress Blount? It's rather like a large tomcat considering the plump and pretty little finch before him."

Cecily giggled. "Philippa, you are dreadful! Elizabeth Blount is a charming girl, and I have never known her to be mean like Millicent Langholme."

"The king calls her Bessie when he thinks no one else is listening. I have heard him do it myself," Philippa murmured. "Watch his face when she dances for him again some evening."

"She's named after the king's mother," Cecily said. "Her mother was a Peshall, and her father fought for the old king at Bosworth when he defeated King Richard III. She comes from Shropshire, and isn't that almost as far north as your Cumbria?"

"You will notice that she doesn't live in Shropshire," Philippa said dryly. "Like me she is a creature of the court, and she has excellent connections too."

"It doesn't hurt that she is quite pretty either," Cecily remarked. "But you are right. Her cousin, Lord Montjoy, is quite in the king's favor. And the earl of Suffolk and Francis Bryan like her too. Have you heard her sing? She has quite a lovely voice."

"I should like to be like her," Philippa replied wistfully. "She is so popular, and everyone notices her."

"Especially the king, as you have noted," Cecily said. "What if he should . . . well, you know. Wouldn't she be ruined? I mean, who would wed a girl who had . . . well, you know, Philippa."

"A lady does not refuse a king," Philippa said. "And kings take care of their mistresses. At least King James did. Do you think our good King Henry would do any less for his mistress? It would be unchivalrous, and our king is the most honorable in all of Christendom, Ceci. Remember last summer when the sweating sickness struck England, and the king moved the entire court from London to Richmond, and then Greenwich until it had subsided. How he feared for his people. He is a great king." Then she grew glum once again. "Are people talking about me, Ceci? Because of your brother?" She sighed deeply. "What am I to do? I am not the most eligible marriage prospect with my northern estates. Let us be frank. Your brother was a big catch for me, and my estates would have given him his own lands."

"All the girls feel awful for you," Cecily said. "Except, of course,

Millicent Langholme. Yours was really an excellent match, but now she will do nothing but brag on Sir Walter Lumley and his estates in Kent. He is negotiating with her father, you know, and she expects to be married by year's end."

"You will be married by then too," Philippa said. "And then I shall have no one here to confide in, Ceci. We have been friends, it seems, all our lives, even if we really only met when we were ten. But then the best part of my life, I think now, has been here at court. I never want to leave it."

"I am not being married until late summer," Cecily said, "and Tony and I will be back at court in time for the Christmas revels. And you will probably have Maggie Radcliffe, Jane Hawkins, and Annie Chambers to keep you company while I am gone. And Millicent will be in Kent as lady of Sir Walter's estates."

Suddenly Philippa's lips turned up in a wicked smile. "Millicent can have her Sir Walter, but only after I have finished with him," she said. "Now that your brother has jilted me, I am as free as a bird."

Cecily's blue-gray eyes grew round. "Philippa! What are you planning to do? Remember, you must consider your reputation if another suitable husband is to be found for you. You are not some earl's daughter. You are an heiress from Cumbria. Nothing else. You must not behave in a rash and foolish manner."

"Oh, Ceci, do not fret yourself. I merely mean to have a little bit of fun. I have surely been the most chaste of the queen's maids until now because of my loyalty to Giles. I need consider your brother no longer. The king is being attracted to Mistress Blount. This means her other admirers will retreat back into the shadows. I mean to step into the empty space created by her loss. Why shouldn't I? I am prettier. I have inherited my Welsh father's singing voice, which I haven't used at all except at the mass when I must sing discreetly. And while I will admit that Elizabeth Blount is the best dancer next to the king and his sister here at court, I dance well enough to be considered graceful. My mother will indeed find me another husband sooner than later. But given where she lives he will be a country gentleman, and it is unlikely I shall ever see the court again." Philippa sighed sadly. "So before I am shackled and bound to wifedom I shall amuse myself, Ceci."

"But flirting with Sir Walter Lumley?" Cecily said tartly.

"Why not?" Philippa chuckled. "I do it not just for me, but for all of those who have had to suffer Millicent Langholme's poisonous tongue and snide remarks over the last three years. I shall be hailed as a heroine by all the other maids of honor."

"But what if Sir Walter should decide he wants you for his wife, and not Millicent?" Cecily asked. "Surely you don't really want him?"

"Never!" Philippa declared. "But do not distress yourself, Ceci. I shall not be the kind of girl a man like Sir Walter would marry even at his most lustful. Like Millicent, he is a fellow who takes very seriously how he is perceived by the court. I shall toy with him just enough to anger and frustrate Millicent. Perhaps I shall even let him kiss me, making certain she knows about it, of course. Then I shall abruptly move on to another gentleman, making Sir Walter look like a fool, and glad for a girl like Millicent Langholme. Actually the wench will owe me a great debt of gratitude."

"I doubt she will see it that way," Cecily laughed.

"Perhaps not," Philippa agreed with an arch half-smile.

"I never suspected that you could be so wicked," Cecily remarked.

"Neither did I," Philippa agreed with a grin. "I rather like it."

"You must be careful lest the queen catch you at your mischief," Cecily said, looking about to see if anyone was near enough to hear them, but they were at the far end of the queen's antechamber.

"She would not expect it of me. Perhaps I shall begin my flirtation this evening. The king has arranged for us to picnic by the riverside in the long twilight. There will be paper lanterns, and before it grows too dark we shall shoot arrows at some butts being set up. Sir Walter is noted for his marksmanship. I think I shall be very bad at archery, Ceci. And I shall stand near him. Being chivalrous, he will certainly want to help me."

"But you are an excellent archer!" Cecily protested.

"Well, it is unlikely he knows that," Philippa said. "And if he does I will pretend that it is dust in my eye, spoiling my aim."

"If Millicent sees it she will be furious," Cecily remarked.

"Yes," Philippa giggled, "but she can do naught about it for the match has not been completely set yet. Nothing is signed. Believe me, if it were we should not hear the end of it. She will not be able to scold her intended husband quite yet. Poor fellow. Were he not so pompous I should almost feel sorry for him."

"Well, he is pompous," Cecily said. "I wonder if you shall be able to lure him at all. You are not important at all, Philippa."

"Ah, but I was good enough for the earl of Renfrew's son before he decided to take holy orders," Philippa answered. "He will be curious enough to be tempted."

Cecily shook her head. "I think Giles is well rid of you," she teased her friend.

Philippa swatted at her with a chuckle. "Perhaps, yet he still hurt me by being so dishonest, and allowing me to believe we would wed when I turned fifteen. I think he knew at least a year ago what he really wanted. Would that he had been brave and honest enough at the time to say so. He has really placed me in a most difficult position."

"It will be alright," Cecily soothed Philippa. "It was not meant to be." Then changing the subject she said, "There are some gypsies camped off the London road. Let us go tomorrow, and have our fortunes told. I know Jane and Maggie will come too."

"What fun!" Philippa exclaimed. "Yes, let us go," she agreed.

In late afternoon the servants began setting up the tables by the riverside. Though they would be dining alfresco, white linen was spread on each board. Poles were driven into the ground for the lanterns. A pit had been dug earlier, and even now the venison was being turned slowly on its spit. The archery butts were set up. There were small punts drawn up on the shore for those courtiers who would enjoy a small excursion on the water in the early evening. A small platform was laid on the lawn, and chairs brought. Here the king's musicians would seat themselves so that the court might dance country dances on the grass in the long twilight. It was the next to last day of May, and they would soon be removing to Richmond for a month until it was time for the summer progress to begin. The court would not be back in London until late autumn, for the air in the city was considered noxious and conducive to disease.

In the Maidens' Chamber Philippa and her companions refreshed themselves, and dressed for the afternoon and evening's entertainment. Despite her modest background Philippa Meredith always had the most elegant gowns, it was acknowledged among the queen's maids. They were never the most lavish, but they were always the pinnacle of fashion and her good taste was greatly admired, and in some cases envied.

"I don't know how she does it," Millicent Langholme grumbled as she watched Philippa and her tiring woman. "She cannot be rich. Her mother is a sheep farmer, I am told. I don't know why she is here at all, for her birth is so low."

"You are jealous, Millicent," Anne Chambers said. "Philippa's father was Sir Owein Meredith, a simple knight 'tis true, but one who stood in great favor with the king, and the king's father, for his deep and abiding loyalty to the house of Tudor. He was a Welshman, and served the Tudors since his childhood."

"But her mother is a peasant!" Millicent persisted.

Anne laughed. "Her mother was the heiress to a great estate. She is hardly a peasant. And the gossip goes that she did the queen a great kindness at her own expense many years ago. The lady of Friarsgate spent part of her youth here at court in the company of two queens, both of whom call her friend, Millicent. You would be wise to consider these facts. Philippa Meredith is most popular among our companions. I know of no one who dislikes her, or says ill of her but you. Beware lest you be sent home in disgrace. The queen does not like those who are mean of spirit."

"I shall be leaving soon anyway," Millicent huffed.

"Is your marriage agreement then set?" Anne inquired.

"Well, almost," Millicent replied. "There are a few trifling matters that my father insists be settled before he will sign the betrothal contracts." She brushed her white blond hair slowly. "He does not say what these matters are."

"I have heard it said," Jane Hawkins chimed in, "that Sir Walter wants more gold in your dower than your father has offered, and your father has had to go to the goldsmiths to borrow that gold. He is obviously anxious enough to be rid of you to put himself into debt, Millicent."

"Oh, is that it?" Anne Chambers said innocently. "I had heard something about several bastards Sir Walter fathered, and one of them on the daughter of a London merchant who will have remuneration for his daughter's lost virtue, support for his grandchild, and Sir Walter's name for the lad."

"That is an evil untruth!" Millicent cried. "Sir Walter is the most honorable and virtuous of men. He would never even look upon another girl now that he is to be betrothed to me. As for any women he may have approached in his youth, they are guilty and culpable whores who are no better than they ought to be. Do not dare to repeat such slander, or I shall complain to our mistress, the queen."

Anne and Jane moved off giggling. They were more than aware of Philippa's plan for Sir Walter, a pompous gentleman known for a lustful nature that he attempted to conceal. They had deliberately baited Millicent Langholme, knowing that she would be closely watching Sir Walter, and that she would be able to do nothing but fume when he succumbed to Philippa's blandishments, which they were certain he would. None of Philippa's friends had ever considered that she might do something like this, but she was changing before their very eyes. It was, of course, the result of her hurt feelings over Giles FitzHugh. But Millicent deserved what she was about to get.

Philippa had dressed carefully this afternoon. She was more fortunate than most of the maids of honor in that she had her uncle Thomas's London house in which she might store a larger than usual wardrobe for herself, as the queen's maids had but minimal space for their possessions, which had to be packed up at a moment's notice and moved to the next royal dwelling in which Katherine would take up residence. Philippa was generous enough to share this luxury with her friends, Cecily, Maggie Radcliffe, Jane Hawkins, and Anne Chambers. Her own tiring woman, Lucy, would be sent to fetch whatever was needed when it was needed.

Philippa had chosen to wear a pale peach-colored silk brocade gown. It had a low square neckline edged with a band of gold embroidery, and a bell-shaped skirt. The upper sleeves of the gown were fitted; the lower sleeve was a wide, deep cuff of peach satin, lined in the peach-colored silk brocade, and beneath which could be seen a full false undersleeve of the sheerest natural-colored silk with a ruffled cuff at the wrist. From Philippa's waist a little silk brocade purse hung on a long gold cord. On her head Philippa wore a little French hood, of the style made popular by Mary Tudor, edged in pearls, with a small sheer veil that hung down her back. Her long auburn hair was visible beneath the veil, and was so long it actually hung below it. About her neck Philippa wore a fine gold chain with a pendant made from the diamond and emerald broach the king's grandmother had sent her when she had been born.

"You are not wearing a high-necked chemise," Cecily noted, seeing no contrasting fabric beneath her friend's gown.

"No," Philippa said with a mischievous smile. "I am not."

"But your breasts are quite visible," Cecily continued nervously.

"I need bait sufficient if I am going hunting," Philippa returned wickedly.

Cecily's eyes widened, and then she giggled nervously. "Oh, please, remember your reputation, Philippa! I know Giles hurt your feelings, but losing your good name is no way to get back at him. I suspect no man is worth a woman's losing her character."

"Frankly, from my little talk with Giles I am certain he would not care what happened to me, Cecily. He never loved me at all or he would have treated me with more kindness. If the church means more to him than marriage to me, so be it. But he did not consider the difficult position into which he was thrusting me. He thought only of himself. And that I cannot forgive," Philippa said. "I have kept myself chaste for marriage. I have never even allowed a boy to kiss me, as you well know, although others have. You have! Soon enough my mother will find some propertied squire, or my stepfather will bring forth the son of one of his Scots friends. I shall have to marry, and I shall have had no fun at all! And worse, I shall have to leave court. So what if I am a little bit naughty now. What matter if I gain a slight reputation for myself. The squire or the Scot will never know. I will retain my virginity for my husband, whoever he may be."

"Well," Cecily allowed, "you have really been far better than the rest of us. And now that the king's minions are out of favor thanks to Cardinal Wolsey, I suppose it is safe to trifle with a few of the young men here at court."

"Starting with Millicent's Sir Walter," Philippa replied. "I shall teach the little bitch to talk behind my back. And the best part is that while she will be angry at Sir Walter, she will still have to wed him, and she will want to for the prestige such a marriage will bring her." Philippa chuckled.

"Poor Sir Walter," kindhearted Cecily said. "He is marrying a shrew."

"I do not feel sorry for him at all," Philippa responded. "He is in the midst of a negotiation to marry, yet he will be easily tempted by just a glimpse of my breasts. I do not think him an honorable fellow at all. He and Millicent deserve each other. I expect they shall be extremely unhappy together."

"Have you no pity then?" Cecily asked.

Philippa shook her head. "None. If a man cannot be honorable, then what is there? My father, they say, was an honorable and gentil knight. So is my relation, Lord Cambridge, and my stepfather, Logan Hepburn. I would certainly not settle for anything less in a man."

"You have become hard," Cecily responded.

Philippa shook her head. "Nay, I have always been exactly what I am."

Chapter 2

❦

"Come, my girls," called the assistant mistress of the maids, Lady Brentwood. "The picnic is beginning. The queen has said you may wander at will this afternoon as long as two or three of you remain by her side. You will take turns, of course, to be fair."

The queen's maids of honor hurried from the Maidens' Chamber chattering and laughing. A picnic by the river was a wonderful treat, and the formality of the court was always dispensed with on such an occasion. The day was a beautiful one. The skies were blue, and there was just the tiniest of breezes ruffling the flowers in the gardens. It was much too early to execute her plan, and so Philippa volunteered to remain by the queen for a time. She did not see Sir Walter yet, and she would want him to be just slightly drunk.

"How pretty you look, my child," the queen told Philippa. "I am quite reminded of your mother when we were girls." She held her squirming daughter in her lap, for the little princess had been brought forth from her nursery to join the festivities. "Mary, sit still, poppet. Papa will not be pleased."

"Would you like me to take her for a walk, your highness?" Philippa inquired politely. "And I can play with her for a short time. I always helped mama look after my sisters and little brothers."

The queen looked relieved. "Oh, Philippa, would you? The

French ambassador is coming this afternoon to see her that he may write his master, King Francois, of Mary's progress. Now that she is betrothed to the Dauphin the French watch her. I should prefer she be wed to my nephew, Charles. Yes, take her away, and try and keep her clean."

Philippa curtseyed. "I will do my best, madame." Then she held out her hand to the little princess. "Come, your highness. We shall walk about and admire all the lovely costumes that people are wearing today."

Mary Tudor, thirty-nine months of age, slipped from her mother's lap, and dutifully took Philippa Meredith's outstretched hand. She was a pretty child with auburn hair much like Philippa's, and serious eyes. She was dressed in a miniature gown that matched her mother's royal garb. "Your gown is pretty," she told Philippa. She was extremely intelligent, and despite her youth she could now carry on simple conversations in both English and Latin.

"Thank you, your highness," Philippa said.

They walked down by the river, and the little girl pointed to the punts. "Go!" she told Philippa. "I want to go in the boat."

Philippa shook her head. "Can you swim, your highness?"

"No," little Mary responded.

"Then you cannot go into the punt. You must be able to swim if you go in the punts," Philippa explained.

"Can you swim?" The oddly adult eyes looked at her.

"Yes," Philippa replied with a smile, "I can."

"Who taught you?" the princess demanded to know.

"A man named Patrick Leslie, who is earl of Glenkirk," Philippa answered.

"Where?" the child questioned.

"In a lake on my mother's lands," Philippa said. "He taught my sisters Banon and Bessie too. We thought our lake cold, but he said the lochs of Scotland were far more chill. I went to Scotland once, but I never swam in a loch."

"My auntie Meg is the queen of Scotland," little Mary said.

"Not any longer," Philippa corrected the princess. "As a widow who has remarried she is now known as the king's mother. But I visited her court with my mother when she was queen. It was quite a fine court."

"Better than my papa's court?" the princess inquired slyly.

"There is no court as grand as King Henry's," Philippa quickly answered. "You know very well, your highness, that your papa is the grandest and the handsomest prince in all of Christendom."

"Such delightful flattery!" the king said, coming up to them.

Philippa curtsied low, her cheeks pink with her blush.

"Papa!" Mary Tudor cried, laughing as he swept her up into his embrace.

"And how is the most beautiful princess in all the wide world?" the king inquired of his daughter, bussing her heartily upon her rosy cheek.

The child giggled happily even as the king's eye turned to Philippa.

"You are Rosamund Bolton's daughter, are you not, mistress?" God's wounds, how her pretty and innocent face took him back.

"Aye, your majesty, I am." Philippa did not look directly at him. It was not polite to stare at the king, and he was known to dislike it.

The king reached out, and tipped Philippa's face up with his index finger. "You are every bit as lovely as your mother was at your age. I knew her then, you know."

"Aye, your majesty, she has told me." And then Philippa giggled, unable to help herself. She quickly bit her lip to contain her laughter.

But the king chuckled, a deep, rich sound that rumbled up from the broad chest beneath his rich jewel-encrusted velvet doublet. "Ahhh," he said, "then you know all. But of course I was a lad then, and filled with mischief."

"And there was a wager involved as well," Philippa replied mischievously.

"Ahah! Hah! Hah!" the king chortled. "Indeed there was, Mistress Philippa, and my grandmother collected the ante, which she put in the poor box at Westminster. I learned then never to allow my pride to dictate a wager." He set his daughter down. "I have heard that Renfrew's younger son has decided to take holy orders. I am sorry."

Philippa actually felt the tears welling up in her eyes, and hastily she brushed them away. "It is obviously God's will," she said, but her voice lacked conviction, and the king heard it.

"If I can be of help, Mistress Philippa," Henry Tudor said quietly. "I still count your mother among my friends, for all she married a wild Scot."

"Thank you, your majesty," Philippa replied, curtseying. "But I would not have you think ill of my stepfather. Logan Hepburn is a good man."

The king nodded. "Take my daughter back to her mother now. Then go and join your friends so you may have some fun, Philippa Meredith. That is a royal command!" And he smiled down at her. "I remember your father also, my girl. He, too, was a good man, and as loyal a servant as the house of Tudor ever had. His children have my friendship. Remember that, Philippa Meredith. Now, run along! 'Tis the last of May, and the day is for divertissements."

"Yes, your majesty," Philippa responded, and she curtseyed once more. Then taking little Mary's hand she moved off in the direction of Queen Katherine.

The king watched her go. Was it possible that Rosamund Bolton's daughter was that old now? Old enough to marry, and have her heart broken. And there were two other Meredith girls, and his sister had said there were sons by her Scotsman. And what did he have? One little daughter, and a wife who was too old to bear him the boys he needed. The queen had lost a child six months ago. When she carried a babe to term it was born dead, or lingered but a few days before dying as they all had but for Mary. Something was very wrong. The physicians said she could have no more children. Was God trying to tell him something? He looked across the lawns to where his wife sat. Her once fine skin was sallow now, and her beautiful hair was faded. She was spending more and more time on her knees in prayer, and less and less time on her back doing her duty. And surrounding herself with such pretty girls did little to make her enticing.

His eyes swept the bevy of maids keeping the queen company. It lingered on Montjoy's cousin, the delicious Elizabeth Blount. Petite and round where a woman should be round. Blond and blue-eyed. And she was the finest dancer next to his sister, Mary, that he had ever encountered. And she sang like an angel. She was quite a favorite with his closest friends, for she had a quick wit. Yet she was also docile in the face of authority, he remembered Montjoy saying. Bessie, Montjoy once remarked, would make the most perfect wife. The king's small blue eyes narrowed. Bessie Blount. She would make a wonderful armful, and being an obedient lass by nature if Montjoy was to be believed, she would yield to her sovereign's passion. Henry Tudor smiled. What a lovely summer lay ahead of them. If, of course, the plague and sweating sickness did not strike again this year. He moved across the lawns greeting his guests jovially.

Philippa returned with the little princess to the queen's side. "We have had a fine walk, your highness. The princess wanted to go on the river, but I did not think it wise."

"Nay," the queen agreed, "you were right, my child."

"What did the king say when he stopped you?" Millicent Langholme asked meanly. "He engaged you in conversation for some time, Philippa Meredith."

"The king's care and interest were for his daughter," Philippa replied quietly. "And he asked after my mother, and her family in Cumbria. They knew each other as children. Why are you interested, Millicent Langholme? Is your own life so uneventful then? But then it would be, wouldn't it, for Sir Walter has yet to make any decision in the matter of a possible betrothal between you." And what fun I shall have with the gentleman right beneath your turned-up nose, Millicent, Philippa thought. And you will be able to do naught about it except fume.

The queen smiled silently as the Langholme girl sputtered her outrage but was unable to reply. "How is your mama?" she asked Philippa.

"Well, I believe, for I have not heard otherwise. Do you think, madame, that there might be a place at court for my sister, Banon? She is a charming girl, but could certainly use the polish time in your service would give her. She has her own estates at Otterly."

"If Millicent Langholme weds, then aye, I would be happy to receive her into my service," Queen Katherine replied graciously. "Banon. 'Tis an odd name to my ears."

"It means queen in the Welsh tongue. She is Banon Mary Katherine Meredith, madame. My father wanted her called Banon," Philippa explained.

"Of course he would honor his own heritage," the queen said, thinking that Philippa had become quite a creature of the court, even soliciting a place for her sister.

The afternoon began to wane. Some people were dancing the country dances before the platform where the musicians were seated at their instruments. The archery butts were being well-used by several gentlemen who had removed their doublets, and were in their shirtsleeves. The punts upon the river contained mostly young couples, along with their boatmen. Philippa's eyes carefully surveyed the gathering. Ahh, there was Sir Walter Lumley. He stood among a group of gentlemen who were dicing. Philippa moved off toward the gathering. She saw Bessie Blount there too, so it would not be so unusual that she joined them.

Bessie smiled as Philippa approached. She was a very good-natured girl who had even less to recommend her in marriage than did Philippa. "Come, and see what luck Tony Deane is having!" she called to Philippa.

"Does Cecily know you have a penchant for the dice?" Philippa teased Sir Anthony Deane, Cecily's betrothed husband.

He grinned up at her, and shook his head. "But as long as I'm lucky, can she complain?" he asked. Then throwing the bones he made his point once again, to the cheers of the onlookers.

Philippa wedged herself into the group next to Sir Walter. "Do you dice, sir?" she asked him, looking up at him with a small smile.

"On occasion," he admitted, his eyes going immediately to her shadowed cleavage. And he unconsciously licked his lips approvingly.

"I have never played at dice," Philippa said innocently, instantly attracting the attention of Sir Walter and several other gentlemen. "Is it hard?"

"Not very," Sir Walter replied, smiling toothily as she looked up at him, her hazel eyes wide with curiosity. "Would you like me to show you, Mistress Meredith?"

"Oh, would you," Philippa cooed sweetly. "What shall I wager?" She reached for the little purse that hung from the cord about her waist. "Oh, I hope I have enough."

Both Bessie Blount and Tony Deane looked sharply at Philippa. They knew she was not the silly girl she was playing at, but they remained silent, curious to see what would happen.

"Oh, we must not take your precious coin," Sir Walter said gallantly. "Let us play for a kiss instead, Mistress Meredith."

"I have never been kissed," Philippa declared. "Would it not endanger my reputation and my good name to be so bold, sir?"

Sir Walter looked stymied. To tell the girl her character would remain pure if she diced for kisses would be an outright lie. But by God he did want to kiss her now, knowing she was untouched. And fumble those adorable little round breasts she was so boldly displaying.

"I am not of a mind to relinquish the dice when I am on a winning streak," Tony Deane said finally. "Why not watch how it is done, Philippa. Then later you may try, but wager a ha'penny, and not your good name."

"Yes, yes, " Sir Walter agreed, "I shall explain it all while Tony plays on, Mistress Meredith." He put an arm about her narrow waist, and was pleased when she leaned against him rather than pulling away.

"Very well," Philippa responded. She looked up at him. "I am ever so grateful for your tutelage, Sir Walter. I think you are most kind." This was better than the archery butts, she considered.

"Nay, my dear, 'tis nothing at all," he told her. Her fragrance was delightful.

Philippa had seen the lust in his eyes. What a fool, she thought, but Millicent will take him most firmly in hand, and his life will be hell. He deserved it. Most men did. "It doesn't look really hard," she said, looking up at him with limpid eyes.

"Nay, it isn't at all," Sir Walter assured her. He was simply unable to take his eyes off of her breasts. The girl he was to wed, Millicent Langholme, had hardly any breasts at all. And she didn't smell as nice as did Philippa Meredith at all. But she was a good match for him, and he knew it. Her blood was nobler than his, and she was an only child. In all likelihood he could arrange for her father's baronetcy to pass to him when the old man died one day. Yes, Millicent Langholme was the perfect match for him, but Philippa Meredith was ripe for seduction, and she was such a trusting little country lass. His arm tightened about her supple waist.

Philippa stiffened, and suddenly pulled away from Sir Walter. "Perhaps I should not gamble," she said. "I really have not the means for it."

"A wise decision," Tony Deane said. What mischief was Philippa up to, he wondered? He had never known her to act like such a silly flibbertigibbet.

"I had best rejoin the queen," Philippa said breathlessly.

"If you have decided not to dice," Sir Walter purred, "then walk with me by the river, Mistress Philippa. The water is lovely with the reflected sunset."

"But will that not cause gossip, sir? You are said to be betrothed to Millicent Langholme," Philippa murmured.

"There is nothing settled yet, Mistress Philippa," he assured her. "And 'tis no more than a walk in plain view of all the court."

"Oh, I am not sure." Philippa wavered. "I would not hurt Millicent's feelings."

"Just a short walk," Sir Walter said, taking her arm, and moving off with her.

Bessie Blount chuckled. "Why, the wicked baggage," she said, grinning.

"What is she up to?" Tony Deane wondered aloud, gathering his winnings, and leaving the dice to the next player.

"I don't know," Bessie said, "but I can assure you that neither she nor Millicent would do the other a kindness. Millicent is always as rude as she dares to be towards Philippa Meredith. But I know who will know. Your betrothed, Cecily FitzHugh. She and Philippa are the best of friends."

"I think it better I don't know what mischief is about to transpire," Tony said. He was a tall young man with ash brown hair and mild blue eyes, with an estate in Oxfordshire.

Bessie laughed. "Well, I for one am perishing from curiosity. I shall go and find Cecily right now." She hurried off, leaving the young man to his own devices. She came upon Cecily who was now with the queen. Millicent was there too. She sidled up next to Cecily. "What is Philippa Meredith doing?" she murmured softly.

"Getting even," Cecily said low. And then in a voice heard by all around them, "Millicent, isn't that Sir Walter walking by the river with Philippa Meredith?"

"It cannot be," Millicent replied. "What business would he have with her?"

The women about them laughed, and even Queen Katherine smiled.

"Well, it most certainly is Philippa," Cecily insisted. "And look how close they are, and how he bends down when he speaks with her. Ohhhh! I think he kissed her! No, wait. He didn't. He is just speaking with her, but my, their lips are very close."

Millicent glared angrily in the direction of the river. "I do not believe it is Sir Walter at all," she said, but she knew it was, and worse, everyone else knew it was too. The wretch was embarrassing her before the entire court! How could he? She would tell her father! He would not allow her to marry a cad. But then Millicent thought of Sir

Walter's estates in Kent, and his beautiful house, and the fact that he had a great deal of gold with the London goldsmiths. She knew what her father would say to her. That men needed to sow their wild oats, and a wise woman looked the other way. But how could she look the other way when Philippa Meredith was flirting so outrageously with Sir Walter? She would smack the shameless wench the first opportunity she got. Her eyes went to the riverbank again, and she scowled.

Philippa was laughing up at Sir Walter. "You, sir, are an outrageous flirt. I wonder if your Millicent knows it," she teased him.

"A man's entitled to admire beauty, Mistress Philippa," he said.

"You would kiss me, wouldn't you?" Philippa responded provocatively.

"To have the honor of your first kiss would please me," he agreed.

"I must think on it," she told him. "I saved that kiss for the man I was to wed, and now he has deserted me for a life of celibacy. Should I not continue to save my kisses for him who will one day be my husband?"

"While I admire your virtue, Mistress Philippa, and I do not believe a comely maid should be free with her lips, a wee bit of experience in the art of kissing cannot be considered wrong, or put you in disrepute. Would you tell me that all of the queen's maids are as innocent as you are? For I know it not to be true." He smiled a smile at her that was almost a leer.

"You argue your case well, sir, but now I wonder if kissing a man I know to be soon betrothed a wise thing. Would I not be thought a bold baggage to do that? I must consider carefully the man I will give my first kiss to, Sir Walter." She smiled at him sweetly and teasingly. "Now I think it wise we return to the others. I should not like any gossip to ensue over this interlude." And picking up her skirts Philippa ran back up the lawn leaving Sir Walter Lumley alone, and most dissatisfied.

Cecily came forward, and linking her arm through her friend's they walked together among the others. "Millicent is fuming. I managed to point out that you were strolling with Sir Walter. She denied it was him, but she knew it was."

"I am deciding if I shall let him kiss me," Philippa replied. "You know I have never been kissed. I was saving that for your traitorous brother."

"Oh, don't let Sir Walter be your first kiss. I have heard he kisses badly. You must let Roger Mildmay be your first kiss. He kisses deliciously," Cecily said.

"Was he your first kiss?" Philippa asked.

Cecily nodded with a small smile. "He is such a nice fellow too. Ohh, I wonder if he might make a good husband for you, Philippa. His estates are near Tony's in Oxfordshire. But then I have heard it said he will eventually wed a neighbor's daughter whose lands match with his. Still, he would be good for a first kiss. Shall I ask him?"

"Cecily!" Philippa was rosy with blushes.

"Well, you had best kiss him, or Sir Walter will not be deterred. You've annoyed Millicent enough for one day. She really isn't worth your trouble, Philippa." She took her best friend's hand. "Come along now, I see Sir Roger Mildmay over there with Tony. I'll ask him for you."

Philippa began to laugh. "I am fifteen, and have never been kissed. And now my best friend must ask a man to do the honors? 'Tis pitiful, Ceci, and I shall look the fool."

"Nay, not with Roger. He is very kind and understanding. He will admire the fact that you were saving yourself for Giles. Come on!" She pulled Philippa along across the green lawns until they finally reached the spot where her betrothed husband, Sir Anthony Deane, and his friend, Sir Roger Mildmay, stood talking. Standing on tiptoes, Cecily whispered something in Sir Roger's ear. Then she let go of Philippa's hand, and took Tony's to lead him off.

Sir Roger Mildmay chuckled softly.

"This is ridiculous," Philippa said. "What has Ceci said to you?"

"That if I do not give you your first kiss, Walter Lumley will. Surely you do not fancy him, Mistress Philippa?" Sir Roger was a young man of medium height and stature, with warm brown eyes and sandy hair.

"No," Philippa said. "I have only been flirting with him in order to make that wretched Millicent Langholme jealous. They will shortly be betrothed."

"Why have you never been kissed? You have been here at court for three years now, I know, for you came with Cecily FitzHugh. Do you not want to be kissed?"

"I was saving myself for Giles FitzHugh, who was to be my husband," Philippa said. "Now was I not the fool, sir?"

"How charming of you, and how old-fashioned. You will make the right man a good and faithful wife one day, Mistress Philippa, but you are no longer attached, and therefore you are free to pursue love as all young girls do." He smiled at her.

"You do not think such behavior loose, sir?" Philippa asked him.

"Aye, if taken to extremes, but a lass's curiosity should be satisfied to a certain point before she is leg-shackled to a husband," he told her. "I propose that we keep company, Mistress Philippa, and if the occasion arises I shall kiss you, and you will learn what the mystery is all about. 'Tis said I am an excellent kisser," he chuckled.

Philippa laughed. "Ceci is right. You are nice," she said.

"Then we are agreed? I shall have your first kiss. And several others I hope," he replied. "But first I would tell you that I know your family will be in the market for another husband for you. I cannot, alas, be he. I will return home at the end of summer to wed the daughter of a neighbor. We have been pledged since childhood, and I am content to marry Anne Brownley. I would not lead you astray." He looked directly at her, and smiled a small smile. "I know your young heart must be broken by what has happened, and I would not add to your miseries."

"Ceci said you were a true gentleman, and she did tell me that you were pledged to another. Besides, it is unlikely anyone will offer for me now. I am fifteen, and my estates are practically in Scotland they are so far north. My stepfather is a Scot, and he and my mother spend part of the year in England and part of the year in Scotland."

"But you are very beautiful," Sir Roger told her. "Certainly the right man will come along for you."

Philippa shook her head in the negative. "My mother will want a man who will live at Friarsgate, and husband it as well as me. She never enjoyed the court as much as I do, and she loves her lands. I, on the other hand, do not want to live at Friarsgate. I want to live at court, or at least be near enough to visit it regularly," she told him. "If only my estates were nearer London." She sighed. "I have not a great name, nor important family connections."

"How came you to court?" he asked, for he was curious.

"My mother was the heiress of Friarsgate. She was orphaned at three of both of her parents, and her older brother. Her father's uncle came to be her guardian. He married her to his five-year-old son, but when mama was five her little husband died. Several families would have had her for their sons, but her uncle wanted Friarsgate for himself and his heirs. He married my mother off to an elderly knight in order to keep her from anyone else. He meant to marry her to his younger son eventually. The old knight, however, thought of mama as a daughter, and taught her how to manage her own estates. Then before he died he wrote a will, and he put his widow into the care and keeping of King Henry VII. Mama's uncle was foiled, and most angry about it, but it was then that my mother came to court. She was first in the care of Queen Elizabeth, and after she had died she went into the household of the Venerable Margaret, our King Henry's grandmother. Her two best friends were Margaret Tudor and the princess of Aragon."

"How fortunate for her," Sir Roger murmured, impressed.

"Mama went home again when Margaret Tudor became queen of Scotland, but first a marriage was arranged between her and my father, Sir Owein Meredith. My father was Welsh, and had been raised in the Tudor household, serving them since he was six. He was well thought of by all. They traveled much of the way home to Friarsgate in the queen of Scotland's wedding train. My father loved Friarsgate every bit as my mama. They were a good match, and it was a tragedy when he died so suddenly in a fall."

"And your mother remarried?" Sir Roger inquired.

"Several years later," Philippa said. "Mama and the two queens always kept up their friendship, which is why I was given a place at court. Mama brought me to court when I was past ten. I loved it right from the beginning, and Queen Katherine said I should join the maids of honor when I turned twelve. And so I did."

"No wonder some of the girls are jealous of you, Mistress Philippa. For a girl of little importance you have traveled high up the social ladder. The loss of an earl's son is a serious privation for your family. I can understand your difficulty, but I will wager that if your estates were nearer London it might be easier to find you a suitable match," Sir Roger said.

"I know," Philippa agreed sadly.

Seeing her attitude flagging he said, "Come, lass, and let us dance. The lanterns are now lit, the air is soft, and the evening fair. I know you like to dance, for I have seen you with the other maids at other revels."

They joined the circle of dancers forming, and Philippa was soon caught up in the music and the rhythm. She danced well, and when Sir Roger lifted her high and swung her about Philippa laughed happily, her sadness gone now. She was totally unprepared when, the dance finally ended in much merriment, Sir Roger quickly kissed her pretty lips.

"Oh!" Philippa gasped in surprise, and then she laughed again.

With a wicked grin he took her hand, and they slipped into the darkness near the river. "Your lips are sweet," he told her. Then stopping, he gathered her into his arms, and kissed her well and truly.

When he finally released her Philippa smiled up at him satisfied. "That," she told him, "was most pleasing, my lord. Will you do it again?" And when he had obliged her Philippa said, "I am a fool for having waited so long to be kissed. In retrospect I wonder how a maid can know if her husband kisses well if she has not some small experience. Ceci says you kiss well, and while I lack any comparison, I am inclined to agree with her. I hope you will continue to offer me your kisses while you are yet unmarried."

Sir Roger Mildmay laughed aloud. "Mistress Philippa," he said, "I think I am envious of the gentleman who will one day husband you. Now let us return to the others lest we be gossiped about for our absence. Kissing is an innocent pastime, but I would not have your reputation disputed or misunderstood by remaining here with you in the dark for much longer."

"I think I should like to go on kissing you for some time, sir," Philippa told him.

He smiled. "I shall be most happy to oblige you, sweetheart, but when we are in a less public venue," he told her as they returned to join the rest of the court.

In the bed they shared in the Maidens' Chamber later that night Philippa and Cecily spoke softly behind the drawn curtains, and Cecily giggled as her friend recounted her kissing adventure with Sir Roger.

"Didn't I tell you?" Cecily said. "He really is the nicest man. It is too bad that he is promised to another."

"I don't care," Philippa replied. "I just enjoy kissing him, but I cannot see him as my husband. Now tell me, was Millicent angry? What did she say?"

"Not a great deal, for the queen was there, but I know she was angry that Sir Walter was paying such close attention to you. When I pointed it out she pretended it wasn't him at all, but then one of the other girls said it was. She was very silent, but she watched you both like a hawk, and when you disappeared by the river for a brief time you could tell she was angry. After you had left him she excused herself from the queen's presence, and ran to find him. But I could tell she was not scolding him. Her position is not yet that secure with him. She clung to his arm, and gazed up at him. She looked quite like a ewe sheep gazing at her lamb, I vow." Cecily giggled. "Will you play with Sir Walter again, or are you now satisfied? Tony told me you pretended not to know how to dice. You are the best player amongst us girls!"

"You were right earlier when you said Millicent is not worth bothering with. She isn't. I have far more important things to do now. I want to kiss as many men as I can so that when I am forced back north to marry some bucolic dullard I will have wonderful memories of my last days at King Henry's court!"

"Sir Roger has certainly inspired you," Cecily said with a small laugh. "He really is a darling. Now let's get some sleep while we may. Tomorrow we move on to Richmond before the summer progress. I think we go north this year."

The following day the court decamped Greenwich for Richmond. To everyone's relief there was no sign of the sweating sickness or the plague now. It seemed to be dying out. Many of their companions began to depart the court as the time for the progress drew near. Some of the girls were going home to marry as Millicent and Cecily soon would be doing. The thought of losing her best friend began to tell on Philippa, and she began to grow more reckless in her behavior: dicing with the young gentlemen of the court, losing just enough to keep them coming back; paying off her debts with kisses, and of late if the gossip were to be believed, cuddles. Her servant, Lucy, scolded her but it did no good. Lucy would have written to her mistress's mother but she did not know how to write, and had not the means to hire someone to do it for her.

The queen was more tired now than she had been recently, and it was being said that it was her age. Her last pregnancy had worn her out entirely, it seemed. The queen intended to retire alone to Woodstock for the month of July rather than accompany the king on his progress. Henry was most displeased by this, but agreed. There were few to tell the maids of honor what to do now, not that Philippa would have listened.

Cecily would not be going to Woodstock. She would be returning to her family's home where she would be wed in August. It had originally been planned that Philippa come with her, but now with Giles having repudiated any match with Philippa Meredith, the earl of Renfrew and his wife felt it best that Philippa not come.

"I fear a visit to our hall at this time would but bring back memories of Giles for you, my dear," Edward FitzHugh had told Philippa. "Your previous visits were such happy ones. Your righteous sorrow, and your anger over my son's decision, or any attempt you might make to conceal it, would but put a pall upon Cecily's wedding day. I know you would not want to do that to she who has been your best friend, even as I know you will understand this decision that the Lady Anne and I have made in this matter."

Wordlessly, quick tears running down her cheeks, Philippa nodded. He was right, of course, but still to miss Cecily and Tony's wedding day . . .

"I have told my daughter of our decision, Philippa. I did not wish to put that upon you, my child. I am so sorry. My son's thoughtlessness has made it difficult for us all. You know that my wife and I would have gladly welcomed you as our daughter, Philippa. I have told your mother I will help in any way I can to provide you with another match."

Suddenly Philippa found herself angry. "I believe, my lord, that my family is quite capable to finding me another match without your help," she said coldly. "I will return now to helping Cecily pack for her departure tomorrow." She curtseyed stiffly, and turning, walked away from the earl of Renfrew.

A small smile touched Edward FitzHugh's lips. What a simpleton Giles was. This proud young girl would have brought so much to their family. And then he thought that perhaps Philippa was too good for his foolish son. It was a great loss, and he forgave her her rudeness.

She had borne up remarkably well in the face of her great disappointment and the embarrassment she had been caused by his younger son.

Philippa returned to find Cecily weeping. Sitting down on their bed next to her best friend, she put an arm about the girl's shoulders. "Your parents are right," she began. "Damn your brother for this new unhappiness he has visited upon both of us this time. You will write me and tell me all about the wedding, Ceci. And Mary and Susanna will not have to feel you are neglecting them for me."

"I am closer to you than to my sisters," Cecily sniffed.

"You will come to my wedding someday," Philippa said. "Believe me, my mother is already seeking eagerly for just the right bumpkin to husband Friarsgate, for it is far more important to her than I am."

"Will you go home this summer?" Cecily asked.

"Heavens no!" Philippa exclaimed. "I only went for a few weeks that first year because the queen insisted. I have never been more bored in my life. Nay, I shall not go back to Friarsgate unless forced to it."

"Your life will not be particularly exciting this summer, as you must go to Woodstock with the queen rather than on progress," Cecily noted.

"I know," Philippa groaned. "We leave in just a few days, but you go tomorrow, Ceci, and I shall be devastated by your going."

"Tony has promised that we will come back to court for Christmas. Until then we will live on his estate."

"Will you go there after the wedding?" Philippa asked as she folded up several pairs of sleeves, and tucked them into Cecily's little trunk.

"Nay. We will go to Everleigh, the original manor of the FitzHughs, in the Marches. We are to remain a month, and then move on to Deanemere, which will be our home," Cecily said. "Everleigh is quite remote, and small. It will suit us perfectly, as we will be unable to entertain any visitors. My family hasn't lived there in some time, but the house has always been kept up and in good repair."

"I will miss you," Philippa said.

"And I you," Cecily responded.

"It will never be the same again between us now that you are to be wed, and I am not," Philippa remarked.

"But we will always be best friends," Cecily replied.

"Always!" Philippa agreed.

Chapter 3

Cecily FitzHugh was gone. Even the detestable Millicent Langholme was gone. All of the younger girls had gone home now. Only Elizabeth Blount and Philippa Meredith remained. And in two days they would be moving with the queen to Woodstock. Dull, quiet, boring Woodstock for a dull, quiet and boring summer. The king and his remaining friends, for many had gone to their own estates now, would go on to Esher and Penhurst. They would spend their days hunting, and their nights in eating and laughter. The queen would spend her days in gentle pursuits and prayer. They would retire early. There would be few, if any, visitors. Oxfordshire was a pretty place, but without the company of a gay court it lacked interest for Philippa. But the queen loved its bucolic charms, and Woodstock's five chapels where she might worship. She was particularly fond of the Round Chapel. Philippa despaired.

"Come," said Bessie Blount the evening after Cecily's departure. "We must have some amusement with the remaining gentlemen before we are off to the queen's convent for the summer." She handed Philippa a small goblet of wine.

"Where did you get this?" Philippa inquired.

"I stole it," Bessie answered with a laugh. "It was some of that particularly fine Spanish Madeira wine Maria de Salinas left behind

47

when she married last year. No one has used her rooms here at Richmond ever since. It was in a corner, on a shelf, in an alcove. It was obviously overlooked. I left it there until now. It would be a shame to waste it, and I think we need it considering the summer before us. God's foot, I wish we were going with the king! Woodstock is so dull without him."

Philippa downed the contents of the little goblet, and held it out for more. " 'Tis good. I always wondered what this particular wine tasted like." She sipped a bit more slowly on her second portion.

"Some of the lads are still here," Bessie said. "I'm going to join them. 'Tis probably the last time we'll have the company of young men for a while. Would you like to come with me?"

"Who is here yet?" Philippa wanted to know.

"Roger Mildmay, Robert Parker, and Henry Standish," Bessie said.

"Why not," Philippa agreed. "I am already bored by the lack of lively company. I never thought I should miss even Millicent Langholme."

Bessie laughed. "I know," she said. "Come on then, and bring your goblet, for I am bringing the wine." She stood and started out the door of the empty Maidens' Chamber, turning to make certain that Philippa was behind her.

"Where are we going?" the younger girl wanted to know.

"To the top of the Canted Tower. No one will find us there," Bessie said mischievously. "We don't want to be caught dicing and drinking now, do we?"

"Nay," Philippa agreed. She sipped from her goblet as they hurried along. The Spanish wine was so very good. It felt like sweet silk on her tongue.

They walked across the Middle Court, joined by the three young men as they went. The summer twilight lasted for hours, but they still carried a small lamp. The Canted Tower was four stories high. It was one hundred and twenty steps to the top. They made the climb, stopping now and again to giggle as the wine began to take its effect upon the two young women. The roof of the tower gave a fine view of the river and the countryside to the southwest of London. The roof was filled with azure and gold weather vanes adorned with the king's arms. The men knelt, and began to dice. Soon both Bessie and Philippa joined them. The wine jug was passed around.

"I have no more money," Philippa complained after a time. The dice had not been favorable to her this evening.

"Then let us bet with items of our clothing," Henry Standish suggested, mischievously grinning.

"I'll bet a slipper," Philippa said, taking off her left shoe and tossing it into the center of their playing field. But soon she had lost her shoes, her stockings, and two sleeves. "Unlace my bodice for me, Bessie! My luck must turn soon," she said. Bessie did not hesitate, and the bodice was shortly lost as well. Philippa began to struggle with the tapes holding her skirt up, but she was drunk now; and her fingers were clumsy.

Just as tipsy but a little more experienced, Bessie decided it might be wise to stop the younger girl from her rash action. The three young men were laughing uproariously. They, too, were half-undressed at this point. Only Elizabeth Blount seemed to be blessed with good fortune this evening. She had lost but two slippers.

Philippa began to sing a bawdy song she had heard in the stables one day, and her gentlemen companions joined in.

> *The cowherd cuddled the milkmaid. He cuddled her in the hay.*
> *He kissed her in the hedgerows, for that is where they lay.*
> *And then he swived her merrily, for it was the month of May!*
> *With a hey nonny nonny, and a hey, hey, hey!*

They collapsed laughing in a heap, delighted with their own drunken humor. Even Bessie was laughing, her hair undone and about her face.

"Hush, hush," she said to them. "We shall be found out!"

"By whom?" Philippa demanded to know. "Everyone who might be fun except us has gone home to their own estates."

"And why have you not gone home, my pretty maid?" Lord Robert Parker leered at her, his eyes going to her chemise, which was now open and revealing her breasts.

"To Cumbria? With naught but the company of sheep?" Philippa responded. "Even being closeted with the queen at Woodstock is better than that."

"Cum-cum-Cumbria," Lord Robert singsonged. "Poor Mistress Philippa! Who wants a lass with a Cumbrian estate and flocks of sheep?"

"Let's have another drink!" Roger Mildmay said, taking a swig from the jug, and passing it around to his companions.

"I . . . hic . . . hate Cumbria!" Philippa declared. "Let's dice, and see who will win my skirts. Or perhaps I can win back my bodice from you, Hal Standish." She threw the bones, and then sighed, disappointed. "Well, have my skirt then. What is a bodice without its skirt?" She stood, and struggled with the garment's tapes again. The skirt fell about her ankles.

"What the hell is going on up here?" a familiar voice roared, and the king stepped out onto the roof with Charles Brandon. His outraged glance swept the quintet of young courtiers. "Mildmay! Standish! Parker! Explain yourselves immediately."

"We're dicing, your majesty," Philippa said tipsily. "And I can't seem to win back my clothing. Luck is against me tonight, I fear. Hic!" And then she giggled.

Charles Brandon swallowed back his laughter. The girl was obviously drunk as a lord. "Hardly the proper young lady her mama was, eh, Hal?" he murmured low.

The king scowled. "Mistress Blount. You will help your companion back on with her garments, and then see that she goes to bed. And you will bring her to my privy chamber tomorrow morning after the mass. Is that understood?"

Elizabeth Blount was pale, and suddenly very sober. "Yes, your majesty," she whispered low. She began gathering up Philippa's discarded clothing and aiding her to dress, but Philippa was very drunk now. She began to sing about the cowherd and the milkmaid once again.

The king looked horrified. The three young men, also shocked into sobriety, struggled to restrain their hilarity, but when Charles Brandon burst into hearty guffaws they were unable to do so. The masculine laughter rang in the deepening twilight as it finally slipped into night. But when Philippa, hastily but fully clothed now, was pulled to her feet by Bessie Blount her legs gave way beneath her, and she slowly sank into a heap at the king's feet, her auburn head using his boots as her pillow.

"So tired," she murmured. "Tired. Hic!" And then in the sudden silence her actions had brought about they heard her begin to softly snore.

After a long moment in which no one seemed to be breathing, the king said in a weary voice, "Mildmay, take the little wench to her bed. Standish, you and Parker carry her down the stairs, then give her to Sir Roger. Mistress Blount, escort them, and you are both to remain in the Maidens' Chamber until you bring Mistress Meredith to me in the morning. As for the three of you young gentlemen, you will return here where I will give you a lecture on the stars that can be seen tonight from this tower top. That way I can be certain that you are not in the Maidens' Chamber. Mistress Blount, you will bar your door and I shall check it when I come down again. Do you all understand me? There will be no more nonsense here tonight. And as for you three gentlemen, I will expect you to be gone back to your own estates within the next two days. I am going to Esher, and you are not invited. Is that understood?"

"Yes, your majesty," the trio chorused as one, looking very chastened already.

"You may come back at Christmas if you will," the king continued, "but I do not wish to see you until then."

"Yes, your majesty," they said again. Then Lord Parker and Lord Standish picked Philippa up, one taking her feet, the other her shoulders. Followed by Sir Roger and Elizabeth Blount, they descended the Canted Tower with their burden.

Charles Brandon laughed again when one of the young men was heard to complain, "Jesu! The wench weighs more than I would have thought." And another voice said, " 'Tis deadweight, you fool!" The duke of Suffolk turned to his brother-in-law. "By God, Hal, Rosamund Bolton would have a fit if she knew how badly her daughter has behaved. What are you going to do?"

"The poor girl is heartbroken over the damned FitzHugh boy," the king said. "And then Renfrew and his wife would not let her come to their daughter's wedding for fear the Meredith lass's sadness would spoil Cecily FitzHugh's day, yet the two girls are the best of friends. I never expected that she would react in such a lewd manner. I must speak with the queen, although I believe I know what must be done."

"And will you really make certain the Maidens' Chamber is bolted and barred?" Charles Brandon teased the king.

"I will!" the king replied.

"Mistress Blount is a charming girl, isn't she?" the duke of Suffolk noted.

"Aye," the king answered him, and his gaze was thoughtful.

In the morning Philippa awoke with the worst headache she had ever had in all of her life. The morning light was hurtful. Her temples throbbed unbearably. She could barely move, but Bessie forced her from her bed. "I am going to die," she insisted.

"Nay, you are going to get dressed, and we are going to mass. It is not like it is when all the girls and the other ladies are here. The queen will miss us if we do not appear. She can count those near to her right now on one hand."

"What happened?" Philippa asked. "How did I get to bed, and in my shift?"

"Don't you remember?" Bessie replied, grinning.

"Nay," Philippa said, groaning faintly as she shook her head.

"You were gambling with your garments when you ran out of coins," Bessie began. "Your luck was not running well last night. You lost your slippers and stockings. Both of your sleeves and your bodice. We sang bawdy songs, and drank a great deal. And then you lost your skirts as well."

"I was only in my chemise?" Philippa looked horrified. "Oh, Jesu!"

"That was not the worst of it," Bessie continued cheerfully. "The king came up to the roof of the Canted Tower with the duke of Suffolk to explore the heavens. He caught us. You sang him the same bawdy song with which you had earlier entertained us. He had me clothe you properly, and then before we might take our leave you collapsed, and fell asleep on his boots, snoring."

"Ohh, sweet Mother Mary," Philippa moaned. "I am ruined!" Her complexion looked almost pale green. "What happened next?" she asked nervously.

"The king had you carried downstairs to the Maidens' Chamber. He told Roger and the others they were to go home and not come back until Christmas. He wants to see you after the mass in his privy chamber. I am to escort you there."

"I am going to be sick," Philippa said suddenly.

Bessie grabbed an empty chamber pot and, giving it to the younger girl, turned away as the sound of Philippa's retching was heard. When it seemed as if all was well again she turned about. "We're going to be late for the mass," she said. "Rinse your mouth with rose water, and let us go. But whatever you do don't drink any water right now. It will only make you vomit again. I'll get you some wine later."

"I will never drink wine again!" Philippa declared.

Bessie laughed. "Trust me. A bit of the hair of the dog who bit you will solve all of your problems. Well, perhaps not your headache."

"I am going to die," Philippa repeated. Then she rinsed her mouth, but she could not rid herself of the sour taste.

They hurried to the Chapel Royal, reaching it just as the queen was entering. Katherine turned, and looked at Philippa. Then turning away, shaking her head, she walked to her place. She knows, Philippa thought. Three years without a misstep, and now I have disgraced myself well and good. And all over a man who decided that he would prefer to be a priest rather than my husband. What was I thinking? Was I thinking at all? I don't want to live at Friarsgate for the rest of my days. I want to stay here at court. What am I to do if I am sent away? I'll never see Ceci again. Oh, damn! And all over Giles! I am a fool! A great and featherheaded booby. Oh, Lord! I think I'm going to be sick again, but I can't. I just can't! She swallowed back the bile in her throat, praying she might keep it down, and not embarrass herself further.

The mass was finally over and, escorted by Bessie Blount, Philippa made her way to the king's privy chamber. The two girls stood waiting in the antechamber among petitioners and secretaries and foreign merchants seeking an audience with the king. Finally a page in the king's livery came to fetch them.

"The king says that you may go, Mistress Blount," he told Bessie, bowing politely to her. "Mistress Meredith is to follow me."

"Good luck!" Bessie said, giving Philippa's cold hand a quick squeeze, and then she hurried off to find her breakfast.

"This way, mistress," the page said, leading her to a small door. He knocked upon it, and then flung the door open to usher her inside. Then he closed the door behind her.

"Come, my child," she heard the queen's voice say.

"Yes, come forward, Mistress Meredith, and explain to me your behavior of last night," the king said sternly.

The royal couple were seated side by side behind an oak table before her. Philippa curtseyed, but she thought her head would fall off when she did. She swallowed hard, attempting to find her voice, and finally said, "There is no excuse for my wretched behavior, your majesty. But in my defense I can say I have never before acted in such a terrible manner, and I can assure your majesty that I never will again."

"I should hope not, Philippa Meredith," the queen said softly. "Your mama will be most upset to learn of this breach of good manners on your part."

"I am so ashamed, your highness," Philippa told the queen. "I remember little. Bessie Blount told me what happened when I awakened this morning. I have never done anything like that before. You know that to be so."

"You were drunk," the king said quietly.

"Yes, your majesty," Philippa admitted, hanging her aching head.

"And most disorderly as well," he continued.

"Yes, your majesty." She felt the tears beginning to run down her face.

"You sang bawdy songs. A song I was surprised to find you knew," the king said.

"I heard it in the stables," Philippa told him.

"You gambled with your clothing, and had I not come upon you when I did who knows what else might have happened," the king scolded her. "Why would a girl of such a good family endanger her reputation so? I knew your father, Philippa Meredith. He was a most honorable fellow. And your mother has always been a good subject as well, despite her marriage to a Scot. Her own service and kindness to this house ensured you a position with our queen. Would you throw away this chance given you?"

Now Philippa began to sob noisily. "Oh, no, your majesty! I am so proud that I serve my queen. I always want to serve her. I am so sorry! You must forgive me, your majesty. I cannot bear it that I have disappointed you so!" And she wept, her small hands covering her face.

The king looked uncomfortable. He did not like crying females. Getting up, he came from behind the oak table and put an arm about Philippa. He took out his own silk pocket square, wiping her eyes and face. "Do not wail, lass. It is not the end of the world," he assured her. Then leaving the pocket square with her he retreated behind the table once again.

Philippa struggled to pull herself together. This was terrible. One did not howl like a baby in front of the monarch. But her head was aching so terribly, and her belly was roiling horrifically. "I . . . I am so afraid you are going to send me away," she finally managed to say. She wiped her wet face, and straightened her carriage.

"We are," the king said, and he held up his hand to still further defense of herself. "But you will be allowed back, Philippa Meredith, when your family believes you are ready to come. The queen and I think you need to return to your family for a time. You have not been home in several years. We can see that your disappointment in Giles FitzHugh has unnerved you badly. And then to be forbidden your best friend's wedding was a cruel disappointment as well. Your mother will need to see and speak with you about a possible new match, for you must certainly be married within the year, my child. And when your heart is at peace again, Philippa Meredith, and your mother is content to let you return to court we will welcome you gladly. We have arranged for you and your servant to begin your journey tomorrow. You will go with the queen's party as far as Woodstock, and then continue on under our protection."

I cannot argue, Philippa thought silently to herself. One does not argue with the king. And they have said I may come back. She curtseyed. "Thank you, your majesty."

"Be thankful few remain here at Richmond, Philippa Meredith," the king said, "that few know of your indiscretion. It will be forgotten by the time you return, I am certain." He held out his hand to her, and Philippa took it, and kissed the king's ring.

"Thank you, your majesty. Your highness. Please accept my apologies for my unthinkable behavior of last evening. It will not happen again." She curtseyed.

"You will carry a letter to your mother," the king said, and then with a wave of his hand he dismissed her.

With an almost audible sigh of relief Philippa backed from the little privy chamber.

The queen turned to her husband. "Be as diplomatic as only you know how, my lord, when you write to Rosamund Bolton. I do want to see Philippa back at court in the future, and I know she does not wish to live her entire life in the north as her mother does."

" 'Tis strange," the king remarked. "Rosamund never really liked the court. Her heart and her thoughts were always with her beloved Friarsgate. She could scarcely wait to return to it each time she was forced to visit the court. But her eldest child adores court, and is, I suspect, a born courtier. I wonder what will happen when mother and daughter meet this time. Philippa will not be content to remain in Cumbria."

"But she is Friarsgate's heiress," the queen noted.

"I suspect that matters not," Henry Tudor replied.

Philippa hurried back to the Maidens' Chamber where she knew Bessie would be waiting. "I am being sent home," she declared dramatically as she entered the room.

"What happened?" Bessie wanted to know. "You will be allowed back, won't you? It would be terrible if you were exiled forever."

"Aye, it would," Philippa responded, "but I am to be allowed back eventually. The decision will rest with my mother, but I shall make her see reason. Both the king and the queen were there in his privy chamber. They scolded me roundly."

"Did you cry?" Bessie asked.

"I did," Philippa admitted. "I was so embarrassed to do so before them too."

"You were probably spared worse because you did. I have heard it said that the king hates a weeping woman," Bessie told Philippa with a grin. "So, when do you depart?"

"I'm to go with the queen's party as far as Woodstock, and then I will be escorted to Friarsgate from there," Philippa explained. "Lucy has almost finished the packing. She will be delighted to learn we are going home. She, at least, has missed it."

"Is it really so dreadful, this Friarsgate?" Bessie asked. "I come from

Shropshire, you know. 'Tis said we have the worst winters in all of England. And my family name is not particularly great either. While I, too, love the court, I am always happy to see Kinlet Hall, and my mother. And I have not your good fortune in being the heiress to my family's estates."

Philippa sighed. "I know I am probably foolish, but I would gladly settle for a small estate in Kent, or Suffolk, or even Devon. My mother's lands need especial tending. She and my uncle Thomas, who is Lord Cambridge, raise sheep, from which cloth is woven at Friarsgate, and then transported by means of their own ship to several countries for sale. They control, if I understand it correctly, just how much of their cloth they will sell, and to whom. While I am grateful for the revenues raised, most of it goes back into their business, and into Friarsgate itself. If I have learned one thing from my mother, it is that when you have responsibilities such as hers you must tend to them yourself. There are few, if any, who can be trusted to shoulder your burdens, even in part. I don't want to spend my time in such labor, Bessie. I don't want Friarsgate, because to possess it I must take responsibility for it. The court is where I want to live, in service to the king and the queen. I want a husband who is a man of the court, and will understand that because he also is in service to the monarch. My father, Sir Owein Meredith, was in service to the house of Tudor from the time he was six. He was knighted on the field of battle. I can just barely remember him, Bessie, but I loved him, and I admired him. I am probably more like him than I am my mother. In fact I am not at all like mama except in our features. Some at Friarsgate who remember back say I am like a great-grandmother of mine, but I would not know that."

"Yours has always sounded like a loving family. Will your sisters join the court someday?" Bessie wondered.

"Banon is certainly old enough," Philippa said. "She is the heiress to Lord Cambridge's home, Otterly Court. And then there is my littlest sister, who like you is called Bessie. I don't know them anymore, I fear."

"But you will soon reacquaint yourself with them both," Bessie Blount replied.

"Aye, and my little stepbrother, John Hepburn, and my mother's sons by my stepfather. I shall certainly be a stranger to them all now," Philippa remarked. "It is very strange having a stepbrother, and half brothers who are Scots, and not English."

"Your summer will be interesting then," Bessie concluded, "unlike mine, which will be uneventful. I had thought Maggie, Jane, and Anne were to remain with the queen this summer."

"Jane's mother grew ill, and she was needed at home. I am not certain if she will return. Maggie's mother is Irish. She asked the queen for her daughter's company so they might visit Maggie's grandmother in Ireland. She is elderly. As for Anne, her family may have found a suitable match for her. They wanted her home so the gentleman in question might inspect her, and she him," Philippa explained. "Aye, I fear your summer may be very dull, but I shall try and get back as quickly as I can."

"I thought you said it was your mama's decision as to when you return," Bessie Blount said.

Philippa smiled. "I shall not be happy at home. If I am not content then no one will be content until they allow me to return to court, and the company of civilized folk."

Bessie shook her head at her companion. "You really should learn to be more biddable, Philippa Meredith. Men do not like headstrong women."

Philippa laughed. "I do not care. I am what I am, and no more. At least I am honest, unlike some. Millicent Langholme simpers, and blushes, but we both know that once she has a ring on her finger, Sir Walter will have one through his nose by which she will lead him to her ways and none other."

Bessie laughed. "I cannot argue with you there," she agreed.

The following day the queen and her party departed for Woodstock, while the king and his friends moved on from Richmond to

Esher, where they would go hunting. Philippa was given a day to rest once they reached Woodstock, and then she departed with her servant, Lucy, for Friarsgate. She carried little luggage, for she had left most of her clothing at Lord Cambridge's house near London. Her beautiful court garb would have no place at Friarsgate. And while she did not relish several months at Friarsgate, Philippa did not look forward to the long trip, and believed that with less baggage they would move more quickly.

Late in the afternoon before her departure Philippa was called to the queen's privy chamber where a gentleman stood waiting by Katherine's side. The queen was seated, and looked rather pale today.

"Come in, Philippa," the queen beckoned her.

Philippa entered, and curtseyed to the queen.

Katherine smiled. "This is Sir Bayard Dunham, my child. He will escort you and your servant safely home to Friarsgate. He has his instructions, and carries a letter for your mother. You will be accompanied by a dozen men-at-arms from my own service. You will leave at first light in the morning."

"Thank you, your highness," Philippa replied, and curtseyed again.

"You will take with you our kindest regards to your mother, and tell her that I hope you will be returned to my service by the Christmas revels," the queen said. "If you are ready, of course, and cured of your malaise over the FitzHugh boy."

"Yes, madame!" Philippa smiled broadly. She was already cured of her pique over the duplicitous Giles FitzHugh, for her little adventure at the top of the Canted Tower had done that, but the queen would not believe it, she knew.

"Go along now, my child. May the Blessed Mother protect you in your travels, and bring you safely home," Katherine said.

"And may God and his gracious son, our lord Jesu, protect your highness, and give you your heart's desire," Philippa said, curtseying a final time as she backed from the room followed by Sir Bayard Dunham.

The queen acknowledged the girl's prayer with a gracious nod of her head.

In the queen's antechamber Sir Bayard said, "I hope you understand that first light means just that, Mistress Meredith. We shall not waste half the day away waiting for you to finish your toilette. How large a baggage cart will you have?"

"My court clothing is hardly suitable to Cumbria," Philippa said quietly. "Both my servant, Lucy, and I will carry what we will need, sir. I am not fond of long journeys, and while I do not relish a summer on my mother's estates I am anxious to get there. We will ride until dark each day, I hope. And I assume you have arranged for our accommodations along the way, Sir Bayard."

"I have," he said, not in the least offended by her tart manner. Then he bowed neatly. "I shall see you in the morning then, Mistress Meredith."

Philippa curtseyed to him politely and then, turning, walked away. Finding Lucy she told her, "Our escort is Sir Bayard Dunham. He's a tough old bird, and I have seen him about the court. We are to leave at first light, and he means it."

"I'll see we're up, and have some food in our bellies," Lucy responded. She had matured since that day she rode into Edinburgh with Philippa, both of them openmouthed at the sight of the first city either had ever seen.

"Will you come back to court with me, Lucy?" Philippa asked suddenly. "I know you have missed Friarsgate far more than I have."

"Of course I'll come back with you!" Lucy exclaimed. "If you brought someone new they would be of no use to you at all. A few months at Friarsgate, and I'll be cured of any desire to remain there indefinitely." The tiring woman chuckled, patting her young mistress's arm. "Why, I can already smell the stink of the sheep!"

Philippa laughed. "Aye, just thinking about it I can too."

In the morning with the sun not even up yet, but their stomachs full of good oat stirabout, freshly baked warm bread that had been covered in butter with plum jam, and the queen's finely watered wine, they awaited Sir Bayard by the stables where the grooms held their horses, and a troupe of armed men were already mounted. Their escort rushed up, obviously embarrassed that he had overslept.

Philippa and Lucy mounted their animals, and Philippa said, "Where is the food basket, please?"

"Right here, m'lady," the captain of their guard said, pointing to the back of his saddle where a wicker container had been strapped.

Philippa turned to Sir Bayard. "Are we ready then, sir?"

He glowered at her, certain she was mocking him, but her face showed no sign of humor, and so he nodded first to her, and then to the captain. They left Woodstock Palace, moving through the town of the same name, and out onto the road north. When they had ridden for about an hour Philippa reached out to touch Sir Bayard's sleeve. Startled, he looked at her. She handed him a small wrapped napkin, but said nothing. Opening it as they rode along he saw a thick piece of buttered bread with a sliced egg and a piece of ham atop it. Philippa had already looked away, and was engaging her servant in conversation. His belly rumbling, Sir Bayard Dunham ate the breakfast she had so thoughtfully provided for him, thinking that perhaps this young girl was not as flighty as he had assumed she was. As were all the queen's maids of honor usually.

They traveled almost the same exact route Philippa had taken when she had come to court. The route her mother had taken those many years ago. They rode through beautiful Warwickshire with its great castle and green meadows. The justly famous dreadful roads in Staffordshire had not changed at all, and while it did not rain, the river crossings were still difficult.

"Outrageous! No excuse for this!" Sir Bayard muttered to himself.

When they reached Shropshire Philippa remembered that Bessie Blount had said that her father's hall was there. "Will we stay at Kinlet Hall?" she asked.

"Nay, worse luck," Sir Bayard responded. " 'Tis not on our direct route."

At that moment a large flock of black-faced sheep began to cross the road, and her escort swore beneath his breath.

"Get those damn animals out of our path!" he ordered the men.

"No, no!" Philippa cried. "If you scatter the flock the shepherd will have a difficult time gathering them all up, and they may lose some of the beasts. We must not cost the farmer who owns them any of his animals. We can wait."

"You are knowledgeable about sheep?" Sir Bayard said, curious.

"My family's wealth comes from sheep, and their wool," Philippa answered him. "These are a breed named after the county. Their wool is particularly fine. My mother has several flocks of them."

Sir Bayard Dunham looked surprised by her answer. Then he said, "I knew your father, you know."

"I can still remember him even though he died when I was very young," Philippa said.

"A good man," Sir Bayard replied brusquely. "Loyal. Honest. Knew how to do his duty. He had no sons?"

"Nay," Philippa answered. "Not living."

The flock of sheep had finally crossed over the road, and the shepherd gave them a friendly wave as he pulled his forelock in a gesture of thanks. They moved on north and west towards Cumbria, going through the flat county of Cheshire and into the forested Lancaster. The desolately barren hills they next traversed told Philippa that they were finally in the tiny slice of Westmoreland they needed to go through.

"We should be in Carlisle tomorrow," Philippa said. "And then just another day and a half of travel to reach Friarsgate. We have been extremely fortunate, Sir Bayard, for it has not rained upon us one day."

"Aye," he agreed, nodding. "Traveling at this particular time in the summer is usually dry."

"Will you join the king at Esher when you return?" Philippa asked him.

Sir Bayard shook his head. "I was assigned some years ago to the queen's service," he told her. "I am no longer young enough to keep up with the king."

Reaching Carlisle the next afternoon they stayed in a guesthouse that belonged to the monastery of St. Cuthbert's. Philippa's great-uncle, Richard Bolton, was prior, and it was by chance that he was in Carlisle when they arrived. Hurrying from the church to the guesthouse, he greeted her. He was a tall, distinguished man with bright blue eyes.

"Philippa! Your mother did not say you were coming home. Welcome!" He lifted her down from her mount.

"I have been sent home, great-uncle, but whether in disgrace or not I shall not know until my mother reads the queen's letter. I am, however, invited back to court at Christmas to resume my former duties." She kissed his cheek.

"Well, if you are invited back," Richard Bolton said, "the infraction cannot be too serious, I suspect. Would it have to do with Giles FitzHugh, my child?"

Philippa's hazel eyes grew stormy. "That dastard!" she told her great-uncle.

"Ahh, then it does," he replied, the tiniest of smiles touching his lips at her expletive. "My dear Philippa, when God calls, as I can certainly tell you, you must listen. There simply is no other solution, and Rome can weave a magnificent spell. I understand he will have a place in the Vatican itself. Obviously the church sees great things for Giles FitzHugh. I am afraid that marriage and a northern estate pale in comparison."

"Obviously," Philippa responded dryly. "I have gotten past my disappointment, great-uncle, but the second son of an earl was quite a coup for mama. What she will do now I do not know. There are no young gentlemen of my acquaintance who want a girl with estates like mine. Far from court, and a vast responsibility. And I am now past fourteen. I am, I fear, doomed to spinsterhood."

"I am certain that Rosamund will find a solution to your problem, my child," the cleric answered her quietly. "Perhaps this is God's way of bringing you home to us."

"I will be returning to court, great-uncle. Of that you may be certain," Philippa said grimly. "I shall not be shackled to some bumpkin because my mother thinks he will take good care of her beloved Friarsgate. I know it means more to her than I do, than anything else does. But I am not my mother."

Richard Bolton's eyes grew troubled. Philippa might not love Friarsgate, but she was every bit as stubborn as his niece, Rosamund, was. It would not, he suspected, be a peaceful summer for the extended Bolton-Meredith-Hepburn family.

Chapter 4

*P*hilippa looked down from the hills surrounding the valley of Friarsgate. The lake sparkled in the afternoon sunlight. The fields looked well tended as always. The sheep, cattle, and horses grazed in their meadows. Her mother had obviously added to her flocks, for there were more sheep than Philippa remembered.

"It looks a prosperous and peaceful place," Sir Bayard said.

" 'Tis both," Philippa noted dryly, and Lucy snickered. Philippa nudged her mount, and they began to descend the hill. The peasants in the field stared openmouthed at the beautiful young woman passing by. Only a few recognized her after two years, for Philippa had grown from a young girl into a young woman.

Sir Bayard Dunham had spent most of his life as a courtier. The landscape around them was indeed lovely. The people looked content. Yet he suddenly realized that he himself could not possibly be happy in so quiet a setting for very long, and he had sympathy for his charge. Philippa Meredith was a creature of the court, and not the country.

Arriving at the house they were immediately greeted by stable boys who came to take their horses, and the door to the house swung open to reveal Maybel Bolton, wife to Edmund, Friarsgate's bailiff. Edmund and his brother, Prior Richard, had been the eldest born of Philippa's great-grandfather's sons, but both were bastards of the same mother.

Their births had occurred prior to their father's marriage, which had also yielded two sons. Philippa's grandfather, Guy Bolton, was the eldest legitimate son. He had perished along with his wife and son, leaving Philippa's mother, Rosamund Bolton, an heiress, and Rosamund's uncle Henry, his younger legitimate brother, his daughter's guardian.

Maybel gave a shriek of surprise, turned as if to go inside, and then reversed herself. She came from the house, enfolding Philippa in her arms, sobbing. "My baby is home at last!" she wept noisily. "Why didn't you tell us you were coming, you bad lass?"

"Because I didn't know myself until several days ago," Philippa said. "You might as well know, Maybel, that I have been sent home to recover from my broken heart, although it is already healed."

"Oh, my poor baby," Maybel sniffled. "To be jilted by the likes of that dreadful Giles FitzHugh! Bad luck to him, I say."

"Maybel, this is Sir Bayard Dunham, my escort. He is the queen's man, and we have the men-at-arms to feed and house as well for the next few days. Where is my mother? And my sisters?"

"Your mother is up at Claven's Carn with the Hepburn. Banon is at Otterly being the lady of the manor. Bessie is about somewhere however," Maybel said. "Come into the hall, child. And you also, Sir Bayard." Maybel looked out at the dozen men-at-arms. "You lot as well." She gestured towards them.

They entered the hall, and Maybel was quickly ordering the house servants to set up the tables and benches for the men. "And feed them now. 'Tis late and they will be hungry." She turned to Sir Bayard. "The weather is warm enough for your men to sleep in the stables, sir. I don't think it proper they remain in the house with my master and mistress away."

"I agree," Sir Bayard said. "When they have eaten I shall take them out myself."

"You may remain here, sir," Maybel responded. "I'll have a servant make up a nice bed space for you. You are not in the flush of youth any longer, and need the warmth the hall will provide."

"Thank you, madame," Sir Bayard said. This country woman was most bluntly spoken, but kind. He could not remember the last time someone had shown a care for his personal well-being. The thought of a warm bed space to sleep in was very comforting.

"Perhaps you should send for mama," Philippa said. "Best to get it all over with as soon as possible. I'm sure she has much to say to me. I do not intend remaining at Friarsgate for long. I am asked to return to my position. The queen will need those of us with experience in her service. Many left this summer to be married. Banon may be invited to court, Maybel. I think she would like that."

"Banon to go into the queen's service too? Oh, my dear child, what an honor, and all because of your mama's friendship with the queen," Maybel gushed.

At that moment a little girl came into the hall. She was all arms and legs, and her long blond hair was unruly. She wore a gown that appeared to have seen better days, and that hung straight on her shapeless form. She stared at Philippa and Sir Bayard.

"Come and welcome your sister Philippa home, Bessie," Maybel said.

Elizabeth Meredith came forward, and with great dignity curtsied to Sir Bayard and her sister. "Welcome home, Philippa," she said.

"Why are you dressed like some peasant child?" Philippa said sharply.

The younger girl looked at her oldest sister. "Because I have no grand garments like you, sister, and what good gowns I have I prefer to keep clean. One can hardly herd animals done up for court."

"I am hardly done up for court," Philippa replied. "I left all my beautiful gowns in London at Uncle Thomas's home. And why are you herding animals?"

"Because I like to," Bessie replied. "I do not enjoy being useless, sister."

"I am a maid of honor at court, and believe me I am not useless," Philippa snapped. "To be in service to Queen Katherine is an honor, and we maids scarcely have time to sleep, we are kept so busy."

"Do you enjoy the court? But of course you must, for you have not been home in ages, sister," Bessie remarked.

"King Henry's court is the center of the world," Philippa said, her eyes shining. "I cannot wait to go back!"

"Why did you bother coming home then?" Bessie queried.

"That is not your business," Philippa said in lofty tones.

Bessie laughed. "It is because of that boy, isn't it? Boys are stupid. I shall never involve myself with a boy, sister. Worthless fellows, except perhaps our little brothers."

"You don't know what you're talking about, Bessie Meredith," Philippa replied. "Someday you will be married, although who will marry you I don't know. You have no land of your own, and a woman must have land to be an acceptable match for a good family. But why would you know something like that? How old are you now?"

"I am eleven," Bessie said, "and any man who marries me one day will do so because he loves me, and not because I have or have no land."

"Girls, girls, cease your quarreling. What will Sir Bayard think?" Maybel scolded them. "Bessie, go and wash the dirt from your hands and face."

"I'll only get dirty again when I go back outside," Bessie said, but she was already moving up the stone staircase to her chamber.

"I am surprised that mama allows her to be so rough," Philippa noted as her youngest sister disappeared from her sight.

"She is the youngest of your father's children," Maybel explained. "Now your mama has a new family, and they need her too. So does her husband."

"Bessie should not be allowed to run wild as she is obviously doing," Philippa said primly. Then she turned to Sir Bayard. "Come, sir, and sit at the high board with me. The servants will bring us supper too."

Edmund Bolton came in, and greeted Philippa warmly. He thanked Sir Bayard for his careful shepherding of the girl from Woodstock to Friarsgate. He saw that a messenger was dispatched to Claven's Carn across the border. Then when Philippa and her sister had gone to their beds he sat with Sir Bayard and his wife by the fire, drinking the fine whiskey that Rosamund's husband brewed up.

"It seems odd to me," Sir Bayard began. "An English landholder, a friend of our queen's, married to a Scots laird."

"There are many such marriages here on the border," Edmund responded. "And our Rosamund is also a close friend of Queen Margaret."

"I am told she is now called the king's mother," Sir Bayard said.

"By some, but never in this house," Edmund replied. "The lady of Friarsgate would not tolerate such disrespect of her old friend."

"The Scots make fine whiskey," Sir Bayard noted.

"Aye," Edmund agreed with a small smile.

Rosamund arrived two days later, just as Sir Bayard was preparing to depart. She thanked him for his care of her eldest daughter, and insisted he have a small purse for his troubles. While he demurred at first, he took the purse as he kissed her hand, and bid her farewell. Rosamund watched as he rode off with the dozen men-at-arms. Then turning, she reentered her house. "Where is Philippa?" she asked Maybel.

"In her chamber, sulking," came the tart answer. "I do not know what has happened to our sweet child, Rosamund. She is disdainful of everything, and fights constantly with Bessie. And that Lucy ain't much better, with her airs. They brought virtually nothing with them, and Philippa has had the seamstress run ragged altering several of her old gowns which barely fit her because she has grown breasts. She has been wearing the same clothing in which she traveled. When I asked her why she brought no luggage with her she said 'twas because she would not be here long, and did not wish to take any longer getting to so distant a place than was necessary. The Philippa I helped you raise is long gone, I fear, and I am not certain I like this girl who bears her likeness and name."

"It is the court," Rosamund said quietly, putting an arm about her old nursemaid.

"We went to court, and did not come back all hoity-toity," Maybel said.

"Remember the Bolton family motto, Maybel?" Rosamund said quietly. "It is *Tracez votre chemin*. Make your own path. That is, I think, what my daughter is doing.

"But she is young yet, and she has been hurt. Not so much in the losing of Giles FitzHugh, but in the embarrassment he has caused her at court."

"The gentleman who escorted her home brought a letter for you from the queen. I imagine there is much in it that Mistress Philippa has yet to share with us," the older woman said. "She has been anxious for you to come home on one hand, but on the other not in so much of a hurry to see you." She handed Rosamund the packet.

Rosamund laughed. At twenty-nine she was still beautiful, although she was even now ripening with a seventh child that would be born in February as her ewe sheep were dropping their lambs. "Well, I suppose it is better to get it over with, Maybel. Send one of the girls up to bring my daughter down into the hall."

"Mama!" Elizabeth Meredith ran into the large chamber. "I saw your horse being led to the stables. You didn't come alone, I hope. Papa will be furious."

"Nay, my darling Bessie, I was escorted by several of our clansmen." She cocked her head, and looked closely at her youngest daughter. "Well," she said, "I see no outward signs of violence."

Bessie burst out laughing. "I am too quick for Mistress Fussy-Prissy, mama. I don't remember Philippa being so mean. I really don't think I like her anymore."

"Be patient, my darling Bessie," Rosamund counseled her child. "Philippa is unhappy right now, and so we must be kind. The match that was to be made for her was a particularly good one, and it will be difficult to replace Giles FitzHugh. Philippa has lived at court long enough to know that. Beneath all her anger and superiority she is frightened. Fifteen is the age many girls wed. To find herself unexpectedly bereft of a proposed husband at this time is a catastrophe in her mind, but Friarsgate is an excellent dowry, and she will have gold and silver as well. She is more than well dowered enough to attract the right man. We must just be patient."

"Philippa says she hates Friarsgate, mama. She says if her lands weren't so far north Giles would not have deserted her," Bessie replied.

"Telling tales already, brat?" Philippa entered the hall. She was dressed in a plain green gown. "Mama, I am happy to see you. But gracious! Are you breeding yet again?"

"Bessie, pet, go to the kitchens and tell cook I am home. Philippa, come and sit by the fire with me. And aye, I am breeding again. The bairn will be born in February. It will probably be another lad, for Logan, it seems, can sire only lads on me." She sat down, the packet Maybel had handed her still unopened. She saw Philippa eye it warily.

"Will you tell me what is in the queen's letter, or shall I open it now, and read it before we speak?" she asked her daughter.

"Do what you will, mama. I'm sure the queen has overreacted to my situation. She seems to believe that I am pining for Giles FitzHugh, and I am not! I hate him for discarding me in so hasty a fashion. Now I am to be the old maid of the court. I am not happy, mama, but I am not weeping over that pious fool."

Rosamund broke the seal on the queen's letter, and opening it out began to read. Once or twice her left eyebrow lifted itself. Once there was almost the hint of a smile about her lips. She actually read the queen's missive twice to make certain she understood Katherine's position. Finally she set the letter aside on the bench where she sat and said in a quiet voice, "Were you anyone else's daughter, Philippa, I expect that you would have been dismissed from the queen's service, and sent home in total disgrace with no invitation to return."

"But I have been asked back! At Christmas, and I am to resume my old place in the ranks of the queen's maids," Philippa said quickly.

"Because the queen values our small friendship, Philippa."

"The king stood up for me too. He was so kind," Philippa told her mother. "They say Inez de Salinas once caught you in a compromising position with the king, and that you got her dismissed from court when she gossiped about it, but the queen forgave you."

"That is a lie," Rosamund said. She would not share her secret history with her daughter. It was not Philippa's business. She continued calmly. "I knew the king as a boy when I lived in his grandmother's care. You know all of that. You are foolish to listen to gossip, Philippa, especially such old gossip, but we are not speaking of my days at court. We are speaking of your shameless behavior. What possessed you? Drinking to excess? Dicing, and removing your clothing when you lost as payment for the debt? How am I to find you a respectable husband when you exhibit such behavior? King Henry was kind to you? Aye, he would be. He well remembers your father, and Owein Meredith's faithful service to the house of Tudor. Would that his eldest daughter could prove as honorable.

"And the queen says while she hopes you may return at Christmas, that decision is to be mine, and mine alone, Philippa. I am very angry at you, and I do not know if I shall ever allow you back at court!"

Philippa jumped up from the chair where she had been seated. "I will die if I am forced to remain in this backwater, mama! Is that what you want? Do you want me to die? I must return to court! I must!" Her eyes were wild with open distress.

Rosamund remained seated. "Sit down, Philippa. I can see why the queen was concerned. You have lost all sense of proportion, and your behavior is out of control. I am not pleased with you, my daughter. What Giles FitzHugh did was childish, selfish, and thoughtless. He might have written his father of his decision before he returned home to announce it to one and all."

"I lo-loved him!" Philippa began to weep.

"You barely knew him," her mother replied bluntly. "You saw him first when you were ten and I took you to court to present you to the king and queen. A match was proposed that I did not decline, but neither did I accept. I said we must wait until you were older. By the time you returned to court Giles was on the continent studying. You have built up this romantic fantasy in your mind about Giles, Philippa. I suspect it is a good thing that Giles is not to be your husband, for I honestly doubt that he could live up to that dream lover."

"Mama!" Philippa sniveled, "I never thought of him like that!"

"Didn't you? Then he was absolutely not the man for you. A woman should lust after the man she is to wed. I might have been shy, but I could scarcely wait for your father to bed me. And believe me when I tell you that I lusted greatly after Patrick Leslie, and Logan Hepburn. Do you not remember the passion between Glenkirk and me?"

"I thought it wonderful, but odd," Philippa admitted. "Most people do not love like that, mama. A good marriage is intended to improve your family's connections and wealth, and for the purpose of procreating children. That is what the queen teaches the maids."

"Does she?" Rosamund said. "Well, I suppose it must be enough for a princess of Aragon who weds a king of England. But it would not have been enough for me, nor should it be for you, Philippa." She reached out and brushed the tears from her daughter's cheek. "Giles has hurt you, my darling girl. Accept it, and then when your heart is once again content we will find you a young man you can love as I have loved the men in my life. You are no queen, Philippa. You are simply the heiress to Friarsgate."

"You don't understand," Philippa said, drawing away from her mother. "I don't want Friarsgate, mama. I don't want to live here for the rest of my life. That was your dream. I love the court! I love the excitement, the pageantry, the intrigue, and the color. It is the center of the world, mama, and I want to be there forever!"

"You are upset, Philippa, and you do not understand what you are saying," Rosamund said calmly. Not want Friarsgate? Certainly Philippa didn't mean it. Of course she wanted Friarsgate. She was just distressed, and now was certainly not the time to discuss it. "I am sending to Otterly for Tom, and your sister Banon," she said, turning the subject away from what was obviously an uncomfortable place for both of them.

"I hope Banon is cleaner than Bessie is. And better bred," Philippa told her mother sourly. "How can you allow your daughter to run about barefoot and dirty, mama? She spends all of her days in the meadows with the sheep. I never found sheep to be of great interest. Does she not take lessons any more with Father Mata?"

"She is far better read than you are, Philippa," Rosamund said. "She is extremely proficient in several languages including Latin and Greek. She can speak Dutch, and German, which I certainly cannot."

"Why would she speak Dutch and German, mama? French is a far more cultured tongue," Philippa replied. "My French is much improved by my service at court. I know papa would be very proud, for he taught you to speak it. Who is there to teach Bessie such clumsy and coarse tongues?"

"Bessie is much interested in our wool business. She has accompanied me to the Netherlands twice. We have a factor in Amsterdam now who apprenticed his son to us. The boy's name is Hans Steen. He is learning the business of wool from the sheep onward. And he teaches your sister the languages she will need to deal with northern Europe. I don't think Bessie will ever want to go to court, Philippa."

Philippa looked absolutely scandalized. "Bessie would prefer to act like a man of business, mama? Oh, how can you permit it? We are not common merchants. I should be totally ruined socially if anyone knew my sister behaved in such an unladylike fashion. You cannot really want her to do this. I know we are not old nobility, mama, but we have certainly climbed the social ladder a short ways since your birth."

"Your youngest sister is landless, Philippa. While she will have a good dower portion thanks to my cousin, Tom, she would not make a good farmer's wife. But she will one day be a valuable spouse for a successful merchant's heir. Besides, she is intelligent, and would be unhappy being an ornament for some man."

"I cannot believe that you would allow my father's child to fall so low," Philippa replied disapprovingly.

"Philippa!" Rosamund exclaimed. "Where do you think your own wealth comes from, you foolish lass?"

"Uncle Thomas is rich," Philippa said naively.

Rosamund laughed. "And where do you think his wealth came from? Trade. Tom's great-grandfather and mine were twins. Martin Bolton was sent to London to wed the daughter of the merchant to whom he was apprenticed. They married, and she bore a son, but she was a pretty girl, and King Edward IV saw her, and seduced her. She killed herself in shame. King Edward felt guilt over the matter, especially as Martin Bolton and his father-in-law were staunch adherents of this king, and had been generous financially to him. So the king gave Martin Bolton a peerage, and that is how it came into the family, Philippa. But trade of one kind or another has always kept this family prosperous. I am sorry you do not understand that, and think it shameful to earn one's bread. You have lost your sense of morality and ethic while you have been at court. I think you will not go back until you have regained these virtues, my daughter. And do not scowl at me, Philippa. My mind is made up, and you will only change it when I see a change for the better in your attitude."

"You do not understand, mama!" Philippa cried. "You have never been young!"

"Only in years, Philippa, but then I was never allowed to be young. The burden of Friarsgate was on my shoulders from the tender age of three. There was little time to be young as you know it. Perhaps, my daughter, I have been too generous to you. You have come to believe it is your right to be spoiled and selfish, but it is not! Now go to your chamber. I am disappointed in you."

"I will go back to court at Christmas if not before!" Philippa cried. "Even if I have to ride all the way to Greenwich myself! I will not stay here. I hate Friarsgate, and I am near to hating you, for all you can see is this damned estate. You do not understand me, and you never have!" Then Philippa ran from the hall, and up the stairs.

Rosamund sighed deeply, and taking up the queen's letter read it a third time. She had known from the first time she had taken Philippa to court that her daughter was lost to her. That was why she had kept Philippa from going until the summer she was twelve. And in that time before her daughter's first visit and departure Philippa had practiced her French and Greek and Latin. She had struggled with her embroidery until it was perfect. She had learned every dance that anyone could teach her. She sang, and she played upon her lute and small Irish harp until her music was almost angelic. She bathed far more often than either of Rosamund's other daughters, and tended to her complexion as if it were the rarest of flower gardens. Each morning and each night she had Lucy brush her long auburn tresses one hundred strokes. Everything she did was to prepare her for court, and her position as one of the queen of England's maids of honor. And when she was fifteen she would be betrothed and married to the second son of an earl. Philippa's life was exactly as she had wanted it. Until now.

"You have weathered the storm, I see," Maybel said, reentering the hall and coming to sit by Rosamund.

"Barely," Rosamund replied. "She is very angry. I have told her she will not go back to court until I see a change in her demeanor. She has replied she will go back even if she has to walk the whole way by herself. I do not ever remember being that headstrong, Maybel."

"You were," Maybel responded, "but your passion was for Friarsgate, and those for whom you were responsible as its lady. Philippa has become selfish. Perhaps she always was selfish, and we did not notice it because she was a child. I fear for Friarsgate, for your eldest daughter has absolutely no interest in it at all. Her passion is for this court of hers, and for herself. If you could but see, but of course you will, how scornful she is of Bessie who loves the land so greatly."

"I must speak with Tom," Rosamund said.

"Not your husband?" Maybel was surprised.

Rosamund shook her head. "Nay. Logan may be my husband, but

he has never really understood me where Friarsgate is concerned. It is his one weakness." She smiled. "Tom understands, and he will know what we are to do about Philippa. Logan would marry her off to the first suitable husband he could find, and devil take the hindmost. My husband will most certainly not put up with my daughter's bad behavior. Nay, Tom must come quickly, for if I remain too long here right now Logan will come. He will not put up with Philippa's haughty ways. As her stepfather he has the right to beat her, and I have no doubt he would take a hazel switch to her bottom should he feel she needed it. And though I would never admit it, I think she does."

"Surely the man would not beat his children," Maybel said, horrified.

"He's a rough man, Maybel, and while he is not cruel, he has taken a switch to Alexander once or twice. And my wee Jamie as well. Rowdy laddies both, I fear. 'Tis his John who is the gentle lad. Nay, we must send for Tom right away."

"Edmund did, when he sent for you," Maybel told Rosamund. "He should be here if not late today, tomorrow for certain, and Banon with him. Mistress Philippa will certainly have her nose put out of joint when she sees our Banon, for she is surely the most beautiful of your lasses. When she was young I thought she would resemble you as does Philippa, but she has grown into a mix of both you and lord Owein, may God assoil his good soul. With those blue eyes of hers you would think she was the laird's child."

"My uncles have blue eyes," Rosamund noted. "But aye, Banon is lovely even at thirteen. Imagine what two more years will do for her."

"Another one to find a husband for," Maybel said almost grimly.

"I am leaving that to Tom," Rosamund replied. "She is his heiress. Let him choose the man who would husband Banon, and be the next lord of Otterly. It is not my concern, although I will want some small say in the matter, of course."

The evening meal was a grim one. Philippa hardly spoke a word except to criticize her little sister. And Elizabeth Meredith was not one to sit meekly with her hands folded and accept the unkind words her sister spoke. At first Rosamund attempted to keep the peace between her eldest and her youngest daughters, but finally she gave up.

"Go to your beds, both of you! I am not of a mind to listen to your quarreling. If you cannot be civil to one another then I do not want you at my board."

The two sisters departed the hall, still quarreling angrily with one another.

Rosamund sat back and closed her eyes for a long moment. Life had been so peaceful before Philippa arrived home. She was beginning to feel some strong antipathy towards the second son of the earl of Renfrew. This was really all his fault. If the life that her eldest daughter had envisioned had vanished in a puff of smoke, with Philippa's return so had the life that Rosamund now led and loved. The girl was contentious beyond all belief. "I am going to bed," she said to no one in particular, and then she stood up and left the hall.

In mid-morning the sound of a horn was heard from the hillside, and Sir Thomas Bolton came riding down the road accompanied by Banon Meredith. Ahead of them rode a young man blowing a trumpet, while sleek greyhounds and a wolfhound loped along beside the riders. Lord Cambridge and his heiress were accompanied by six men-at-arms. Up to the front door of the house they rode, where Rosamund, alerted, was already there to greet them. Lord Cambridge slid from his mount, and lifted Banon from hers.

Banon Mary Katherine Meredith was a beautiful girl on the brink of young womanhood. She was dressed in a deep blue silk riding gown that matched her eyes. Her auburn hair was simply dressed beneath a gabled hood that had been set back to display her hair, and from which hung a small neat lawn veil. "Mama!" she said, slipping from her uncle's grasp. She kissed Rosamund sweetly. "Where is Philippa? I am anxious to see her!" She smiled, and Rosamund was reminded of her mother whom she could but barely remember.

"Wait, my child," Rosamund advised. "Philippa is not as you remember her. She is unhappy, and angry."

"She is selfish and mean," Bessie Meredith said, overhearing as she ran up to greet Banon. "Banie! How lovely you look!" Then she turned and flung herself at Tom Bolton. "Uncle Thomas! What have you brought me?"

"Bessie!" Rosamund gently scolded her daughter, but Tom Bolton laughed.

Reaching into his elegant velvet doublet he drew forth a sleepy kitten, of a deep orange hue. "Will this do, madame?" he asked her.

Squealing with delight Bessie took the kitten, holding it up to admire its golden eyes, and kissing its nose. "How did you know I wanted a kitten?" she demanded of him.

Thomas Bolton laughed. "You always want some living thing to love, Bessie, and I have brought you enough puppies to make a hunting pack. I thought a kitten for a change would suffice your greedy nature."

"Oh, thank you!" Bessie said, and turning, she put an arm through Banon's, and walking off began to whisper most earnestly.

"Now what is that all about, dear girl?" Lord Cambridge asked his cousin.

"Philippa, if I don't miss my guess," Rosamund said as they walked into the house. "She has come home angry, and argues constantly with Bessie, of whom she very much disapproves now. I am worried, Tom, and I need your advice on how to deal with my eldest child. I am at a loss as to what to do."

"Where is Logan?" her cousin asked. He took a cup of wine from the servant holding the tray, and sipped slowly as they entered the hall to seat themselves.

"Up at Claven's Carn with our lads, and may he remain there, Tom, for I know he would beat Philippa if she spoke rudely to him, and she is that way with everyone now. She says she hates Friarsgate, and she almost hates me as well for loving it more than I do my children. There is no reasoning with her at all, I fear."

"And all because of Renfrew's lad? They are a nice enough family, but I would not have thought any of them could arouse such passion in a woman's breast, dear girl. It has to be more than just that," Tom Bolton said, sipping thoughtfully at his wine.

"She was sent home, Tom," Rosamund said low. "Oh, she has been asked back when she has recovered from her disappointment, but that decision is to be mine."

"And why was she sent home?" His look was both curious and amused.

"She and some friends, three young men and another lass, climbed to the top of the Canted Tower where they got drunk and were caught gambling. My daughter had lost all her coin, and so was pledging items of her wardrobe. She had divested herself of both shoes and stockings, her bodice, and had just stepped from her skirts when the king and the duke of Suffolk arrived to study the constellations."

Thomas Bolton burst out laughing. "My dear, dear girl, I should have never suspected that Philippa had such devilment in her. How too too amusing!"

"Oh, Tom, it is not funny at all! If I were not considered a friend of the queen's Philippa might have been ruined. Fortunately just about everyone had left court for the summer, having no wish to tramp from one hunting site to another with Hal, and needing to be on their own lands. The incident could have been a disaster. We need to find a husband for Philippa, and I simply do not know where to begin!" Rosamund declared.

"Why, cousin," he said, "I have not seen you so distressed in a long time. This is indeed serious then. I think I must speak with Philippa, and hear what she has to say before I can make any decision as to how we may surmount this difficulty that has arisen. I trust that Logan will remain on the other side of the border while we consider the problem. Your wicked Scot has a good hot temper on him, and if Philippa is as out of control as you believe, then there must not be a clash of wills between the two."

Rosamund nodded. "I will have one of the servants fetch Philippa to you. I will leave the hall, for she and I cannot speak these days without quarreling. I am breeding another son for Logan, and I do not enjoy controversy." She arose. "I will be in the garden if you wish to speak further with me before the dinner hour."

Thomas Bolton watched as his cousin glided from the hall. He sometimes thought it was a pity that he was not a man for marriage with a woman, for his cousin would have been a good wife for him. They had from the first gotten on, and she always seemed to come to him with her problems, but not so much of late. Well, it was only proper that she confide in her Scotsman. But this was obviously an issue that would require the most delicate finesse to solve. And Logan Hepburn had never been a man noted for finesse.

"Uncle."

Thomas Bolton looked up and saw Philippa standing before him. He gave her a quick smile, and then said, "My darling girl, while I am ecstatic to see you, the gown you are wearing is a total disaster! Surely this is not the new fashion at court?" He looked genuinely distressed, and not just a little appalled.

A tiny smile touched the girl's lips, but it was as quickly gone as it had come. "I left my court gowns at the London house, uncle. I would not bring them here. They would be most unsuitable, and besides the journey with all its dusty summer roads would have ruined them."

"Then what on earth is it that you wear, my darling girl? It is most unattractive."

"I had some old gowns I left behind in my trunks altered," Philippa explained.

Thomas Bolton shook his head wearily. "Your figure has, um, er, ripened in your time away, Philippa. There is obviously not enough fabric in the gown to do you justice. It will not do. No, no, darling girl, it will not do at all! We must have new gowns made at once. Not the kind, of course, that you are expected to wear at court, but gowns for a country visit that will at least fit you properly. God's foot, my dear, what you are wearing makes your shoulders look quite broad, like a peasant girl who pulls the plough for her husband." He shuddered with distaste.

Philippa had to laugh. "Uncle," she told him, "finally I have a reason to be glad I am here. Why do you persist in isolating youself here in Cumbria when once you so loved the excitement that only being at court can engender?"

"Indeed, darling girl, I did once very much enjoy the court. When I first came to Friarsgate I was astounded that your mother could love it here so. But after a time the glory of the court pales when one sees a winter's sunrise from a hillside, or the first of the spring flowers pushing through the snow to catch the eye with splashes of quick color. Perhaps it is my age, dear Philippa, but I far prefer Cumbria now myself, else I should not have sold my house in Cambridge."

"Yet you kept your houses in London and Greenwich," Philippa noted.

"I kept them for you, darling girl," he told her. "I saw what you were from the first time we took you to court."

"Oh, uncle, I knew you would understand!" Philippa cried. "Mama does not understand, for Friarsgate is her whole life. But it is not mine! I love the court! I want to remain there, but how can I now? I will soon be too old to be one of the queen's maids of honor. As the wife of Giles FitzHugh I might have been able to remain at court. Now what is to happen to me? The queen will have me back, but for how long? And Cecily is to be wed shortly, and soon all my friends will be gone while I remain, an old maid."

"Is that the problem?" Lord Cambridge asked Philippa.

"Just part of it, uncle," she answered him. "How am I to find a husband at court when my estates are so far north as to be practically in Scotland? Giles himself said he would not have been able to live here because it is so far from civilized company. And mama will never approve a match for me if the man does not agree to husband this land one day. And she is right there. Friarsgate is a great responsibility, but I do not want it. I am a creature of the court, and content to be such."

"You are certain you do not want Friarsgate, Philippa? It may be in a northerly clime, darling girl, but it is a most impressive inheritance," Lord Cambridge said.

Philippa sighed. "I cannot have Friarsgate and a life at the court. If I must choose then I choose the court. I know mama thinks I am simply speaking out of pique. While her great ardor is for this land, mine is not. I could not wait to get away. I would have gone the day I reached twelve years, and the few weeks she made me wait after my birthday were an agony. I lived in terror that mama would change her mind."

He saw the difficulty now, and it was going to break Rosamund's heart, but Thomas Bolton could see that Philippa was as determined in her fervor for the court as Rosamund was and always had been for Friarsgate. He nodded. "I must think on this, dear Philippa," he told her, "but I will help both you and your mother to resolve what would appear to be an insurmountable problem. Will you trust me to do this?"

"Yes, uncle, I will," Philippa replied, and she smiled.

Chapter 5

‌ ⁂

*L*ogan Hepburn rode across the border with his clansmen. Riding with him on matching black-and-white ponies were his two oldest sons, John, aged five and a half, and Alexander, aged four. Before him on his saddle the youngest of his sons, James, sat proudly. Jamie was just beginning to learn to ride his own pony, and had been furious that his elder siblings would make the trip to Friarsgate on their own beasts, while he would be forced to ride with their father. He had kicked and shrieked upon learning it, but a smack on his fat little bottom had quickly sobered him. But Logan had grinned behind the child's back, well pleased by Jamie's temper. While John was a quiet lad like Jeannie Logan, his mother, who had been the first wife of the Hepburn of Claven's Carn, Alex and Jamie were more fiery. Logan Hepburn had always known that Rosamund would give him strong sons. And come midwinter there would be another bairn, he considered, well pleased.

He didn't like being apart from his wife. It was, he thought, his one weakness. She had received a message that her eldest daughter had come suddenly home, and she had gone at once to Friarsgate. But she had been gone a month now, and while there had been brief messages, she gave no indication that she would return soon. Logan Hepburn wanted his wife home, and she had not explained to his satisfaction why she was making no plans to return any time soon. The summer was almost over. And so he had come to bring her back, but suspecting it might not be as easy as he hoped, he had brought his lads along. Having all her children in one place at the same time, from oldest to youngest, could have a softening effect on her heart. Rosamund could be a very determined woman when she chose to be. He smiled. That was one of the reasons he loved her so deeply.

Rosamund had anticipated he would come, for she knew he was not happy without her presence for very long. When Bessie came running to inform her that her stepfather was coming down the hill road, and the lads were with him, Rosamund chuckled.

"Do not be so smug, dear girl," Thomas Bolton said with a grin. "The man has always been totally mad over you, and you know it. 'Twill be a lovely visit, I have not a doubt, if we can but keep Philippa from quarreling with him. Of all your girls he is fondest of Bessie, and will tolerate no cruelty towards her."

"He has come to bring me home to Claven's Carn, and I cannot go until I have settled the dilemma over Philippa. First he will take her side, and try and cajole me into sending her back to court. When that fails he will begin to consider the sons of his friends as possible mates for my daughter. Oh, Tom, have you thought of nothing that can help Philippa? I do not like arguing with Logan."

"I have something in mind, but I am not yet certain. Let us welcome your bold borderer to Friarsgate first. This is not quite the time for what I am considering," Lord Cambridge said. "And Philippa must agree as well. She may decide to stay in the north and settle for a Neville, a Percy, or a Scot, even as her mother did."

"Never!" Philippa said, entering the hall. "Logan is here, mama. Will you be leaving soon then? And may I please rejoin my mistress at Woodstock?"

"I will not quarrel with you now that Logan is entering the house," Rosamund said through gritted teeth. "I must discuss your situation with your stepfather."

"Have you not written him then?" Philippa pressed.

"Aye, I have. But your future is a matter of great importance. Logan and I must speak face-to-face on it, Philippa. And when we have, we will inform you of our decision in the matter." Then she arose from her seat by the hearth and, turning, went forward to greet her husband as he entered the hall.

"Logan will persuade her to let me go back," Philippa said smugly.

"She will not be moved until she is certain whatever is decided is what is best for you," Lord Cambridge told his young relative.

"Logan wants her back at Claven's Carn. She has been gone from him for several weeks. In order for her to go back she must let me return to court. He will cajole her into doing just that," Philippa told Thomas Bolton.

"Go and greet your stepfather. Then come back to me and we will speak on this, Philippa. Know this, dear girl. I am the only one who can persuade your mother to allow you to return to the queen's service. And I am the only one who can make certain you have everything that your heart desires."

"Uncle?" Her look was curious.

"Go!" he told her sharply.

Philippa turned, and hurried across the hall. Her heart was beating very rapidly, and she felt almost faint. For as long as she could remember Thomas Bolton had been the maker of magic in this family. How could she have forgotten it? He was the only one who could help her! Her mouth turned up in a smile. "Logan," she said, and standing on her tiptoes she kissed his rough cheek. "I think I am now too old, stepfather, to call you papa." She gave him another warm smile. "Have I grown up, do you think?" She pirouetted before him, almost dancing.

"Indeed, lass, you've become a fine young lady," Logan Hepburn told his stepdaughter. "I would hae nae recognized you did you nae look so much like your mother when I first knew her." He kissed Philippa on her forehead.

"You will want to talk with mama, of course," Philippa said sweetly, curtseying.

"Aye, I do, but first, lassie, come and greet your brothers. They will nae remember you, for Johnnie was just three when you went away, and Alex still in leading strings, and our Jamie not even born. Here, lads! Here is your oldest sister, Philippa. Show her that you all remember the manners your mam has taught you."

John Hepburn marched up to Philippa, took her hand, and kissed it with all the grace of a courtier even as he bowed. "I can just remember you, sister, but barely. I will not forget you now, however. You are much like our mam."

"And you, like the mother who birthed you, Johnnie Hepburn," Philippa said. "I remember Jeannie Logan, and she was most fair, and kind too."

"I do not remember her at all, but I thank you for your words," John Hepburn said. Then he pulled his two younger siblings forward. "This is Alexander, and this Jamie. He cries a lot when he does not get his own way."

"Do not!" Jamie Hepburn yelled, and he hit his eldest brother with a small hard fist. "Take it back, Johnnie!"

"Greet our sister, you little buffoon," his elder said.

"I do not think you a buffoon, Jamie Hepburn," Philippa said. "You would appear to be a brave lad to attack one larger than you."

The little boy looked up at her. He had his father's dark hair, but his mother's amber eyes. "You're pretty," he said.

" 'Tis all the greeting you'll get from him," Alexander Hepburn told Philippa. "I do not remember you, but I am happy to have such a pretty sister." His father's blue eyes met Philippa's hazel eyes. "I'm Alexander Hepburn."

"Do not Banon and Bessie make you happy too?" Philippa mischievously baited him with a grin.

"Sometimes, and sometimes not," the lad told her plainly, and he grinned back.

Philippa curtseyed again. "I will leave you and mama to your reunion, Logan. Brothers, you must go to the kitchen where cook has a treat for you after your long ride. I must go and speak with Uncle Thomas." She shooed her brothers in the direction of the kitchen stairs, and then moved gracefully across the hall to where Lord Cambridge awaited her return, seated in a tapestry-backed chair, a goblet of wine held in his elegant beringed hand. Philippa sat down opposite him, and looked questioningly at him.

"How can you help me so I may escape the tedium of this glorified sheep farm?" she demanded of him.

"You are so impatient, dear girl," he said in an amused tone. The jewels on his fingers twinkled as he raised the goblet to his lips to drink.

"Uncle, I am bored. I have been home these six weeks now. August is coming to an end. I want to go back to court."

"And so you shall, my pet, for I can see quite clearly that Friarsgate is not the place for you. How diverting I find that, remembering your mother in her youth. There she was in the midst of the center of the earth, as you so succinctly put it. And what did she want? Nothing more than to return to Friarsgate while you, her eldest child, want nothing more than to escape it." He chuckled, and then he grew serious. "Now tell me, Philippa, do you mean it when you tell Rosamund that you do not want Friarsgate? Do you mean it truly, or is it just that you are having an attack of exasperation over the disappointment Giles FitzHugh visited upon you? I want the truth, Philippa. What I do to help you will depend upon what you tell me now."

"I do not want Friarsgate, uncle. I do not!" Philippa said.

"It is a great inheritance, dear girl. Are you sure you would give it up?" he queried her further.

"Aye, I would give it up! What good is it to me? It is far too far from the king and the court. I prefer living at the court. But if Friarsgate becomes my responsibility I cannot live at court. I know the obligations involved in being the heiress of an estate like this, uncle. I do not want those duties. I prefer to serve the queen."

He was silent and thoughtful for a long few minutes. To his surprise Philippa remained quiet as well. Finally Lord Cambridge said, "If you do not want Friarsgate, my darling girl, then what do you want other than to live at court, and serve the queen?"

"Oh, uncle, I know that you and my mother have made a success of your cloth trade. Could you not spare some of your combined wealth for me? A respectable dower and a small income would suit me well. And it is all I need to live at court, and to pay my servant her yearly wage."

"What of a husband, Philippa?" he asked her.

She shook her head. "I have spoken enough with my mother over these last weeks to know that I have never really been in love with anyone, least of all Giles FitzHugh. If he had come home to wed me I should have done so, and thought myself happy. Perhaps for a few years, but perhaps forever. Who can say, uncle? But while I have been considered an heiress, a northern estate is of no use to me. So I will content myself with a smaller portion. If one day there is a man who will love me, and I him, then at least I may offer that man a respectable dower portion. There are plenty like me at court, uncle, as you would certainly know from your own time there. My father was such. His marriage to mama took him from loyal obscurity to the rank of a landowner. Perhaps there is a man at court with a small home who would be happy to have a wife like me. I do not scorn marriage."

"But you are a proud girl, Philippa," Lord Cambridge reminded her. "Would simplicity truly suit you, I wonder."

"What other choices do I have, uncle?" she asked him frankly.

"We shall see, darling girl," he told her. "Now, promise me, Philippa, that you will trust me to aid you. That you will cease quarreling with your two sisters, for Banon is my heiress, and I will have no one gainsay her. And Bessie is your stepfather's especial pet, being the only girl at Claven's Carn. If you wish to have your own way in this matter then you must allow me to resolve it."

"And I will go back to court, uncle?" she asked him anxiously.

"You will go back, and in time for the Christmas revels, I promise you, darling girl," he said. "Now tender me your pledge, Philippa Meredith, and give me your hand in token of that pledge." He offered his own hand, and she put her small one in it.

"I will trust you, uncle, and I will try not to be so difficult," she promised him.

"Good!" Lord Cambridge answered her.

"Can you tell me what it is you plan?" Philippa asked eagerly.

"It is far too soon, and there are certain things I must set in motion first," he said.

Across the hall Rosamund watched her cousin as he engaged her daughter in earnest conversation. What was he planning? It had best be soon, for Logan was already importuning her to come home to Claven's Carn. It was difficult to say no to him when he caught her gaze with those blue blue eyes of his that had always been her weakness. She had tried to explain how disappointed Philippa was over the FitzHugh boy, and how she had said she didn't want Friarsgate.

"The lass is daft with her displeasure," Logan said. "Let her go back to court. She'll come to her senses soon enough."

She hadn't told him but now she had to. The tale of the Canted Tower was recounted, and Logan then said exactly what she had expected.

"I know several lusty young men, sons of friends, who would gladly take the next lady of Friarsgate to wife. Obviously the lass needs to be wed, and quickly."

"Nay. It is more complicated than that, Logan. But Tom says he can solve the problem if we will but allow him. I would, for he has always been right in his judgments of difficult situations, my love."

The laird of Claven's Carn nodded. "I must be honest with you, lovey. Philippa has always frightened me a wee bit, though I am shamed to admit it. She is but a lass, yet that air of determination she wears would terrify a stronger man than me. If Thomas Bolton believes he has a suitable solution to the problem then let him offer it, I say. I am willing to listen to anything he has to say. And then we may go home."

"Bide here with us a few days, my dear lord," Rosamund said. "It is yet a few weeks to grouse season," she teased gently. "Once I am home again I think I will be loath to travel abroad until I have birthed this son of yours that I carry. I am heavier and more tired with this bairn than with the others. I would name him Thomas, after my cousin, if you will. I think it is time I called a child for him who has been so good to me through all these years. Would you agree?"

He nodded. "Aye. Tom is a good man for all his odd ways."

"Then you will be patient with me?"

"Till the end of September, madame, and then you will come home to stay," he told her with a small smile.

Philippa's conversation with Lord Cambridge had brought about a change in her attitude. She wasn't certain what he was planning, but she knew whatever it was, it would be to her advantage. And so she tried her best to be kind to her sisters, but Bessie, it seemed, went out of her way to irritate Philippa and bait her into conflict. Banon, however, was a different personality, and the two sisters renewed their acquaintance while carefully avoiding Bessie and her wicked tricks.

Banon loved hearing about the court. "I suppose I should go for a brief time," she said one day as the two sisters sat together in the early September gardens. Around them the Michaelmas daisies were coming into early bloom. Above the plants fat bumblebees droned lazily while collecting pollen from the delicate blooms.

"You would love it!" Philippa enthused.

"Perhaps I would, but I must keep in mind that Otterly, like Friarsgate, is a northern estate. I will marry a man of the north, but a brief stay in the queen's service would but add luster to my reputation, would it not, sister?" Banon's blue eyes looked at Philippa, thinking her deliciously sophisticated even in her simple country gown. Uncle Thomas had insisted Philippa have a country wardrobe made when he had first arrived. Banon always enjoyed being around Lord Cambridge when he was choosing fabric and discussing gowns with the seamstress. He had the most exquisite taste. "It is your hairstyle, I believe," Banon suddenly said. "That is what gives you that air of glamour."

"I wear it down as do others," Philippa said, "but I like that French style Annie showed to Lucy so long ago. It is very elegant."

"Uncle Thomas says I am too young yet for such a style," Banon told her older sister. "Do you think he is right?"

"Wait," Philippa counseled her sibling. "There is time to look older, for that is what you want to do, isn't it?" She smiled at Banon.

Banon nodded. "How did you know?" she asked.

"Because I felt the same way when I went to court for the first time, but Lucy advised me to keep my hair down always so I might look younger, and none would trifle with me. She said I needed to learn the ways of the court first, and that would give me time. She was right, of course, but when you come to court you will have me to watch over you. And my friends too."

"You are anxious to return, aren't you?" Banon said.

"Aye!"

"When will it be?" Banon asked.

"I do not know. Uncle Thomas has said I must be patient, and he will solve the difficulty. I must trust that he will although I will admit to growing impatient of late," Philippa admitted.

The end of September came, and Logan Hepburn announced on Michaelmas that he would take his family home on the first day of October. "You are welcome to come, Philippa," he told the girl.

Stricken, she looked to Lord Cambridge.

It was time, Thomas Bolton thought, and then he began to speak. "I think I have the answer to the difficulties that the FitzHughs have unwittingly caused our own family," he began.

"Tell us!" Rosamund said eagerly.

"The solution may not please everyone, but it will please Philippa, dear cousin, and it is her happiness we must concern ourselves with now. Would you not agree?" His eyes met hers sympathetically, and Rosamund knew she was not going to like what he said, but she nodded in the affirmative. "Philippa has said most strongly that she does not wish the burden of Friarsgate on her shoulders. She feels her happiness lies at court, and not here in Cumbria. We have discussed this several times over the last few weeks, and her mind is quite made up in the matter."

"Not want Friarsgate? The lass is daft!" Logan said, half angrily, and knowing how this was hurting his beloved Rosamund. What the hell was the matter with Philippa? He should have made a match for the lass himself, and had her married off with no nonsense about it, but Rosamund would not allow it. Now look what was happening!

"And what conclusions have you come to, Tom?" Rosamund asked her cousin. She was very pale, and her voice was almost frail.

"We must allow Philippa to find her future at court, which is what she wants. As she has pointed out to me, cousin, you and I have profited very well from our cloth trade. We will take some of this profit and give Philippa a generous dower portion. And I will find a small estate in the south that I can purchase for her. That way she will be landed as well as dowered. Under those circumstances a husband can certainly be found for her, for she must be wed like all respectable lasses. And she will have the time she needs to choose a man who, like her, prefers life and service at court. There are many such couples at court, dear girl, as we both know. I think this is the perfect solution to all our problems. Will you agree?"

"But what of Friarsgate?" Rosamund said softly.

"What of Friarsgate?" Philippa exploded. "What of me, mama? Can I not just this once come before your damned Friarsgate?" She was near to tears.

Rosamund looked stricken at the rebuke.

"Do not speak to your mother in that tone, Philippa Meredith!"

Logan Hepburn roared. He put a protective arm about his wife. "She has given her life to Friarsgate and its well-being. Yet you stand there boldly and throw the gift she would give you back in her face. I do not understand you, lass."

"Nay, you don't," Philippa agreed angrily. "None of you do except Uncle Thomas! What is so difficult for you to understand? I am like my father, Owein Meredith. I am happy to be in service to my queen as he was content to be in service to his king. But I cannot do that if I am burdened with Friarsgate." She turned to her mother. "You will, God willing, live many more years, mama, but the truth is that you are spending less and less time at Friarsgate, and Friarsgate needs its mistress. Your husband is a Scot. Your sons are Scots. Two of Owein Meredith's daughters are grown now, and Banon is already mistress of Otterly. She is happy to be so, and has told me she will wed a northerner one day. I wish to remain in the south. Please, I beg of you, let me do so. I would rather be dead than take on the responsibility of Friarsgate. Let me go, mama. Let me go, and be happy as you have been, as you are, happy." Philippa's hazel eyes were wet with unshed tears. She held out her hands in supplication to her mother.

Her daughter's words had been like knives cutting her to pieces. What had it all been for if not for her children? She had so carefully husbanded and protected Friarsgate and its people. What had it all been for then? But Philippa's face told Rosamund that she could not, would not, be moved in her determination. Well, there was always Banon. She could one day care for both estates. But now was not the time to discuss it, Rosamund knew. She was tired with this confinement, and depressed by what was happening. She didn't want to discuss it any longer. She focused her amber eyes on her eldest child. "You are certain?" she asked, knowing, as she did, the answer.

Philippa nodded.

"Then go and find your own happiness, Philippa. I will not stop you." She turned to her cousin. "What would I do without you, Tom? You will handle all the arrangements in this matter?"

Thomas Bolton came and sat next to Rosamund. He took her hand in his, and kissed it tenderly. "I will make everything perfect, darling girl," he promised her, keeping her little hand in his embrace. "Why, it is long past time I paid a visit to court. I find I am growing bored, and need the company of clever amusing people for a time again. And Banon must come with us. A bit of polish will do her no harm. And who knows? One of the northern families may be at court seeking to find a pretty, rich wife for one of their younger sons. The match must be made when we can make it, Rosamund. Your hesitation with Philippa was a mistake. Would you not agree?"

She nodded. "Aye, it was."

"But I will repair the damage done, darling girl," he told her cheerfully. "Now you must go home to Claven's Carn, and be cosseted by this man of yours until this next son of yours is born. I think you have borne enough bairns now, Rosamund." He kissed her little hand again and released it, turning to Logan Hepburn as he did so. "Four healthy sons is more than many men have, Logan. Remember that you must provide one way or another for them all. And think how lonely your old age would be, my good friend, if you were alone."

"I suspect I will never be alone as long as you live, Cousin Tom," the laird of Claven's Carn said with a grin, "but I agree that four lads is a goodly number."

"Rosamund?" Lord Cambridge looked at his cousin questioningly.

She nodded. "Neither of you will be without me in our old age," she said, and the color was coming back into her pale cheeks, and a small smile was turning up the corners of her mouth. "Forgive me for frightening you both. I am just more tired this time than I have been in the past. I must remember I am no longer a girl." She laughed. "And too, the shock of Philippa's decision has not been easy."

Philippa came and knelt by her mother's knee. "Mama, I am sorry for my words. You know that I love you, but I am different than you are. Strange, isn't it, that you who raised me with such a strong sense of duty should be surprised when that duty would take me elsewhere.

Yet it has, and my sense of responsibility in my service to the queen is every bit as strong as yours is for Friarsgate. Can you understand that?" The young woman looked anxiously into her mother's face for some sign of comprehension.

"I suppose," Rosamund said softly, "that that is a mistake many parents make. They expect their children to be as they are because they have raised those children with their values. Yet when a child interprets those values differently we are surprised." She smiled at Philippa, and put a gentle hand on her face. "You have fought every bit as hard for what you want, my daughter, as I did for what I wanted. I cannot fault you then, can I? You go with my blessing, Philippa Meredith, even if I am saddened by your decision. You were born of the love I had for your father. I would do his memory a great disservice if I did not allow you that which would make you happy."

"Thank you, mama!" Philippa said, and the joy in her voice was most evident.

"Well, thank heavens that is settled now, my darling girls," Lord Cambridge said with a feigned sigh of relief. "God's foot, my dear! There is ever so much to do before we dare show ourselves in public. Banon must have a whole new wardrobe of gowns for court, wouldn't you agree, Philippa dearest? And I shall have to dig into my coffers for jewelry. And while I know your garments are awaiting you at the London house, Philippa, surely you could do with a few new gowns yourself, my pet? And men's fashions have certainly changed in the last several years. Philippa, you will have to direct my tailor. I will not appear before the king unless I am certainly dressed as has always befitted my reputation as an elegant gentleman. Will you come with us to Otterly so all these preparations may be effected? It is a bit south, so you will be even closer to your beloved court." He chortled. "Rosamund, my angel, it is just like the bad old days, and I can hardly contain myself considering the adventures to come!"

Rosamund burst out laughing. "Oh, cousin," she said, "I am not certain I should entrust my girls to your tender care. They will have far too much fun, and begin to believe that their lives should always be filled with merriment and beautiful clothing."

"Did I not care well for you?" he reminded her.

"Oh, yes," she agreed. "No one was ever kinder and more generous to me, dearest cousin. I almost envy my daughters the wonderful times they will have with you. Almost," she finished with a little smile. She suddenly felt happy again.

Logan Hepburn was not in the least offended by his wife's words, for he knew them to be the truth. No one had ever taken such loving care of Rosamund until her cousin, Tom, had come into her life. They were more older brother and younger sister in their affection for one another. "Then we shall go home to Claven's Carn tomorrow, and your heart will be at rest, lovey, knowing that Philippa's future is safe with Tom."

She nodded.

That evening their supper in the hall was merrier than anyone had known in a very long time at Friarsgate. Philippa was quite the story-teller, entertaining them all with amusing anecdotes of her life at court. Banon was filled with questions that her mother, her eldest sister, and Lord Cambridge answered. The Hepburn sons, though little, had been allowed at the high board tonight as a treat. When they became restless they were allowed to play before the fire. Jamie shared his beef bone with one of Thomas Bolton's dogs, taking a bite, and then offering a bite to the canine, an enormous wolfhound with a fortunately gentle disposition. The little boy's innocent actions set his elders to laughing.

"Why, the beastie could eat the lad in two bites," Maybel cackled, "but is the bairn not sweet, sharing his dinner with the creature?"

Elizabeth Meredith sat and watched her family with curiosity. It had been a long time since the hall had rung with laughter, longer still since her whole family had been together. And tomorrow they would all be gone again, and she would be alone. Though sometimes she accompanied her mother to Claven's Carn, she had decided she preferred her own home at Friarsgate. She didn't care that she would be alone. She would have Maybel and Edmund to watch over her. Father Mata would continue to teach her, although he said she was learning faster than her sisters had, and there would soon be little left he could teach her. And there was Hans Steen, who was continuing to teach her German and Dutch. She would be happy to see them all gone, Bessie thought, so her life might get back to normal. She still had not come to like Philippa again, and she had nothing in common with Banon any longer. They were sisters in blood only. And that was enough.

The following day dawned clear. Rosamund was ready at first light to begin her trek home to Claven's Carn. She bid each of her daughters farewell individually, and in their turn. "I will make no decision regarding Friarsgate for now," she told Philippa. "I know you think you won't, but you might change your mind about it. I just want you happy, my daughter."

"I won't change my mind, mama, but I think you wise to wait before deciding what you will do. It is a valuable inheritance for whoever will get it. I am happy in my choices, but remember that I always love you." Philippa hugged her mother. Then lowering her voice she said, "I know what Uncle Thomas was saying to you yesterday. Can you prevent conceiving another bairn after this one is born?"

Rosamund nodded. "I'll tell you someday when the time is right. If you marry, Philippa, bring your husband to meet me. I know Tom will guide you in your choices."

"I will," Philippa promised. Mother and daughter hugged a final time.

"Now, Banon," Rosamund said to her second daughter, "listen to your uncle, and obey his advice. He is a wise man. Wiser than your sister, though she thinks she knows it all. She doesn't. Take your uncle's counsel first."

"I will, mama," Banon replied. "Philippa's choices will not be my choices. And I shall be home to Otterly in the spring, for I take my responsibilities there seriously. Uncle Tom says the manor could not have a better mistress than me," she finished proudly.

"I am certain he is right," Rosamund said. "Send to me when you return."

"I will," Banon said, and hugged her mother. "And send to me, mama, when you have birthed my new brother."

Rosamund nodded, and turned to Bessie. "Are you sure you won't come with me?" she asked her youngest daughter.

"Nay," Bessie replied. "I am happiest here, although I am happier when you are with me, mama."

Rosamund fondled one of Bessie's thick blond braids. "If you change your mind, send to me. There is plenty of time before the snows come."

Bessie smiled at her mother. "If I change my mind I will," she said, but they both knew she wouldn't. She kissed her mother's cheek, and moved away.

"Now don't you go weeping," Maybel said tartly, coming up to Rosamund. "I'll take good care of the lass, and you know it."

"I hate to burden you at this time in your life, Maybel," Rosamund said. "You are no longer young. You are already several years past a half century."

"Well, some may be old at my age, but I ain't!" Maybel declared. "And for your information, Mistress Hepburn of Claven's Carn, your uncle is still a most vigorous fellow, and he's four years my senior. I have more than enough energy to raise another lass. What would I do if you took our Bessie away from me? Don't you even think about it, Rosamund! Would you break my heart?" Her weathered face sagged with sadness.

"No, no!" Rosamund cried, and she hugged Maybel. "I just did not want to encumber you if you could not do it. Bessie is not an easy child."

"She is a perfect little darling," Maybel protested.

"Then she is yours," Rosamund laughed. She turned to her uncle. "As always I know I can entrust you with Friarsgate's safety."

"You can," Edmund Bolton said quietly.

"Come, darling girl, your bold borderer is chafing at the bit to be on his way, and your rowdy sons are every bit as bad. You have said your farewells to everyone but me. I adore you, cousin! I shall look after our lasses. I shall make everything right for Philippa, and Banon shall have a wonderful time at court. Write to me." He kissed both her cheeks heartily, and then led her outside to help her onto her horse. "Farewell! Godspeed!" And he smacked her horse lightly upon its rump while giving Logan Hepburn a broad wink. "Farewell, dearest Logan! Until we meet again," he called as the Hepburns of Claven's Carn went on their way. Then turning to the others he said, "I am ravenous, Maybel! Is the food ready? My lasses and I must soon be on our way as well."

"Well, why are you standing there posing then?" she demanded of him. "Come into the hall, my good lord!"

Rosamund turned to look back at her family, and she could not help but laugh. There stood Maybel shaking a finger at Tom. Banon and Philippa had linked arms, their heads together as they talked. And there was her Bessie dashing off towards the meadows, and the priest running after her, his long skirts flying, as his voice carrying on the wind called Elizabeth Meredith to her studies. They didn't need her, any of them. She sighed, and turned her face back towards the border, and Claven's Carn. She was surely needed there.

Lord Cambridge departed Friarsgate shortly afterwards with his two charges and Philippa's servant, Lucy. Once at Otterly Court the preparations had begun for Philippa's return to court, and Banon's first visit. True to his word Lord Cambridge had both the manor seamstress and a tailor from Carlisle working frantically to outfit them all. Even Lucy was to have two new gowns, and they were the first made, being the simplest. Lucy helped work on them herself, delighted. And there was material for her to have new caps as well, and aprons of fine lawn.

"I must have several short coats with pleated backs," Thomas Bolton said to his tailor. "My legs are still quite handsome, even considering my age. And the sleeves must be fur-lined, or padded. The royal palaces are never as well heated as they might be, I fear, dear Master Tailor."

"Your codpieces must be decorated, uncle. It is all the fashion now," Philippa advised him.

"No! Well, why not, dear girl? A man's assets must surely be as well displayed as a lady's, n'est-ce pas?" And he chuckled.

"What is a codpiece?" Banon asked.

" 'Tis a flaplike appendage at the front of a man's breeches," Philippa explained. Here in the country men did not wear such things, their garments being more utilitarian.

"But does that draw attention to . . ." Banon stopped, blushing.

"Of course! That is the whole idea. The bigger the codpiece the larger the manhood, or so it is believed," Philippa answered. "After all, women display their breasts, sister. But to leave a manhood dangling in plain view would be rude, and so the codpiece is now an important piece of fashion."

"A dangling manhood would certainly spoil the line of the garment, do you not agree, Master Tailor?" Lord Cambridge said drolly.

"Indeed, my lord, and in some cases it could spoil a gentleman's illusion of himself, I fear. I am glad I am but a simple tailor, and need not dress myself so."

"I will want my codpieces all bejeweled," Lord Cambridge said, and the two girls giggled behind their hands.

They celebrated Martinmas in mid-November with goose and roasted apples. Philippa found Otterly Court a very elegant house. I shall have a house like this one day, she thought. Not like Friarsgate, which is so ordinary with its old hall. But a modern house like Otterly with fine glass windows, and a fireplace in every room. Banon is very fortunate that she will inherit Otterly one day.

And then finally the day of their departure came. Philippa was almost sick with her excitement. She had waited forever, it seemed, for her return to court. Cecily and Tony would be there. They had said they would come for the Christmas revels. She would introduce Banon to everyone, and serve the queen again as she had previously. They would travel slowly, for they had two full baggage carts, and Lord Cambridge had arranged for them to stop each night in either a fine religious house or the house of some noble family that he knew. There might even be others joining them on their journey to London. And Banon's serving woman, Susan, would also come with them. Lucy was already explaining to her how it would be. And they were to have two dozen well-armed men from Otterly escorting them, and remaining with them until Banon returned in the spring. It was all going to be wonderful, Philippa thought happily. It would be the best Christmas revels ever.

Chapter 6

They rejoined the court in mid-December only to learn that Queen Katherine had been in extremely delicate health these past few months. The king was firmly told by a group of physicians that the queen would never conceive again. Henry Tudor was not pleased. The Christmas revels had a pall over them as far as the king was concerned. He had no son. Henry Tudor had no heir. Why had God denied him? Was he not a faithful Christian? A good king? He was, by the rood, and yet he was being denied a son to follow him! His wife was old, and dried up. And she had never been able to sustain enough life in her babies that they lived, but for their one daughter, Mary. He was to be followed by a girl? No, by the rood! He would have a legitimate son and heir! He must! His thoughts went to his new mistress, who had eased his distress by whispering in his ear that she was carrying his child. A child to be born sometime in early summer.

Philippa was disappointed the revels would be subdued, but more for Banon than herself. "The Christmas Court is always marvelous. After Twelfth Night it seems that Lent is always just upon us. You will go home in the spring, and have had no fun."

"Think of your poor mistress," Banon said. "My heart broke for her the other day when you brought me to meet her. She is so frail, and she looks so sad. Yet she greeted me with kindness and a smile. I think she must have been pretty when she was young."

"So mama has always said. But she also said Queen Margaret was prettier," Philippa noted. "Hurry and get ready, Banie. We are due at court by afternoon. Dress warmly. The river will be cold."

"Do you think that Cecily and Tony will return to court for the Christmas revels?" Banon wondered aloud.

"I hope so," Philippa answered her sister, as she carefully adjusted her cord and chain belt with its dainty pomander case about her waist. Her gown was a violet-colored velvet with a panel of violet, cream, and gold brocade showing. It had a square neckline. The sleeves were narrow to the elbow, running into a wide deep cuff of rich fur with a false undersleeve of the brocade that had a frilled lace edging. She wore a French hood that was trimmed in tiny seed pearls and lace, set back on her head with a small back veil of delicate lawn. Lucy fastened a fine gold and pearl chain with Philippa's emerald and pearl broach, now made into a pendant, hanging from it. Philippa was very proud of this piece of jewelry, for it had been given to her by the king's grandmother when she was born. Anyone who admired it was told the story. Fastening gold and pearl earbobs into her ears, Philippa completed her toilette and turned to see if Banon was ready.

Banon's gown was of peach-colored quilted velvet with an underskirt of cream and gold brocade. Her sleeves were slashed to show cream silk beneath the velvet, and tied with gold cords. The neckline was square like her sister's but with a pearl edging, and she had a twisted gold belt with a long tassel attached to it. Like her older sister she wore a French hood with a back veil. About her neck was a long strand of pearls with a gold and pearl pendant in the shape of a cross, and from her ears hung pearls.

They joined Lord Cambridge in his hall, which overlooked the river.

"Uncle!" Philippa exclaimed, seeing him. "Your clothing today is even more magnificent than yesterday! Next to the king you are surely the most stylish gentleman at court," she teased him.

"I am more splendid than King Hal," Lord Cambridge replied, "but we shall not quibble the point, darling girl. Do you like my hose? I thought to keep it plain so as not to detract from the glory of my doublet and my short coat." He spun about so they might admire him, flashing his embroidered sleeves at them. "And what do you think of my shoes? I had them dyed to match my coat! And my embroidered gauntlets too."

"Sky blue, gold, and white suit you, uncle," Philippa said. "I particularly admire the pleated edge of your shirt collar, and your cap and plume."

He grinned at her. "The whole suit was made to complement my fair coloring. There are few men who are true blonds as I am. Banon, have you nothing to say?"

"Uncle," she told him, "you astound me with your incredible sense of fashion. While you have always dressed well, when we were back in Cumbria I would have never imagined you capable of such sartorial splendor."

He chuckled. "Nay. Otterly is not the place for such garments. I had almost forgotten how much I enjoyed wearing clothing like this. Alas, it will not be for long."

The servants were bringing them fur-lined cloaks, and setting them on their shoulders so they might exit the house for Lord Cambridge's barge.

"Do you regret coming north, uncle?" Philippa asked him.

"Nay, darling girl, I do not. Court is far too exhausting now for a man of my age, and your mother means far more to me than gallivanting about after the king. Nay. At this time in my life Otterly suits me well, as does the quiet life. I have but come back to court to make certain that you are well settled, Philippa Meredith."

She kissed his cheek. "I love you, Uncle Thomas," she told him.

He smiled, pleased. This would be their second visit to court. They would soon be leaving London for Greenwich. Thomas Bolton was just beginning to slip into the thick of the court intrigue again. He had already picked up one delicious little rumor that the king's new and very discreet mistress was the delightful Mistress Bessie Blount. It was also said that Bessie was expecting a child. Tom did not discourage Philippa from pursuing her friendship with the charming Bessie. Indeed, he went out of his way to seek out her company as well. Henry Tudor would not be jealous of him, particularly if Lord Cambridge were paying extravagant court to the girl, helping to defuse any serious rumors that might reach the queen's ears which could cause Bessie to lose her place in the queen's household. She would lose it eventually, of course, but now was not the time. Katherine was very fond of Thomas Bolton, Lord Cambridge, and if she had heard any gossip regarding his unorthodox inclinations she had refused to listen to them, for she saw nothing untoward in the man's behavior. She would judge him by the Thomas Bolton she knew, and not the scurrilous whispers of other people.

The Christmas kept at Greenwich was simple and quiet. The feasts for each of the Twelve Days were subdued in consideration of the queen. But the king, yet angry, danced openly with all the pretty young women, and more with Mistress Blount than any other. Bessie was not a malicious girl, and so she continued to treat the queen, her mistress, with the utmost deference and respect, hurrying quickly back to her side when the music would end. Some thought her a simpleton for it. But Queen Katherine knew in her heart what was happening although she showed no indication of it. She was grateful for Elizabeth Blount's good manners and good heart. Bessie's natural sweet nature made it difficult to dislike her or be angry with her. The king had chosen her, and Bessie had been raised to obey and listen to her king.

On the first day of the new year 1520 Lord Cambridge overheard a bit of news that piqued his interest. Lord Melvyn had died, and there were no heirs to his small estate in Oxfordshire. The land would either revert to the crown, for it had a fine wood for hunting, or it would be sold for the benefit of the crown. It was near enough to London so that Philippa might continue her service to the Tudors. And it was a prosperous estate. Lord Melvyn's apple orchards were famous for the excellent cider that came from them, and his pastureland was rented at an excellent fee to a neighbor who raised cattle. This was the information that Lord Cambridge had been able to obtain from one of the king's secretaries, William Smythe.

"And if I were interested in obtaining ownership of the late Lord Melvyn's estate?" he queried Master Smythe, a tall, lean man with a bland and ageless face.

"The king is interested in having it for the deer park," Master Smythe said.

"The king has many deer parks," Lord Cambridge replied.

"That is true, my lord," the secretary said. "Perhaps it could be sold, for the king values a full purse as well as a good deer park, and Woodstock is near."

The meaning was clear. "I would, of course," Lord Cambridge murmured, "want to pay a finder's fee for any consideration on your part. A generous fee," he finished.

"There is another gentleman interested in the estate," Master Smythe said. "He is the gentleman who has been renting Lord Melvyn's pastureland."

"I will pay more," Lord Cambridge said bluntly. He reached into his doublet and drew out a small chamois bag which he handed to Master Smythe. "A small token of my esteem, which I will leave with you until I have returned from inspecting Lord Melvyn's property in Oxfordshire. And I shall tell the king of my interest in the property so there will be no difficulty for you."

"You know his majesty well enough to speak with him?" Master Smythe's voice held a new note of respect. Not all courtiers knew the king well enough to speak with him. Most, in fact, did not. He took the small bag of coins from Lord Cambridge.

"I have been speaking with the king for many years, Master

Smythe, and my cousin, the lady of Friarsgate, for whose eldest daughter I wish to purchase Lord Melvyn's estates, is a good friend of the queen. This daughter is in service to her highness." Thomas Bolton smiled, and flicked an imaginary bit of dust from his ornate doublet.

"There shall be no sale of Lord Melvyn's property until you have returned from inspecting it, my lord," the secretary said. "But you understand that I must accept the highest offer for my master, the king. That is my duty." He was even now tucking the little bag into his own doublet. It was of a pleasing weight.

"Of course," Lord Cambridge said, and then he withdrew from the small room where this one of many secretaries was ensconced. The bribe had been generous. Generous enough to ensure him more than enough time to see the property in question. January was not a month for travel, but Thomas Bolton could travel rough if necessary, and it was necessary. Explaining to Philippa that he must see to some business and would be gone for several days, he left the court in the company of two Otterly men-at-arms, and rode to Oxfordshire.

Lord Melvyn's estate, Melville, was located northwest of the town of Oxford. The town was full of good accommodations with excellent food and drink. Lord Cambridge took the best quarters that could be found at the King's Arms, a large comfortable inn on the edge of Oxford. If they departed early in the morning, he told his men, they could easily reach Melville and be back into the town by dark. And luck was with Thomas Bolton. After a good night's sleep he awoke to a cold but clear and windless winter's day. Taking food for the midday meal with them they rode out, and by the time they had returned that evening Thomas Bolton knew he had found Philippa Meredith a new dower portion. Lord Melvyn's house was in poor repair, but that could be modernized and repaired. The next morning, to the surprise of his men, he was up early and eager to ride for London.

"I believe I have found you an estate in Oxfordshire," he told Philippa. "But I shall not be satisfied until it is settled. I am at the mercy of one of the king's secretaries. And there is someone else who seeks Melville as well. He cannot possibly have as much money as I do, however. Still, I shall not crow until the matter is settled."

"Is that where you were, you old dear?" Philippa asked. "You missed an important event. Banon has met a young man. He is a poor Neville, but educated and with charming manners. You will like him."

"Do you like him, darling girl?" Lord Cambridge asked. "And what does Banon say about him? Is it possible one of my problems is already solved?"

"Aye, I do like him, and Banon, while reticent to say a great deal, likes him too, I am certain," Philippa replied. "But tell me about my new estate, uncle."

"Nay, my pet, not until I am certain it is yours," he told her. "I do not want you disappointed. Master Smythe, one of the king's secretaries, says there is another who would have Melville. I have not yet learned if this is so, or if he seeks to get a better price off of me which he will then skim for himself while accepting my generous bribe as well. These lower echelon servants can be both greedy and ruthless. This is a good property, Philippa, my angel, but I prefer not to be cheated and taken for a fool, for if I am it will cause your mother and me no end of difficulties in our business dealings. I will meet with Master Smythe on the morrow to hopefully conclude the negotiation."

"Thank you, uncle," Philippa told him. "No one else has ever been so good to me as you. Mama says it too about you."

"You are my only family," Lord Cambridge said. "I would be lost without you."

Immediately after the mass, and before the morning meal, the lord of Otterly Court met with the king's secretary. There was another man with him, soberly dressed, his face windburned like the visage of someone who worked out of doors. He stared openmouthed for a moment at Lord Cambridge in his scarlet velvet knee-length coat with pleats from its high yoke, and the flared, fur-lined sleeves. Then the man's eyes went to Lord Cambridge's slashed and beaded leather slippers that had been dyed to match his coat.

"Good morrow, Master Smythe. I assume you are prepared to do business," Thomas Bolton said pleasantly, nodding at the other man.

"This is Robert Burton, the earl of Witton's secretary and agent, my lord. He will be bidding on Lord Melvyn's property for his master. Would you care to open the bidding, my lord?" The secretary smiled rather toothily, which was a surprise to Lord Cambridge. He did not believe he had ever seen one of the king's secretaries smile.

"One hundred and fifty guineas," Thomas Bolton said. It was a more than generous price, and he was not of a mind to dally with the purchase. He saw Robert Burton swallow hard.

"Two hundred guineas," the agent finally said.

"Three hundred guineas," Lord Cambridge answered.

"My lord! The property is not worth that price," the agent cried.

"Ah, Master Burton, but it is to me," Lord Cambridge replied.

Robert Burton shook his head, and looked at Master Smythe. "I cannot offer more than I have, sir."

"Then the property is won by Lord Cambridge," Smythe replied. "May I see the color of your coin, my lord?"

Thomas Bolton drew a large leather bag from his doublet, and handed it to the secretary. "Count it out, Master Smythe, and take another ten guineas for yourself. I was prepared to pay more if I had to, but the earl of Witton obviously was not. I will wait while you tally up my purchase."

"My lord, may I ask why you want this property?" Master Burton inquired politely.

"It is a gift to a relative," Lord Cambridge said quietly.

The agent nodded. "My master will be most disappointed," he said. Then with a small bow he withdrew himself from the little chamber.

"I would speak with you privily, Master Burton," Thomas Bolton called after him.

The agent raised his hand to signal that he had heard as he closed the door.

"What do you know of this earl of Witton?" Lord Cambridge asked the secretary.

"Precious little, my lord. He has been in his majesty's service, but other than that he is a stranger to me." He finished piling up several stacks of coins he had removed from the leather bag. Then slowly and deliberately he counted out the ten additional pounds. Carefully closing the bag he handed it back to Thomas Bolton, along with a bill of sale and the deed to the property known as Melville.

Lord Cambridge accepted it all, smiling. "You knew I should be the high bidder, Master Smythe," he said. "You are a clever fellow."

"You will find while the bill of sale is in your name, my lord, the property has been put in the name of your young cousin, Mistress Philippa Bolton," the secretary said.

Now Thomas Bolton was truly impressed. "Are you content in the king's service, Smythe?" he asked the man.

"It is difficult for a man in my position to gain the advancement he desires. I am not one of the cardinal's men, my lord. I was recommended to my current position several years ago by Lord Willoughby, who wed with the queen's friend, Maria de Salinas. But I have no powerful patron to aid me."

"You have not answered my question, Smythe. Are you content in the king's service? Or would you prefer employment somewhere where you might have more responsibility and respect?" Lord Cambridge said.

"If such a position should become available, if it were offered to me by the right master, I could leave the king's service with a clear conscience," Master Smythe said. "I am not important, but simply one of many."

"And I am not an important man," Lord Cambridge replied. "But I am a rich man with a bent for trade and possibly the need for someone like you. We shall talk again, William Smythe, before I return north. Would you mind living in the north?"

"Not at all, my lord," said Master Smythe and smiled for a second time that day, surprised that Lord Cambridge had remembered his Christian name, and suddenly being absolutely certain that despite his foppish airs, Thomas Bolton, Lord Cambridge, was a most clever and astute gentleman.

Lord Cambridge nodded, and then without another word he left the secretary, going out into the corridor where he found Robert Burton. "Thank you for waiting, Master Burton. Let us go someplace where we may speak in private." They found a secluded alcove with a window seat overlooking an inner court, and settled themselves. "Now, Master Burton, tell me about your master, the earl of Witton. He has served the king in some capacity? And why did he wish Lord Melvyn's lands?"

Robert Burton hesitated. He had waited out of curiosity, but he was anxious to return home to tell his master of the fact they had lost the land to a stranger.

"Come, come, Master Burton," Lord Cambridge said quietly. "I may be able to assuage your disappointment if you give me the correct answers. Is your master wed?"

"Nay, sir," came the reply.

"How old is he?" The next question snapped.

"I would not know, sir, but he has only been earl this year past since his da died of the sweat. My master is not an old man, but he is not a youth either."

"Why is he not wed?"

"My lord! I would not be privy to such information. I am merely a secretary," Robert Burton replied.

"Come, sir, servants know more than their masters, and that is certain," Thomas Bolton said with the hint of a smile. "Have you not lived on the earl's estate since your birth? Can you recall when your master was born?"

"Aye, I was twelve when his lordship was birthed," Master Burton said.

"And how old are you now, sir?" was the next question.

"I am forty-two this September past, my lord," came the answer.

"Then your master is thirty, Robert Burton. 'Tis a good age. Now tell me, do you know if your master is betrothed to any woman?"

"Oh, no, sir, but he be looking, or so my sister who serves in the house says," came the reply.

"Good! Good! Now one other question, Robert Burton. Is your master sound of body and mind, and fair to gaze upon?"

"He is a good and fair master, my lord, and the lasses say he is handsome," the bailiff said.

"Why does your master want Melville?" Lord Cambridge asked.

"We have been renting the pasturage on Lord Melvyn's lands for years, my lord. When he died with no heirs my master thought it was a good time to purchase the land. Who else would want it? But alas, you did! The earl will be most disappointed."

"Perhaps I may assuage his disappointment," Lord Cambridge said. "Tell your master to come and see me. There may be a way that he can obtain Melville. I am Thomas Bolton, Lord Cambridge. My home is on the river near Richmond and Westminster. Bolton House. Any wherryman will know."

Robert Burton stood up. "Thank you, my lord, I will tell my master what you have said to me. I believe he will come, for he very much desires old Lord Melvyn's lands. A new owner might wish that pasturage for themselves, and would not rent it." He bowed politely and hurried off, leaving Thomas Bolton considering that he might very well have all their problems solved, providing of course that the earl of Witton was amenable.

Robert Burton left London as quickly as he could and rode north and just slightly west for the earl of Witton's lands, which were called Brierewode. He pushed himself, stopping when it grew dark only to eat and rest his horse for a few hours. At the first light he was up and riding once more. Reaching his master's estates after several days, he gave his exhausted horse into the keeping of a stable boy and hurried into the house to find the earl in his library.

Crispin St. Claire looked up as his secretary entered the room. "How much did it cost us, Rob?" he asked.

Robert Burton shook his head. "We lost it, my lord."

"What?" The earl of Witton was astounded. "Did I not tell you you could bid up to two hundred guineas?"

"There were three bids, my lord. The first was for one hundred and fifty gold guineas. It was made by a Lord Cambridge. Two hundred, says I, not wanting to prolong it. Three hundred, says this other gentleman." He shrugged. "My lord, what was I to do?"

"The property isn't worth all that gold coin," the earl exclaimed.

"That's what I told Lord Cambridge," the secretary replied. "Well, it is to me, he says. Then while the royal secretary is counting out the price plus an additional ten guineas Lord Cambridge says he should take for himself, he tells me to wait. So I did."

"And what did he say to you afterwards?" the earl asked, curious.

"He asked a lot of questions about you, my lord. Then he says if you will come and see him there may be a way for you to obtain the property in question. He says any wherryman in the London vicinity will know Bolton House, his home. His name is Thomas Bolton."

"He probably wants to sell me the property at a profit," the earl said, irritated. "He may even be in league with the royal secretary in this matter. I will not be diddled by some scheming courtier, damnit!"

"I don't think he is that, my lord," the secretary responded. "His garments are grand, and say he is a fop. But his manner is assured and direct. I cannot reconcile the two, but I must tell you that I liked him. I did not think him dishonest."

"Interesting, Rob, for you are a good judge of character, and always have been," the earl noted. "Shall I go then, and meet this Lord Cambridge?"

"It is winter, my lord. The land is lying fallow. The cattle are in the barns, and there is little to do right now for any of us. Is winter not the time when the nobility go to court? What harm can it do you to speak with Lord Cambridge? You can be no worse off after you have spoken with him than before, I am thinking."

"I could be in great debt, Rob," the earl told his secretary.

"The land is worth no more than I offered, my lord, and you would be foolish to go into debt to obtain it. I deposited your coin with your goldsmith in London, and there it will remain until you have need of it."

"I will admit to being curious," the earl said slowly, "and you are here to act on my behalf, Rob. Yet I swore I would not go back until I had found a wife."

"You are more apt to find one at court, I am thinking," the secretary said, "than here. None of our near neighbors have daughters of an age to wed."

"I do not want some spoiled lass who thinks only of gowns, and how to spend my coin. A man must have a wife he can speak with now and again. These girls at court are naught but dancing, preening feather-heads in my opinion. They giggle, and flirt, and kiss every gentleman they can find in whatever dark corners they can find. Still, there might be just one who would suit me. A biddable lass who would manage my home, and bear my children without complaint. And not waste my coin on fripperies."

"You'll never know, my lord, unless you go back to court," Robert Burton said. "You know the king would welcome you. You served him well for eight years."

"I did," the earl agreed. "Being a diplomat for Henry Tudor is not an easy task, Rob, but I served him with honor both in San Lorenzo after that idiot Howard was called home, and in Cleves as well."

"And you never found a lass in either place, my lord? 'Tis a pity, I think. We would have been happy to see you bring a bride home. Even a foreign lass."

"In San Lorenzo the ladies of the south were too free with their favors to suit me," the earl said. "And in Cleves they were too large, and too straightlaced. Nay, give me a good English wife. If I can find one."

"Go back to court for the rest of the winter, my lord," the secretary advised his master. "See what Lord Cambridge desires of you. And see if there is a pretty lass there who would suit your lordship." Robert Burton was a servant of long and good standing with his master, and so was able to speak so freely to him.

"Well, I must go to London if for no other reason than to see what Lord Cambridge desires from me, and whether I can cajole him into giving me the lands that are rightfully mine. If only I could have convinced Lord Melvyn to sell me his properties, but towards the end there he became dotty, and convinced that everyone around him was stealing from him. I could not reason with the man at all."

"He was very old, my lord," Robert Burton reminded the earl. "They get that way sometimes when they are so old. Not all, but some."

The earl of Witton departed for court a few days later. By the time he reached London the court was up from Greenwich and settled at Richmond again. Presenting himself first to Cardinal Wolsey's major-domo, he begged a place to stay from him. It had been the cardinal who had assigned him to his various missions and postings for the king. The earl of Witton doubted if King Henry would even know who he was, but the cardinal did. He was given a small cubicle where he might leave his few belongings and lay his head at night. His food would be his own concern. He might eat in the cardinal's hall if he could find a place. The earl of Witton thanked Cardinal Wolsey's head of household, insisting he take a little bag of coppers for his trouble.

The morning after his arrival he dressed carefully, but soberly, and hailing a wherryman asked to be taken to Bolton House. The boatman nodded, and began to row upstream with the incoming tide. They were well past Richmond when the wherryman began guiding his boat towards the shore where a fine slate-roofed house of several stories, set in a garden, was situated. They drew up to a little dock, and the earl got out, tossing the wherryman a large coin.

"Shall I wait, me lord?" the wherryman asked.

Seeing the two barges tied to the other side of the dock, the earl shook his head. "Nay," he said. "I suspect my host will get me back when I need to go." He watched as the boat moved back off, now fighting the tide as it came upriver. He walked up the carefully raked gravel path towards the house, and he was halfway there when a servant hurried forth. "I am the earl of Witton to see Lord Cambridge," he said.

"Yes, indeed, my lord, my master is expecting you. Please come with me," the servant said, and moved quickly up the path and into the house.

The earl followed, and was surprised to be brought into a wonderful room that appeared to run the entire length of the house. There were windows along one wall overlooking the river. The room was paneled with a coffered ceiling, and the wood floors were covered in the finest eastern carpets the earl had ever seen. At one end of the room great iron mastiffs flanked the huge fireplace where a fire roared. The fine oak furniture was polished, and there were bowls of potpourri. On a large sideboard was a silver tray with matching goblets and crystal decanters.

Suddenly a door in the paneled wall opened, and a gentleman stepped into the room. He was wearing a burgundy velvet midcalf-length coat that was obviously lined in fur. It had full puffed sleeves and black silk undersleeves edged in lace. There was a fine fur collar enclosing the neckline of the coat. "My dear lord St. Claire," the gentleman said, extending an elegant hand with more rings than the earl had ever seen in all his life. "Welcome! Welcome! I am Thomas Bolton, Lord Cambridge. Please, let us sit by the fire. Are you thirsty? I have some excellent Spanish wine, but no, perhaps afterwards to toast our agreement."

The earl took the extended hand, and was surprised by the firm handshake. Then he sat down, frankly overwhelmed by Lord Cambridge. "What agreement are we going to toast, my lord?" he managed to ask.

Thomas Bolton chuckled. "The one we make so you may have Lord Melvyn's lands, which is what you want. In exchange you will give me what I want. It is really quite simple, my lord."

"I do not know if I can raise more than you paid for Melville," the earl said.

"Dear boy, the land wasn't worth what I paid for it," Thomas Bolton laughed.

"Then why did you offer such a ridiculous amount?" the earl asked.

"Because you wanted it, of course," Lord Cambridge said to the surprised earl. "I am delighted that your agent was able to convince you to come. He is a good man, and serves you well, I expect. And since he returned to Brierewode, for that is the name of your estate, isn't it, I have made some inquiries about you."

"Have you?" the earl said weakly. This was the oddest conversation he had ever had with anyone, he thought.

"You are the fourth earl of Witton. Your family is old, and loyal to whoever is on the throne. A wise course to follow, I might add," Lord Cambridge said, and then he continued. "You have served Henry Tudor in the capacity of ambassador and negotiator on the continent for several years. Your mother died when you were two. Your father died a year ago, which is why you came home. You have two older sisters, Marjorie and Susanna. Both are wed to respectable men, but not great names, of course, for their dower portions were modest. You are known to be an honest man, intelligent, and scrupulous in your dealings. You have never been married, or even betrothed."

"There has been no time for it," the earl said as if defending himself, and then he wondered why he would defend the fact he was in service to his king.

"Have I forgotten anything?" Lord Cambridge asked aloud. And then he answered himself, "No, I think not."

The earl laughed in spite of himself. "What is it you want of me, my lord?"

"I want to give you Lord Melvyn's lands, dear boy. Isn't that what you want?" Thomas Bolton said, smiling at the earl of Witton.

"And what do you want in exchange, my lord?" Crispin St. Claire asked, piercing Lord Cambridge with a direct look. "What is it you want so much of me that you would pay such an exorbitant sum for Melville?"

"You need a wife, my lord earl. Are you willing to take one in exchange for Lord Melvyn's lands? Which by coincidence now belong to my young cousin, Philippa Meredith."

The earl of Witton was more than surprised by Lord Cambridge's words. He didn't know what he had expected, but it was certainly not this. Warily he asked, "What is wrong with the lass?"

"Nothing at all. She is fifteen. Fair. Intelligent. Chaste. And her dower, in addition to Melville, has both gold and silver coin, jewelry, clothing, linens, all that a young woman who is marrying is expected to have."

"I repeat, what is wrong with her? Has she been seduced, and her reputation compromised? I will have no slut for a wife." My God! Surely he wasn't even considering such an outrageous proposal, but his gray eyes were thoughtful.

"Philippa Meredith is the heiress to a great estate in Cumbria. She was to wed the second son of the earl of Renfrew," Tom began. "Unfortunately the lad decided after his time in Paris and Rome that he was more suited to the priesthood. He came home to announce this right after Philippa's natal day. Philippa serves the queen as one of her maids of honor, and has for several years. She is pure, I guarantee you. But she is also, if I am to be honest, stubborn. She decided that Giles FitzHugh had so desperately sought to escape living at Friarsgate that he became a priest rather than wed her."

The earl laughed again. "Poor lass," he said. "But if she has this great estate in the north, why do you want Melville?"

"She has renounced her inheritance in Friarsgate, although her mother refuses to accept it yet. So because I adore my cousin,

Rosamund, and her daughters, I looked for an estate nearer to the court for Philippa. I chose Lord Melvyn's estate. But Philippa needs a husband. And you desire those same lands, but you cannot afford them. I see a marriage between you as a perfect solution," Lord Cambridge said. "You have an old and respected name. Philippa has wealth. It would appear to be a perfect match. I know Rosamund and her husband, the laird of Claven's Carn, would agree. They trust me in matters such as this."

"The girl is half Scots? Oh, no, my friend. No!"

"Nay, the laird is Philippa's stepfather. Her late father was Sir Owein Meredith, a knight in service to the house of Tudor since his childhood. Her mother, Rosamund Bolton, the lady of Friarsgate. King Henry VII was Rosamund's guardian for a time. It was his mother who arranged the marriage between my cousin and Owein. My cousin is held a friend by both Queen Katherine and the Scots queen with whom she was raised. That is why Philippa has a place in the queen's household."

"But the girl's family is hardly the equal of mine," the earl said.

"No, it is not," Lord Cambridge agreed. "Yet you have no family but two sisters, my lord. Philippa Meredith's mother has produced seven children, of whom six live, and she is with child again even now. Think! I offer you a nubile young girl of good family, in favor with the king and queen, whose dower is rich in everything you desire."

"It is tempting, my lord," the earl said, "but you will understand that I am not of a mind, even in order to gain Melville, to agree easily to your proposition. I would meet your young cousin. Get to know her. We must suit, for whatever she possesses I will not have discord in my house. I want a biddable wife who will obey me."

"I can promise you that Philippa would be a good wife, but she is intelligent, my lord, and educated as many of these young courtiers are. She will not always be agreeable to you, but then I have never known a wife who was, have you?"

"You argue your point well. I will not say nay, but neither will I say yea. Let us be introduced, and we shall see what comes of it, Lord Cambridge. Is the girl in the house now?"

"No, she is at court with her mistress," Thomas Bolton said. "She is devoted to Queen Katherine in her service, as her father was devoted to the Tudors."

The earl nodded. "It speaks well of your young cousin," he said. "When then shall I meet her?"

"I have a barge at my disposal," Lord Cambridge said. "If you do not mind waiting while I change my garments, we shall go to Richmond together, my lord. My servants will bring you something to eat. Where do you reside in London?"

"I was given a cubicle at the cardinal's home," he said. "But food is another matter entirely. I would welcome something to eat, but why would you change clothing? Your gown is most handsome."

"Dear boy, I should not appear at court in my house garb!" Lord Cambridge cried. "I have a reputation to keep up, as you will soon learn. The servants will bring you food and wine while I am preparing myself. We shall talk on the way to court." And arising from his chair Thomas Bolton retreated through the door by which he had entered the chamber, leaving his guest both slightly amused, and bemused.

The servants now entered, bringing with them a tray upon which the earl found a dish of poached eggs in a cream sauce flavored with marsala wine, a thick slice of a country-cured ham, a small cottage loaf which had obviously just come from the ovens, a crock of sweet butter, and a little dish of cherry jam. A little table was brought to him and draped with a white linen cloth. The tray was set before him. A goblet was placed at his right hand.

"Wine or ale, my lord?" a male servant asked him politely.

"Ale," he replied, and set about to eat the little meal that had been brought to him. He was, he found, very hungry, having come straight to Bolton House this morning. Lord Cambridge's care for his person showed a delicacy of manners that impressed Crispin St. Claire. If his young cousin were as careful of her guests it could be that she would

make a good hostess, a good wife, a good countess of Witton. It surprised him that he was actually considering an alliance with the
daughter of a northern landowner, and an ordinary knight. His own
family had arrived in England several centuries earlier with King
William the Norman. He had Plantagenet blood, for one of his ancestors had wed one of King Henry I's bastard daughters.

Still the girl in question—what was her name?—Philippa, yes!
Philippa Meredith had the property he coveted, and if Lord Cambridge were to be believed, she also had wealth. He saw no reason not
to believe Thomas Bolton. Was there anyone else that he would have
preferred to wed? The truth was there was not. There was no one. He
knew he had to take a wife. His sisters told him often enough. He was
the last male St. Claire in his line. But since his return home after his
father had died he had made no effort whatsoever to seek a match
with any female. This girl, it seemed, was providence. Her family was
respectable. Her connections were good. She had the land he sought
after, and she had wealth. What more was there that a man could ask
of a wife? And if she were pretty it would be but a bonus, but she need
not be. He did not have to say anything further to Lord Cambridge.
The man was astute, and he knew that after enough time to salve
Crispin St. Claire's dignity, the earl of Witton was going to accept his
proposal. He was going to marry Philippa Meredith, and make her his
countess. Looking the wench over was nothing more than a formality.
The earl mopped his plate with the last piece of bread, and drank
down the remainder of his goblet. He pushed back his chair, and
sighed contentedly. It was going to be a good day. It was going to be a
very good day. The main door to the beautiful hall opened, and Lord
Cambridge stepped through into the chamber. "You have eaten well,
dear boy?" he asked solicitously.

"I have!" the earl of Witton said, and then he stared with amaze-
ment.

Thomas Bolton chuckled at the look on the younger man's face.
"Yes," he said, "I am quite magnificent, am I not, my lord?" His short,

full, pleated coat was of midnight blue velvet brocade lined and trimmed with pale gray rabbit fur. His shirt collar had a delicate pleated edge. His sky blue doublet showed cloth of gold through artfully done slashings. His hose was finely woven wool in alternating stripes of the contrasting blues, and he wore a gold cord garter on his left leg. His codpiece was ablaze with gemstones. His square-toed shoes were the same velvet brocade as his coat. About his neck was a large chain made from squares of Irish red gold.

"By the rood, my lord," the earl said, "if your cousin is half as beautiful as you are I shall marry her at once! The garb you wear now does make plain your burgundy house coat." And he laughed. "I did not think it possible that any man could dress so well. Even the king, though you did not hear me say it."

"And you, my lord, did not hear me tell you that the king frequently consults with me as to his wardrobe. Now, if you are ready, my dear Crispin, we shall leave for court so you may inspect Philippa Meredith, but I have no doubt you will have her to wife."

Chapter 7

❦

"There she is," Lord Cambridge said quietly. "There is my darling girl, and her younger sister, who is my heiress. She sits by the queen's knee. Her highness is most fond of Philippa Meredith. She looks much like her mother, and I believe she reminds the queen of her youth. Of course that youth was not always a happy one, but Philippa's mother, Rosamund Bolton, always remained steadfast in her loyalty to the queen."

"The girl in green?" the earl asked, to be certain.

Lord Cambridge nodded. "Aye. Tudor green," he said and he chuckled. "Not yet even sixteen, and Philippa is a consummate courtier. What do you think? I offer you wealth, the land you desire, and a very pretty girl for your wife, dear boy."

Crispin St. Claire looked while attempting not to stare. She was lovely. Her features were delicate, and while not of noble blood she could not be considered coarse by any stretch of the imagination. "She is fair enough," he acknowledged, "but I will want more in a wife than just beauty."

"She has both manners and education," Thomas Bolton said.

"But has she wit, my lord?" the earl asked.

Thomas Bolton felt a slight stab of irritation prick at him. "Come, sir," he said rather more sharply than he had intended to. "If she were of a more baronial family would you be quite so fussy? Those lasses have a tendency to die young, and be poor breeders. For a family such as yours to survive it is necessary for you to wed outside of your usual realm every few generations. However, if you care not to have my young cousin to wife you have but to say so now, and we will part friends."

"I need a wife with whom I may carry on an intelligent conversation now and again, my lord," the earl said in defense of himself. "I would sooner not marry at all, and allow my earldom to disappear, than marry a woman who can speak of nothing but children, and her household. Do not tell me a woman like that would interest you."

Lord Cambridge could not help but laugh. "Nay, sir, a woman like that would not interest me. But you need have no fear. Philippa is a girl of many and varied opinions. While she may drive you to distraction, she will never bore you. She may anger you; she may make you laugh; but you will never, ever be bored by her, or with her, I guarantee it, my lord. Now, are you interested in meeting Philippa Meredith, or shall we go our separate ways, my lord?"

"You tempt me with your words, sir," the earl admitted. "You make this girl seem most intriguing. Aye, I should like to meet her."

"Excellent! I shall speak with her, and we will arrange it. I think a less public venue than the babbling court, eh?" Thomas Bolton said.

"Not now?" The earl of Witton was surprised, and perhaps a little disappointed.

"In matters of so delicate a nature," Lord Cambridge said, "it is best to go carefully, and prepare the way. Philippa was quite angered by Giles FitzHugh's decision. It placed her in a most embarrassing position, and her feelings were hurt. She even considered taking the veil, but her great-uncle, the prior of a small monastery, thought it not wise, and spoke with her on the matter. However, she has come to distrust men, I fear."

"Did she love him that much then?" the earl asked.

"She did not love him at all, although she was certain that she did.

She hardly knew him," Lord Cambridge said, and then he explained. "She met him as a child, and fancied herself in love with him from that moment onward. He was the older brother of her best friend, and young Cecily innocently helped to feed Philippa's dreams as best friends are wont to do. Then Giles came home, announcing he was being ordained into the priesthood when he returned to Rome, and all of Philippa's girlish dreams came crashing loudly down around her. Everything she had planned her life would be was gone. I think it would have been better had the lad died rather than desert her for the church."

"Is she still angry?" the earl asked.

"She says nay, but I think she is," Lord Cambridge replied. "But it is now eight months since the unfortunate incident, and it is time for Philippa to move on with her life, my lord. Wouldn't you agree?"

The earl nodded slowly. "When may I meet her then?"

"In a few days' time. You must stay with me, dear boy. A cubicle in Cardinal Wolsey's residence sounds appalling. We will not be caught unawares. Philippa and her sister live at court as maids of honor. She comes to my house now and again for fresh wardrobe, as the space assigned her here is very slight."

"Agreed," the earl responded, "and I thank you. Were I still in service to the king I have no doubt my accommodation would have been better, but it was grudgingly given, and it is without a fire. And of course I am not invited to Wolsey's table either."

Lord Cambridge shuddered. "The man may be clever, and a cardinal, but blood will tell in the end. He has no manners, nor does he have any common sense. His palaces at York Place and Hampton Court are larger and grander than any the king possesses. One day Henry Tudor will stop to consider that. No man, even a cardinal, should put himself above the king. One day the cardinal will make a slip, and his enemies will be quick to point it out to the king. He is not a well-loved man though he be useful to the king. His rise has been great. His decline will be greater."

"But he is extremely intelligent, and crafty," the earl said. "While I served the king my instructions always came through Wolsey. Some say he manages the country while the king plays, but knowing both men I see it differently. The king uses Wolsey as anyone would a good servant. The king takes the glory, and the cardinal the contempt."

"Ah, you have surprised me, my lord earl," Thomas Bolton said. "You are obviously more astute than I would have taken you for, and I find that pleasing. Now, however, I am going to join a few friends. If you wish to leave before me just send the barge back, and I will do the same." Lord Cambridge bowed, and moved off into the crowd, smiling and greeting people as he went.

An interesting man, the earl of Witton thought. Odd, but interesting. He moved into a recessed alcove, and looked for Philippa again. She was no longer seated next to her mistress, but dancing a boisterous country dance with a young man. When he swung her up and around with great vigor she threw her head back and laughed. The earl smiled. It was obvious she was having a good time, and why not. She was young, and fair. His interest was piqued further when the next dance began, and the king partnered Philippa Meredith. The king only danced with those he considered the best dancers in his court. Consequently his partners were limited, as many young women were afraid to dance with him lest they displease him. But Philippa Meredith wasn't one bit afraid of Henry Tudor. Holding her skirts up she pranced daintily next to her monarch while the musicians played. She was graceful, and the smile on her lips never wavered. When the dance was over and done with, the king kissed the girl's hand and she curtseyed, then backed away to rejoin her mistress. She was flushed, and a single tendril of auburn hair had slipped from beneath her elegant French hood. He found it charming.

Before he left court that day Thomas Bolton sought out his young cousin, and begged a moment of her company from the queen who graciously gave it, smiling warmly at Lord Cambridge. He took Philippa's small hand in his, tucking it in his arm, and they left the great anteroom where the king and the court were now amusing themselves. Walking quietly through a gallery hung with magnificent tapestries, Lord Cambridge began to speak.

"My darling girl, we have had the most incredible piece of luck!"

"Were you able to obtain the property you sought, uncle?" Philippa asked him.

"Aye, and it is already in your name, but that is not the half of it. There was someone else who sought the property. A gentleman whose lands match with Melville. He is the earl of Witton, and he is unattached, and seeking a wife."

Philippa stopped. "Now, uncle, I am not certain I like where this is going," she said nervously.

"You can be the countess of Witton, darling girl! Think on it! Your husband would be an earl, of an old and illustrious family," Lord Cambridge gushed.

"What is the matter with him, for there must be something wrong with an earl who would take a plain knight's daughter to wife," Philippa replied suspiciously.

"His name is Crispin St. Claire," Lord Cambridge said. "He has been in service to the king as a diplomat. His father died last year, and he has come home to take up his responsibilities. There is nothing wrong with him."

"Then he is old, uncle. Do you want me shackled to some graybeard?" Her look was almost fearful.

"He is thirty, Philippa, and I could not by any stretch of the imagination call him a graybeard. He is a mature man, and ready to take a wife. Can you not see what an incredible piece of good fortune this is for you? He wants Melville, and it is a part of your dower portion, darling girl."

"He must be desperate to have it then, that he would offer to wed me," Philippa replied.

"He did not," Thomas Bolton said, deciding that his young cousin needed a bit of cold water thrown upon her fine opinion of herself.

"He tried to buy Melville from me, but I paid a ridiculous price for it in order to get it when I learned this earl was wife hunting. I told him if he would have the land he must have you to wife to get it."

"Uncle!" Philippa's pretty face grew red. "You deliberately ensnared this man?"

"I wanted the estate for you. It is within an easy distance of London and the court. When I learned afterwards that the earl wanted it too I simply took advantage of the situation. You mother would fully approve my actions," he responded.

"Your audacity, you mean," Philippa said. "What must this earl of Witton think of you? Of me? I cannot believe you would do such a thing, uncle!"

"Nonsense, darling girl!" he said, unaffected by her criticism. "The earl of Witton's is an old and an honorable family, but they are not a great family. He is not poor, but neither is he wealthy. Your father was a knight, Philippa. Your mother is a woman of property. Your connections here at court are impeccable. Even without Lord Melvyn's property you are a most respectable prospect. A marriage with this man gives you a title. It ennobles your children. And in return he gains the lands he wants to add to his own, and a wife with a large purse. It is a perfect match." He smiled at her.

"But where is the love, uncle? If I must be shackled to this man should there not be something between us other than money and property?" She was very pretty in her concern, her hazel eyes thoughtful.

"First you must meet him," Lord Cambridge said. "I would not force you into any marriage, darling girl. Let us see if you and the earl are compatible, for if you are not you shall not be his wife. I want you happy, as does your mother. But think, darling girl! An earl instead of the second son of an earl. All the advantage would have been for Giles FitzHugh had you wed him. What advantage would you have gained by such a match? Oh, once I thought it a good possibility, before you came to court, but this prospect is so much better. And you are in the queen's favor, and the king's. I saw him dance with you this evening, Philippa."

"Oh, that was because he could not dance with Bessie, and she said he should dance with me. That I was a fine dancer," Philippa explained.

"Why would Mistress Blount not dance with the king?" Lord Cambridge was curious at this turn of events.

"She does not feel well, uncle. She says her belly makes her ill these days," Philippa answered innocently.

He debated a moment, and then he said, "You know the rumor, darling girl?"

Philippa bit her lower lip, and a blush suffused her cheek. "That she is the king's lover, uncle? Aye. I have heard it, but if it is so, what am I to do? I love the queen, but I do so like Bessie Blount."

"You continue on as always, my dear. You are respectful and loving of your mistress, but you are also kind to Mistress Blount. You would be foolish not to be, for she is in the king's favor without a doubt. And something else you should know, darling girl. It is most likely that Mistress Blount is expecting the king's child. She will shortly, I am certain, disappear from the court, for the king will not embarrass the queen by allowing his mistress to parade her big belly about, especially now that it has been determined the queen will conceive no more."

"I had heard the whispers, uncle, but I could not believe them. Who will have Bessie Blount to wife now that she has disgraced herself?" Philippa wondered.

Thomas Bolton smiled to himself. Philippa's naivete was sometimes charming, and it reminded him of how truly innocent she was. "The king will be generous to Mistress Blount, darling girl, and particularly if she births him a son. She will have a husband as a reward, and a pension, I have not a doubt. And the king's child will be given certain honors, particularly a son."

"I feel almost guilty retaining my friendship with Bessie in light of the queen's distress," Philippa said slowly.

"Do not make the mistake so many at court do of taking sides, darling girl," he warned her. "Royalty are changeable as the winds, and it is best to blow with the wind rather than against it. The king favors Mistress Blount, who behaves with respect and discretion towards the queen. Both king and queen behave as if naught is amiss between them. And that is how you will behave. Does the queen show any anger towards Mistress Blount?"

"Nay," Philippa said, "although others of the queen's women have begun to shun her, uncle. And some are outright mean."

"Do not follow their example, Philippa. Behave towards both Bessie and the queen as you always have. No one knows what tomorrow will bring."

Philippa nodded.

"Now, darling girl, let us get back to the subject of the earl of Witton. I have asked him to stay with me at Bolton House. I will ask the queen to allow you home in a few days, and you will meet each other then. Will that please you?"

"A countess," Philippa mused. "I would be the countess of Witton. Millicent Langholme would be pea green with envy. She is only just wed to Sir Walter Lumley. And Cecily would be certain that Giles knew. And Giles's parents, who forbade me my best friend's wedding, would certainly be impressed, especially if Witton has better estates than Renfrew. Imagine, Renfrew offered to help me find a husband. He could not have found a husband such as you have found for me, uncle." Philippa was beginning to consider the situation, and it was not unpleasant.

"Nothing is graven in stone, darling girl," Lord Cambridge warned her. "He must like you, and you must like him."

"He wants my land," Philippa said dryly. "Is there any doubt that I should not please this earl of Witton?"

"He wants Melville, it is true, darling girl, but he is a man of honor," Lord Cambridge said. "He will not marry just for the land."

"Neither will I, uncle," Philippa told him.

He grinned at her. "Darling girl, I suspect you will enchant Crispin St. Claire. This is a great coup, should you manage it. An earl. A diplomat. And a man who will enjoy coming to court every bit as much as you do. But of course you must do your duty by the man first, and give him an heir."

Philippa stopped. "Children," she said slowly. "I had not thought about children, uncle. But, aye, if I am in any way like my mother it is that I know my duty."

Lord Cambridge smiled and nodded. "Aye, you will delight the earl, darling girl. Of that I am absolutely certain."

"I shall come home in two days' time, uncle. May I explain to the queen that you are negotiating a match for me?" she asked.

"Mention no names," he advised her. "The queen will understand."

"Of course," she agreed. They had come to the end of the gallery. "I must get back, uncle," she told him. "The queen is a kind mistress, but I should not take advantage."

"Tell me quickly how Banon does?" he said.

"She has found favor, but like mama she longs for the north, and is anxious to return to Otterly," Philippa told him. "The Neville boy's grandfather was a first cousin of our Bolton grandmother, who was born a Neville. Such a liaison seems promising, uncle. You should speak with Banon."

"I shall," he promised her.

She stopped, and kissed his cheek. "I must fly," she said, and hurried away back down the gallery.

Suddenly Thomas Bolton was exhausted, and felt every bit of his forty-nine years. He sighed. He was surprised to realize that he did not enjoy the court any longer. He wanted to be home at Otterly, snug by his fire and heedless of the Cumbrian winter outside his windows. While the business of seeing that Banon and Philippa were well matched interested him, it was the cloth trade that he and Rosamund had created that was of more interest to him. How could he watch over their commerce in London? And Rosamund was at Claven's Carn awaiting the birth of her child. Would she be paying attention to their endeavor as she should?

"Lord Cambridge?" William Smythe had appeared from the dim recesses of the gallery. He was soberly dressed in a black velvet midcalf-length coat which Thomas Bolton noted was a bit worn, and dusty in color.

"Ah, Master Smythe," he greeted the younger man.

"I did not want to disturb you when you were with your cousin, my lord," William Smythe began. He offered Lord Cambridge a smile.

Why, what a pretty fellow, Thomas Bolton thought suddenly, and he smiled in return. "Most thoughtful," he replied.

"I have been considering what your lordship intimated when we last met. Perhaps I misunderstood your lordship, but were you implying that I might benefit from a change of employment?"

"You would have to reside in the north," Lord Cambridge said. "And there would be occasions when I would require you to travel. Our cloth trade grows larger, and more profitable. My cousin and I can no longer manage without help, but of course I would want someone sophisticated in the ways of business to aid us. You would live at Otterly. At first in the house, and later on if you decided to remain in my service I would see you had your own cottage in the village. You would be paid fifty gold guineas each Michaelmas for your year's service, and you would have a space in the church cemetery."

William Smythe could not keep the surprised look from his usually emotionless face. "My lord! 'Tis most generous. More than anything for which I could have hoped."

"You must consider my offer carefully," Lord Cambridge said. " 'Tis an honor to be in royal service. And what of your family?"

"I have no family left, my lord. And I am merely one of many here, with little chance for advancement. I know my own worth. I am a clever man with little chance to show off my talents. Yet you saw them, and are willing to offer me this opportunity." All the haughtiness of their previous encounter was gone. "I need not consider any further. If your lordship will have me in his service, I will be content, and I will work hard for you." He knelt, and grabbing up Thomas Bolton's hand, kissed it.

"Give your notice, William," Lord Cambridge said. "Then come to me at Bolton House. I do not know when we shall be ready to return home to Otterly, but you should begin your new duties as soon as possible." He reached into the purse beneath his ornate doublet and drew out a coin which he handed to the younger man. "Pay your debts," he said. "You must come into my service unencumbered."

The secretary arose, saying nervously, "One thing, my lord. I have a cat. She has been my most faithful companion for several years now. I would bring her with me."

"A cat?" Lord Cambridge laughed aloud. "Of course you may bring the cat. I can see that you will get on quite well with my young cousin, Bessie Meredith." He laughed again. "I like cats myself. It is a good mouser, William?"

"Oh, yes, my lord. Pussums is an excellent mouser," he answered.

"I will send my barge to bring you to Bolton House when you are ready. You and Pussums." Lord Cambridge chuckled, and then turning away, he continued down the gallery. He was tired, but this visit to court was proving quite entertaining in the most unexpected ways.

Philippa had returned to the queen's side now.

Katherine looked up. "Everything is alright, my child, is it not?"

"Aye, madame. My cousin wanted to tell me that he may be ready to make a match for me, but first he would like me to meet the gentleman in question. In two days he would like me to come to Bolton House, if your highness can spare me."

"Can you tell me the name of the gentleman in question?" the queen asked softly.

"My cousin has said until the arrangement is agreed upon he would prefer I say naught, madame. He hopes your highness will understand," Philippa ventured nervously. She could not imagine saying no to the queen, her mistress, but in effect that was just what she was doing.

"Of course," the queen agreed, to Philippa's surprise. "You do not want to embarrass the gentleman in question, or yourself, my child." Then she smiled a small conspiratorial smile. "I shall not even tell the king."

That night Philippa lay with her sister in the bed they shared in the Maidens' Chamber. Banon was filled with excitement, for her Neville suitor's father was going to speak with Lord Cambridge regarding a betrothal between his son and Banon Meredith.

"Uncle Thomas will say yes, of course," Banon confided. "Robert may be a younger son, but he is a Neville."

"So was our grandmother. Uncle will not necessarily be impressed," Philippa said. It galled her somewhat that her younger sister was to be betrothed before she was.

"Do you know that small lake that borders Otterly lands?" Banon replied. "It belongs to the Nevilles. Robert's father has said he will give it to Robert, and a strip of land on its far side. It will belong to Otterly if we wed."

"Lord Neville loses nothing by that gesture," Philippa told her sister. "After all if Robert marries you, then Otterly becomes his."

"Otterly will belong to our eldest son," Banon said.

"Who will be a Neville, not a Bolton or a Meredith," Philippa countered. "The Neville family will increase their holdings by their younger son's marriage to you."

"But I will be happy!" Banon said. "Why do you always make everything so difficult, Philippa? You are just jealous because I am to be betrothed, and you are not." She turned away from her older sister, dragging the coverlet over her shoulders.

"Uncle Thomas has found a possible husband for me," Philippa replied. "And I shall not have to leave the court if I marry him."

"Who?" Banon did not change her position.

"I cannot say yet," Philippa responded. "I could not even tell the queen, but in two days I will go to Bolton House, and meet the gentleman."

"He won't be a Neville," Banon said.

"No, he won't. He will be someone who loves the court even as I do, sister. You had best hope that we suit one another, for mama will never allow you to marry until I am married. I am the eldest, and I must wed first."

Banon sat up in their bed, and glared at her sister. "If you spoil my chance at happiness I shall never forgive you, Philippa Meredith!" she cried softly.

"You like Robert Neville, Banie. I must like this gentleman as well. I shall not marry simply to facilitate your plans," Philippa snapped.

"Ohh, you are sometimes so hateful and spiteful!" Banon said angrily.

"You had best pray for me, little sister," Philippa teased her sibling. Then she turned away from her sister, and fell into a dreamless sleep, while beside her Banon lay fuming and angry.

Two days later Philippa made her way to her uncle's barge which had been sent for her. She was dressed in a golden brown velvet brocade gown with a tightly fitting bodice. The neckline was low and square, and filled in with a soft natural-colored linen pleating. The sleeves were tight, with cuffs of rich brown beaver. A silk girdle embroidered in gold and copper threads hung from her trim waist. Upon her head was a matching gable hood with a golden silk gauze back veil, and about her shoulders a beaver-lined brown velvet cloak.

Lucy grinned. "Well," she said, "he ought to be impressed with you, mistress."

"What do you mean he?" Philippa said nervously.

"The gentleman that Lord Cambridge wants you to meet with an eye towards marriage, mistress. That is why you're going to Bolton House, isn't it? Mistress Banon says that's what it's all about."

" 'Tis true that Uncle Thomas would introduce me to a gentleman, but there is nothing been discussed yet. We are just to meet away from the curiosity of the court."

"Aye," Lucy agreed. "Too many gossips and sharp eyes here, Mistress Philippa."

"You will say nothing, Lucy," she said, and her tiring woman nodded in agreement.

Philippa was glad that she was wearing several heavy warm petticoats beneath her gown. The day was cold, and dreary. There was the hint of snow or an icy rain in the air. The barge was rowed up the river with the tide, and it seemed no time until she could see Bolton House coming into view. She was frozen despite the fur lap robe upon her knees and the flannel-wrapped hot bricks at her feet. And her mind was racing madly.

What would he be like, this earl of Witton? At thirty he was just about twice her age. Would he still want to come to court? Would he permit her to come to court? Or would she be expected to remain in Oxford producing heir after heir for him? She had to wed sooner than later. She was facing her sixteenth birthday. Cecily had not returned to court. She was expecting a child, she had written Philippa. They would remain at Everleigh until after the child was born, as Cecily wanted to be near her mother now. Even the obnoxious Millicent Langholme was with child. Sir Walter had arrived at court on Twelfth Night to brag on his prowess. Bessie Blount was with child, although that was hardly something spoken about. Her baby would be born in June, she had told Philippa. She would be leaving court shortly, before Lent, in fact. I shall be alone but for my sister, who will certainly marry as soon as she may. But I must wed too. Philippa sighed, and then started as the barge bumped the quai of Lord Cambridge's house.

Immediately a footman was there to help her from the vessel. "Your cousin is awaiting you in the hall, Mistress Philippa," he said, ushering her up through the gardens, Lucy following. Inside he took her cloak, and she hurried off, knowing the way well.

"Uncle," Philippa called, entering the lovely room. It was warm, and welcoming, and the dreary day did not seem quite so bad now. She held her hands out to him.

"Darling girl!" Lord Cambridge greeted her, coming forward to take her hands in his and kiss her on both cheeks. "Come now. There is someone whom I should like you to meet." He led her down the chamber to where a tall gentleman awaited them by the fireplace. "Mistress Philippa Meredith, I present to you Crispin St. Claire, the earl of Witton. My lord, this is my young cousin Philippa, of whom we have spoken." He released his grip on the girl as he spoke.

Philippa curtseyed politely. "My lord," she said, eyes lowered, but dying to get a look at him. There simply had not been enough time to decide if he were handsome.

Aye, she was even prettier close up, the earl thought as he raised Philippa's hand slowly to his lips, and saluted it with a light kiss. "Mistress Meredith," he said.

His voice was deep, and had a slightly rough edge to it. Philippa felt a small shiver race up her spine. She snuck a quick peek at the man still holding her hand, and as she did she said, "May I have my fingers back, my lord?"

"I am not certain yet if I wish to return them," the earl said boldly.

"Well, well, my dears, I see you will get on quite famously without me, and so I will leave you to become better acquainted," Lord Cambridge murmured, and turning about, he left them. It was going to work out! He sensed it.

As Thomas Bolton had spoken Philippa's startled gaze had met that of the earl.

"Ah," Crispin St. Claire said, "you have hazel eyes. I wondered when I saw you at court from a distance what color eyes you would have. Your auburn hair was visible, but I wondered if you might have brown eyes like so many with reddish hair."

"My mother's eyes are brown," Philippa replied. "I have my father's eyes."

"They are pretty eyes," he told her.

"Thank you," Philippa said, blushing.

It was then he realized that while Philippa might have thought to marry the FitzHugh lad, she had never been courted. He was still holding her hand, and now he led her to one of the window seats overlooking the Thames. "So, Mistress Meredith," he began, "here we be, in an awkward situation. Why is it that those who seek to do us kindness never realize that by doing so they place us in a difficult position?"

"You want Melville," she said frankly.

"Indeed I do. I have pastured some of my herds on that land for several years. I need it. But not enough to wed where I would not be happy. Nor the lady either," he told her as candidly. "Now for pity's sake, Mistress Meredith, look at me, for you have wanted to ever since you entered the room. I am not the king who cannot bear to be perused by a direct glance. Do you know my age? I am thirty. I am sound of both limb and mind, I believe." He released her hand, and stood up. "Look upon the earl of Witton, mistress."

Philippa looked up. The man before her was tall and slender. He could not be called a handsome man, but neither could he be said to be ugly. His nose was too long, and narrow. His chin was pointed, and his mouth too big. But he had fine gray eyes edged in deep brown lashes. His hair was an ash brown. He was elegantly but simply dressed in a medium blue velvet knee-length pleated coat with flared and fur-lined sleeves. She could see a fine gold chain beneath lying upon his blue brocaded doublet. They were the clothes of a gentleman, but not necessarily a courtier. Still, his manner was if anything too assured. For some reason it irritated her.

She stood up. "You tower over me, my lord."

A slight smile touched his lips, but was quickly gone. "You are a petite girl," he told her. "Is your mam as delicately made, Mistress Meredith?"

"She is, and has birthed seven children, six of whom are living, and is expecting to give birth any day now to her eighth," Philippa replied. "I, too, am capable of bearing my husband an heir, my lord."

"Some women who prefer court life do not enjoy children," he remarked.

"I am the eldest of my siblings, my lord, and I can assure you that I like children," she told him. "If it should be decided that a match between us would be suitable, my lord, then I am prepared to do my duty."

"And who would raise your children, mistress?" he probed.

"I serve the queen, my lord. I must be at court some of the time else I lose my place," she told him.

"But if you wed," he said, "you will no longer be a maid of honor. Have you considered that? Would there be another place for you among the queen's women?"

She had not thought of that. It had not occurred to her until he had said it that her place among the queen's maids would be gone. None of the girls with whom she had grown up at court had returned once wed. "I had not thought . . ." she began, and suddenly found herself close to tears.

He quickly took her hand again to comfort her. "I would not keep you from the court if you were my wife, Philippa Meredith, but I would expect you to be at Brierewode enough to oversee any children we would have. Many among my class are content to have their children raised by servants, but I am not. We might come to court to hunt in the autumn, and then return for the Christmas revels. We would remain in Oxford for the winter, and then join the king in the spring before going home for the summer. While you were at court you might offer your services to her highness, but for the first time in your life you might enjoy just playing."

"You make it sound most pleasant, my lord," she told him.

"It could be," he replied, and then they sat together again.

"To be your wife would be a great coup for my family," Philippa said, "but while some might think me foolish, I must know the man I wed before I wed him."

"I agree," he said, "for I must know the woman I would wed before we take vows. Still, I believe we have made a good start today, Mistress Meredith."

"And I believe that under the circumstances in which we find ourselves, my lord, you may call me Philippa," she told him.

"Who are you named after?" he asked, "For I am certain it is a family name."

"My mother's mother, Philippa Neville, though I never knew her," the girl replied. "She died with my grandfather Bolton and their son when mama was three."

"Neville is a well-known name in the north," he noted.

"They were a less distinguished branch of that family," Philippa quickly said. She would not have him thinking she sought to make herself better than she was.

"You are scrupulous in your history, Philippa. It is a quality I like in both men and women," he told her.

"Women can be honorable, my lord," she responded stiffly. This was a difficult conversation, Philippa thought. They were both being so formal and polite. Did he know how to be any other way? He was, after all, thirty. Yet there were men at court his age and older who possessed a sense of fun. The king was older, and he did.

"What are you thinking, Philippa?" he asked her.

"That this meeting between us is strained," she admitted.

He chuckled. "Do you always answer a question so truthfully?" Her small hand was cool in his. "It is difficult," he admitted. "We are strangers, and it is proposed that we marry." He rubbed the little hand between his two big hands to warm it. "It has been a long time since I paid court to a woman, Philippa. I suppose I am clumsy at it, for the truth is I was never very skilled at courting."

"Is that why you have never married?" she inquired.

He nodded. "And there was no time, for my service to the king was primary in my life, Philippa. I know you understand that kind of duty, for you too give faithful service to the monarch as did your late father, I am told." Her hand was now warm in his.

"Tell me about your family," she said.

"My parents are dead. I have two older sisters, both married, and both sure that they know what is best for me," he told her.

Now it was Philippa who laughed. "Families are strange things, my lord. You love them always, but there are times when you wish they would be silent, and evaporate away so you might be alone to live your life in peace."

He chuckled again. "You have old thoughts for a girl so young."

"I am not young!" she declared. "I shall be sixteen at the end of April."

"Will you? Then we must consider the possibility of a match between us quickly before you grow much too old for me," he teased her.

"Oh, you do have a sense of humor!" Philippa cried. "I was so afraid you would be an old sobersides, my lord. I am certainly relieved that you are not."

The earl of Witton laughed aloud. "Lord Cambridge promised me that you would never bore me, Philippa, and from this brief encounter today I can certainly see that he did not prevaricate. So now we have met, and we have spoken together. Shall we continue on, or would you prefer not?"

"I must wed, and you must wed," she told him. "If you be willing, my lord, then I am content that you court me. But might we wait just a little while before any formal betrothal is settled between you and my family?"

"Of course," he agreed. "But I shall ask the queen's permission to take you to visit my home in Oxfordshire, Philippa. I will want Lord Cambridge and your sister to come as well. And you will want to see Melville, the property that is now yours, I am sure." He raised the hand he had been holding all this while to his lips, and kissed it again. "Now," he told her, "you may have the return of your pretty fingers."

And she blushed again, not looking at the hand. "Will you remain in London long, sir?"

"Just long enough to speak with the queen, Philippa, and then I will want to return to Brierewode to see that it is prepared to show at its best when you come to visit me," he told her. "The winter is coming to an end now, but it would be best to travel before the roads become waterlogged. Brierewode is beautiful even in the late winter."

"If we agree upon a match, my lord, I should not want to be married until after the court visits France in early summer. I have never been to France, and while I am certain that our king and queen are the brightest stars in the firmament, I should like to be able to tell our children that I have also seen the king and queen of France."

"If we agree, then of course you may serve your mistress a final time in France, but I will come with you, Philippa. You are young, and despite your veneer of sophistication you are an innocent. I do not want you eaten up by a handsome French courtier. They are sly, the French. I will come with you, and protect you from harm."

"I do not need to be protected, my lord. I am quite capable of fending for myself," Philippa declared indignantly.

"Have you ever met a Frenchman?" he asked her.

"Well, no," she admitted. "I have not, but they cannot be any more crafty than an English courtier, I am certain."

"They are far craftier, and will have your gown off you before you are even aware of what is in their mind. French courtiers, both male and female, are the masters of seduction. I cannot have the future countess of Witton's reputation compromised in any way, Philippa. You must trust to my experience in these things."

"You will make me look the fool," she cried unhappily.

"What then, do you seek to be seduced? For if you do, I will be most happy to oblige you," the earl of Witton said, his gray eyes narrowing dangerously.

Philippa shrank back from him. "Oh no, my lord! I simply do not wish to appear the baby. I promise you I will be most careful."

"Aye, you will, for I shall be by your side, my lass, and all will know that you are to be my wife, that none attempt to tamper with your virtue," Crispin St. Claire told her.

"As if I should allow such a thing!" Philippa said sharply. "Do you assume that, having been a part of the court for three years, I have allowed myself to be compromised, my lord? Fie, and shame!"

"Can you tell me that you have never kissed any of the young men at court?" he demanded of her.

"Of course n . . ." Philippa stopped in midsentence. Sir Roger Mildmay. But how could she explain that to the earl of Witton? "I was not kissed until last spring," she finally said. "I had saved myself for Giles, and then he rejected me. Cecily said I should at least have been kissed at my age, and so I allowed a friend that privilege."

"You acted from anger then," he said quietly. "You must learn never to allow your emotions to dictate your actions, Philippa. Such behavior could lead to a fatal mistake, I fear. Who was the gentleman in question?"

"Sir, I do not kiss and tell! It was only Sir Roger," she exclaimed. "And 'twas just kissing. He took no other liberties. He is a friend. But Cecily said he was her first kiss, and he is considered the best kisser at court."

The earl of Witton didn't know whether to laugh, or scold her. The queen was obviously not in complete control of her maids, although given her difficulties, poor lady, it was a wonder there were not more scandals. "Before we wed, if we wed, you will cease your experimentation in kissing. If you wish to be kissed, I shall kiss you."

"I don't know why," Philippa pouted. "What harm is there in innocent kissing?"

"Your reticence but arouses my curiosity, and I cannot help but wonder why you would deny me," he told her.

"Because you will make a fool of me. You can't call out this man for the simple act of a few kisses last year before you and I even met," Philippa said.

"Call him out?" The earl was astounded. "Why would I call him out?"

"Do you not think my behavior has dishonored you, and you wish to restore your family's honor?" she asked him naively.

"Nay, Philippa, I do not wish to call out a young man for offering to console a disappointed girl with a few kisses before I even met this girl. I am sorry if you misunderstood me."

"Oh," Philippa responded, feeling both foolish and disappointed. "Then why would you insist on being by my side if I go to France?"

"If you are to be my wife, Philippa, I cannot leave you to yourself if we accompany the court to France. It simply is not done. I must be by your side to escort you as your future husband."

"What if we are not formally betrothed until we return from France?" she asked him slyly.

"If we are not betrothed before you go to France, Philippa, then I expect we will not be betrothed at all. You say you are to be sixteen in April. Well, I shall be thirty-one in early August. Neither of us can wait. I will want an heir as soon as possible. I am willing to allow you the latitude of going to France with the court, but if you are to be my wife I must be by your side. And we will wed as soon as we return. If you cannot agree to that here and now, then I see no reason for our acquaintance to continue further."

Chapter 8

"You would not believe what he said to me!" Philippa told Lord Cambridge, and then she repeated the conversation she had just had with the earl of Witton. His declaration had surprised her so, she had run from the hall.

"I agree with him, darling girl," Thomas Bolton said.

"He behaves as if he didn't trust me, uncle! I cannot wed with a man who does not trust me," Philippa said angrily.

"Even if Crispin knew you well enough to trust you, Philippa, he would still not allow you to go to France unescorted. It is unseemly. Now let us go back into the hall, and straighten this matter out."

"Uncle!" she protested, pouting.

"Philippa, this is an amazing match for you. If indeed you have not put the earl off with your childish behavior. We shall return to the hall immediately!" His voice was stern, and she looked surprised. In all her life she had never heard Thomas Bolton speak in such a sharp, commanding tone.

"Did you ever speak to my mother like that?" she demanded of him.

"I never had to speak to your mother like that," he told her. "Now, girl, to the hall!" And he gently pushed her from his library, through the corridor, and into the hall again where the earl of Witton stood staring out at the river morosely.

The earl turned as they entered.

"Philippa has come to apologize for her behavior," Lord Cambridge said, "and she will gladly agree to your escorting her to France this summer. Philippa?"

"Oh, very well," Philippa grudgingly muttered. "I apologize, my lord."

"There," Lord Cambridge said, almost purring. "Now you two will be friends again. Being of an independent turn of mind you must both learn to compromise, eh?"

"I agree," responded the earl, looking towards Philippa.

"I am sorry I left you so precipitously," Philippa allowed stiffly. "I was upset that you did not trust me, my lord. No one has ever questioned my veracity."

"And I did not mean to, if indeed that is what I did," he replied. "I am simply concerned for your good name, Philippa. I am happy we are to be friends again now, and that you will accept my company in France without complaint."

She nodded. "We are, and I will," she told him.

"Excellent, excellent!" Lord Cambridge said, smiling broadly. "Now, my dears, I am absolutely ravenous, and you have both been so busy arguing that you never noticed that the board is set and ready for us. Philippa, you will remain the night. There is an icy rain falling outside now, and I do not wish to compromise your health by sending you back to the palace this evening. The morning is time enough."

They sat down to an excellent meal. Lord Cambridge's cook was a true artist. They began with salmon, sliced wafer thin, and lightly broiled with dill. There were fresh oysters, and large prawns steamed in wine and served with lemon. Next came a fat duck dripping its juices, and swimming in a gravy of rich red wine; a rabbit pie; a platter of chops, and another with half of a country-cured ham. Philippa's eyes widened as a silver platter filled with lovely plump artichokes was offered.

"Uncle! Where did you get these?" she asked him. "I thought the king kept them all for himself. You know how he adores artichokes."

Lord Cambridge smiled craftily. "Why, darling girl, I have my little ways as you well know. I, too, adore artichokes."

"It is not the season for them," the earl said, helping himself from the platter.

"Nonetheless I manage to obtain them," Thomas Bolton said, tearing off a piece from the warm cottage loaf, and buttering it lavishly before taking a large bite.

"Miracles are born in Uncle Thomas's kitchens wherever he may be living at the time," Philippa said.

"You have more than one house then?" the earl asked.

"Here, and at Greenwich, and of course Otterly in Cumbria," Philippa responded before her cousin might. "And each house is identical both inside and out, for Uncle Thomas does not like a great deal of change." She laughed. "Is that not correct, uncle?"

"It is," he agreed. "My life is far less complicated that way. It matters not where I may be living, everything is in exactly the same place."

"But the upholstery is different," Philippa put in, smiling.

"One must have some small variety," Lord Cambridge said drolly.

Their meal ended with a tartlet of winter pears and a bowl of clotted Devon cream. The goblets had been kept filled, and all at the board were feeling mellow as outside the rain poured down, a certain indication of the spring to come.

"Philippa plays a fairly good game of chess, Crispin, dear boy," Lord Cambridge said. "I taught her myself. As for me, I am exhausted, and must seek my bed." Arising from the high board he bowed to them, and departed the hall.

"He is not very subtle," Philippa said when he had gone.

"But most hopeful, I think, that you and I will not quarrel again," the earl replied.

She smiled. "As a child my mother ruled me. These past few years at court I have felt as if I were the mistress of my own destiny, although I know it to be not fully true. Now I face the prospect of a husband who will be master over me. And while I know that is how it should be, it is something with which I must come to terms. Does that make any sense to you, my lord?"

He nodded, thinking that taking a wife was much like taming a wild creature, at least where Philippa was concerned. "I shall try not to prick you too hard, Philippa," he promised her with a small smile. Then he arose from the board. "Come, and play chess with me, madame. 'Tis a game I very much enjoy."

She fetched the board and the pieces from their place within the sideboard. Then she set them up neatly on a small game table she had instructed him to bring to the fireside. "White or black, my lord?" Philippa asked him as they seated themselves.

"Black," he said. "I have always enjoyed being the black knight."

"And I the white queen," she quickly parried, and moved her first pawn.

He laughed, then studying the board carefully for a moment, he too moved a pawn.

They were, he quickly found, quite equally matched. She did not play like other women, filled with emotion, and weepy when she lost a piece. Philippa played coolly and with a sharp intellect. She was careful with each move she made, and he was quite astounded when she checked his queen. They spoke virtually not a word, and not easily did he finally defeat her, checkmating her king.

And she laughed when he did. "Ah, at last I have found a worthy opponent," she told him. "I shall not allow you such leeway the next time we play."

"Ahh," he replied with a small smile, "then you think you can beat me, eh?"

"Perhaps," Philippa hedged. Men, as she recalled, did not like being bested by a woman. She had foolishly allowed her tongue to run away with her.

"Only perhaps?" he taunted gently, wondering why she had suddenly drawn back.

"Nothing is ever certain, my lord," Philippa said quickly in reply.

He laughed again. "You think you can beat me, but you have decided to spare my masculine feelings, Philippa. Is that it? Well, do not bother. If you think you can beat me, then let me see you do it." He did not believe she actually could, but he was very much enjoying teasing her, seeing the range of emotions play across her lovely face.

Without a word Philippa set the chess pieces in their proper place again, and then playing with intense concentration she proceeded to beat him in a far quicker period of time than he would have imagined. When she checked his king, and set it next to his queen, his knights, and his bishops, she looked across the table at him. There was not even the hint of a smile upon her face when she spoke.

"You were correct, my lord. I sought to spare you. You cannot live at court as I do, and serve the monarchs as I do, and be a total ninny. Neither the king, the queen, or those who surround them in their more private moments during the day would tolerate a bad chess player. And while I have carefully held back with his majesty so that he always wins our matches, I play hard enough with him that he believes he has actually bested me. It delights him, for I have bested his brother-in-law, the duke of Suffolk, and others of his favorites on many occasions. I have even played and beaten the cardinal twice."

The earl of Witton nodded slowly. "Lord Cambridge said it. You are a consummate courtier, Philippa. I am most impressed by your acumen."

"But am I the sort of girl you would want for a wife, my lord? Unlike others of my sex I am a poor dissembler," she responded. "What you have seen this day is what I am. I have a temper. I have a passion for beautiful things. But I am not a giggling or silly turnip head."

"Will you always obey me if I am your husband?" he asked her candidly.

"Probably not," she told him so quickly that he smiled.

"You are honest, Philippa. I count honesty among the greatest of virtues along with loyalty and honor," Crispin St. Claire said. "Well, I can always beat you if you are truly disobedient. And there are other more pleasurable means of bringing a fractious wife to her husband's will."

"Are you flirting with me, my lord?" she asked. Her cheeks felt warm.

"Aye, I am," he replied. "I like to make you blush, Philippa. To find that I can discommode you reassures me that I will have some small advantage."

"You speak as if the matter between us is settled, my lord," she responded, feeling a small prick of irritation. There was an arrogance about him that troubled her.

"Can you find a better match than an earl of Witton?" he asked seriously. "I could probably find a girl with better bloodlines, but as Lord Cambridge has reminded me, an over-bred girl would be a poor breeder. If you are like your mother you will prove more than worthy, Philippa. Aye, it is settled between us, and you will be my wife."

"I have not said it!" she cried, jumping up from her chair so suddenly that the game table between them shook, and several chess pieces fell to the floor.

"But you will, Philippa," he taunted her. "You will agree to be my wife."

"It is the land you want," she flung back at him.

"In the beginning, aye. But not now," he told her. "I beheld you for the first time at court the other night, and decided the matter then and there."

"Do not dare to say you love me!" she cried.

"Nay, I do not, for I barely know you," he responded. "Perhaps we shall learn to love each other one day, Philippa. But few go into a loving marriage. You are not a fool, as you have so carefully pointed out to me. You know that marriages among people like us are arranged for a variety of reasons. Land. Wealth. Status. Heirs. We will respect one another, Philippa. We will make children together. And if we are very fortunate the love may come. But you will make me a good wife, and I will make you the countess of Witton, and a good husband. Do you find me unattractive, or unpleasant to be with, Philippa?"

"Nay," she admitted. "You are not a beautiful man, but neither are you an ugly one. And you have wit, and intellect, both of which I value far more in a man than a handsome face. But I think you arrogant also, my lord."

"Aye, I can indeed be arrogant, but nonetheless I believe we have made a good beginning, Philippa." Then reaching out he drew her from behind the table, and wrapped his arms about her. "I want the betrothal papers drawn up soon," he said, looking down at her, his fingers tipping her face up to his. "I find I do not choose to wait long for you."

He had taken her by surprise when he enfolded her into his embrace. She felt herself blushing once again. Worse, her heart raced at the proximity of their two bodies, though her skirts protected her from too great an intimacy. He was going to kiss her, she realized. His head was descending. Her eyes closed slowly of themselves. Her moist lips parted slightly. She sighed as his mouth touched hers, and her head spun with the pleasure the kiss offered. It had certainly not been anything like this with Roger Mildmay. Philippa was astounded. And then his lips were gone, and she felt a sense of deep loss. She almost cried out a protest as her eyes flew open.

"There," he said. "The bargain between us is sealed now, Philippa."

"But," she protested once again, "I have not said it!"

"You will," he promised her in his deep voice, and he released his hold on her.

Philippa almost stumbled when he did, but she recovered herself quickly. "I must go to bed," she told him. "I will have to arise early to be back at the palace in time for the early mass. The queen always expects her maids to attend the first mass of the day with her. Good night, my lord." She curtseyed to him, and almost ran from the hall.

He watched her go, and then walking to the sideboard he poured himself a silver goblet of rich red wine from the decanter there. Seating himself by the fire he considered the evening that they had just spent together. Was he mad to wed such a young girl? Perhaps a girl of twenty would suit him better, but nay. He wanted Philippa Meredith. And he was not of a mind to wait the next several months or a year to wed her. She had admitted to kissing another, and yet the touch of her lips on his had sent his senses reeling. Her mouth had not the experience of a courtesan. Indeed there was a charming innocence about it. He would let her go to France, but while she could not know it yet, she would go as his wife. Tomorrow he would seek an audience with the cardinal, and offer Wolsey his services for this great meeting that was to take place in the coming summer between King Henry and King Francois. Crispin St. Claire knew there would be a need for skilled diplomats at this endeavor. The cardinal knew what was needed, but he had not the patience to work out all the tiny details that would need to be settled. A minuter of details that would decide where each king's pavilion would be set; how many horses each man would have; how much, and what kinds of foods and wines; how many courtiers each king would bring with him. And then there would be the similar preparations for Queen Katherine and Queen Claude. Nothing would be left to chance. Each of these kings was filled with his own self-importance. Each considered himself the first among rulers. Each would have to be catered and cosseted equally. It would require much patience, and a great deal of planning. And not just before the event transpired, but during the event and afterwards, as both Henry Tudor and Francois Premiere sought to claim that they were the greater of the duo and had gained the upper hand at this event.

Philippa departed early the following morning before either Lord Cambridge or the earl was up. She did not want to see or speak with either of them until she had had time to consider all that had happened in the few short hours she had been with the earl. She had slept badly. Her time with Crispin St. Claire had left her somewhat confused. He was a strong-willed man, she quickly divined. He was used to having his own way. So was she.

Her father had died when she was so young, Philippa thought. She had been raised in a house of women. Edmund Bolton was a quiet man, and while the management of Friarsgate was left to him, in the hall he was relatively silent while her mother and Maybel had ruled the roost. And Uncle Thomas never interfered with her mother. Indeed, if anything they had been close companions and confidants. And while she had been at home when her mother had wed Logan Hepburn, her stepfather never interfered with her mother's rule at Friarsgate, and Philippa had rarely gone to Claven's Carn with them, as she was considered the heiress to Friarsgate.

She was simply not used to having a man tell her what to do, and how to do it. But he really hadn't, she reconsidered. He would simply exercise his rights as the man of the house. His house. Why was she chafing like an unbroken mare at her first bridle? This was an incredible match for a girl like her. And when he had kissed her . . . Philippa felt herself grow warm with the memory of it, and she smiled to herself. She had enjoyed kissing him. She had almost wished he would kiss her again, and perhaps not stop for a brief time. She wondered what Crispin St. Claire would have thought of that.

The earl of Witton entered the hall at Bolton House that morning to find it empty but for the servants. Lord Cambridge would not make an appearance until afternoon, the earl knew. But where was Philippa? Certainly she hadn't returned to the palace this early? He stopped a servant.

"Where is the young mistress?" he inquired of him.

"Gone back to Richmond, my lord," the man replied. "It were barely first light when she called for her barge. May I bring you breakfast, my lord?"

The earl nodded. He had hoped to speak with her before she left. Had she fled him? Or was it that she really did want to be back in time for the first mass of the day? Would the queen really have minded if she had not been there this one time? He ate the meal placed before him, and then spent a restless morning until Lord Cambridge finally made his appearance dressed to the nines, and obviously preparing to return to court himself. The earl had noted that the Bolton barge had returned, and was bobbing in the river waters by its quai.

"Dear boy, how long have you been up?" Thomas Bolton asked his guest, taking a goblet of watered wine from the tray a servant was holding.

"Several hours, Tom," he answered.

"Did you see my darling girl before she departed back to her duties?"

"She was long gone when I came down into the hall. A servant told me it was barely first light when she left," the earl answered his host.

"So faithful in her duties, my young cousin," Lord Cambridge murmured.

"I want the betrothal papers drawn up as soon as possible," the earl began. "Philippa will accompany the queen in a few months' time, but I have decided I would prefer it if we were man and wife before we leave for France. I am going to Wolsey this morning to offer my services for the event. The king will take only a chosen few, so I must put myself in the cardinal's service if only for a brief period of time."

"And is Philippa as eager to be wed as you are, dear boy?" Thomas Bolton asked.

"I have not discussed it with Philippa. It is not her decision when we wed," the earl told Lord Bolton.

"Tch, tch, dear boy!" Lord Cambridge clucked, shaking his head. "You cannot simply announce to my cousin that you have set your wedding date. I will have the papers drawn up for you, and I will seek the king's permission for the match, but you must tell Philippa that you desire to wed before the summer progress to France. Surely you learned last night that she is not a meek creature whom you may treat like a little ewe lamb. I believe you will have to use all your diplomatic skills to get her to agree, but then I will remind her that Banon cannot wed until she is wed. And Banon and Robert Neville want to marry soon. If Philippa will settle herself, her sister can be married at Otterly in the autumn or early winter. You, of course, will wed my cousin here. Her mother will be disappointed not to be with her daughter at such an auspicious time in her life, but Rosamund will understand. Besides, she will have delivered her child by now, and not be fit to travel so far from Claven's Carn."

"Can you act on the lady of Friarsgate's behalf?" the earl asked.

"I can, and the king is aware of it. Still, my dear Crispin, I will not force Philippa into marriage with you. Her mother would never allow it. Rosamund was brought three times to the altar by others. Her fourth husband was her own choice, and she has always said she wanted her lasses to have the choice as well. Would she approve of you? Oh, my, indeed she would! But it is not Rosamund whom you must convince. It is her daughter, Philippa. Be assured that I will speak in your favor, and I am not against a marriage before the summer journey to France. Actually I believe it would be better for Philippa to have the protection of a husband."

"Will you go with the court?" the earl inquired.

Lord Cambridge shook his head. "This is an enormous undertaking, the meeting between England's king and France's king. Only the crème de la crème will be invited. I have wealth, and am considered amusing by my betters, but I will not be asked to accompany Henry Tudor and his queen. I am simply not important enough. Nor will Philippa's sister go. I will return north with Banon Meredith and young Neville. My heiress's betrothal agreement will be executed, and the marriage celebrated sometime in the autumn. Perhaps you will be able to come north then to meet Philippa's family. I know that she will want to be at her sister's wedding."

"You are certain that Philippa will be invited to go with her mistress?" the earl said. "I should not want to offer my services to Wolsey only to find myself separated from my wife for the next few months."

"Philippa is an especial favorite of the queen's despite her own humble birth," Lord Cambridge said. "The queen will want her by her side. She cherishes that link with her past, and Philippa is very good with her when the queen grows sad. She soothes her. Oh, yes, I can be certain that Philippa will be invited to go with the court to France. And what an adventure it will be for her, my dear Crispin! She has visited Scotland with her mother, and God only knows that is a foreign enough place, but to go to France! Ahh, dear boy, that is something she will never forget. The memory of it will surely sustain her during her first confinement, eh?" He chuckled. "Now, however, all you must do is convince the little wench to wed you before the summer progress. Do you think you can do it?" Thomas Bolton smiled. He knew Philippa far, far better than Crispin St. Claire. The task that the earl had set himself was almost Herculean, but he would support him, for he did believe it was better Philippa wed before the journey.

"I don't know," the earl admitted in a moment of rare candor. I have not said it! He could hear her voice in his head. How was he to approach her? Directly? Stealthily?

"If the decision were mine," Lord Cambridge suggested, "I think I would woo the lass with all the skills at my command. Poetry. Little gifts. But most of all, passion. Virgins are skittish, but they are curious, and rarely immune to passion, dear boy."

"Surely you aren't suggesting that I seduce Philippa," the earl said slowly.

"If it were me," Lord Cambridge murmured, "I would do whatever I had to do to gain the fair maid's consent, dear boy. A skillful seduction is a marvelous way around a stubborn lover."

"I think," the earl said slowly, "that Cardinal Wolsey has lost a skillful and wickedly clever servant in you, my lord."

Thomas Bolton barked a sharp laugh. "I would think, dear boy, that I am far too wise to involve myself in the political dealings of any nation or government. I leave that to those others who need to enhance their own self-importance."

Now it was the earl of Witton who laughed. "Are you a cynic or a skeptic, Tom Bolton?" he asked.

"Neither," Lord Cambridge responded. "I believe I am a realist. And so must you be if you are to win Philippa over in time to go to France. Court her, but do not underestimate her, dear boy."

And just how was he going to do that, the earl asked himself as he prepared to join Lord Cambridge at court that day? And next to Thomas Bolton he looked like a sparrow beside a peacock. But then, so did most of the court but for a very few.

"I shall seek appointments with both the king and the queen," Lord Cambridge said as they exited his barge at Richmond.

"Won't that take time?" the earl replied.

"Under normal circumstances it would, but I have a new friend among the ranks of the king's secretaries, and a fat purse. Both will gain me a few minutes with the monarch and his spouse today, so we may not have to wait."

"Then I shall go and offer my services to the cardinal," the earl said.

The two men separated, each going in a different direction. The earl of Witton found his way to Cardinal Wolsey's apartments. There he told one of the cardinal's men that he wished to speak with his old master. "Today," he emphasized strongly. "I come to offer my services for this great meeting to be held between our good King Henry and the French king."

The cardinal's second secretary to whom he spoke knew who the earl of Witton was, and of his service to his master. "You do not need much time then," he said, his gaze anxiously scanning the earl's face. "He is frightfully busy with all of this."

"Five minutes," the earl told the second secretary.

"You will have to wait, but I will get you in," was his reply.

Crispin St. Claire sat down in a tall-backed chair, and waited. Having been in the cardinal's service before, he was more than well aware of how busy Wolsey was. Wolsey served a hard master in the king. It was no easy task to do his bidding, to keep ahead of him, to be seriously useful to Henry Tudor, to dodge his detractors. And Thomas Wolsey had more against him than stood for him. A brilliant and hardworking man, he had an unfortunate inability to tolerate fools. But worse, he was arrogant, and thought nothing of keeping the high and the mighty cooling their heels in his antechamber. Even the earl of Witton now waited, more patiently than most.

Finally the secretary beckoned to him, and rising quickly he followed the man into the cardinal's sanctum. "My lord, the earl of Witton," the secretary said, and then scuttled back through the door where they had entered.

Thomas Wolsey did not bother to look up from the papers on his desk. "I am told you wish to offer me your services once again, my lord."

"Only briefly," the earl said. "I want to go to France with the court, but know I am not important enough to be invited merely for my charm."

"Why?" Wolsey snapped.

"I am planning on marrying one of the queen's maids of honor. Hopefully the nuptials will be celebrated prior to the summer progress. Whether they are or not, I do not wish to have Philippa in France without me, my lord."

"Philippa?" The hooded eyes looked at him briefly.

"Mistress Philippa Meredith, my lord," the earl responded.

The cardinal thought a long moment, and then he said, "Her father was Sir Owein Meredith, and her mother a Cumbrian heiress." He stopped, then continued. "Rosamund Bolton, I believe she was called. The Venerable Margaret arranged the marriage. This is their daughter? Surely you could do better, my lord?"

"The girl suits me, my lord cardinal. She has beauty, wit and intellect."

"That in itself would recommend her to a lesser man, Witton, but certainly there is something else that has attracted you." Thomas Wolsey was no fool.

The earl smiled briefly. "Her dower contains land that matches mine, and that I would possess," he answered truthfully. "Her family will not sell."

"Hah!" the cardinal responded. "How did a northern family like hers gain such land? Wait! I see the fine hand of Thomas Bolton in this. Of course! He would be a dangerous fellow if he chose to enter the political arena seriously, and God will bear witness that I have difficulty enough with the king's minions as it is. He arranged this match, didn't he?"

Again the earl of Witton nodded truthfully.

The cardinal was silent for a time, and then he said, "Very well. I could use a pair of eyes and ears among this summer progress. One that would not be suspected of me. There are always plots, and plotters abound. This is an enormous, an incredible, and a dangerous undertaking, but his majesty would meet with the French king, and Francois would meet with Henry Tudor. You must wed the girl before we depart in May. The queen is most fond of this maid, and will have the girl with her. I will perform the ceremony myself for you. Choose a date. I will convince the queen that while she may certainly have her favorite with her, we cannot separate newly wed lovers. There is your excuse to be with the court."

"Thank you, my lord cardinal. You do me honor," the earl said. "I will report anything of interest to you."

"Of course you will, Witton. You were ever the consummate diplomat while you were in our service." He waved his hand at the earl. "God bless you, my son."

He was dismissed. The earl bowed, saying, "Thank you, my lord cardinal," as he backed from the cleric's presence. In the antechamber he placed a coin upon the table where the secretary sat. Then saying nothing, he departed, as the sound of the coin scraping across the wood reached his ears.

Choose a date. The cardinal's words echoed in his ears. I have not said it! Philippa's words rang in his head. He almost laughed aloud. How was he to get her to accept their betrothal, and agree to an almost immediate marriage? It would take a miracle, and he had never before asked God for a miracle, but now was as good a time as any. He sought out Lord Cambridge, but he could not find him. He did see Philippa, however, in her usual place by the queen's side. He walked towards her, and when she looked up and blushed he was hard-pressed not to chuckle, but he didn't.

Instead he bowed to Queen Katherine. She nodded, giving him permission to address her. "Your highness, might I steal Philippa away from you briefly?" he asked.

The queen smiled. "I am told there is to be a betrothal, my lord," she said.

"There is, madame," he answered her.

"I am well pleased by such a match," the queen told him. "Philippa Meredith is a most virtuous maid. She will be a good wife to you, my lord. Aye, you may walk with her for a short time." The queen gently pushed Philippa forward off her stool. "Go along with your betrothed, child."

Philippa stood, and curtseyed meekly to the queen. She did not flinch openly when the earl of Witton took her hand and tucked it into his arm as they moved away.

"Go into the gardens," the queen called after them. "You will have some privacy if such a thing is possible at court."

"It is March," Philippa murmured low. "I hardly think the royal gardens conducive to a romantic ramble in March."

"It is not romance I seek at this moment, Philippa," he replied softly. "We need to speak with one another, and for that privacy is essential."

"The day is chill, and I have no cloak at hand," she responded. "Come, the chapel will be empty."

"What if someone comes to pray?" he asked her.

Philippa laughed. "At court? Most of them go into the chapel for the morning mass, and then only to be seen by the king and queen. The chapel will be empty even of the queen's priests, who are usually napping or gambling, and in some rare cases bent on seduction at this time of day." She directed their steps.

He was surprised by her acumen once again. She might be untried in the ways of love, but as Lord Cambridge had pointed out, Philippa was a consummate courtier. She was a female, and a young female at that, but he decided he must take her into his full confidence from the start. She would not be fooled by half-truths. They had reached the chapel. It was, as she had predicted, quite empty. He watched with astonishment as Philippa peeped into the confessional to make certain it was empty. Then she chose the exact middle of the room to seat herself.

"It will be difficult to be overheard from either end of this chamber if we are here," she told him.

He sat down next to her. "You are amazing," he told her, and he kissed the hand he still held.

To his surprise she did not blush this time, but she gave him instead a genuine smile. "Since your purpose is not romantic, my lord, and you wished privacy, I can only assume you have a more serious matter to discuss with me."

He nodded, and then he said, "I must know I can trust you, Philippa, and you are really still a girl in many ways."

"I have learned how to keep a confidence, my lord," she told him quietly, "but the decision you must make is yours alone. If you require me to be silent, you have but to ask it of me, and I will be silent."

"We need to marry in haste," he told her, and wasn't at all surprised when her eyes grew wide.

"Why?" The single word was tinged with both curiosity and trepidation.

"I must go on this progress, but I am not important enough to be asked, and so must have an excuse. The queen will want you with her. You are her favorite among the maids though you are yourself unimportant. If we are newly wed she will make certain we are not separated, for she is a romantic lady at heart. I will be able to accompany you and the court to France."

"As an agent of the cardinal, I take it," Philippa said.

"Aye," he admitted. "He wants someone no one will suspect, with eyes that are trained to see and ears sharp enough to hear. He did not say it, but I know him well from my many years of service. He thinks he smells a plot of some sort on the wind, though he has yet to learn exactly what it is, or if it even really exists, but his instincts have always been infallible. By chance I came to him at the right time to offer my services, but of course no one must learn I am in his service. And none will suspect that the bridegroom of the queen's favorite maid is in France for anything more than a summer of love."

Philippa giggled. She simply couldn't help it. "A summer of love, my lord? Gracious! You make it sound most salacious, but then that is nothing new at this court."

He smiled back at her. "Perhaps I did not phrase it properly."

"Oh, I quite liked your phrasing, my lord," she assured him, grinning up at him.

He was very tempted to kiss her adorable mouth, but he did not. "The cardinal has said he will marry us himself."

"Thomas Wolsey would perform the ceremony? Nay, my lord, I think it not a good idea. It will draw attention to us, and if you wish not to be noticed I think it better the great cardinal show no favor to two unimportant people lest others ask why. I am certain that one of the queen's priests would, with her gracious permission, perform the sacrament of marriage uniting us," Philippa said.

Again he was surprised by her. "You are right, Philippa!" he said. And then he realized that she had not protested the idea of a quick marriage. "You are willing?"

She nodded. "My lord, I needed time to consider all that has happened. A match between us is a good thing. I ask only one favor of you."

"And that would be?" What could she possibly want of him?

"I do not really know you, my lord. While I see the advantages to us both in this match, I am inexperienced in the ways of love. I cannot yield myself to you wholly simply because we are man and wife. I would not deny you your rights, my lord. I just want some time to learn more about my husband before we unite our bodies. Can you understand that?" She had looked him directly in the eye while she had spoken.

"Aye, I can understand, Philippa. And I am willing to give you a certain amount of latitude in this matter. We will wed first, and then we will court as lovers do. But the marriage will be consummated on our wedding night for obvious reasons."

"I do not really understand the nature of courting," she told him.

"There is kissing, and touching," he replied.

"Oh, I have heard that, but what else is there to courting?" she wondered. She was purposefully ignoring his statement regarding consummation.

"I am not certain myself," he admitted. "I have never paid serious court to a girl before, Philippa. We shall explore this mystery together. Now, when shall our wedding day be? I shall leave it to you to choose the date."

"The queen's nephew, the emperor, is coming to England at the end of May, and then we depart for France in early June. My birthday is the twenty-ninth of April. Let us wed the day after, on the last day of April, my lord. It will give me time to prepare properly. Would that suit you?"

"Tom says your mother will not be able to come," he said. "Would you not prefer to go home for your marriage?"

"There is no time. Mama will have a new bairn, and knowing my stepfather he will not want her to travel even to Friarsgate with it. She nurses her own children, you see," Philippa explained. "We shall, with your permission, my lord, go north for my sister Banon's wedding in the autumn. If you are content with that, then so am I."

"I am content," he agreed.

"One thing I must tell you before the betrothal is signed, and the marriage celebrated," Philippa said. "I am my mother's heiress to Friarsgate, but I have told her I do not want it. Her lands and her flocks are great. She has a commercial enterprise in cloth that she and Lord Cambridge manage. I don't want any of it. I should have to live in Cumbria, and while I find it beautiful there, I do not want to live there. And an estate like Friarsgate must be watched over by its mistress or master. That is why Uncle Thomas purchased Melville for me. And in addition I have a most exceptional dower portion in gold and silver coin, as well as plate, jewelry, and all the possessions that a respectable girl would have. I am very well dowered, my lord, as you will see. But I renounced Friarsgate, and you must know it before this match is settled between us."

"I should have little use, Philippa, for a large northern estate that requires tending," he told her. "You will find Brierewode is more than enough for me."

"Do you have sheep?" she asked him.

"Cattle and horses, only," he told her.

"Thank God!" Philippa exclaimed, "for I cannot abide the stink of sheep."

Chapter 9

*L*ord Cambridge had managed to catch the queen before the midday meal to tell her of the impending betrothal of Philippa Meredith. "With your highness's blessing, of course," he had said, bowing. And the queen had been delighted, and sent him to the king to impart the happy news. He had caught the king at his dinner, and been allowed to stand just to one side of the royal diner while he spoke his peace.

"Will Rosamund agree?" the king wanted to know.

"I have her permission to arrange a match for Philippa, aye, my lord."

"How did you manage it, Thomas Bolton? An earl, and one who has never wed, and is young enough to get children on the girl. You are obviously more clever than I would have given you credit for, but then Wolsey has always said it." The king took a bite from a small haunch of venison in his grip.

"I purchased the late Lord Melvyn's estate. It matches with Witton lands," Lord Cambridge said simply.

The king laughed. "You are fortunate he wanted it."

"He has been pasturing his cattle on it, so I thought he might," Lord Cambridge answered with a small smile.

Henry Tudor chortled. "Wolsey is always right." He took a gulp from the large footed wine goblet by his right hand. "And the queen approves?"

"Aye, my liege, she does."

"Then I must approve as well, and I do," the king replied. "When will the marriage be celebrated?"

"I shall ask Philippa, and return with her answer, majesty," Lord Cambridge said.

"I shall stand witness to the event even as I did to the betrothal of her mother to our good servant, Sir Owein Meredith," the king said. "I was but my father's son then, and I recall he remonstrated with me when I boasted that one day Rosamund could say her betrothal was witnessed by a king and a queen. My sister, Margaret, was already Scotland's queen, but my father was still king."

"I know that both Philippa and the earl of Witton will be honored by your gracious presence," Thomas Bolton said, and then he withdrew to seek out his young cousin and Crispin St. Claire. He found them walking in the gallery near the royal chapel.

"We have agreed on everything, Uncle Thomas," Philippa greeted him.

"And what is everything?" he replied, kissing both her cheeks.

"Why, our marriage, uncle. We have decided to marry on April thirtieth, the day after my sixteenth birthday. You must have the papers drawn up at once."

"You do not wish to go to France then?" Lord Cambridge asked.

"Oh, I shall go, for the queen wants me with her, and she is certain to allow my husband to accompany me, for she would not separate a newly wed couple. Her heart is too kind. It shall be the most glorious summer, and when we have returned we shall travel north to Otterly to see Banie married to her Neville," Philippa concluded.

Lord Cambridge looked to the earl. "And you agree, my lord?"

Crispin St. Claire grinned. "I dare not disagree," he said. "Philippa's flawless planning is but an indication of the skills she possesses, and will be put to good use at Brierewode when she becomes its mistress. My house can use a competent chatelaine."

"You will be pleased to learn the king approves your match, and has offered to stand witness to your formal betrothal."

"Ohh!" Philippa clapped her hands together. "He and Queen Margaret were witnesses to my parents' betrothal. Wait until mama hears of it! I must go and write her this very minute." She curtseyed to the two men and, turning, hurried off down the gallery.

The two men strolled together. "How did this all come about so easily, my dear Crispin?" Thomas Bolton asked his companion.

The earl shrugged. "I am as mystified as you are, Tom. I asked the queen's permission to walk with Philippa. You had obviously already seen her for she was aware of our impending betrothal and marriage. She was most gracious, and sent us off suggesting we go into the gardens. Philippa, however, being sensible first rather than romantic, said no, for it was too chill. She led me to a small chapel where we spoke. She said she had departed early because she needed to think about our situation. And then she announced to me the date of our wedding, and that we would go north to her sister's wedding when we returned from France. She said it was best to be married at the end of April because the emperor would be here in May, and then in June we would embark for France. She is a practical girl. There will be no need now to visit Oxford this winter."

"Practical. A kind word for bossy," Lord Cambridge said with a smile. "But then that is Philippa. When she makes up her mind to do something she does it. You are content with the arrangement then?"

"I am. Have the papers drawn up so we may act on them," the earl said.

"Dear Crispin, it will be done before the week is out," Lord Cambridge promised.

The two men parted, and Thomas Bolton hurried to his barge that he might be rowed home as quickly as possible. It was the time between the tides, and the river was as smooth as glass. The craft skimmed along the Thames, and its passenger thought that he could smell springtime in the air. Arriving at Bolton House he found a message from the north awaiting him. Opening it he read the contents, his eyes widening a moment, a smile creasing his face. Rosamund had delivered twin sons, to be named Thomas Andrew and Edmund Richard, on the last day of February. The lads were both healthy, strong, and suckled well. He was to be godfather to his namesake along with Rosamund's stepson, John Hepburn. The other twin would have his mother's uncles for godfathers. The boys had, according to custom, already been baptized, she wrote. If he had been at Otterly where he belonged, she scolded him, he might have been there. When was he coming north? And what of her daughters?

"Is the messenger still here?" Thomas Bolton asked his majordomo.

"Yes, my lord, in the kitchens, eating. He arrived but an hour ago. He is one of the laird's own men."

"Send him to me when he is finished. There is no rush, for I must compose a letter to his mistress," Lord Cambridge said. "Bring me my writing box."

"At once, my lord!" The servant moved off to do his master's bidding.

When he had returned, Thomas Bolton sat down to write his cousin. He and Banon would be coming home in early June. The clever child had settled on a Neville, a descendant of her grandmother Philippa Neville's family. He would be accompanying them, and they would stop at his family's home to visit the Nevilles, who had expressed their delight in the match. And the church had approved. The lad was a younger son, and this would be an excellent match for him. There should be no difficulty given Banon's dower portion and the fact she was to inherit Otterly. The marriage would be celebrated in the autumn. Here Thomas Bolton paused. He wished he might explain Philippa's situation to Rosamund himself, but he could not. Picking up his pen again he continued. He had obtained a splendid match for Philippa with the earl of Witton. Philippa was delighted, but the marriage would be celebrated on the last day of April at court. And the king would bear witness to the betrothal agreement as he had to Rosamund's all those years ago. The need for the haste was that the queen wanted Philippa to accompany her to France with the summer progress, and in order for the earl to go as well they must be wed. Philippa would be released from her service when they returned from France. The pair would then come north to meet the family. And when he got home, Lord Cambridge promised his cousin, he would explain in exacting detail how Philippa's match had been obtained. He went on to say that he was both amazed and delighted by the birth of his namesake and his namesake's twin. But he did hope that, now that the laird of Claven's Carn had five legitimate sons, he would be content, and Rosamund would take the precautions he knew she was aware of to prevent future children for whom provision would have to be made. Then he went on to say he would be bringing with him a secretary he had poached from the court, one William Smythe, who he believed would be most valuable to them and their commercial enterprise. He was eager, he wrote, to return home. Court no longer held the same luster for him as it once had. He closed by sending her his love.

Laying the quill aside Thomas Bolton considered if he had left anything out of his missive, but deciding he had not, he folded the parchment, sealed it, and pressed his signet ring into the hot wax. It would have to do. He had more important tasks ahead. The betrothal papers must be drawn up, the date for the signing set at the royal convenience. And his darling girl must have two new gowns: one for the betrothal ceremony, and the second for her wedding day. He began to consider fabrics and color. The door to his library opened, and William Smythe entered.

"I have just learned of your return, my lord," he said, and then spying the folded letter on the desk, he continued. "I would have written your letter for you."

" 'Tis for Rosamund, Will, and I prefer to write her myself."

"The messenger is outside, my lord. These Scotsmen must have arses like leather, for while he ate I could see naught beneath his kilts but a pair of rather large balls," the secretary told his master.

"I am curious as to how you obtained a peek, dear Will, but I shall not embarrass you with my query. Send the man in, please," Lord Cambridge said with a small grin.

The Hepburn clansman was known to Thomas Bolton. He bowed and waited.

"You and your horse will rest the remainder of the day, Tam. Eat your fill, and sleep. My cook will give you food for your journey to-morrow. You will carry this message to my cousin the Lady Rosamund at Claven's Carn. Your master is well?"

"Aye," the clansman said. "And right pleased wi' his two new lads. His lady is a good breeder, she is, my lord." Tam grinned broadly.

Lord Cambridge nodded. "Five sons should be enough for your master," he noted dryly.

"Och, my lord, a man can nae have too many sons," was the reply. Then the clansman bowed. "I thank you for your hospitality," he said, picking up the folded parchment. "I'll see this delivered safe." Then he bowed again, and left the room.

"Will, send for the mercer. I will want to choose fabric for my darling girl's wedding gown."

"At once, my lord," the secretary said, and departed the library.

Thomas Bolton closed his eyes, leaning back in his chair. The day was but half over, and he was absolutely exhausted. It was obvious that what he had written to Rosamund was truth. He had simply not the stamina for court any longer. Court was for young creatures like Philippa. He wondered what she was doing now.

Philippa was speaking with her sister Banon as they separated colored threads in the queen's workbasket. "Have you kissed Neville?" she wanted to know.

"Of course," Banon replied. "How was I to know if I could tolerate him if I did not kiss him? He kisses well in comparison to the others I have kissed," she concluded.

"You kissed other lads?" Philippa sounded shocked.

"Oh, sister, you can be such a prude." Banon laughed. "Much of the fun of being a girl is getting to kiss the lads. I know that you kissed none until the FitzHugh boy deserted you. And now that you are to wed with the earl of Witton you cannot kiss any lest you spoil your chances, and shame the earl."

"I have done my share of kissing," Philippa said. "Enough to know that the earl kisses very well, Banon."

"You have already kissed him?" Banon was surprised, given her oldest sister's reticence.

Philippa nodded. "I would swear that my toes curled, Banie," she said.

Banon giggled, and then she replied, "Just think, Philippa, this time next year we will both be married women with big bellies. Mayhap you will have even delivered by then. Imagine! We will be mothers, Philippa."

"Because we are wed does not necessarily mean we will be enceinte at once," Philippa told her sister.

"Mama says that every time Logan drops his trews she finds herself with another bairn in her belly," Banon confided. "I will admit that our stepfather is a fine figure of a man. I wonder it took mama so long to wed him."

"Mama loved another man," Philippa said. "I do not believe you can so easily get over the kind of love she and Lord Leslie had, Banon."

The days were much longer now, and the air was warming. The gardens were beginning to green up, and the court was looking forward to its May move to Greenwich. The queen's nephew, the Holy Roman Emperor, Charles V, would visit England before the meeting with King Francois of France. He would be returning home to Spain following his coronation as emperor at Aachen in Germany. Katherine wanted her husband and her nephew on good terms. She far preferred a strong alliance with Spain and the empire to one with France, but she was to be disappointed in her hope.

Much to her irritation the king regrew his beard because he had been told that King Francois had a fine beard of which he was very proud. Katherine did not like her husband with a beard.

"I do it to honor France's king," Henry Tudor said. "Remember that his son will one day husband our daughter. Mary will be France's queen as well as England's. What a coup, Kate! Imagine our little girl queen of two such great nations."

"Indeed," the queen said, but her voice definitely lacked enthusiasm. She had not wanted a betrothal with France, and she did not want a meeting with them. She wanted her daughter aligned with Spain, and she knew England could not be ally to both.

The betrothal papers would be signed on Philippa's birthday, with the wedding to follow on the next day. She had been allowed more latitude in her service to the queen in order to prepare for these two important events in her life. And she was allowed to meet with the earl of Witton more frequently now. Philippa still thought him arrogant, but Lord Cambridge had laughed at this assessment.

"The difficulty, I believe, is that you are both alike," he told her.

"That is not so!" Philippa declared vehemently.

"Come, darling girl, and choose the fabric for your betrothal day," he coaxed her.

"The violet silk brocade," she told him. "That particular shade is flattering to my hair, I believe. And I shall have the ivory silk brocade for my wedding gown with an underskirt of that ivory and gold velvet brocade. And matching French hoods and veils, uncle. Am I being too greedy?"

"Nay, darling girl, not at all, but while the hoods can be made for you, you will not need them either day, for your hair must be left loose as befits your maiden state."

"Banie must have a new gown too," Philippa said.

"And so she shall. I think that rich rose velvet most flattering to your sister," he replied. "Remember she will have new gowns when we return north, for she will soon be a bride too, darling girl." He stood up. "And now that we have settled these most important details, I shall return you to the palace with the earl. Was he too distressed that we would not allow him with us while we considered this important decision?"

"He said he suspected you were far more suited to the task than he was, and besides he said there is something about not seeing the bride's gown before the wedding," Philippa answered, and she stood up. "Thank you, Uncle Thomas. I know I shall be the most beautiful bride at court thanks to you." Then kissing his cheek, she curtseyed and left him to join Crispin St. Claire, who awaited her in the hall of Bolton House.

They left the house, and walked through Lord Cambridge's garden down to where the barge awaited them. The earl was becoming used to the marble statues of the well-endowed young men set about the garden, and Philippa seemed not to notice them at all. Settling themselves, they sat back as the barge skimmed down the river back to Richmond.

He put his arm about her shoulders, and she leaned her head against him. "You grow most used to me," he said teasingly.

"Since we are to be wed, I suppose I ought to," she replied.

He tilted her face up to his, and kissed her a long slow kiss. Her lips were like rose petals, soft and perfumed beneath his own. His hand caressed her breasts for the first time, and Philippa stiffened, drawing away, startled.

"What are you doing?" she said, and there was a nervous edge in her voice.

"What it is my right to do," he told her quietly.

"You promised you would wait," she reminded him. "Wait until we got to know one another better."

"Do you think that one day we will simply awaken, and know one another better, Philippa? We are to be married in just a few weeks' time. We become familiar with one another not just by innocent kissing, but by touching as well." His fingers tightened on her chin. "You are very lovely, and I find I am beginning to consider the delights of possessing you completely. We cannot wait forever. Our families will expect you to produce an heir within a reasonable amount of time."

"Have you made love to other women?" she asked him.

"Of course, Philippa. No healthy man is celibate at thirty," he told her.

"Were they whores? Or were they noblewomen?" she pressed.

The question surprised him, but he answered her candidly. "Some were whores, but also noblewomen as well. And in my youth, girls on my estate who were willing. I have never forced a woman."

"Do you have any bastards, my lord?" Her look was curious.

"Two little girls," he surprised her by saying. "I give their mothers a yearly stipend, Philippa, and will continue to do so when we are wed."

"Then you are experienced in the amatory arts, my lord," she said.

"Aye, I am well skilled," he told her. "Now, madame, enough of your questions."

"The boatmen," she said, pointing to the four stout men before them.

". . . do not have eyes in the back of their heads nor can they see through the curtains," he responded with a chuckle. His arm tightened about her, and he looked down into her face. Her eyes had grown very large as his hand began to smooth itself over her gown. Her clothing was a most distinct barrier to his rising passion, but the barge was not the place to unlace her bodice, he thought. Instead he bent his head and kissed the soft swell of her bosom as it rose above the neckline of her gown. Her scent, lily of the valley, was utterly intoxicating, and his senses spun as the fragrance filled his nostrils.

For a moment as his mouth touched the soft flesh Philippa didn't think she could breathe. The gentle but firm kisses he pressed onto her unresisting form made her heart beat rapidly and her head spin with excitement. She felt the tips of her breasts harden. She didn't want him to stop. But she was not certain he should be doing this. Should he? She had seen her stepfather fondle her mother in such a fashion when they were not aware they were being observed, but they had been wed. She had no one to ask about such things. Her mother was far away, and her only friends were not at court any longer.

"Philippa, what is the matter?" the earl asked her. He was cupping one side of her face with his big hand.

"I have been told that a man wishing his own way with a maid will swear that what he is doing is acceptable," she said. "I have also been told that a man who obtains cream from the cow for naught is less apt to purchase the creature. I have kept my reputation by being chaste, my lord, not by allowing myself to be fondled in a barge."

"I am relieved to learn it," he answered her seriously. "It would make me most uncomfortable to learn that you had an unsavory reputation, Philippa. I may assume then that there is nothing in your girlish past that would disturb me should I learn of it."

"You are making fun of me," she pouted.

"Nay, I am merely inquiring of you as you have just inquired of me," he told her, and there was a twinkle in his eye. "Nothing at all?"

"My character cannot be faulted," she said haughtily. Why did he look as if he wanted to burst out laughing?

"Yet I have heard the tale of the Canted Tower from your own lips," the earl said mischievously. "Now let me see if I can recall it. Some young ladies and some young gentlemen were caught playing a rather naughty game by the king himself."

"I had had too much wine to drink!" Philippa protested. "It is not in my nature to overimbibe or be risqué, my lord. And most of the court was gone so there was no scandal."

"Lord Cambridge found it very amusing, as did I."

"There was nothing funny about it, my lord! My behavior was shameful, and only the timely arrival of the king prevented me from a worse fault," Philippa cried. "Why do you fling this indiscretion in my face now?"

"Philippa, Philippa! You are an innocent young girl whose heart was broken. You were made the butt of many jests in your plight. Finally you reacted with what for you was inappropriate behavior, but I know that is not your nature. And it was not so dreadful a sin you committed. I tease you because I am shortly to be your husband, and I want to make gentle love to you, but you resist me." He caressed her face. "Do not resist me, Philippa. I mean you no harm."

She put her head against his shoulder, and began to weep. "I want to be loved by the man who caresses and kisses me," she said piteously. "You do not love me. You want Melville."

"Aye, I do, and you are correct when you say I don't love you. How can I? I barely know you, Philippa. And you hold me off in your shyness. We are to be married soon, and it would not be honorable to steal the cow's cream if I didn't mean to buy the beast." He held her against him, his hand now stroking her back.

She sniffled softly. The big hand caressing her was very comforting. Even if he didn't love her he was kind, she thought. "Kissing," she said. "It is all I know."

"And you do it very well," he told her.

"I have heard of touching, but I have not listened closely. And I have never allowed any man to touch me. The incident at the Canted Tower was foolish, but fate prevented anything untoward from happening, my lord."

"We all have some incident in our youth that we would rather not discuss or recall, Philippa," he told her. "Now dry your eyes, and we will kiss and make up."

She pulled a small lace-edged handkerchief from her sleeve, and mopped her face with it before restoring it to its place. "I don't think I want to kiss you now," she told him. "You have mocked and teased me, my lord. You must be kinder to me."

In a single swift move Crispin St. Claire swept Philippa into his arms in a low embrace that left her helpless to his will. "I do not believe for one moment, my dear Philippa, that your feelings are damaged by our conversation. But you are behaving like a silly little court ninny. That is not what I want in a wife. I want the girl you really are. The one with wit and intellect. Now I have given you my word that I should not rush you along passion's path, but we will be wed in a few weeks' time, and I will delay no longer than that, Philippa. So if you do not wish to be shocked upon our wedding night, I should suggest you learn to accept my embraces now." He kissed her, a hard kiss. "You have no idea how delicious, how delightful, passion and lust can be when it is unbridled. I will not allow you to indulge in the queen's Spanish moral reticence." He kissed her again. "I will have you warm and naked in our bed, Philippa. I will fondle you at my leisure, and you will not close your eyes and say your rosary when I do, but you will sigh with the pleasure I offer you." He kissed her again, now a slow, deep kiss that left her breathless. "We will join our bodies as the God who created us intended us to do. You will cry out with the joy our mutual desire gives you, and you will beg for more." His hand now smoothed over her bodice, fondling her young breasts. "Now say 'Yes, Crispin,' " he commanded her in a low and fierce voice.

"No! I will fight you!" she declared.

"Why?" he demanded.

"Because . . . because . . ."

"You have no reason, Philippa. You will belong to me, but I will belong to you."

"I could hate you!" she whispered.

"But you won't," he told her, and he kissed her a final time before sitting her up again. "You're very pretty when you are confused," he told her.

"You are so arrogant!" she told him half angrily.

"And you are utterly adorable in your confusion," he assured her, grinning.

The barge bumped the palace quai, and Philippa was aided in disembarking.

"I must rejoin the queen now," she said, and hurried away from him.

He watched her go, amused by their encounter, but he had meant what he said. She was like a finely bred and unbroken young mare. But he would break her to his bit. He was not in the least sorry that they were to marry. She was going to make a fine countess of Witton. He entered the palace seeking out some gentlemen with whom to play cards, and to his surprise he encountered his eldest sister as he walked through a gallery. "Marjorie!" he said. "What are you doing here?"

"I am told you are finally to marry, and I must learn it from a friend down from court. I came up to London as soon as I could. Who is she, and why have you kept it a secret from me? Does Susanna know?"

He took his sister's hands in his and kissed them both. "I have hardly had a moment to myself, Marjorie, since I decided. The betrothal papers will be signed on the twenty-eighth, and we will wed on the thirtieth."

"Who is she?" his sibling demanded. "I am told she is a maid of honor."

"Her name is Philippa Meredith," he began.

"Meredith? Meredith? I do not recognize the name. Who are her people?" his sister wanted to know.

"Come and sit with me," he invited her, and ushered her into an alcove where two chairs were set. "Her father was Sir Owein Meredith. He served the Tudors from the time he was a small child until the Venerable Margaret herself arranged his marriage with the heiress to Friarsgate, Rosamund Bolton."

"Bolton? 'Tis a northern name, Crispin. They are absolutely uncivilized, those northerners. Surely you could do better than that?" Lady Marjorie Brent looked askance at her brother. She was an extremely beautiful woman, with light blue eyes and deep brown hair. "Her dower will have to be excellent to overcome her deficiencies."

He laughed. "You are going to be very surprised when you meet

Philippa. Her mother lived at court as a girl. She gained the friendship of both Queen Katherine and Queen Margaret. That is why Philippa was given a position in the queen's household. Her highness is most fond of Philippa Meredith. And as for her dower, it is rich enough to be almost obscene, and it includes Melville, dear sister."

"Ahh," Lady Marjorie Brent said, "so that is the attraction the girl has for you, Crispin. Well, I cannot fault you for wanting Melville, but could you have not purchased it, and married better?"

"I am not a wealthy man, Marjorie," he reminded her. "And her cousin, who is her guardian here in London, would not sell the property for any price."

"Oh," his sister laughed, "you paid his price alright, little brother."

"It was time for me to wed, and Philippa is lovely. You will like her. She is mannerly, and a consummate courtier, Marjorie," he told his sister.

"I shall reserve my judgment, Crispin," she told him. "I have sent for Susanna to come from Wiltshire. You cannot wed until we have both met this girl."

"I have told you the wedding is set for the thirtieth of the month," he said.

"Why such unseemly haste? Have you already lain with the wench, and put a child in her belly? Did she entrap you in this way, brother?"

He laughed aloud. "Philippa is almost overly chaste, Marjorie. The marriage is being celebrated quickly because Philippa will go with the queen to France this summer. The only way I could remain with her, for you know that only the highest will be chosen to accompany the summer progress, was to marry her. The queen promised I should go with them then, for her heart is soft and she would not separate a newly married couple."

"Hmmm," his sister said.

"With luck she will return enceinte, and I will have an heir by this time next year," the earl said. "Isn't that what you and Susanna want to see?"

"Well, I certainly do," Lady Marjorie said. "As for Susanna, I think she always anticipated you choosing her second son for your heir should you not wed. I believe she has almost counted upon it."

"And you did not consider my title for your son?" he teased her.

"My lad has his own title. He did not need another," Lady Marjorie said dryly.

"Can you be certain this girl is fertile and capable of bearing children?"

"Her mother has birthed five sons and three daughters by two of her husbands," he told his sister. "Only one of the lads died."

" 'Tis most promising, Crispin," his sister said thoughtfully. "I am beginning to feel more reassured by what you have told me."

"The king will witness the betrothal signing," he said, knowing this would impress her even more.

"No!" Lady Marjorie exclaimed. "You are telling me the girl is that important?"

"She is not important, but both the king and the queen have known her mother since their shared childhoods, and the friendship has never been broken. Philippa's uncle asked both the monarch and his wife for their blessing on this union between me and Philippa. It was freely given, sister."

"Well, perhaps I need not have come up from Devon after all," Lady Marjorie Brent said, "but since I am here I may as well remain until your union is celebrated."

"Where are you sheltering?" her brother asked.

"I thought to find a place here in the palace, Crispin."

"Nay, there is too much going on with preparations for the summer progress to France, and the queen's nephew, the emperor, arriving at the end of May. You will stay at Bolton House with me. It is owned by Philippa's cousin, Thomas Bolton, Lord Cambridge. You will find him a most hospitable gentleman, Marjorie, and Susanna will stay as well."

"There will be room enough?"

"Aye, and knowing how you love your food, sister, I am happy to tell you that Tom Bolton's cook is a marvel. He travels with his master from Cumbria to London to the Greenwich house," the earl said.

"The more I learn of this girl's background the more I am pleased, Crispin. Will her parents be here for the marriage celebration? I am most anxious to meet them."

"Sir Owein is long dead, I fear, and Philippa's mother has just recently been delivered of twin sons, Marjorie. But one of her sisters is here at court in service to the queen as well. She will shortly wed a Neville. She is Lord Cambridge's heiress."

"Perhaps this is not a bad match after all, Crispin," his sister opined. "The St. Claire family is an old one, but we have never been particularly distinguished in the history of our country. We are in fact rather dull. We have always obeyed the law of the land, and I believe the only time we took a stand against a ruling monarch was with the other barons against King John. We remained clear of the Lancaster/York squabbles, and supported the Tudors when they took the throne."

"All of which has allowed us to survive as a family," he said quietly. "And while we are not rich, neither are we poor."

"I should have trusted to your judgment, Crispin," Lady Marjorie Brent said, "but since I am now here I shall make the best of it."

"The queen has been generous to Philippa, allowing her more time away from her duties recently. You will pay your respects this evening, and meet Philippa then," he told his sister. "And then I shall bring you back to Bolton House. Lord Cambridge may come to court today, or not."

Thomas Bolton did come to court that day. He had departed his house and taken the smaller of his barges, the one he had had built for Rosamund long ago, into London, where he had seen his goldsmith first, and then visited his tailor and the tailor's wife, who was a seamstress of extraordinary talent. It was the tailor's wife who would be sewing the gowns for Philippa's betrothal and wedding day, as well as Banon's new gown. He was then rowed to the palace, and for some reason he did not dismiss the smaller barge and send it home.

In the queen's antechamber he found the earl of Witton with an older woman, and was introduced. "Madame," he told Lady Marjorie, "I knew your husband once. I was devastated when he wed, but seeing you I can understand his eagerness to leave the court behind." He kissed Lady Marjorie's hand while smiling his most endearing smile.

She was instantly charmed with him. "You are too kind, my lord," she gushed.

He smiled at her again. "Have you met my cousin Philippa Meredith yet, madame?" he asked her, still holding her hand.

"I am to shortly," she told him, smiling back, and more than well aware that he had not yet released her hand. What a delightful man he was, she thought.

"She is a dear girl, madame, and if I may be permitted to say it, she will make your brother a fine countess," he murmured.

"Everything Crispin has told me reassures me," Lady Marjorie said.

The door to the queen's privy chamber opened. Philippa hurried out and over to them. "Is everything alright?" she asked. "One of the pages said you needed to see me, my lord," she addressed the earl.

"This is my sister, Lady Marjorie Brent," the earl of Witton said. "She has surprised me by coming up from Devon, where she lives. She had heard of our betrothal through a friend just returned from court."

"Had you not written to your sisters, my lord? That is most bad of you, and our wedding to be celebrated so soon," Philippa gently scolded him, curtseying.

"Oh, dear Philippa, that is so typical of my brother, but I can see that you have manners," Lady Marjorie said. She embraced the girl warmly. "May I welcome you to our family."

"I thank you, madame," Philippa replied. "I regret that I have so little time to give you, but alas, my duties must come first."

"My dear Philippa, I completely understand," Lady Marjorie said.

"Then you must excuse me," Philippa replied, curtseying once again, and turning away to hurry back to the queen.

"Wait," Tom Bolton said to the girl, who turned questioningly.

"You must come home tomorrow afternoon, for the seamstress will be there to begin your two gowns. Bring Banon with you, darling girl."

Philippa nodded, and then was gone.

"You will stay with me, of course," Lord Cambridge said to Lady Marjorie.

"How kind you are," she replied, not mentioning that her brother had already asked her, but then it was not his house, was it?

"I cannot imagine being anything but kind to you," Lord Cambridge murmured, and Lady Marjorie tittered, well pleased. "If your business here is finished, dear lady, then perhaps you will accompany me back to Bolton House in my barge. Crispin, dearest boy, the small barge will be here for you." He took Lady Marjorie's arm and led her off.

Crispin St. Claire, watching them go, was hard-pressed not to laugh. He was not certain exactly what kind of man Thomas Bolton was, although he had his suspicions, but Lord Cambridge had obviously sized up his sister, and knew just how to handle her. The earl wondered if his host really knew his brother-in-law. He decided he would not ask. The answer might prove too disconcerting.

Chapter 10

The twenty-eighth of April dawned wet. The court was preparing to leave for Greenwich on the twenty-ninth. The betrothal ceremony would be held at Bolton House, and the papers signed there. The great hall had been decorated with flowering branches. A small feast would be held following the formalities, although neither the king nor the queen would stay for the festivities. They would drink a toast to the couple and then return to Richmond.

Philippa had been sent home to Lord Cambridge's house the previous evening so she might sleep in her own bed. The queen had learned from the mistress of the maids that she was not resting well. Bridal nerves, both women had concurred. But she had slept no better at Bolton House. Her soon-to-be sisters-in-law could not, it seemed, stop chattering, and she found them irritating. Both Lady Marjorie Brent and Lady Susanna Carlton adored their younger brother, and insisted on imparting to Philippa what they considered good advice on the care and feeding of Crispin St. Claire. Philippa felt near to screaming, and seeing it, Banon took charge.

She arose from the high board, smiling as she said, "Philippa must really go to bed now and get her rest, my ladies. We share a bed at court, and I can tell you that she has hardly slept at all these past few weeks with all her duties. I do not know why the spring should seem more busy than the winter, but it does. You will excuse us, please." And she took her older sister's hand in a firm grasp, leading her from the hall.

"What a charming girl," they heard Lady Susanna say, and they giggled as they hurried up the staircase, sharing a conspiratorial glance as they went.

"Thank you!" Philippa said to Banon as they reached her bedchamber. "I do not know why, sister, but I find Crispin's sisters annoying. And they are both really good ladies." She sighed. "I don't know what is the matter with me lately." She opened the door to the chamber, and they entered together.

"You are being married in two days," Banon replied in practical tones. "You are merely suffering an attack of nerves. I would be nervous too. Why, you hardly know the man, and I have watched you go out of your way to avoid him at court these past weeks. I do not believe you have been alone with him once. The papers are not yet signed, Philippa. You do not have to marry him if you do not want to marry him. You yet have the opportunity to cry off."

Philippa shook her head. "No. It is an incredible match for me, and an honor for the family that I enter the ranks of the nobility. And if I cried off now you could not be wed in the autumn to your handsome Neville. Do you love him, Banon?"

"I think so," Banon replied. "I am not certain really what love is, or is supposed to feel like, sister. But I like being with him. I like the thought of having his children. I suppose I shall ask mama about love when I see her in a few weeks."

Philippa looked agitated, but then she said, "Have you kissed many times? Has he touched your breasts?"

Banon was about to protest so intimate a question, but then she realized that her older sister was not asking for prurient reasons. For some reason she needed to know. "Aye, we have kissed a great deal," she said. "Robert loves to kiss me, and I must admit to enjoying his kisses. And aye, he has caressed my breasts, and I have caressed him. It gives us pleasure, Philippa. Does it not give you pleasure to kiss and caress with the earl?"

"We have kissed but a few times, and I have resisted his caresses," Philippa admitted. She was very pale. "I did not want him to think me a bawd, behaving as so many of the young girls and women of the court do. And now I am terrified, for I must bed a stranger in two nights' time. I do not want to cry off. Yet I am afraid, Banie."

Banon Meredith shook her head. "Philippa, you may be the oldest of us, and you may know how to do your duty, but even Bessie has more sense than you would appear to have. I have watched you avoid the earl these past few weeks, and I will wager he has not once found you alone. What were you thinking, sister? This man is to be your husband. You had precious little time in which to get to know him, and you wasted it. Crispin does not seem a monster to me. Indeed he appears to be a kind man. I can offer you no advice, Philippa, but to trust to his kindness."

"I don't know what I am supposed to do!" Philippa wailed.

"Well, neither do I," Banon said. "How could I?" Then she grinned. "Ask Lucy. She will have some knowledge, you may be certain."

"Lucy?" Philippa was genuinely surprised. Her tiring woman seemed always to be there for her. How could she know of men and women?

"The serving women at court always know such things. They are freer with their favors than we should be," Banon explained. "Lucy," she called, and the young woman came into the bedchamber from the wardrobe where she had been seeing to her mistress's gown for the morrow.

"Yes, Mistress Banon?"

"My sister needs knowledge of what transpires between a man and a woman. Since mama isn't here, you must tell her what you know." Banon's blue eyes were twinkling with mischief.

"And what makes you think I would know such a thing?" Lucy demanded, her hands on her broad hips.

"Oh, you know," Banon replied. "I've seen you with that manservant at court. Will you tell me that you were simply meeting to discuss the weather and the latest fashions?" She giggled.

"Oh, you're a bad 'un!" Lucy scolded her. "Well, I'll tell my mistress what she needs to know, as her own mother can't do it for her, but you'll have to go to your own bedchamber, Mistress Clever, for you ain't being married in two days' time, and you don't need to know until you are wed, and your mam will tell you what you must know then. Shoo now!" And she pushed Banon from Philippa's chamber. Then she turned back to her mistress. "Let's get you ready for your bed, and I'll tell you what you need to know."

Philippa nodded. "Will there be time for a bath in the morning?"

"Aye," Lucy said. "We must arise early, for the king will be very punctual in his coming as his days are always busy." She unlaced her mistress's bodice and unfastened the tabs holding it to her skirts. She untied the ribbons holding her petticoats up.

Philippa stepped from the pile of velvet and silk while Lucy put the bodice away. She sat down, and Lucy took her dainty slippers off and, rolling her stockings down, removed them. Standing, Philippa walked over to the oak table where a basin of scented water was set. She washed her face, hands, and neck, then scrubbed her teeth with a rough cloth. Clad only in her chemise she walked over to her bed and climbed into it.

Lucy had finished putting away Philippa's garments and shoes. She had emptied the basin out the window. Now she came and sat down on the edge of the bed. "Tell me what you do know," she said.

"I know nothing," Philippa admitted. "Banon has scolded me for not kissing the earl more, or letting him touch my breasts. I think she is right."

"Well," Lucy said in practical tones, "that may be true, but you didn't, and now you are faced with bedding a husband, mistress. However, there is little to it if you wants my opinion. He'll be happy you're ignorant. Tells him he's the only one to get between your legs. These lords like their wives to be pure when they first has 'em, or so I am told. You're unique, mistress. Most of your companions has been naughty and lewd with the courtiers. But your reputation is chaste."

"But what do I do?" Philippa asked her tiring woman.

"Why, you do nothing, mistress. He'll lead the way, and that's as it should be for a good lass like yourself. The way it's done is that your husband will put you on your back and get between your legs. There's a hole deep between your nether lips into which he'll fit his manhood. He'll move it back and forth for pleasure's sake. There ain't nothing more to it. When he's emptied his love juices into you he'll withdraw from you."

"What about the kissing and the touching, Lucy?"

"Depends how eager he is for you. That will determine the kissing and the cuddling." Lucy chuckled. "One thing you should know, though. There might be pain for a brief moment that first time. If your maidenhead is lodged tightly you will feel it more. And there will be a little bit of bleeding when he breaks your maidenhead. Don't be frightened by it."

Philippa nodded. It all sounded very pragmatic. Having heard Lucy's explanations, she didn't understand what all the fuss was about. "Thank you for telling me, Lucy. I did not want to appear the ninny before the earl."

"Mistress Banon says you ain't been sleeping well," Lucy replied. "I expects this has been weighing on you." She arose and tucked the coverlet about Philippa's shoulders. "Now there's nothing to be frightened of, mistress. You just close your eyes and go to sleep. You're safe in your uncle Thomas's house."

After Lucy had tiptoed away to her own cot in her little chamber next door, Philippa thought she would again be awake the night, or most of it. Her mind raced with her concerns. She had never been to Brierewode. What kind of a house was it? Would it be easy to manage? Would the servants resent her, or would they be happy for a new mistress? Would she be a good wife, a good countess of Witton? How could she balance her duties as Crispin's wife with her duties at court? But then to her surprise Philippa felt herself growing sleepier. Why was she torturing herself with questions? Everything was going to work itself out perfectly. It always did. And she wouldn't see Brierewode until sometime in the autumn anyway. Her eyes grew heavier. There was nothing to worry about. Nothing at all. She slept.

When Lucy gently shook her awake Philippa could hear the sound of rain outside of her window. Well, it was April. She lay quietly hidden behind the curtains in her bed while her tub was set up, and the male servants, each carrying two buckets apiece, trekked in and out of the chamber with hot water for her bath. Finally they finished, and Lucy closed the door firmly. Philippa heard her pouring oil into the water, setting the towel rack by the fire, and then her bed curtains were opened.

"Come along, mistress," Lucy said. " 'Tis all ready for you, and piping hot just as you like it." She helped Philippa from her bed and quickly drew off the girl's chemise.

Philippa climbed into her tub, sighing as the heat penetrated her body. "Ohh, that feels good," she said. "Let's do my hair first, Lucy." Then she sat quietly as the tiring woman washed and rinsed her hair with the scented water. When Lucy had finished she wrapped her mistress's head in a towel, as Philippa took the soap from her and began to wash herself. She was quick, for the morning was chilly, and she wanted to mop herself off so she would not catch an ague while she brushed her hair dry. Wrapping herself in a bath sheet, she sat by the hearth and began to ply her hairbrush.

Lucy hurried to the kitchens to fetch her mistress's breakfast. She returned with a tray with a slice of ham, a hard-boiled egg, a small cottage loaf, and a Spanish orange that had been peeled and sectioned and placed in a little bowl, along with butter and jam. "Cook apologizes for the meal, but he is busy preparing for your betrothal feast, mistress." She set the tray down on the oak table. "Come and eat now. I must do your hair before you dress. What a lovely gown it is too!"

Philippa felt her mouth turn up in a small smile. It was a lovely gown. Pinning her almost-dry hair up, she put her brush down and came from the fireplace to sit down. "The meal is suitable to the occasion, for I am not that hungry," she told Lucy.

"Well, eat it anyway. There's no romance in a rumbling belly," Lucy replied. "And cook sent up some of that nice cherry jam you like too," she coaxed.

To her surprise Philippa ate everything on her plate and downed a small goblet of breakfast ale. She remembered how her mother would not let her have ale at breakfast until she was twelve. Until then she was only allowed watered wine. Her favorite cherry jam was most tasty on her tongue. She finished most of the cottage loaf and the butter with it. Clean, rested, and well-fed now, Philippa felt she could face this important day in her life. She rinsed her mouth with minted water. "Let us begin my toilette," she said to Lucy.

Lucy brought forth a clean chemise of pale ivory silk. It had full sleeves, and the cuffs were edged with delicate lace. The neckline was round and sat upon the collarbone. The tiring woman slipped the gown on over her mistress's head, guiding her arms into the sleeves.

"I love the feel of silk against my skin," Philippa purred. She drew on the stockings that were handed to her. They were plain creamy silk. She attached simple ribbon garters to them.

Lucy smiled, and setting a shake fold with two silk petticoats layered over it upon the floor, she helped her mistress to step into them. Then she drew up the undergarments, tying them neatly. Next she drew the skirt of the gown over Philippa, settling it atop the petticoats and the shake fold. Philippa smoothed her palms over the rich violet brocade. Lucy offered her mistress the gown's bodice, drawing it on and carefully lacing it up the back. The squared neck was banded with gold embroidery. The upper sleeve of the bodice was fitted, but the lower part of the sleeve had a wide turned-back cuff of violet satin and velvet brocade. The chemise sleeve with its lace-ruffled cuff shone. Lucy fastened a gold and violet embroidered girdle about Philippa's waist.

"There!" she said in satisfied tones. "Now you have but to step into your slippers, and I will do your hair. The master says it must be brushed and loose. He has given me this to sprinkle in it." She held out a small box to show Philippa.

Philippa chuckled. "It is gold dust," she said, "and most rare. How extravagant of him. Use but a little. I will want some on my wedding day as well." She slipped her feet into her soft violet leather slippers, which had been embroidered in pearls.

"Stand still now," Lucy instructed as she climbed up on a small footstool, hairbrush in hand. She brushed her young mistress's clean hair until it shone with its auburn lights. When she was at last satisfied she sprinkled some of the gold dust upon the brush, and worked it into Philippa's hair. "Well, if that don't beat all," she said. "That gold dust adds just enough sparkle. We should save it, and use it again at the Christmas revels this year," Lucy opined. "You would create a sensation, mistress."

"I do not know if married women are supposed to create a sensation," Philippa laughed. Then she turned about and stepped back. "How do I look, Lucy?"

"You are even more beautiful than your mother," Lucy replied admiringly.

There was a knock upon the door, and before they might answer it Lord Cambridge entered the bedchamber, his face wreathed in a smile. Reaching into his doublet he drew out a long rope of perfectly matched ivory-colored pearls and matching earbobs. "For you, darling girl," he said, and dropped the pearls over her head with one hand as he handed her the earbobs with the other. "And wear the gold and pearl chain with the gold and pearl crucifix," he advised as Philippa fastened the two fat pearls into her ears. "I obtained these pearls specifically to go with it."

"Has the king arrived?" Philippa asked.

"Gracious no, darling girl. You and I must personally greet him as he steps across the threshold. I do not believe he has ever been to

Bolton House. Thank God it is small and simple, lest I be classed with the cardinal and find myself giving Bolton House to the monarch to keep his jealousy at bay."

"Uncle Thomas," Philippa giggled. "What a wicked tongue you have, and so early in the morning as well. Have the chatterboxes been fed yet?"

"Your tongue is as sharp as mine, darling girl," he chuckled. "Aye, they have filled their bellies from my bounteous board, and are already in the hall. Both are atwitter with the thought of meeting the king. Neither ever has. And I cannot seem to stop bragging about the Bolton family's long association with the Tudors." He grinned. "The more I gossip with them the more suitable this match becomes to them."

Philippa shook her head, and then she said, "As if they really have anything to do with it. Crispin will have Melville, and were I one-eyed and snaggle-toothed we would still be wed. I refuse to allow myself any illusions about this marriage. I shall not be disappointed then."

"I think you do your earl an injustice, darling girl. I know he is a man of honor. Aye, it was Melville that brought you to his attention, but I firmly believe he would never marry you just to have the land. Have you not noticed how he stares at you when he thinks no one is looking?"

"You are imagining it," Philippa said.

Lucy hurried to answer a new knock on the door. Outside of the portal William Smythe stood, soberly garbed in his usual black.

"My lord, the king's barge is approaching the quai," the secretary said with a bow.

"Thank you, Will. Come along, darling girl," Lord Cambridge said, and he took his young cousin's arm. "Is the hall ready, Will? Are the sisters close to swooning?"

"Indeed, my lord, they are," the secretary said with a small smile. "I believe only the arrival of the young mistress and you will calm them down. The earl is looking most uncomfortable and nervous."

Philippa and her cousin hurried downstairs and through the corridor leading to the door that opened onto the gardens. They watched from the open door as the royal barge was docked, and the king stepped out. He turned to help his wife and, sheltered from the rain beneath a canopy held by Lord Cambridge's servants, the royal couple made their way through the gardens to where Lord Cambridge and his cousin waited to welcome them. The royal couple were followed by one of the queen's priests.

Thomas Bolton bowed low as Philippa curtseyed, her lovely skirts blossoming about her like the petals of a flower.

"My liege, I cannot tell you what an honor it is to have you here," Lord Cambridge said as he ushered the king and the queen through the door.

"From the river it is a jewel of a dwelling, Tom, if small. It suits you." The king's voice boomed. Then he turned an approving eye to Philippa. "Your mother would be most proud of you, my dear. Raising your family to the ranks of the nobility is quite an accomplishment, especially considering your stepfather, but then neither you nor your sisters have any Scots blood in you. I have heard that your sister is to marry a Neville."

"Aye, your majesty. Banon will marry Robert Neville in the autumn. His grandfather and my grandmother were related by blood."

"You have the church's permission?" The king turned to Lord Cambridge.

"Indeed, my liege, we do," Thomas Bolton said. "The cardinal himself has obtained the permissions from Rome."

"Excellent!" the king said. "Well, let us get on with this betrothal. Both the queen and I have a long day ahead of us. We leave for Greenwich tomorrow."

Lord Cambridge and Philippa led the royal couple into the hall where the earl of Witton and his sisters awaited them. Lady Marjorie and Lady Susanna were introduced to the monarch and his wife. Both were overwhelmed, and seeing it the king was kind, gently teasing them, and giving each a hearty kiss upon their rosy cheeks. Queen Katherine was gracious, and the earl's sisters were much taken with her gentle manner.

The servants quickly brought wine. They had all from the humblest kitchen boy to the majordomo himself gathered in the back of the hall to catch a glimpse of their king and their queen. William Smythe brought the betrothal papers and spread them carefully and neatly upon the high board. He set the inkwell, the sand shaker, and the quill by them. Two great gold candlesticks had been set on the board, each with a thick beeswax candle. The hall fires burned high and warm so that the flowering branches gave off their scent. And outside, the April rain beat against the windows.

"It is time, my lord," the secretary said.

Lord Cambridge nodded. "Come," he invited them, "to the high board where we will formalize this betrothal between my cousin, Philippa Meredith, and Crispin St. Claire."

They gathered around the board, and William Smythe carefully offered the pages first to the earl, handing him the inked pen. The priest stepped forward.

"Crispin St. Claire," he said. "You agree to this betrothal?"

"I do, holy father," the earl responded.

"Sign here," the secretary said, pointing.

The earl of Witton signed, handing the pen back to William Smythe.

The secretary inked the quill and offered it to Philippa as he put the papers before her.

"Philippa Meredith," the priest spoke again. "Do you agree to this betrothal?"

"I do, holy father," Philippa replied, and swallowing hard, she signed her name. Then she handed the quill back to the secretary, who sanded both signatures so the ink would not be smeared, rendering the signatures illegible.

The priest then signaled the pair to kneel, and blessed them.

"It is done then," the king said jovially as the earl helped Philippa to her feet. "Let us have a toast to the bride and her bridegroom!"

The wine was quickly brought, and a long life and many children was toasted.

"Her mother is a good breeder," the king said with a meaningful glance at his wife. "You'll probably have an heir within the year."

The queen bit her lip with her distress, but then she said, "I have asked Frey Felipe to perform the sacrament in my chapel at Richmond on the thirtieth. You will come to Greenwich afterwards to join us."

"Nonsense!" the king boomed. "We do not leave for France until early June. You can be spared one maid of honor, Kate, for a few short weeks. Philippa and her husband will go to his seat in Oxfordshire and then join us at Dover on the twenty-fourth of May. They have had little time to themselves since this arrangement between their families was made. Did we not have a sweet honeymoon all those years ago, Kate?" And he gave his wife a kiss upon her lips, causing the queen's sallow skin to grow rosy momentarily.

"Yes," she agreed. "Of course, Henry. Why did I not think of it myself?"

"But your highness," Philippa protested weakly. "Do you not need me?"

"Do you see?" the king boomed again, pleased. "She is devoted to her duty even as her father, Owein Meredith, may God assoil his noble soul, was devoted to his." He turned to the earl's sisters. "Did you know that Sir Owein served the Tudors from the time he was six years old? He was a page in my great-uncle Jasper's household. He was knighted on the battlefield." He turned back to Philippa. "Nay, sweeting, you must spend some time privily with your new husband. I command it, and there is an end to it."

"Yes, your majesty," Philippa said, curtseying. Spend time with the earl? They hardly knew one another. What would they talk about? Her heart sank. It was her own fault. She had deliberately avoided him these last weeks when she could have been getting to know him. Now she would be this stranger's wife in two days' time.

"It is time for us to leave," the king announced. "Since I will not be at the wedding I shall kiss the bride now." He took Philippa by her shoulders and bussed each of her blushing cheeks in turn. "God bless you, my dear! We will see you at Dover." Then he turned, shaking the earl's hand and that of Lord Cambridge, kissing the hands of Lady Marjorie and Lady Susanna as the queen bid first Philippa and then the others a farewell. Then, escorted by Thomas Bolton, the royal couple and the priest departed.

There was a long silence, and then Lady Marjorie and Lady Susanna both began to speak at once.

"Blessed Virgin, he is so handsome!"

"His beard tickled me when he kissed my cheek!"

"The queen doesn't like his beard," Philippa said. "He has grown it because King Francois has one, and he wishes to honor him."

The sisters looked fascinated at this piece of information. They had seen how the king and the queen had treated their new sister-in-law. It had been with a familiarity they would have thought reserved for the high and the mighty, not a girl from Cumbria. They each had children who would one day need an ingress into court. Could Philippa possibly provide them with such a service? This marriage was indeed fortuitous.

"If my ladies would enjoy seeing the royal barge," William Smythe said, "it is now departing from my lord's quai."

Lady Marjorie and Lady Susanna rushed to the windows overlooking the river, and at once began ohing and ahing. The royal barge with its rowers all in their Tudor green livery was quite magnificent.

"I've never seen its like before!"

"Nor are we apt to see anything like it again!"

"Can you see the king, Susanna?"

"Nay," came the disappointed reply. "They have drawn the draperies."

Lord Cambridge reentered the hall and, coming over to Philippa, kissed her soft cheek. "You look exhausted already, and the day is yet new," he told her. "You must go into the gardens with Crispin and get some fresh air, darling girl."

"In the rain?" she asked him.

"The rain has stopped. There is even just tiny rays of sunshine peeping through the clouds," he said. "It is two days until you are formally wed, and it is past time, Philippa," he advised her meaningfully.

"How is it you know me better than I know myself?" she asked him, and he gave her a small smile and a wink. Then turning, he said to the earl, "A quiet stroll would be just right now, I think. I will send a servant for you when the feast is ready to be served."

Without an utterance Crispin St. Claire took Philippa by the hand and led her from the hall. "Bring me a cloak, and have Lucy fetch her mistress one," he told the servant in the corridor. As the servant scuttled away the earl took Philippa by her shoulders and kissed her gently. "We did not kiss to seal our betrothal," he said with a gentle smile. "In fact we haven't kissed in some days, Philippa. Do you find kissing me distasteful, little one?" His gray eyes were staring directly down into her eyes as he tipped her face up.

"Nay, my lord, I like kissing you," she admitted softly, "but I would not have you think me a brazen girl."

"You are many things, I can see, Philippa, but brazen is not a word I would apply towards your behavior," he told her, his arms tightening about her. He liked the feel of her petite form against his body.

"Because you were told of the unfortunate episode of the Canted Tower . . ." she began.

"I know what was involved in that incident, Philippa. I have already told you that I found it amusing. You are reputed to be the most chaste of the queen's maids," he said.

"How would you know such a thing?" she wondered. What was that scent emanating from his velvet doublet? He looked so elegant this morning in his burgundy velvet, and his hose was a most fashionable parti-colored black and white.

"I asked," he said simply. "I have learned in my thirty years that the best way to discover the answer to your query is to ask."

"Oh," Philippa responded, feeling slightly foolish.

"Your cloaks, my lord." The servant was at their side holding the requested garments. He handed the earl Philippa's as he set the cloak meant for the earl about his shoulders. Then he retrieved Philippa's cape and set it about her shoulders.

The newly betrothed couple walked out into Lord Cambridge's garden. The rain had indeed stopped, and the sun was beginning to peep through the clouds.

"Oh, look!" Philippa cried, pointing. "A rainbow! 'Tis good fortune to see a rainbow. And on this day of all days!"

He looked to where she was pointing and saw the broad arc of color bridging the river Thames. He smiled. "Good luck on our betrothal day is more than welcome."

"Are you afraid?" she asked him as they walked.

"Of what?" he countered.

"Of marriage. Our marriage. We don't know each other," Philippa remarked.

"We would have known each other better had you not avoided me these past few weeks, and do not cry it was your duty, or deny it. Your actions were deliberate, and I do not understand why," he replied. "You have agreed to this marriage from the beginning."

Philippa sighed. "I know," she said. "I agreed, and then I became afraid. You are nobility, my lord. And I fear that you cannot love me, that it is only the land you seek."

"If it were practical, Philippa, I should give up Melville to prove to you that it is not just the land. But I need those grazing pastures. Besides, all marriages are arranged for sensible reasons. The emotion called love has little to do with most matches. But we could come to love one another someday, little one. For now, however, we are finally betrothed, and in two days will be wed. Let us become friends. The king has graciously allowed us some time alone. It is a few days' journey to Brierewode, and I would show you your new home."

"But we are going to France!" she said. "I would go with the queen, my lord."

"And so we shall, Philippa. We shall be at Dover on the appointed day. We shall spend the summer in France with the court before returning home to visit your mother, and then wintering at Brierewode."

"We must join the Christmas revels," she told him.

"If you are not with child, we will," he said.

"With child?" Philippa swallowed hard.

"The purpose of our union is children," he told her gravely. "I need an heir. If you prove to be as good a breeder as your mother I shall sire several sons on you."

Philippa stopped dead, and then she stamped her foot at him. "Do not speak as if I am some superior breeding stock," she cried angrily.

"Whether you are superior breeding stock or not remains to be seen," he replied dryly, his gray eyes suddenly cold.

"You promised me that you would wait," she said.

"And so I have, for almost a month, while you have gone out of your way to escape my company, Philippa. Not a kiss or a cuddle have I been allowed. But in two nights' time, little one, you will do your duty because you will be my wife. Do you understand me?"

"You are the most arrogant man I have ever met!" she declared furiously.

He laughed. "I probably am," he said agreeably. Then he reached out and yanked her into an embrace, wrapping his arms tightly about her. "That mouth of yours, Philippa, would be put to better use in this manner rather than sparring with me." His head descended, his lips meeting hers in a hungry kiss.

At first her knotted fists beat against the embroidery on his burgundy velvet doublet. The kiss had rendered her weak, and her head was spinning. But she liked it. Oh, yes! She liked it very much. Her mouth softened beneath his, and she sighed. Her fists ceased their tattoo.

He raised his head, looking down at her through silver slits. "You are so ready to be loved, Philippa. Why do you fight it? I will not be unkind to you."

"I need to know you better before I offer myself body and soul," she murmured against his mouth.

"You have these two days, little one. There is no more time," he told her, pulling her into the shelter of a large pruned bush, and drawing her down onto a marble bench. Then he began to kiss her again, and one kiss fed into another until she was certain that her lips would be visibly bruised. His fingers loosened the laces on her bodice. His hand pushed beneath her neckline reaching for, finding, fondling a sweetly rounded breast.

Philippa couldn't breathe. Her heart was beating furiously. His hand was warm and gentle as he cupped the captive breast. Her head lolled back against his shoulder. His touch was the most exciting thing she had ever experienced. "You mustn't," she feebly protested. "We are not wed yet."

"The betrothal legalizes our union," he groaned low.

"The queen says a woman must be chaste even in the marriage bed," Philippa whispered.

"Bugger the queen," he said, half angrily. "Is it she who is responsible for your reticence these last weeks?"

"My lord!" Philippa was shocked by his words. "The queen is an example of wifely perfection to all of her women."

"Mayhap that is why the queen has borne no live son," he responded, and his thumb rubbed the nipple of the breast he was fondling. "Healthy children come from passion, not saintliness, Philippa!"

"I cannot concentrate when you do that, my lord," she protested.

"You are not meant to, little one," he said, laughing low. Then he began to kiss her again even as he continued caressing her breast. "You are meant to lose power over your composure, and yield yourself to the delicious feelings coursing through your veins at this moment." His lips touched her forehead, her cheeks, her throat with heat.

Philippa pulled her head away from him. "Oh, my lord, you must not assault me so sweetly. My head is spinning with your caresses and your kisses. I cannot think!"

He laughed, and then he smiled at her. "Very well, little one, I will cease momentarily. I suspect from this brief encounter that there is a deep well of unexplored lustful passion within your innocent soul. I shall very much enjoy awakening it, Philippa." His hand removed itself from her bodice.

"My lord," she said disapprovingly, "such speech is unseemly in a gentleman. My mistress, the queen, would never approve of the words you so freely use."

"Your mistress, the queen, is a good woman, and she has struggled to be a good wife to the king. But your mistress, the queen, is a prude, Philippa. She cannot help it. She was raised in Spain to have a devotion to her duty. A strict piety to the church first and foremost. A fidelity to her position as a Spanish infanta, and secondly as England's queen. And her last allegiance is to her husband. Duty does not belong in the marital bed, Philippa."

She gazed up at him, obviously puzzled.

"A man wants a woman in his bed who enjoys being there," he explained. "A woman who opens herself to their shared passion and trusts that her lord will lead the way to a pleasure they may both enjoy. I know you are a virgin, Philippa. It pleases me that you have been chaste. But the time for purity is past. For the short time we have before our marriage you will yield yourself to my will, little one. And you will not regret it. That I promise you."

"The queen . . . ," Philippa began, but he placed two fingers against her lips.

"You are not the queen, Philippa," he told her. "Now I want you to say, 'Aye, Crispin. I will do as you say.' " His gray eyes were dancing with his amusement.

"But you have to understand . . . ," Philippa tried again, and the two fingers were again pressed across her mouth.

" 'Aye, Crispin,' " he gently prompted her.

"I will not be spoken to as if I were a child!" she protested.

"But you are a child where passion is concerned," he told her. "And I am he who will teach you and make you the most skilled pupil, Philippa. Now your first lesson is to kiss me sweetly, and say, 'Aye, Crispin, I will do as you say.' "

The hazel eyes glaring at him were most definitely mutinous. She compressed her lips together into a straight, narrow line. She stood up from the bench. "No, Crispin, I will not say it! You are an arrogant horse's rump!" Then she turned and ran back into the house, the laces of her bodice trailing behind her.

The earl of Witton burst out laughing. Marriage to Philippa Meredith was going to be anything but dull, he decided.

Chapter 11

⟨⟨❈⟩⟩

he day after her betrothal ceremony, Philippa celebrated
her sixteenth birthday. Her sister, Banon, now dismissed
from the queen's service, arrived at Bolton House early with all her belongings. Her blue eyes were sparkling, and she had a more sophisticated air about her now than when she had arrived at court several
months back. Banon had turned fourteen on the first day of March.

"I'm so sorry I couldn't be here yesterday," she said, flinging her
gloves aside as she pulled them from her elegant little hands, "but the
mistress of the maids said since I would be at your wedding it didn't
matter. The old cow!" She hugged Philippa eagerly. "The queen said I
might go this morning, and believe me I was out of the palace even before the first mass. The place is in an uproar with the move today to
Greenwich. Honestly I don't see what you see in living at court. All
that pandemonium and commotion, not to mention the constant
moving." She stopped. "Oh! Happy natal day, sister!" And she kissed
both of Philippa's cheeks. Then stepping back she said, "You look pale.
Are you alright?"

"Uncle Tom says I am suffering from what he describes as bridal
nerves," Philippa answered her younger sister. "I am so glad to see you,
Banon! Come, and let us have something to eat before my new sisters-
in-law come into the hall. They never stop chattering, and they are so

provincial. They are sweet, but I think I am grateful they will not live near us." She took Banon's hand in hers, and together they seated themselves at the table while the servants hurried to bring them food, and set goblets of morning ale before them.

"Ohh, real food again!" Banon enthused. "I found the food at court almost inedible, I fear." She pulled a piece from the hot cottage loaf that had been placed before them, buttering it lavishly and taking a bite. A blissful look came over Banon's face as the butter drizzled down her chin. "Ah, that is pure heaven," she said.

"One day you will get fat," Philippa teased her sister.

"I don't care," Banon said. "I shall have Otterly, my bairns, and Robert. 'Tis all I want in life, sister. And Robert won't care. More of me to love, he always says."

Philippa shook her head. "How is it that you and Robert can speak so easily with one another? You have known him hardly longer than I have known the earl."

"Philippa, you are my older sister, and you know without my saying that I love you, but you have too much of the queen in you. I mean neither you nor the queen any disrespect when I say that, but you should be more like mama. She has a zest for life, and devil take the hindmost. She is not afraid of giving in to passion. The first night she and Glenkirk met he bedded her, and she was more than willing, it is said." Banon dipped her spoon into her trencher of warm oat stirabout, bringing it to her mouth. It was flavored with bits of apple, cinnamon, sugar, and heavy cream.

"How do you know such a thing?" Philippa demanded, surprised.

"Uncle Tom told me," Banon said. "I have lived with him since I turned twelve, after all. And while she resisted our stepfather, she also longed for him," Banon added. "But you have held Crispin St. Claire at bay, whether from shyness or prudery I do not know. But no matter, the effect has been the same, and now you will marry him tomorrow, and you can no longer hold him at bay. You would not be doing your duty as a wife if you did."

"I know," Philippa admitted. "I am so confused, and not just a little frightened."

"Of what?" Banon wanted to know.

"Of him. The earl. He is a very strong-willed man," Philippa explained.

Banon laughed aloud. "You are a very strong-willed girl," she said.

"He took me into the gardens after the ceremony yesterday, and he kissed me again and again," Philippa replied.

"And?" Banon probed.

"He loosened my laces! He fondled my breast! He said I was his pupil, and he would teach me passion, that in two days' time I would be his wife, and I would do my duty towards him," Philippa said. "I ran back into the house and stayed in my chamber the rest of the day."

Banon shook her head. "You are determined to be unhappy, I see. What is the matter with you, Philippa? The earl is a charming man. He is not very well known at court but those who know him speak of his ethic and good nature. No one has forced you to this match. I cannot believe you are behaving like a shrinking virgin, and a ninny."

"I am a shrinking virgin," Philippa protested.

"You are a ninny first, I suspect. I am almost tempted to stay my own betrothal in an effort to aid you. That is what sisters are for, but I will be damned if I hold back from my own happiness because you are behaving like a silly fool," Banon declared. "If I were not in love with Robert Neville I would steal the earl from you and marry him myself!" She drank down half the contents of her goblet in irritation. "He is most preeminent as prospective husbands go."

"Why, thank you, Mistress Banon," the earl said, coming up to join them at the high board. He gave her a warm smile, and then turned to Philippa. "You are feeling better this morning, little one?" He kissed her forehead as he sat down next to Philippa.

"Aye, my lord," she answered him, her eyes lowered.

"Well, I've had all I want to eat for now," Banon said, getting up from the table. "I'm going to go and take a nap. One never gets enough sleep at court, I fear. I shall see you both later."

"I will go with you," Philippa said, and she made to stand up, but the earl would not let her. She turned to him questioningly.

"I don't want you to go with me, you lackwit!" Banon snapped, and she ran from the hall.

"This foolishness must cease," the earl told Philippa.

"I know," she agreed. "I do not know what is the matter with me, my lord. I have never before been a coward." She filled his goblet from the pitcher on the table, and buttered a piece of the cottage loaf for him.

"We will spend the day together," he told her. "We will take Tom's barge out on the river, and row upstream away from the city. We will bring a basket with us and have a picnic, just the two of us. Not my chattering sisters, or your charming sister, or the flamboyant Lord Cambridge. Just us. And you will tell me of your family, and why you have an aversion to sheep," he teased her, "and I will tell you of my early years."

"Oh, I should like that," Philippa said, and she smiled at him.

"You are tired, little one. I can see it. You take life most seriously, and I wonder if you have ever been carefree in all of your life," he said, and he caressed her face with his fingers.

"When I was little, and lived at Friarsgate," she said softly. "Mama watched over all of us and saw we were happy and safe. There were lessons with Father Mata, and we learned to swim in our lake. I remember seeing newborn lambs just from their mother's wombs. Sheep are not very intelligent, and drop their newborns in the worst of winter," she told him.

"It sounds most peaceful and idyllic," he replied.

She laughed. "It does, doesn't it." She stood up. "I am not running away, I promise, my lord, but I would go to the kitchens and tell cook we will need a basket for our picnic. I shall return quickly, and you shall eat while I am gone."

He caught her hand and kissed it. "Do not be long, little one. I find I am coming to quite enjoy your company," he said to her.

What a sweet thing to say, Philippa considered as she hurried off to the kitchens of Bolton House. Banon was right. She was being a ninny. But the queen had instructed all her maids of honor to chaste behavior, and was not the king's wife a shining example of virtue to her kingdom's womenfolk? While Philippa had seen the king give his wife a public kiss now and again, he was far more familiar with some of the court ladies, and Philippa knew that the court was in certain areas a haven for licentious behavior of a salacious variety. She wasn't certain what was right and what was wrong. If indeed there was a right or wrong about it all.

Reaching her destination, she instructed the cook to fill a basket with bread, ham, cheese, and wine. "And some of those delicious-looking meat pasties coming out of the ovens right now," she said, "and oh, I see early strawberries, some of them as well. Pack enough, Master Cook, for the earl is a big man, and likes his food."

"When will you want it?" the cook inquired politely.

"In an hour, or possibly even less," Philippa said. "I'll send Lucy for it."

"There will be just the two of you?" the cook asked.

Philippa nodded, feeling a small blush touch her cheeks. "Aye," she responded, and then departed the kitchens.

Upstairs in the hall she found that the earl was just about finished with his morning meal. He was yet alone, for Lord Cambridge rarely rose before ten in the morning when he was in London. Neither were the earl's sisters in evidence.

"I will wait until Uncle Thomas is up," Philippa said, "so I may tell him where we are going. Would you like to go into the gardens? The day is fair."

"Aye," he agreed, "but first I have a small surprise for you, Philippa. It is your natal day, is it not? You are sixteen today. I have brought you a small gift." He held out a velvet bag to her.

"How kind!" she exclaimed, surprised. "What is it?"

"Open the bag," he smiled, "if you wish to know."

Philippa spilled the contents of the bag into her upturned palm to reveal a delicate gold chain to which was attached a round gold pendant studded with sapphire stars. "Oh," she exclaimed. "It's beautiful, my lord. Thank you so much! The only man who has ever given me jewelry before is Uncle Thomas." She held the chain and pendant up, admiring it as it sparkled in the sunlight of the hall.

"Well, now it will be my privilege to gift my wife with jewelry. Let me put it on you," the earl said, taking the chain from her and turning her about to slip it over her head. "My mother wore this piece, Philippa, and my grandmother. It is always given to St. Claire countesses. I had an ancestor who fought with King Richard. He brought it back from the Holy Land." Then his arms went about her waist, and he dropped a kiss upon her shoulder. His hand adjusted the pendant, his fingers slipping between her breasts for the briefest moment as if by accident, but they both knew it was no accident.

Philippa's pulse raced, but she did not scold him, or even flinch. By tomorrow she would be his wife. Whatever the queen said about the virtue of chastity in a marriage, this innocent play could not be wrong between a man and his wife. The betrothal agreement made them a married couple already according to the law of the land. Once the church rendered its blessing and gave them the sacrament it would be fact. If the purpose of marriage was children, then she must yield to his desires. And why should she not yield to her own desires? There were so many questions she needed answers to, and for the first time in three years Philippa Meredith wanted her mother.

"What are you thinking?" he asked her. "You are very silent, little one."

"I wish my mother were here, for there is much I have to ask her," Philippa said.

"I expect ignorance and inexperience of you, Philippa," he said, guessing the direction her thoughts must be taking. Then to his surprise Philippa laughed.

"You must not read my mind, my lord," she told him. Then she turned and kissed him on the lips without any prompting at all. "Thank you again. The chain and the pendant are lovely, and I will cherish them."

They walked out into the garden to discover that the river was filled with barges making their way from Richmond down the Thames to Greenwich. Philippa recognized many of the vessels, with their colorful flags flying, and their inhabitants as well. She waved at them gaily, and hailed many by name. The royal barge appeared, and as it came even with Lord Cambridge's quai she curtseyed low, as by her side the earl bowed low.

"Philippa! Philippa!" A small figure in a bright scarlet gown waved wildly from the royal barge.

Philippa waved back, and curtseyed again as the earl bowed as well. "It is the princess Mary," she told him. "Safe journey, your highness!" she called as the royal barge moved past Bolton House with stately grace. "We can sit down now," Philippa told the earl, settling herself on a marble bench.

"Does everyone go to Greenwich by barge?" he asked her. "And why, when Richmond is downriver of Bolton House, did we see them at all?"

"In the spring, aye. And of course not everyone can afford to keep a barge, so it is important to have friends that have one, or a friend who has a friend. The court departs when the king decrees, and sometimes the tide is not with them. They come upriver first, turn with the tide, and then go back down again. The king could just as easily wait, but he will not." She smiled. "If you listen you can hear the baggage carts rumbling along the road outside of our gates now. And here and there among them those who could not find seats on the barges, pretending they wanted to ride anyway. One must be very rich or have important relations or friends to succeed at court. I have been very fortunate. From the first time I came to court I knew it was where I wanted to be. I cannot imagine any other life."

"You know I cannot allow you as much time at court as you have had," he said. "You will have other duties to attend to as the countess of Witton. We can go for the Christmas revels, and in May, of course."

"Of course," she agreed amiably, thinking to herself that once the queen recalled her to be one of her ladies her husband could not gainsay her. And the queen had hinted that she would be recalling Philippa eventually. I can wait, Philippa thought.

Lucy came into the garden and, finding them, curtseyed. "Cook says he has your basket ready, mistress. Good morning, my lord!"

"I had best go tell Uncle Thomas that we are going to take the barge, and picnic," Philippa said. "Put the basket in the barge, Lucy, please." She arose and went off.

"Are my sisters up yet, Lucy?" the earl asked.

"I ain't heard a peep out of them or their tiring women, my lord," Lucy replied.

"Do you think you will be happy at Brierewode? It is not Cumbria," he told her.

"I am content wherever my mistress is, my lord," Lucy said, curtseying again. "I must put the basket in the barge now."

He stood up. "I'll take it, lass," he said, taking it from her hand. "Which barge?"

"The one with the Friarsgate blue and silver curtains," Lucy said. "Lord Cambridge had it made for my mistress's mother when she came to court after Sir Owein's death. My sister is in service to the lady of Friarsgate."

"Do you think the lady of Friarsgate will like me?" the earl wondered.

"If you're good to her lass, aye, she will," Lucy responded pertly.

"I am endeavoring very hard to be good to your mistress, Lucy," Crispin St. Claire said with a small smile at the young tiring woman.

"She takes to heart too much what the queen says, my lord, but you never heard me say it," Lucy told him with a broad wink. "If you gets my meaning."

The earl laughed. "I do, and I shall struggle to overcome that influence as swiftly as possible, Lucy." Then he walked away with the basket towards the little barge bobbing on the river by Lord Cambridge's quai.

In the meantime Philippa had gone back into the house and hurried up the staircase to her cousin's apartments. She knocked softly, to be admitted by Thomas Bolton's personal servant.

"Good morning, Mistress Philippa," the man greeted her.

"Is he awake yet?" she asked.

"For over an hour, and already dictating his orders to Master Smythe. Shall I tell him you are here?" the serving man asked politely.

She nodded, and was quickly admitted.

"Darling girl, a most happy natal day!" Lord Cambridge called to her as she entered his bedchamber.

"May I echo his lordship's good wishes, Mistress Philippa?" William Smythe said, bowing to her. He was standing by the bed.

"You may," she told him.

"Darling girl, what is that piece of jewelry you are wearing about your lovely neck? I have not seen it before, and I certainly did not give it to you. Come closer so I may inspect it more thoroughly," he said.

"Isn't it lovely? The earl gave it to me as a gift for my natal day, uncle. He says it belonged to his mother, his grandmother, and all the way back to an ancestor of his who fought with Coeur de Lion and brought it back from the Holy Land." She lifted the chain and pendant from about her neck and handed it to Lord Cambridge.

He took it and examined it, then handed it back to her. "It is quite superior, darling girl," he told her. "I can but hope his taste is as good as his ancestor's."

"I came to tell you that we are going to take mama's barge and picnic somewhere on the river today," she told him. "The court just went by down to Greenwich."

"Why the king will not schedule his goings with the tide is beyond me," Thomas Bolton said. "But he will control everything touching his life, won't he? Go, darling girl, and enjoy your day. I shall keep the sisters amused, you may be certain. Perhaps I shall take them to the tower to see the king's lions. I will wager neither has ever been. Where is Banon? She has arrived already?"

Philippa nodded. "We broke our fast together, and she has gone to nap. She is most delighted to be with you and going home to Otterly. Will Robert Neville go with you, or has he already left for the north?"

"No, no, he is here. He will travel with us, for we must stop at his father's and settle the betrothal agreement and set the wedding date before we may reach home. I expect him at Bolton House before day's end. Is that correct, Will?"

"Indeed, my lord, it is," the secretary replied with a short bow.

"Then I am off," Philippa said. "Pray I can escape into the garden without being accosted by one of my sisters-in-law." Then she was gone out the door. In the upper corridor it was still quiet. Philippa scampered quickly down the staircase, and peeked into the hall. It was empty but for a serving woman polishing the furniture. Moving through the door into the garden, Philippa almost danced her way down to the stone quai where she found the earl awaiting her. Gallantly he handed her into the barge.

"I have given the rowers their instructions," he said as he settled her, and then sat next to her. "We are ready," he called to the two bargemen.

The little vessel moved off upriver, struggling against the tide, keeping close to the shoreline where the current was less treacherous.

"Where are we going?" Philippa asked him.

"I have absolutely no idea," he answered. "This is not a part of the river with which I am familiar. I'll know the spot when I see it." He drew her into his arms.

"How will you be able to see what you're looking for if you're kissing me?" she asked curiously. His gray eyes held an expression she didn't understand, but it didn't frighten her at all.

"I doubt there is a perfect spot so near Lord Cambridge's house," he quickly replied, "so it is best to fill our time kissing, madame. Practice, I am told, makes perfect." His lips brushed hers. "You have been very negligent in your studies, little one." He kissed her softly and slowly.

"I was but waiting for the proper instructor, my lord," she told him coyly when he freed her lips once again. "Are you he, mayhap?" She was flirting, Philippa thought. She was actually flirting with the man she was to marry on the morrow.

He tipped her face up to his, gazing into the hazel eyes that looked shyly back at him. "I am he, Philippa," he told her. "I will teach you with all the skill at my command, not just kissing, but the ways of passion as well. Do you understand, little one?"

"Aye," she whispered, and then she said, "I did not wear a chemise today, and my gown is front-laced, my lord." Then her cheeks grew pink with the bold admission.

He was astounded. "Philippa," he said low. "You do me honor."

"Well, we are to be married tomorrow, and we are formally betrothed," she reasoned. "You are an honorable man, I know. If I am a bit liberal today with the cream, you will still purchase the cow, I am sure now."

"I will," he agreed, smiling down into her eyes.

"You have never before been wed?" she asked him. "Not even betrothed?"

"Nay. While my father lived I saw no need to marry, and my sisters had sons to take the title should something happen to me," he explained.

"But you did not remain at Brierewode," she noted.

"There was naught for me to do, Philippa. My father managed his estates with little help. He and his old bailiff, Roald. He had no intention of sharing his authority even with his only son and heir. I cannot be idle. I drifted into the court and caught the eye of Cardinal

Wolsey. The next thing I knew I was being sent on diplomatic missions. Little ones at first, and then larger ones. And one day I was sent to San Lorenzo, one of those little duchies between France and Italy. The king's ambassador had managed to irritate the duke, and was dismissed by him. I was sent as his replacement, but the duke would have no more Englishmen." The earl chuckled. "I managed to smooth the duke's ruffled feathers, but was sent home nonetheless. My next posting was to the duchy of Cleves. I was there when my father died. It was at that point I left the royal service. There was no time for a wife while I served the king."

"You are younger than your sisters," Philippa said.

"Aye, I am. I am thirty, Marjorie is thirty-seven, and Susanna is thirty-five. My mother was not very strong but she was determined to give her husband a healthy son. The effort sapped her strength. She died right after my second birthday. My sisters mothered me until they wed, and by that time I was old enough to survive on my own."

"I was barely six when my father died," Philippa told him. "I can remember him but barely now, and my sisters remember him not at all. My littlest sister, Bessie, is said to resemble him, but Banon and I are like our mother. And my half brothers look like my stepfather, Logan Hepburn."

"He is a Scot, I am told," the earl said.

"Aye. His home is just over the border from Friarsgate. He has loved mama ever since he was a boy, to hear him tell it. He saw her first with her uncle at a cattle fair. He was very determined to have her to wife. He and his brothers brought salmon and whiskey to my parents' wedding, and they played their pipes. Mama says she was angry, but that papa found it amusing."

"Was your mother much at court?" he wondered.

"Nay, my mother hated court. When her second husband died she was sent into King Henry VII's protective custody. She was only thirteen, I think, and her uncle Henry wanted to marry her off to his little boy to keep Friarsgate in the Bolton family. The king sent my father to escort mama to court where she met the Scots queen and Queen Katherine. They were all girls together in the Venerable Margaret's household. My parents were betrothed, and returned north with the queen of Scotland's wedding train. After papa died, mama visited Queen Margaret, and then Queen Katherine. But she was always eager to return home to Friarsgate. She and Logan move between it and his Claven's Carn."

"But you love the court," he said.

"From the first time I came with mama and Uncle Thomas!" Philippa told him.

"Well, there is something we have in common," he told her. "I like the court too. But of course we must make us an heir before we can spend too much time there."

Philippa nodded. "I know my duty, my lord, and I promise you that I will do it."

"But first," he said, "we need to become more intimate, little one. You know that babies do not come from the fairies, I assume." His big hand cupped her face.

"I am most aware of it, my lord, but I am not yet certain just how it is all accomplished," she admitted candidly.

"I am a patient man to a point, Philippa, which surely you must admit you can understand by now," he began, and his fingers began to unlace her bodice slowly. "We shall attain our goal while giving each other much pleasure." He loosened the laces enough to open the garment, and he gazed with admiration upon her small creamy round breasts. "Ahh, how lovely you are," he told her, a single finger tracing a path between the two breasts.

Philippa bit her lip nervously, and whispered to him so softly that he had to lean nearer to hear her. "The rowers, my lord."

Her warm fragrance rose up to assail his nostrils. ". . . have not eyes in the back of their heads, as I have previously told you, little one." He cupped one breast in his palm. It lay soft and quivering like a young dove newly netted. He touched the nipple with a fingertip, and it immediately puckered tightly. He bent his dark head and licked the nipple slowly, slowly.

Philippa hadn't realized that she wasn't breathing until she exhaled gustily. "Oh!" The sound was small, sharp, and very surprised.

"Did you like that?" he asked her, raising his head from her breast.

She nodded, her hazel eyes very wide. But for the moment she could not speak.

"Would you like me to do it again?" he said.

"Aye!" She managed to squeeze the word out but her throat was tight.

He drew her deeper into his embrace, and now his face pressed itself against the warm flesh bared to his sight. He covered her little breasts with kisses, and at one point felt her beating heart beneath his lips. He licked at the other nipple, and then he took it into the warmth of his mouth and began to suckle upon it gently.

Philippa shuddered with the utter pleasure he was giving her. A low moan escaped her lips, and then he suckled harder and harder upon her nipple until she felt an odd sensation in her nether regions, a tingle, no, a tiny throb, and she was wet but not from pee. It was a warm and sticky substance. She moved against him.

Suddenly Crispin St. Claire lifted his head from her bosom. The look in his eyes was one of unexpected surprise. Clumsily he began to relace her gown. "Are you a witch?" he asked her low.

"I do not understand," Philippa replied. "Why have you stopped? I liked it!"

"So did I," he admitted. "Perhaps too much, little one. I have never considered myself lustful, and yet I believe if we continue on in so intimate a manner I may steal your virginity from you before our union is blessed by the church. You would hate me for it, Philippa, and I do not want you to hate me."

"Let me," she said, and she completed the lacing, tying the bodice neatly in a small bow. "I have never before been touched in so tender and familiar a manner, my lord. I feared it, and yet when you made yourself free with my person, I was not afraid." She sighed. "Indeed I enjoyed it, and regretted it when you stopped."

"When this all began," he told her, "it was for the land. But now I find that I desire you very much. But I honor you as my wife as well. I will not take your virtue in a boat upon the Thames, though were you not a virgin, Philippa, you would have been impaled upon my love-shaft five minutes ago." Then he kissed her hungrily, his mouth exploring hers fiercely, forcing her lips to part, pushing his tongue between them to forage for her tongue.

Startled, she found that tongue caressing her tongue fervently. His hard body was pressed tightly against hers, crushing her breasts until she cried out in pain.

"I'm sorry!" he apologized. "God's boots, what is this magic you have suddenly unleashed upon me, little one?" Jesu! His cock was as hard as stone from what should have been an innocent encounter to prepare his bride for her marital duties.

"Am I magical, my lord?" She was teasing him now, and to her surprise Philippa felt happier than she could ever remember feeling.

He laughed. "Aye, you are enchanting me, little one. And you have no idea at this moment of the power you hold over me, but you do. I think you will become a very dangerous woman one day soon."

"I do not understand, but I will admit that I like the sound of your words, my lord," she responded.

"Philippa, my name is Crispin. An odd, and an old-fashioned name, I will admit."

"It is not odd at all," she told him. "It is from the Latin, Crispis, and he is the patron saint of shoemakers, my lord."

"I should like to hear you say my name," he said to her.

"Crispin," Philippa said, "but there must be more."

"Crispin Edward Henry John St. Claire," he said. "Edward and Henry for the kings, and John for my father."

"Why Crispin?" she asked him.

"It is a family name, and every few generations one male in the family is blessed or cursed, depending on his viewpoint, with the name," he explained.

"I like it, Crispin. Oh, look! On the right bank of the river, a grove of willows. What a lovely place for our picnic! Please tell the rowers to pull in to the shore."

The earl drew the diaphanous curtains aside and gave the order, and the rowers obeyed his command. The little boat touched the shore, and the earl jumped out, turning to help Philippa disembark. One of the rowers handed them the picnic basket, a coverlet for them to sit upon, and several silken pillows.

"There was an inn just downriver, milord," one of the two rowers said. "May Ned and me go back?"

"How long until the tide turns again?" the earl asked him.

"About four hours, milord, and then there is the calm between the tides," the man answered him.

"Come back in three hours' time then, or sooner if you prefer. Let us try and catch the tide downriver before it turns again," Crispin St. Claire said.

"Thank ye, milord," the rower responded, and then jumping back into the barge, he and his mate turned the vessel about and headed back down the Thames to where they had seen an inn.

Philippa had spread the coverlet on the ground beneath a large willow. She set the pillows about and put the basket down. "Will you come and sit by my side, Crispin?" she cooed at him. Why had she ever been afraid of the intimacy between a man and a woman? When he had caressed her it had been wonderful. Before he turned back to her she pulled open the bow holding her laces tied, and quickly licked her lips.

He turned, and caught his breath. She was simply lovely. She wore no cap or veil, and her rich auburn hair flowed artlessly down her back. Her silk gown, a flattering Tudor green, was one piece. Her lips beckoned him on to his destruction. What the hell was the matter with him? Why this sudden burst of uncontrollable lust for Philippa

Meredith? She took a deep breath, exhaled, and the laces of her gown gave way dangerously, and then she sat down upon the coverlet.

"Will you not join me, my lord?" she invited him sweetly.

"This was not a good idea," he said as if to himself.

"Of course it was," she disagreed. "Are we not getting to know one another better, Crispin?" She held out her hand to him. "Come, and sit with me. I want to be kissed and cuddled again. We are alone, and there is no one to see us in our little riverside grove of willows."

He did not take her hand, but he sat down. He was a grown man. A man of experience. He could certainly restrain himself one more day. He was not some green and callow youth who sprayed his seed down his hose in a frenzy of eager desire. "I am hungry," he said, eying the basket. Food would take his mind from his passion.

"So am I," she replied, eying him as if he were some particularly rich sweet that she just had to have. Now.

He felt his mouth struggling not to smile. What had he done with just a few kisses and caresses. It was as if all her ladylike inhibitions were forgotten. "Madame," he said in what he hoped was a stern, warning voice, "you must learn to control yourself."

"Why?" she questioned him, pouting adorably. "I want to be kissed."

"But just yesterday you did not. Why this sudden change in you?" he demanded to know. "First I cannot get you to kiss me, and now you must kiss me."

"We are betrothed now. Our wedding is tomorrow," she said as if that explained it all. "Don't you want to kiss me, Crispin? Are you one of those men who wants what he cannot have until he gets it, and then he doesn't want it anymore?"

"Philippa, I want to kiss you. I want to caress those sweet little titties of yours. But I have discovered to my surprise that what began as a mere lesson in passion to reassure you has whetted my desires so greatly that I am not certain I can control them. I want you a virgin tomorrow night. Our wedding night. I want the servants to gossip about the bloodstain on the bedsheet after we have departed for

Brierewode. In the years to come I want them to remember that you were pure and untouched when I first took you. That you were an honorable woman."

"Oh, Crispin!" she cried. "I should kiss you if you had not already assured me it would release the ravening beast in you. When I have returned to the queen's service I shall proudly tell her of the honorable man to whom I am married. You are just what she would have wished for me. Alas, however, it seems that you have aroused a lustful nature in me that is perhaps not quite respectable. I long for your touch."

"And I for yours, little one, but we will restrain ourselves for now. We will not have to restrain ourselves in another day. So you think the queen would approve of my gallantry, do you? Do you think I am the kind of man your mother would want for you?"

"I doubt it would matter to my mother, as you will not be the master of Friarsgate," she told him frankly. "She will be happy that I am happy, for I know she loves me even if we do not always see eye to eye. You will like her."

"I hope that you will like Brierewode," he said. "The countryside is very unlike your wild Cumbria. The hills are gentle and the meadows green."

"Are we on the Thames?" she asked him.

"Nay, we are to the west of the river, but I have planned with your uncle that we travel home via the river. We shall have his large barge, as he is returning to Otterly with your sister the day after our wedding. We shall go as far as Henley, where our horses will be awaiting us. We will ride cross-country to Cholsey, and then continue on by barge to Oxfordtown itself. After that we will ride home. It should take us about seven days. Your Lucy and my Peter will travel overland with the luggage cart. We will meet them first in Cholsey, and then Oxford."

"Where will we stay at night?" she asked him.

"There are several charming inns along the river, and Lord Cambridge has made arrangements for us," he told her.

"So we shall drift up the river alone, together, with no cares," she said.

"I thought you would enjoy it," he told her. "And had we not suddenly gotten along so famously it would have given us time to learn about one another."

"Shall we make love along the way?" she teased him.

He grinned. "Oh, madame, I have much to teach you, and I am delighted to find in you such a willing pupil," the earl told her. "Now open that damned basket, Philippa, for one of my appetites must be fed this minute or I cannot be responsible for what will happen."

"Yes, my lord," she said meekly. Marriage to this man, she suddenly decided, was not going to be so bad after all.

Chapter 12

April thirtieth dawned bright and sunny. The river at the edge of Bolton House sparkled in the cheerful light of morning. The gardens were abloom with early flowers, and the birds were singing sweetly. Philippa had awakened early enough to watch the sun rise. She had gone downstairs into the gardens in her night garment and gathered dew from the grass which she spread upon her face as if it were May morn. Then twirling amid the fragrant blooms, she ran on bare feet back up to her bedchamber to prepare for this most important day in her life. She realized to her surprise that she very much wished Rosamund were here today. But at the end of April her mother would be busy with the lamb count, the culling of her flocks, and preparing to ship the wool cloth woven by the cotters over the long winter months off to her European markets.

Crispin St. Claire had awakened early too. Going to his window he had seen the lithe figure dancing amid the flowers in the garden below. It was Philippa. He watched her, enchanted, and in that moment the earl of Witton realized that he was falling in love with the girl he would marry this very morning. He smiled, surprised, thinking himself briefly an April fool. She was so innocent and yet so sophisticated. And he had a great deal more to learn about her.

Banon came into her elder sister's bedchamber, rubbing her eyes sleepily. "I vow I shall never catch up with the sleep I have lost these months at court," she complained. "Can I share your bath?" She yawned broadly, and then, sighing, sat down on the bed.

"Lucy has gone to fetch us a meal," Philippa said. "It is a perfect day, Banie. The air has a warmth to it, and smells so fresh."

"I'll be glad to escape back to Otterly before the plague season," Banon remarked.

"We don't have plague every year," Philippa said.

Lucy pushed her way into the bedchamber with a heavy tray which she set upon the oak table in the center of the room. "Come along now, you two, and have your breakfast. I'll get the tub ready, for the footmen are on their way now with the hot water. Wrap your shawls about yourselves. I'll not have either of you flaunting yourselves before those sharp-eyed London lads." She snatched up Philippa's shawl and put it about her shoulders, then scampered into the room next door and came back with a shawl for Banon with which she enveloped the girl.

The two sisters sat and began to eat. There were eggs in a sauce of cheese, cream, and dill. There was ham, and fresh bread with sweet butter and cherry jam. There was a single trencher, neatly hollowed out, filled with oat stirabout. There was honey and cream for the cereal. Philippa and Banon shared the trencher. Philippa might have been at court for over three years, but she had never lost her country girl appetite, and Banon equaled her sister at the board. They ate until there was nothing left. They had sipped goblets of watered wine, for Lucy assured them it was better for the digestion and their nerves this morning than ale, which would only give them the bloat.

The footmen paraded up and down the stairs carrying their buckets of hot water. They had pulled the tall oak tub with its strong iron bands from its wall cabinet and into the room before the fire. When the tub was finally filled, Lucy shut the door to the chamber firmly and set about preparing the water.

"Don't put lily of the valley oil in," Philippa said. "Banie is going to share my tub, and I don't want her smelling of my fragrance."

"I don't like lily of the valley," Banon remarked. "It gives me the headache."

"I'll do damask rose then," Lucy replied, uncorking a narrow flask and pouring a thin stream of oil into the water. "Hurry and get in, you two. You've eaten enough for an army. Not even a crust left for the poor, or a crumb for the birds."

The sisters giggled as they got up from the table. They laid aside their shawls and pulled off their night garments.

"Your breasts have grown," Philippa noted to her sister as she climbed into the tub. "They are bigger than mine, and you are the younger. 'Tis not fair!"

"Yours will grow too when you let your husband fondle them on a regular basis," Banon responded with a grin. "They don't grow when you keep them to yourself. Oh, I envy you, sister! I wish tonight were my wedding night!"

"If your mother could hear the pair of you," Lucy said disapprovingly.

"Oh, Lucy, she wouldn't fuss at us," Banon said. "She slept with our stepfather before they were wed, you know, and she was the earl of Glenkirk's mistress. And your own sister became with child before she wed. All Philippa and I do is speak on passion."

"You were barely old enough to know such things," Lucy said, shaking her head.

"No one pays a great deal of attention to children," Banon said wisely, "but they listen, and they hear."

"Wash your hair, both of you!" Lucy said.

The two sisters grinned, but did her bidding, helping each other to rinse their long auburn hair free of soap, then pinning it up so they might continue their bath. When they had finished they climbed from the tub, one at a time, and Lucy wrapped them each in large towels that she had been heating before the fire. She handed Banon a towel for her hair, but sat Philippa down and began to dry her hair herself. Philippa was, after all, her mistress, not Banon. By toweling and brushing the hair before the heat of the fire Lucy soon had the bride's hair dry.

"I'll dress you first, Mistress Banon," she told the younger girl. "I have your gown all ready." She helped Banon into her stockings and garters, and her round necked silk chemise. Then she held out the bodice for Banon to fit her arms into the attached sleeves which were fitted to the elbow, and then folded back in a wide cuff to show the puffed sleeves of her silk chemise. Finally came the shake fold and the petticoats followed by the skirt of the gown. The garment was rose silk brocade. It had a square neckline embroidered with a band of gold and silver ribbon. The wide cuffs were rose and gold brocade. Banon's slippers were covered in the same brocade fabric as was her neat little English hood with its gauzy short veil. She wore a simple gold chain about her neck with a pearl, ruby, and gold cross.

"That color is so flattering on you," Philippa said. "I think it must be your blue eyes. Our hair is so similar, and yet that shade of rose is not a good color for me at all."

"I want to see your gown now," Banon said. "The material was simply gorgeous."

Philippa had already dressed herself in her stockings and undergarments while Banon was being dressed. She smiled at her sister's comment, and then Lucy fitted the bodice of Philippa's ivory silk brocade wedding gown onto her mistress. The wide sleeves were slashed, and tied with gold cords, but fitted at the wrists and edged with a lace ruffle. The neckline of the gown was square, and decorated with embroidered gold ribbon and pearls. The skirts of Philippa's wedding gown were split in the front to reveal the ivory and gold velvet underskirt which was embroidered and quilted.

"Oh, sister," Banon breathed admiringly, "you simply must be painted in that gown! I so wish mama were here to see you."

"You know the spring is a bad time for her," Philippa said. "She will be at your wedding, and I shall see her then. Crispin and I must marry today, for the queen wishes us to be man and wife when we join the court to go to France."

"Will you always serve Queen Katherine?" Banon asked.

"Of course," Philippa said.

"There have been rumors that the king is not happy with her because she cannot give him an heir," Banon murmured.

"They have Princess Mary to follow the king," Philippa said. "The king has no choice unless the queen dies. She is his wife, no matter her deficiencies, until death."

"I have heard it said the king could divorce the queen should he choose," Banon replied. "That he could wed a new, younger, and more fertile wife. Other Christian kings have done it in an effort to get an heir."

"That cannot be so!" Philippa snapped. "A Christian marriage is until death, Banon. I hope you have not repeated such dreadful gossip around the court."

Banon shook her head. "I listen," she told her older sister. "Nothing more."

"Good," Philippa replied, slipping her brocade slippers onto her feet.

There was a knock, and the door sprang open to reveal Lord Cambridge. He entered the bedchamber and, one hand over his heart, he stepped back dramatically, exclaiming, "My darling girl, you look magnificent! You really must be immortalized in that gown. I shall speak to the earl myself." He took her hand and kissed it.

"Banon said I should be painted too," Philippa responded. Then she stepped up before him, and kissed his cheek. "Thank you, Uncle Thomas, for everything you have done for me. You have obtained a far better match for me than I could have ever hoped for, and I am grateful."

"You seem to like him, darling girl, and I do want you to be happy,"

Tom Bolton said. "And I believe it is more than just the land for him now. He seems quite taken with you after these last few weeks. He is a good man, Philippa. That I know in my heart. I should not let you wed him today if I did not believe that. I promised your mother to look after you, and you know that she is dearest to my heart of anyone else living in this world. I would not fail her nor you." He took a lock of her unbound hair up in his fingers, and kissed it.

"Aye, I know," Philippa replied. Then she smiled at him. "Uncle dearest, you are dressed most soberly today. No embroidered doublet glistening with gold threads and pearls? No brightly colored silk hose or a bejeweled codpiece? Today is my wedding day, and you appear in a midnight blue velvet coat with furred sleeves? If it were not for the outrageous gold chain upon your chest with its great sparkling pendant, I should hardly recognize you," she teased him. "Even your shoes are plain."

He chortled. "Today is your day, darling girl. I would not outshine the bride, but I have seen to your bridegroom's apparel. He is a vision in Tudor green. His sleeves are slashed and embroidered. His shirt collar has a pleated edge. His coat is full, short and pleated as well, and his codpiece! My darling girl, it is a work of art, as you shall soon see! I am most envious of the fellow, and should be quite jealous were he marrying anyone else but you. He is in the hall now, his sisters alternately twittering and weeping about him. I have left young Neville with him. Where are your jewels?"

"I was just about to adorn her when you come in, my lord," Lucy said, and then she put a great rope of pearls about her mistress's neck and affixed the matching pearl earbobs in the girl's ears. "There now, don't they look just fine!"

"Are we all ready then?" Lord Cambridge asked. "Lucy, you too."

"Me? Oh, my lord, thank you! Give me but a moment to fetch my apron," she cried.

"Be quick then, lass!" he told her. "The vessels are ready to take us to Richmond, where one of the queen's chaplains will perform the sacrament. Go along, Banon, and your sister and I shall be behind in but a moment." He gently shooed the girl out the door. Turning, he looked to his young relation. "I should not be the one to speak with you of such things, but who else, darling girl, is there?" He appeared extremely uncomfortable.

Philippa giggled. "It's alright, Uncle Thomas. I know exactly what it is I need to know about such matters. The queen, the other maids, my sister, and Lucy have been most kind about sharing their wisdom with me. And I have been advised by the queen that too much knowledge is not a good thing for a bride."

"Thank God!" He breathed with a great sigh. "I fear I should have swooned before I could have spoken to you of such delicate concerns."

"I'm ready, my lord!" Lucy was back, her simple black silk gown covered with a lace and lawn apron.

"Then we are indeed ready to go," Lord Cambridge decided.

They found everyone else awaiting them in the hall. The earl's eyes met Philippa's, and she gave him a tremulous smile. Lady Marjorie and Lady Susanna admired the bride's gown effusively.

"The barges await, my lord," William Smythe said as he came up to Lord Cambridge's elbow.

"My dears," Thomas Bolton said, "I shall take the blushing bride and her maidservant in the smaller vessel. The rest of you are to go in my own personal barge. Come along now. We mustn't keep the priest waiting."

As always, Lord Cambridge had planned everything perfectly. The river was between tides, and as smooth as glass. Their barges moved easily through the water the distance down to Richmond Palace. There was but one servant at the stone quai, as most of the servants had gone to Greenwich with their royal masters. He helped them from their elegant crafts, and they hurried up the stairs to the palace. Another servant met them at the riverside door, and with a bow escorted them through the silent corridors to the queen's favorite little chapel where the ceremony would be performed by one of the queen's own priests, a Spaniard of indeterminate age, who was waiting for them. Philippa recognized him as Frey Felipe.

She left the wedding party and went to him. "Thank you for remaining behind, Frey Felipe, to perform the sacrament."

"I am honored, my lady," he replied in his accented English. "You are dear to her highness's heart, and you have served her well as has your mother." He gave her a slight bow, and then said, "Shall we begin?"

The earl of Witton stepped forward to take Philippa's hand. He gave it a little squeeze, and smiled at her. Lord Cambridge stood on the other side of the bride with Banon, Robert Neville, Lady Marjorie, Lady Susanna, and Lucy pressing about them. The chapel was very quiet but for the murmur of the priest's voice as he intoned the Latin words of the ceremony. The chamber's windows faced the river, and the sunlight on the dancing waters reflected and flickered upon the stone floor. There was a lace cloth and heavy gold candlesticks with beeswax tapers on the altar. There was a matching carved and jeweled crucifix in the center of the altar. There were crimson velvet cushions for the wedding party to kneel upon. Frey Felipe was aided by a little boy in a fine white linen and lace surplice.

It was suddenly very much like a dream, Philippa thought, as the sweetly scented incense was wafted over them. She reacted instinctively, saying the Latin words she had been taught by Father Mata at Friarsgate. This was her wedding day. The ceremony was even now being performed. A small wave of panic hit her. Was it too late to change her mind? Then she felt the gentle pressure on her hand, calming her, reassuring her. Was she breathing? She opened her mouth perfunctorily to receive the host. She repeated the words as she was instructed. The earl slid a heavy gold ring encrusted with rubies on her finger. Frey Felipe was briefly binding their hands together with a silken band, speaking about their union being unbreakable. And finally he was blessing them, and it was done. Philippa Meredith was a married woman in the eyes of both English law and Holy Mother

Church. She was no longer plain Mistress Meredith. She was Philippa, countess of Witton. The earl tipped her face up to his and gently brushed her lips with his. There was much laughter and clapping.

"You can breathe now," he said softly in her ear. "It's over and done with, and we are properly shackled till death parts us, little one."

And she smiled at him. "It was like a fantasy," she told him as he led her from the chapel. "A maid waits all her life for this day, and then it is done in a trice."

Lord Cambridge had stayed behind to press a small bag of coins into the priest's hand. "Please thank her highness for her generosity towards my young relation," he said.

"My mistress is always pleased to see her maids well matched, and this match was a particularly good one for the girl. She is deserving, my lord, for she has always been chaste and devout and most loyal to her mistress," Frey Felipe said. "More so than many," he concluded.

"The flesh is weak, good father, and men weaker yet, and kings are men too," Lord Cambridge replied.

"Indeed," the priest said dryly. Then he bowed. "Good day, my lord." And, his brown robes swaying, he departed the chapel through a side door.

Thomas Bolton knew to what the priest had referred. Bessie Blount might be gone from court, but the knowledge that her child was due to be born shortly was hardly a secret. Her child, and the king's child. God help the queen if Bessie birthed a healthy boy. There had been rumors, and Lord Cambridge was always privy to the latest gossip when he came to court. The rumors whispered of the king's unhappiness and growing concern that perhaps God was not happy with his marriage. I think I am glad to be going home to Otterly shortly, he thought to himself.

Hurrying to the larger of his two barges, he squeezed himself aboard. "I see," he said archly, "that our lovebirds have already headed upriver back to Bolton House. I have arranged a small feast to celebrate this event. And afterwards I have a wonderful surprise for you all."

"Oh, Uncle Thomas, tell us now!" Banon pleaded prettily.

"Nay, darling girl," he replied. "Philippa and Crispin must hear it too." And he chuckled to himself.

"It is always something marvelous when he chortles like that," Banon told Robert Neville. "He is the kindest and most generous of men, Rob."

The tide had turned, and was with them now. It swept both vessels up the river, making it far easier for the oarsmen who rowed. Philippa and Crispin had already disembarked as the larger barge nosed itself into the quai. Lord Cambridge's servants were there to help their master and the ladies out. They walked chattering through the garden into the house, finding their way to the lovely hall again. Settling themselves at the high board they waited as the servants brought in the feast.

There were raw oysters fresh this morning from the sea. There was creamed codfish, the sauce flavored with celery and dill. There was whole trout lying on beds of watercress and surrounded by carved lemons, and large fat winesteamed prawns. There was duck in plum sauce, lark pies hot from the ovens, a roasted peacock redressed with its tail feathers, a large haunch of beef encrusted in rock salt, and another of venison, as well as a whole country ham. There were platters of artichokes that had been steamed in white wine, braised lettuces, and roasted leeks. The breads had been baked into fanciful shapes, and came to table hot. There were crocks of sweet butter to spread upon them. There was cheese: a French brie and a hard English cheddar.

"I have never seen such a feast in all of my life," Lady Marjorie whispered to her sister, Susanna. "He is odd to my way of thinking, but Thomas Bolton is a host without peer. The food is so fresh, and so beautifully cooked it has little need of spices."

Lady Susanna nodded. "I wonder what his surprise is to be?"

When the main meal had been cleared away the servants brought in jellies, candied violets, and bowls of strawberries with thickly clotted Devon cream. There were sugar wafers served with the sweet wines poured. Several toasts were drunk to the couple's health and happiness. The afternoon was growing late, and finally Lord Cambridge stood up.

"Now, my dears," he told them, "I have a surprise for you. I am taking Banon, Robert, Lady Marjorie, and Lady Susanna to my house at Greenwich. Your trunks are packed, my dears, and already on their way with your servants. We will bid the bride and groom farewell, and depart immediately afterwards." He turned to Philippa. "You shall have Bolton House to yourselves, my darling girl." He looked most pleased with himself.

"Greenwich?" Lady Marjorie gasped. "That is where the court is now."

"Indeed, dear lady, it is. And tomorrow is May Day, and one has never celebrated May Day unless they have done so at court. I will wager you have never been to court on May Day. 'Tis the king's favorite holiday of them all. My house is right next to the palace, and we are invited to join in the celebrations."

"Oh my!" Lady Marjorie said, her eyes wide with anticipation.

"And when you have had your fill of Maying, dear ladies, you can return home, while my ward, young Neville, and I will go north to Otterly."

"Uncle Thomas," Philippa began, but he waved a languorous hand at her.

"Do not thank me, darling girl," he purred, his blue eyes twinkling.

And Philippa laughed. "I do not think I was going to," she told him. "Crispin and I are leaving on the morrow for Brierewode."

"I know, but I felt you deserved your privacy for the rest of your stay. Do you really want the sisters looking archly at you when you depart the hall this evening?" he murmured low. "Banon, young Neville, and I will return but briefly in a few days, and then begin to make our way home."

"I will miss you," she told him. "Life is always more fun when you are around."

He chuckled. "I will see you when you return to Friarsgate with your husband, and at Banon's wedding to young Neville. Her match is not as spectacular as yours, of course, but I believe they care for each other, which is more important, is it not?"

"How would I know such a thing?" Philippa answered him.

"Did you note how he looked at you this morning in the chapel, darling girl? He is a man on the verge of falling in love. Accept his love, and return it wholeheartedly."

"I don't understand this love. God knows I have had a good example of love from my mother, but what does love feel like?" Philippa looked genuinely confused.

"You will know it when you feel it. Now I expect all the gossip, in minute detail, of this summer in France with the two kings when I see you again," he told her, bending to kiss her brow. Then he addressed his guests once more. "Come, and bid Philippa and Crispin farewell. Our barge awaits us, my dears!"

Banon hugged her older sister. "I have enjoyed being with you again, Philippa. Now I have another reason to be eager for my wedding to Rob. I shall see you then." The two sisters kissed. Then Banon moved to speak with her new brother-in-law. "Farewell, my lord. I will be pleased to welcome you to Otterly when you come. Godspeed in your journey in the coming months."

The earl took Banon gently by the shoulders. "Farewell, sister. I, too, look forward to seeing your beloved north country." He kissed her forehead.

Young Robert Neville bid the bride and groom good-bye. He was followed by Lady Marjorie and Lady Susanna, both of whom became teary, hugging Philippa and their brother in turn. Lord Cambridge brought up the rear, smiling.

"Lucy will be here for you, and will travel with you. Crispin and I have arranged the trip. Good-bye, my darling girl! Be happy! I shall see you in October!" And then he was gone, leading his guests from the hall.

235

They stood silent for several long moments, and then Philippa ran to the windows that overlooked the Thames. She watched as the guests were helped into Lord Cambridge's large barge. And then just before he climbed down into the boat, Tom Bolton turned and waved. Philippa burst into tears, surprising her new husband.

"What is the matter, little one?" he asked, not certain if he should hold her, but then enfolding her in a gentle embrace.

"I have just realized that my childhood is over," Philippa sniffled. "I thought it so when I came to court, but I still had my family. Now I am alone! When Uncle Thomas turned to wave at us I suddenly knew it to be so." She pressed her face against his velvet-clad shoulder.

"You have not lost your family, you foolish creature," he told her, laughing. "You will always have them, no matter you are my wife. And you and I will but add to that family as we begin our own. Stop weeping, Philippa. I believe you are having an attack of the nerves, finding yourself with only your bridegroom to sustain you. Have you not considered how I feel? I am shortly to reach my thirty-first year. I have spent much of my adult life in service to the king. Now I suddenly find I have a wife. It is all very strange to me too, Philippa."

Philippa sniffed noisily. She looked up at him, and her dark lashes were clumped in sharp-looking little spikes. Her hazel eyes were wet, her cheeks stained with her tears. "I am not a foolish creature!" she said with as much dignity as she could manage. "You are a man, and it is different for men than it is for girls. You have traveled the world for the king. You are experienced."

"And you are not," he said quietly, "nor should you be. You are a young bride who has just seen her family go off leaving her with a man she hardly knows. But this is the way of the world in which we live, Philippa. You are going to have to learn to trust me, little one, for we are now shackled together for life."

"It was Uncle Thomas turning to wave that unnerved me," she told him. "After my father died he appeared to escort mama to court. He explained his relationship to us; his great-grandfather and mama's great-grandfather had been brothers. He was like nothing any of us had ever seen before."

The earl laughed. "I can but imagine," he told her.

"But he was so kind," Philippa continued. "He and mama came to adore each other as they were better acquainted. Maybel and Edmund loved him too. Suddenly we were a real family again."

"His lands were here in the south, were they not?" the earl said.

"Aye, but he sold them and purchased our great-uncle Henry's home. Of course he tore it down and rebuilt it, for Uncle Henry was a wicked man, and his wife and children were no better. It is a long story, and I will not bore you with it."

"Nay," he said. "I would hear it."

"Then let us go out into the garden," Philippa answered him, "and I will tell you all. And then you will tell me more about yourself, and your family." She turned, and was startled when he took her hand in his. " 'Tis a shame to waste a day so fair," she said.

They went out into the garden and sat with the sun warm upon their backs as Philippa told her bridegroom the story of her family, and of how Henry Bolton had attempted to wrest the Friarsgate inheritance from Rosamund Bolton, its rightful heiress. She told Crispin St. Claire how her mother, with the help first of Hugh Cabot, Owein Meredith, her father, Thomas Bolton, and Logan Hepburn, the laird of Claven's Carn, who had eventually become her stepfather, had foiled Henry Bolton and his family. How Henry the elder had died of a fit when her mother had refused to let his son, Henry the younger, have Philippa for his wife. How Henry the younger had been tricked into an ambush with English borderers, led by Lord Dacre, and killed, thus ending the threat his family had posed towards hers.

The earl of Witton shook his head. "Your mother is a brave and resourceful woman. I hope, Philippa, that you possess some of her virtues."

"My mother's greatest passion is Friarsgate. It always has been, but nay, that is not so. Once my mother loved so deeply, so passionately, that I believe she might have left Friarsgate behind. Sadly for her it was not to be. But then my great-uncle might have had his way, and I be shackled to Henry Bolton the younger, and not you."

"Another story?" he asked, smiling at her.

"For another time," Philippa said. "It would seem I have many stories to tell of my family." She chuckled.

"I am afraid my family is dull by comparison, little one," he told her.

"Crispin," she began, "in fairness you must decide before we travel north in the autumn whether you would really give up the Friarsgate inheritance. It is a very rich birthright and while I do not want it, or the responsibility that goes with it, you may."

"Nay, I have told you that Brierewode with the lands from Melville are more than enough of an obligation. We will go to court, Philippa, for as long as it amuses you, for I have promised you that. But we will not live at court as so many do. I cannot be away from my lands for too long, little one. My cotters and my tenants need to know I am there for them, caring for them. When a man does not oversee his own estates he stands in danger of losing them through mismanagement or neglect or outright theft. I do not approve of these men who just take from their land, but give nothing back to it. I care for Brierewode every bit as much as your mother cares for Friarsgate. Nay, I do not want it. Besides, your mother, according to Lord Cambridge, is my age. She will live for many years, and believe me she will watch over Friarsgate until she dies. And by then she will have found the right person whom she can trust to husband her lands into the future."

"Thank you," she told him. "How odd, but you are just the sort of man my mother wanted me to wed. I see it now."

A light wind had sprung up off the river. The day was waning into the spring twilight. The Thames below the garden was empty of even the simplest of traffic now.

"I think we had best go in now," he told her, drawing her up from the marble bench where they had been sitting. "How perceptive it was of Lord Cambridge to take my sisters down to Greenwich for a few days. It will be a memory that they will cherish forever. They are country wives, and live unaffected lives. Marjorie has six children, and Susanna four. Their husbands are dull, but good fellows."

They walked hand in hand through the gardens back into the house again. The hall had been cleared of the earlier feast, and the fires were burning. Most of Lord Cambridge's servants had gone down to Greenwich, for they always traveled with their master. There were some at Otterly to keep it ready for his return, and the others had been left behind to serve the earl and his bride. A male servant whom Philippa recognized as the majordomo's first assistant came forward and bowed to them.

"A light collation has been left upon the high board, my lord. There is a cold joint, a capon, bread, butter, cheese, and a fruit tartlet. Do you wish to serve yourselves?"

"I will serve my husband, Ralph," Philippa said. "Where is Lucy?"

"Do you require her, my lady?"

My lady! She was now my lady. "Nay, but I will need her later," Philippa answered the serving man.

"I will tell her you inquired, my lady. She is in the kitchens at this time having her supper," Ralph said. He bowed again, and moved off.

"Would you like to eat now, my lord?" Philippa asked the earl.

"Not yet," he said. "I am of a mind to play you a game of chess."

She shook her head wearily. "My lord, 'tis not fair! You would have me beat you again, and on our wedding day?" Philippa teased wickedly.

"Madame, 'tis our wedding night," he reminded, chuckling as she blushed.

"So you are determined not to play fair," she scolded him.

"All is fair, I have heard it said, in love and war," he answered her.

"But which is this, I wonder?" Philippa riposted quickly.

He laughed aloud. "Well said, little one!"

"Why do you call me little one?" she asked him.

"Because you are petite in stature, and you are younger than I am," he replied.

"I like it," she told him, and he smiled.

"Good! I would please you as much as I can," he said.

"And I you," she replied, "and so I shall set up the chessboard."

He stood very close to her. "And you will strive not to beat me too badly, madame?" His lips brushed the top of her head, and when she looked up at him, surprised, he placed his lips on hers, kissing her a long and slow kiss. His arm slid about her slender waist, drawing her closer to him.

Her first instinct was to draw away, but then she remembered he was her husband. She looked into his serious gray eyes, unable to see his emotions. His face was not a handsome one like Giles's had been. Indeed like everything else about him it was hard, lengthy, and narrow. His lips were long and thin, his chin pointed. Her hand reached up to touch his face. "You are not a beautiful man," she said, "but I like your visage."

"Why?" he demanded, taking her hand in his, and kissing the fingers.

"It has strength and nobility in it," Philippa told him, surprising even herself with her own words.

"Why, little one, what a fine compliment you have given me," he replied.

"Men at court are often consumed by their appearance, even the king whom we must consider the handsomest man living. What woman wants to compete in her mirror with her husband, my lord? Nay, you are not handsome, and I am glad for it," she said.

He laughed then, and the magic between them dissolved. It would be ignited between them again, and soon, he knew, but not now. He released her from his embrace. "Set up the board, madame," he told her.

They sat down to play, and as in most of their games Philippa quickly gained the advantage, capturing his rooks and his queen. "You are too impatient," she told him. "You must study the board, and consider at least three moves ahead."

"How can I?" he replied. "I do not know what piece you will move."

"Crispin!" Her tone was exasperated. "There are only so many moves you can make in each play. You must contemplate in your mind which ones they are, and then weigh and balance the best of them."

The earl of Witton was very surprised by her explanation. "Do you do that?" he asked her, and knew before she spoke what she would answer.

"I do. I dislike losing. You must allow me to teach you better, for you are no challenge for me now. There is no fun in playing an opponent you know you will beat," Philippa said in matter-of-fact tones.

"Did no one ever tell you that to best a man at chess is not particularly feminine?" he queried her.

"Yes, they did," she said, "but the queen never lets the king win easily, and more often than not she will beat him. I but follow her example, my lord. I am not nor will I ever be one of those fluttering females lacking intellect, and giggling over the latest gossip making the rounds of the court."

"Nay, I do not imagine you will," he said, "but sometimes women of reason who revel in their sense of intellectual superiority miss the obvious. Check and mate, my dear countess." He grinned triumphantly as he captured her king.

Philippa stared openmouthed, but then she burst out laughing and clapped her two hands together. "I bow to your cleverness, my lord," she told him. "I am beginning to see now that there is more to you than I anticipated."

"Indeed, madame, there is much more," he said meaningfully. He stood up and stretched. "It is time we ate something, madame, for we cannot avoid the inevitable forever." He took her hand, and leading her to the high board he seated her gallantly. "We must be grateful that Lord Cambridge has had the delicacy of manners to leave us alone. I think neither of us would have enjoyed the crudity and general drunken merriment that goes with the bedding of a bride and groom."

Blushing, Philippa nodded silently. Then she carved him several slices of beef and two more of capon, laying them carefully on his plate before she served herself. Her own appetite had suddenly faded away at his careful mention of the night to come. She poured them both goblets of rich and fragrant red wine.

He, however, ate with good appetite, but he saw how she picked at her capon, and how she drank half a goblet of wine down after she had poured it. She was afraid. But how afraid? Philippa was, of course, a virgin. He did not relish the thought of deflowering a reluctant virgin, but the deed must be done this night. He knew very well, even if she didn't want to, that Lord Cambridge would expect to see the proof of Philippa's lost virtue in order to assure himself and his family that the marriage was consummated. He drank deeply of his own wine. The night ahead was going to prove to be a lesson in both diplomacy and his strategic abilities. He hoped that he was up to it.

Chapter 13

❦

When they had finished their meal and the servants had cleared the high board, a long and awkward silence ensued between them. Finally the earl said in a quiet voice that nonetheless brooked no resistance, "I believe we should retire, my dear. I shall remain in the hall until Lucy tells my serving man that you are prepared for bed." He stood up, taking her hand to lead her down from the high board. Then he kissed the icy little hand, bowed, and said, "I am patient to a point, Philippa."

She curtseyed to him, the color drained from her face, and she swayed slightly. But then she took a deep breath, saying, "I will try not to keep you waiting, my lord," and drawing her hand from his, she turned and hurried from the hall. Reaching her apartment she entered her bedchamber and gasped, surprised. "Lucy! What has happened here?"

"Lord Cambridge had the entire room redone today after you left for the church, and while you were all feasting, and this afternoon while you and the earl was in the garden. He had everything prepared and ready. He said that you and your husband should begin on an even playing field. That you should not remember the bedchamber of your girlhood as the place you spent your wedding night. He wanted it all different."

Philippa gazed about her. Gone were the rose-colored velvet draperies that had hung on the windows and curtained the bed. This had been her mother's room once, and then it had been hers ever since she had come to court. The furniture in both rooms of the apartment was the same, except for the bed in her bedchamber which had been replaced by a very large bed that would obviously accommodate two. The draperies were now a rich shade of burgundy reds and the Turkey carpets deep reds and blues. The velvet curtains that would surround the bed were hung from fine shiny brass rings.

"Well," Philippa said, half laughing, "he has accomplished his goal, but I rather liked the rose velvet."

"It was faded and worn, my lady. This is so rich and fine," Lucy said.

"For one night," Philippa said softly, "and all so my memories of the rose velvet room would always be happy ones. Uncle Thomas is the most thoughtful of gentlemen. No one else, not even my mother, would have considered such an extravagance."

"He loves all you lasses very much, does Lord Cambridge," Lucy said. "Come now, my lady, 'tis no use dawdling."

Philippa gave her tiring woman a small smile, and nodded. "It sounds so strange to my ears to hear you call me my lady," she said to Lucy while the older girl unlaced her bodice. Her own fingers undid the tabs holding the bodice to her skirts.

"You're the countess of Witton now, my lady," Lucy said proudly. She worked busily as she spoke, loosening the sleeves and drawing the bodice off by them, laying it aside. Then she unlaced her mistress's skirts, the petticoats and the shake fold beneath them. Philippa stepped from them, and Lucy gathered everything up, bustling off into the small chamber where all of her lady's clothing was kept.

Philippa walked over to her jewel casket, opened it and, removing her earbobs and pearls, put them away. Seating herself she slipped off her shoes and, easing her garters, rolled her stockings from her legs. Lucy came from the other room, gathered them up, and disappeared again. A basin with warm water had been set on the oak table. The young woman bathed her hands and her face. Then she scrubbed her teeth with a mixture of pumice and mint, using a small cloth. She was doing everything as she did it every night before she went to bed. But tonight there would be a husband in her bed.

Lucy came back, and thrust the chamber pot at her. "Pee," she ordered, "and then bathe yourself there."

Philippa's first instinct was to argue she didn't need to pee, but she found that she did. She obeyed her maidservant's instructions. Lucy emptied the pot out the bedchamber window, then rinsed it with the water from the basin, and emptied it the same way. She tucked the chamber pot beneath the bed again.

"Well, you're as ready as you're going to be," she said. Then she curtseyed, and without another word was gone out the door of the bedchamber. Philippa heard the door to her little apartment close as Lucy hurried into the hallway beyond.

"My hair," Philippa said softly, and then she laughed at herself. She was perfectly capable of brushing her own hair. Taking up her brush she sat down in the window seat overlooking the gardens. One hundred strokes was what Maybel and mama had taught her. Each morning, and each night. The boar's bristles slicked rhythmically through her long, thick tresses.

Philippa watched the river as she brushed. There was a crescent moon tonight, and above it a bright star. It was so beautiful. If only it could stay just like this forever, she thought. And then the door to her bedchamber opened, and she heard him as he stepped into the room.

Philippa did not turn about, but her hand stopped midway in a stroke. He said nothing, but he took the brush from her hand and began to skim it through her long auburn hair. She sat silently, barely breathing as he brushed. Finally he spoke.

"Have you kept count? Is it a hundred yet?"

"I lost count," she said, "but it must be, or more."

"Then we have finished," he replied. "You have beautiful hair, Philippa." He took a handful, and bringing it to his lips, kissed it.

He sat next to her on the window seat, his arm sliding about her slender waist. She stiffened and he loosened his grip, but slightly. His hand pushed her long hair to one side, and he gently kissed the nape of her neck. It was a slow and lingering kiss. Philippa shivered slightly. The hand moved around to untie the ribbons holding her chemise closed.

"Please no!" she pleaded softly, her own hands going to stop his.

"I am only going to caress your sweet breasts, little one," he told her, whispering in her ear, kissing it.

"I am so afraid," she admitted.

"Of what?" he asked gently.

"Of this. Of you. Of what must happen between us tonight," she told him, the words spilling out in a desperate rush.

"This," he said, "is simply a caress." He had pushed her hands away, and drawing the chemise aside had cupped her left breast. "I am your husband, Philippa, and you need have no fear of me ever unless you betray me. What must happen tonight between us is to satisfy your family that you are indeed my wife in every way, else I steal your dower, and put you aside for non-consummation."

"But you would never do that!" she cried. "You are an honorable man."

"I am delighted that you understand that," he told her, smiling. "And that is why our union will be consummated tonight, Philippa. Because I am an honorable man. Come, little one, there is nothing to fear. I will join my body with yours, and we will both receive pleasure in the union."

"Why must it be tonight? Could we not wait?"

"How long would you propose we wait?" he asked her, amused.

"I don't know," she said, almost crying.

"Which is why it will be tonight, Philippa. The longer we tarry in our duty the more frightened you will become. Once the deed is done you will see it is not terrible at all. Mayhap you might even want to do it again, and yet again," he teased her.

"The queen says that the union of a husband and a wife is for the sole purpose of procreation, my lord, and nothing more. And that is what the church teaches as well."

"I will have neither the queen nor the church in our bed, Philippa," he said, and his voice had grown hard. "There will be only two in our bed. You and me!" He pulled her roughly into his lap and, a hand grasping her head to hold it still, he kissed her hard.

His mouth worked roughly against hers until her lips parted, seemingly of their own volition. His tongue plunged deep, finding hers, stroking it, subduing it, kissing and kissing her until she was breathless. She shuddered, but to her surprise her arms wrapped themselves about his neck. "I like it when you kiss me," she murmured.

"You were meant to be kissed," he said roughly. "Kissed, and caressed, and made love to, little one. I find I can behave like a gentleman when I am not touching you, but when you lie in my arms like this and I pet those sweet breasts that you possess, then, Philippa, I lose control of myself. I cannot ever remember a woman lighting such a fire of lust in my loins."

She looked up at him, surprised. "You desire me?" she asked him shyly.

The warm gray eyes engaging her hazel eyes gave her the answer even before he spoke. "Aye, I want you, little one," he told her. "And now I am glad you held me off these past weeks, for tonight we shall take a journey of exploration together that can only end in sweet pleasure for us both."

Philippa felt as if every bone in her body had just melted away. She wasn't even certain she had the strength to move, or speak. He tipped her from his lap but momentarily, pushing her chemise from her shoulders. She felt the silk sliding down her body, her hips, her thighs, her legs. He lifted her from the fabric and took her into his lap again as he sat. She was naked! She didn't know where to look. Her throat grew tight.

Only a few women had ever seen her naked. She had never been naked before a man until now. What would the queen say? Had the queen ever been naked before the king? Philippa didn't think so. Katherine even wore a chemise when she bathed.

"This is not fair," she said. "You are taking advantage of my innocence, my lord."

"You are right," he agreed, and tipped her from his lap again. "I should be naked too, and then we are equals once more." He stripped his silk chemise off and tossed it onto the floor near hers. "There," he said.

Philippa's hands flew to cover her eyes. "Oh, my lord!" she cried. "The candles still burn and light the chamber."

"Aye, they do," he replied amiably, and he took her hands from her face, but Philippa kept her eyes tightly shut. "Why are your eyes shut?" he asked.

"Because you are naked, my lord," she told him. "It isn't proper that we see one another naked. God gave us garments to clothe our shame, the church teaches."

"I cannot make love to you, Philippa, if you are clothed," he said reasonably, "and if we are to follow the teaching of the church to procreate then we must be naked, I fear." He was close to laughing, but he did not. Damn Spanish Kate and her over-pious ways. No wonder the king hadn't managed to get a healthy son on her. How could someone so intent on her immortal soul enjoy her earthly body? And without enjoyment it was all for naught. How long had Philippa been with her? Almost four years? Well, he could not in a single night undo all of the queen's foolishness, but he was going to make a very good try at it. "Open your eyes at once, little one!" he commanded her. "I am your husband, and I will be obeyed!"

The hazel eyes flew open, startled by the tone of his voice. They found a place just over his shoulder upon which to fixate. "Yes, my lord," she whispered. Her cheeks were very pink, and her youthful form leaned away from him.

He yanked her hard against him.

"Oh!" She struggled, but he would not give way, and Philippa felt every inch of her husband's lean hard body as it pressed against her. Her gaze met his.

"Now, Philippa," he told her, "I intend caressing every inch of your delicious little body, and I intend that you caress me in return. We will kiss as well. And when our lustful natures have been well aroused, little one, then we shall come together as man and wife, and you will cease this prudish nonsense. The joining of two bodies can, with God's blessing, produce offspring, but it can also offer pleasures unlike any you have ever known before, and that is good. I suspect the queen has never known those pleasures, and for that I am sorry. But you will know them!"

"The queen says a wife should say the rosary and pray without ceasing when her lord mounts her," Philippa informed him primly.

"Not a bead, girl, or a prayer when we come together. The only noise I would hear from your lips should be cries of delight, and pleas for me not to cease. Do you understand, Philippa?" His big hands fondled her bottom, squeezing the twin halves.

Philippa started, surprised, and in an effort to escape those wicked hands pressed against him. But then her eyes widened with greater surprise. There was something hard pressing against her belly. "Oh!" she gasped, and tried to back away but he would not allow her to do so. "Crispin!" she pleaded, using his name.

"Aye?" he responded, his eyes dancing with merriment.

"Please," she said softly.

"Please what?" he replied.

Suddenly a tear rolled down her cheek. "Oh, you are cruel!" she told him.

His tongue reached out and licked the tear away. "Aye, but sometimes a man must be cruel to be kind," he told her.

"I do not understand," she said, and she was trembling now. His tongue on her cheek had been the most sensuous gesture she had ever experienced in all her life.

"Nay, you wouldn't," he answered. "Not yet, little one. But you will." Then he lifted her up in his arms and carried her to the waiting bed, where he gently deposited her.

Her eyes could no longer avoid him. He had an elegant body much like the statues in Lord Cambridge's gardens. It was far more beautiful than his plain face. She cried out softly when that body covered hers.

He had seen the admiration in her gaze when she had looked at him, though her eyes had not lingered on his manhood at all. He was careful to position himself so that he did not crush her. Taking her face into his two hands he began to kiss her again. He was ready, but she was not, and he would harm her no more than was necessary to capture the prize of her virginity. His lips brushed over her lips and her face. To his delight she responded shyly, returning his kisses, her arms going about his neck once again. He rolled them so that he was now beneath her, and she atop him. She gave a little cry of surprise, but did not protest. He drew her forward until her breasts were within easy reach of his mouth. First he buried his face in the valley between those small fruits, and then, unable to restrain himself, he began to lick her nipples, first one, and then the other, back and forth until she was moaning so softly that at first he wasn't even certain the sound was coming from her. His mouth closed over one of those tempting nubs. He suckled hard, and she cried out, but the sound was neither of fear nor distaste. When he had taken all he could from the first nipple he moved to the second, drawing on it with pleasure, taking delight in her as her head moved back and forth, the auburn hair tumbling about her.

"This cannot be right," she gasped.

His teeth grazed the nipple teasingly.

"Oh, Crispin!" But she did not ask him to cease.

He rolled again, and she was beneath him once more. He began to bathe her body with his fleshy tongue. First her round little breasts, then her throat, and he felt the pulse leaping beneath his caresses. He rained kisses from her shoulders to her hands, each in its turn, and sucked suggestively upon her fingers. His tongue then foraged its way across her shapely torso. He kissed the small mound of her belly, considering carefully his next move. He wanted to taste the virgin nectar of her, but she was much too innocent for so powerful a passion yet. Instead he moved to lie next to her, cuddling her, while his hand explored her further, brushing across the curls on her mons, pressing a finger between her moist nether lips.

"Oh, you mustn't," she cried weakly when he did.

"Aye, I must," he told her. He found her sensitive little jewel and began to worry it, gently at first, and then more insistently.

"Oh! Oh!" Philippa half sobbed. What was he doing? And why did it feel so . . . so . . . absolutely wonderful? This could not be right. The joining was for procreation, but then a small part of her reason deliberated that they had not yet been joined. She shivered with the small wave of pleasure that washed over her, not realizing at first that he had pushed a single finger into her love channel.

God's nightshirt, the earl silently swore to himself, she was very tight. And his finger quickly found her maidenhead. It was fully intact, proving her innocence. He moved the finger within her, and suddenly aware, Philippa cried out.

"No!"

"Aye, little one, 'tis time," he said, and he mounted her quickly, pulling her resistant thighs apart and positioning himself for the attack. He had been ready almost from the moment he had entered their bedchamber. He was hard as rock, and he could feel his member throbbing with its eagerness to do battle. He began to move forward.

"No!" Philippa cried again. "No!"

He gently restrained her as his manhood pushed past her nether lips and into the entry of her love sheath. Despite her protests she was very wet with her budding desire. Slowly, slowly. His knob pushed into her, the ring of intimate flesh closing tightly about him as he moved his length forward, pressing deeper and deeper until he was met by the barrier of her maidenhood. He stopped.

"I cannot bear it," she sobbed. "You are too big. You will tear me asunder!"

There was nothing he could say, he knew, that would soothe her.

He must take her virginity quickly. He thrust hard, and the tiny shield of flesh gave way before him.

Philippa shrieked, more with surprise than pain. His manhood filled her full. She had never imagined such a feeling. He was moving in her now, his mumbled words attempting to soothe her, his own passions rising to obscure his reason. Suddenly she relaxed, and gave herself over to his desire. She didn't know what had prompted her to let go of control over herself, but she did. And when she did, her eyes closing, her entire being was suffused with a pleasure such as she had never known. His grip on her had loosened, and unable to help herself she began to caress the big lanky body laboring over her.

"Wrap your legs about me, little one!" He grated out the order in harsh tones.

Philippa obeyed, and felt him driving deeper into her body. She cried out softly with surprise. "Ohhh, Crispin!" she sighed, and she wondered what in the name of all the saints had she ever been fearful of? This was heaven on earth! This was divine! And this was how children were created? She sighed again, and then felt a shuddering beginning from deep within her. It rose up, enveloping her fiercely, and she cried out in fear at this new sensation, but then the warmth swept over her. She felt a rush of hot fluid filling her love sheath, and the earl gave a great groan that was half pleasure and half relief. Then he rolled away from her, but as he did he pulled her into his embrace, kissing her face, her lips, her eyes.

"Little one, little one," he finally managed to say to her. "I thank you for the gift of your innocence, and the pleasure that you gave me. I can only hope I gave you some pleasure as well, though I think I did."

"I forgot to pray, my lord," Philippa said. "I could think of nothing, it seems, when you were making love to me. I think I will not ever tell the queen of my lapse."

The earl of Witton burst out laughing. "Madame, I forbid you to ever pray while I labor over you. Passion is for pleasure, not piety. God help the poor queen who has never known that."

"You hurt me in the beginning," she said.

"The breaking of the maidenhead is said to hurt, I am told," he replied. "Did no one tell you that? But then they would not have, for fear of frightening you."

"But after, it was wonderful. I seemed to be on another plane. I flew, my lord, I will vow that I flew!" she said. "How often will we couple like that?"

"Whenever desire overtakes us, little one," he promised her, "but for now I would have us sleep. Tomorrow we start for Brierewode, and in a few weeks we must depart for France. I want you to see your new home before we do. It has been a long day, Philippa. You must rest now. I will be by your side to keep you safe. I do not believe in the nonsense some practice of a husband and wife sleeping in different chambers, and only coming together for the pleasure. From this night on I shall sleep by your side."

"I am glad," she told him. "My parents always shared a bed, and mama and my stepfather do as well. I am not unhappy with your decision, my lord."

She drew the down coverlet up to cover them both. There seemed no point to getting out of bed to fetch their chemises. She tucked the coverlet about his shoulders, and he was charmed by this sweet sign of her nurturing nature. He was beginning to suspect that he had made a good bargain with Lord Cambridge, and he also suspected that Thomas Bolton had known it. He drew Philippa closer, and she laid her auburn head on his shoulder. They slept.

In the early dawn the earl of Witton awoke. His bride was still cuddled next to him. He studied her carefully, realizing that she was quite a pretty creature. Her skin was very fair, and her auburn hair had golden lights in it, unlike her sister Banon, whose tresses were a deeper auburn in color. Just looking at her aroused him, and he was surprised by it, but then of course she was a new sensation for him. Nay, that was not it. He had never been so roused by any woman. He ran a gentle hand down the curve of her body as she lay on her side by him.

Philippa opened her eyes, startled, and then she remembered where she was. Her eyes met his, and she blushed at the intimacy that surrounded them. She was not used to it, but she supposed in time she would be. She gave him a small smile. He said nothing, pushing her onto her back and mounting her. For some reason it seemed right, and she was to her surprise eager for them to couple again. She slid her arms about him, drawing him down into an embrace as he pushed himself slowly into her eager body. "Ahh, that is good," she told him softly.

"Tell me what it feels like when I am inside of you," he said low.

"It is difficult to explain," she began. "I find I already enjoy the feel of you as you enter my love channel. You fill me, and I feel myself wanting to draw you in further. I want to enclose my flesh about your manhood. I never want to let it go. I lose my identity as we become one, my lord."

"I feel powerful when our bodies are joined," he admitted to her. "I am the aggressor, and yet somehow you control me, Philippa. Ah, little one, to be inside you I find unbearably sweet," he said. And then he began to kiss her mouth.

He kissed her until Philippa's head was spinning. The sensation of his lips on her, his manhood inside her, was almost too incredible to bear. He filled her and his member throbbed, beating against the walls of her love channel until she was moaning with her eagerness to be totally possessed. "Do it!" she begged him. "Do it, and do not stop!"

He moved slowly within her, increasing his tempo and rhythm until Philippa's head was thrashing wildly on the pillows. The sight of her desire for him was almost unbearable. He thrust harder and deeper until she began to scream softly with her pleasure.

Philippa wrapped her legs about him, allowing him deeper access. It was incredible, and she now understood her mother better, she thought, than she ever had before. Her head was spinning, and yet she still managed some control over herself as the pleasure began to burgeon and grow until she knew she was going to die, and she didn't care. Only the desire counted for anything. Her body began to shake from the inside out. She was dying! "Crispin!" she cried his name. "Crispin!" And then her consciousness was sucked down into a whirling dark vortex of heated pleasures.

He heard her crying his name as she clung to him, but he could only concentrate on the emotions battering him. He could feel himself swelling and growing within her until it was almost unbearable and painful. But then suddenly his member released its hot tribute in spurt after spurt after spurt of his love juices. For a moment he thought that his juices would never stop coming. Would his young bride always have this wickedly lustful effect upon him? God's boots, he hoped so, even if in the end it killed him!

They slept again, this time exhausted, sprawled upon the bed, their limbs intertwined, leg with leg. And when they finally awoke the sun was just coming up. Outside in the gardens the birds were singing a May song.

Philippa had awakened first this time. She extricated herself carefully from the tangle of their limbs, her eyes studying her husband, blushing at the memories of their recent passion. He had such a strong and vibrant body. Her gaze went to his manhood, and she was amazed to find it limp, and surprisingly small now considering its earlier state.

"You have only worn it out for now, but it will recover," she heard him say. His eyes remained closed, however.

"Oh!" She blushed at being caught in her perusal. "I have never seen a man's body until now," she weakly explained to him.

He chuckled, and now the gray eyes slowly opened. "I hope it is all that you expected," he said.

"I didn't know quite what to expect, my lord, but I cannot say that I am disappointed in what I have found," Philippa told him.

"Another night I will teach you to fondle it, for it enjoys the touch of a woman's hand, little one, but for now we must arise, although I am tempted to stay abed when I see those adorable little breasts of yours so prettily displayed."

She drew the coverlet up to cover herself, mischievously sticking her tongue out at him. "I have removed the temptation, my lord," she told him.

He grinned. "Only my desire to take you to Brierewode before we leave for France prevents me from spending the day here in bed with you, madame," he explained. "You have proven a most satisfactory armful, Philippa, my lady countess of Witton."

"And you, my lord, have allayed all of my fears of the marriage bed," she replied. She slipped from the bed and, finding her chemise, drew it on. Then opening the door to the dayroom she called, "Lucy! His lordship and I will have a bath now."

Lucy jumped from the chair where she had been sitting awaiting her mistress's call. She had not dared to enter the bridal chamber this morning. "At once, my lady. Where shall I have them set it up? Out here?"

"Aye, 'tis best. Is the fire hot?" Philippa asked her serving woman.

"Aye, 'tis blazing and very warm," Lucy replied.

Philippa turned back into the bedchamber. "We shall bathe this morning, for we shall not have the opportunity along the road. Here is something you must learn about me. Unlike so many at court I bathe regularly, and not just once or twice a year. I should like you to bathe with me this morning, my lord."

" 'Tis not a habit I find distasteful, madame," he answered her. "I will be pleased to share your bath."

"I shared with Banon yesterday, but usually I bathe alone," Philippa explained. "Please be as modest as you can before my tiring woman, my lord."

It took some time, but the tub was eventually ready for them. Lucy waited in the dayroom for her mistress and her new master. She had already asked the earl's valet to lay out fresh clothing for his master in the little chamber next to the bedchamber where Philippa had once slept as a girl. The man moved briskly through the dayroom as the newlyweds washed each other in the large tub. Lucy busied herself in the bedchamber, taking the sheet with the bloodied evidence of her mistress's virtue off the bed, and setting it aside for Lord Cambridge's view. Then she laid out clothing for Philippa. The trunks were already packed, although Philippa would leave all of her court clothing in London where it would be ready when they returned on their way to Dover. Lucy smiled as she heard Philippa giggle, and the earl's guffaw of laughter. The wedding night had obviously gone well, and she was glad for her mistress's sake that it had.

"How long will it take us to reach Brierewode?" Philippa asked the earl as they bathed in their tub by the fire.

"Several days. Lord Cambridge and I arranged the trip together. We will go by barge to Henley and then ride crosscountry to Cholsey where we will take the river as far as Oxford. From there we will ride. It is probably quicker to ride all the way, but I wanted us to have time alone, little one. I hope you are not unhappy with my plans."

"It sounds most romantic, my lord," she told him. "I have never been up the river so far. And it is May. Everything will be coming into bloom."

Finished bathing, they each joined their servants and dressed. Philippa's gown of deep blue light velvet had a filled-in neckline with a little wing collar of linen. The sleeves were fitted from shoulder to elbow and had a ruffled linen cuff. The skirt was of one piece with a cord and chain belt from which hung a pomander case. It was the perfect traveling gown, and she would wear it each day. The earl wore a deep blue coat which was pleated from a high yoke and had a velvet collar and lining. It hung to his ankles. His shoes were embroidered.

Descending to the hall they ate a hearty meal of oat stirabout, sharing a bread trencher from which they dipped the cereal. There was ham, hard-boiled eggs, butter, cheese, and Philippa's favorite cherry jam for the cottage loaf. Remembering Lucy's warning of yesterday about morning ale and the bloat, Philippa drank watered wine as she had when she was a child. When they had finished eating they prepared to embark on the river.

"His lordship's man and I will meet you and the earl at the inn where you will be spending the night," Lucy said.

"You aren't coming with us?" Philippa was surprised.

"No room for a tiring woman and a middle-aged valet on a honeymoon voyage," Lucy chuckled. "There's a basket of food for your midday repast, and the oarsmen have food as well. You'll be fine, my lady."

"Come along, little one," the earl called to his bride, and he took Philippa's hand in his to lead her from the house and down through the garden to the riverside stairs, down to the quai where their barge awaited them.

It was a fair day, a perfect first of May.

"They will already be dancing at court," Philippa noted with a smile.

"Are you sorry not to be there?" he asked her.

"I should like to be there," she admitted, "but only if we might be together, Crispin."

He chuckled. "Lord Cambridge is correct when he says you are a perfect courtier, and I might add that you have a diplomat's tongue, Philippa, and I should certainly know that, having been in his majesty's diplomatic service." He helped his wife down into the beautiful little barge that Thomas Bolton had had made for his cousin, Rosamund, many years before.

It was a pretty little vessel with a cabin containing a bench upholstered in sky blue velvet. There were glass windows that could be lowered on either side of the bench, which was hollowed beneath so braziers of coals could be set there in the winter months. Outside and behind the cabin on the open deck were two upholstered oak chairs, with arms, beneath a blue and gold striped awning. In front of the cabin the two oarsmen sat in a recess in the deck, ready and waiting for their orders. The earl seated his wife in one of the chairs beneath the awning, and sitting next to her called to the oarsmen that they were ready. The barge pulled away from the quai belonging to Bolton House.

The tide was with them, and the barge moved smoothly up the river. Philippa gazed fascinated at the river traffic as it passed them on its way down into London. There were barges carrying early farm produce and flowers. Some barges carried livestock, and others, building materials. Eventually, however, they had the river to themselves. They passed farms, meadows, and small villages. Here and again as the river narrowed their barge glided beneath a bridge. There were waterfowl nesting in the reeds and marshes along the river's edge. There were even several swan couples, with their cygnets swimming neatly in a row between their parents.

"It has been a long time since I have been in the countryside," Philippa noted.

"You do not like the country," he said.

"Nay, I do. I just need to be near enough to court that I may enjoy it as well. My mother's Friarsgate is so very far from London that it takes forever to get back and forth. She never really liked the court. Her passion is for her estates," Philippa explained. "And she and Uncle Thomas set up their cotters in a manufactory to weave the wool mama's sheep produce. They decided it was foolish to send the wool to the Low Countries to be woven when it would provide work for the cotters in the winter. Our wool is exceedingly fine, especially a blue cloth that we do, and so it has been quite successful. They even regulate the amount of that blue the mercers in Carlisle and the European countries can have."

"That is very clever," the earl said. "They keep the demand high by keeping the supply low. Your mother, it would appear, is a very clever woman, Philippa."

"Aye, she is," Philippa agreed, "but you can understand, knowing me as you do, why I did not want the responsibility of Friarsgate."

"You will find Brierewode a less complicated home, little one. You need only manage the household, and our children."

"Not you, my lord?" she asked him mischievously.

He laughed. "I can see we will have a certain number of battles, madame, but you will learn to remember that I am the master of Brierewode, and there can be but one master." Then he kissed the tip of her nose.

"My lord," Philippa said, and her cheeks were flushed with irritation, "I will not be treated like a mindless little flibbertigibbet. I may not want the management of Friarsgate, but I am more useful than you would appear to realize. And I shall be the mistress of Brierewode. And I will be at court serving my mistress, Queen Katherine, for part of the year as well. The queen appreciates my value."

"Your first duty is to produce an heir for me, Philippa," he said. "Do not forget that, little one." The gray eyes met her eyes.

"Are you going back on your promise to go to France, my lord? We are expected!" Philippa cried.

"And we will go. I do not give my word lightly," the earl responded. Then he caressed her face gently. "I may have already put a babe in your belly, madame," he told her, and he laughed softly when she blushed at his words. "You were a most receptive and very passionate little virgin, Philippa." His lips brushed her forehead lightly.

"My lord! Do not speak of such intimacies aloud. We could be overheard by our bargemen," she scolded him primly.

"Twice," he reminded her in a low voice, "twice you drew my seed most eagerly into your hidden garden where babes are first created. God's boots, just thinking about it makes me want you again, little one."

"My lord!" Her eyes pleaded with him for caution.

"I could have you here," he murmured, taking her hand and pressing it against his heated manhood which was covered by his long coat. "Perhaps later I shall set you upon my lap, slowly, slowly pull up your pretty skirts, and impale you on my lover's lance. Then I should teach you to ride your eager stallion while I muffled your cries with my kisses, Philippa. Would you like that, madame?"

"My lord, you make me blush. Your bold words are shameful," she said, but her hand did not pull away from his groin.

"When we get home I shall teach you to hold it and fondle it, little one," he told her meaningfully. Then he put her hand back in her lap.

Philippa turned her eyes to the river again. Her heart was beating furiously. She felt hot all over, and the gentle breeze upon the river did nothing to cool her. She closed her eyes in an effort to calm herself, but all she could think of was her wedding night, and of the pleasure he had given her. She kept remembering what the queen had taught her maids. The coupling of a married couple was for the purpose of procreation, that more souls be born and baptized in Holy Mother Church. The queen had never said anything about pleasure, and Philippa wasn't at all certain that she should be enjoying coupling with her husband as much as she had. Nor was she sure the seductive words he was whispering in her ear should be exciting her so. Or that she should be looking forward to being in his arms again, being possessed so completely by him. She started when he took her hand up again, her eyes flying open to look at him.

He kissed her hand, and each finger on it in its turn, and then her palm. "Do not fret so, little one," he told her. He had seen the play of emotions as they had raced across her lovely face. "It's going to be alright, I promise." Then still holding her little hand in his he turned his own gaze to the river they traveled.

Philippa closed her eyes again, realizing that she was tired. Her position at court allowed for little rest, and these last few weeks leading up to their wedding, and then last night. Aye, she was tired. But she was no longer afraid. She wished Banon were here so she could tell her. But Banon would know soon enough that marriage, whatever God might have intended, promised to be wonderful if you were shackled with the right man.

Chapter 14

⁓⧯⁓

The barge pulled near the shore of the river and anchored so they might eat. The two oarsmen carried the earl and his wife to the riverbank on their backs so they would not get wet. Then they returned to fetch the basket of food.

"Go out of sight of this place," the earl ordered them. "I will call you when we are ready to resume our trip. You made excellent time. We shall be at the King's Head by sunset. You have food?"

"Aye, milord. And our thanks. We'll eat and rest a bit," one of the oarsmen said. They both bowed, and then moved off upstream and into a stand of trees.

Philippa spread the cloth in her basket on the ground and sat down, her skirts blossoming about her. "Come, my lord, and eat," she invited him.

In the basket they found meat pastries baked this morning, wrapped in a linen cloth, and still warm. There were pieces of roasted capon, bread, cheese, and a small pottery crock filled with strawberries, along with sugar wafers. There was a stone bottle, and uncorking it they discovered it was filled with red wine. The air had grown warmer as they had traveled that morning. They ate, emptying the basket of its supplies.

"I think this is one of the nicest May Days I have ever had,"

Philippa told her husband. "And this morning along the river was lovely."

"We will pass Windsor this afternoon," he told her.

"I don't think I have ever seen it from the river," Philippa answered him. "We used the river from Richmond to Greenwich, but I have never been above Bolton House until the other day. I quite like it." She lay back upon the grass, with a contented sigh.

With a smile he lay next to her, taking her hand in his. "I will be honest with you, Philippa. Traveling by barge was Lord Cambridge's idea. He said if the weather was fine we should do it. He said it was romantic, and less troublesome than being in a coach or riding. I was not enthusiastic, but I agreed to go along with his idea. Now I am glad that I did. It is a fine way to spend May Day." Raising himself up on an elbow he looked down into her face, and then he kissed her.

"Crispin," she murmured against his mouth, "the oarsmen."

He raised his ash brown head, and smiled wickedly at her. "Why do you think I sent them out of sight, Philippa? They understood my instructions, and the reasons behind them. Now do not fuss at me, my prim little bride. I have every intention of making love to you in this treed glade. If you do not allow me to satisfy my lust for you here and now, then sometime this afternoon as we are rowed along, I shall have you as I earlier described, little one. The choice is yours to make."

She could see in his gray eyes that there would be no bargaining with him. "I think you are very wicked, my lord. What if a shepherd or a milkmaid should come upon us, and catch us in flagrant delicto?"

He pushed her skirts up, and his palms slid over her milky thighs. "A man with his wife can hardly be called a sinner, madame," he replied. "God's boots, you are deliciously tempting, Philippa!" He kissed her hard, his tongue pressing past her lips.

Why did she feel so weak when he assaulted her senses like this? Her mouth opened to suck his tongue into her mouth. She was acutely aware of his fingers playing between her nether lips. Her breasts felt as if they would burst from her bodice, and she silently cursed the lacing up the back of her gown. He had found that sensitive little nub of flesh, and was now worrying it with a fingertip. Philippa moaned. "Crispin, that is really quite wicked of you. You must stop."

"Why?" he asked low, and pushed two fingers into her love sheath.

"I don't know," she whispered. "Oh, that should not be so good!"

"Why?" he demanded a second time, and his body covered her, his manhood replacing his fingers as he pushed into her.

"Oh Holy Mother of God, it is too sweet, my lord!" She could feel every inch of him as he filled her. She felt his length. His thickness. His warmth.

"It's good, isn't it, Philippa?" he murmured softly, his tongue licking at her ear. "It's very, very good. Tell me you want me even as I desire you, my little one."

"Yes!" she sobbed. "Yes!" And then she cried out softly as he began to move upon her, slowly at first, and then more rapidly until they were both gasping with the pleasure the union of their two bodies was giving them.

Afterwards they dozed for a brief period, and then the earl arose, straightening his gown back into a semblance of order. Philippa opened her eyes and gazed up at him. She had never anticipated that this elegant and urbane man would be so passionate. She had never anticipated that she would be so passionate. Turning, he saw she was awake again, and reaching down he drew her up into his embrace, and kissed her gently.

"We must go now," he said. "I will call the oarsmen."

She nodded. "Is my attire neat?" she asked him.

He brushed her skirts, and then smiled at her. "You are perfect, madame."

"Next time unlace my bodice, Crispin," she told him. "I had difficulty breathing, I fear. Perhaps all my gowns should now lace in the front rather than the rear."

"Perhaps they should," he agreed with a grin. "I missed those adorable little fruits that you possess, Philippa. Tonight I shall apologize to them for my neglect."

"I will not couple with you in a public inn!" she declared indignantly.

"On a riverbank, but not an inn?" he teased her.

"People might hear us," she said.

He laughed. "We will see the accommodation we are given," the earl told her.

"Even the best accommodation will not guarantee us enough privacy, and we are fortunate not to be coming down from the north," she replied. "Uncle Thomas and I stayed mostly at convent and monastery guesthouses where the sexes are separated."

"I should not like that," he responded, and now it was Philippa who laughed.

She gathered up the cloth, folding and tucking it in their basket. There was no food, for they had eaten everything that had been packed for them. The earl sought out their two oarsmen. They were once again carried upon their servants' backs to the barge, and settling themselves, they sat back to enjoy the river views as they once again got under way.

They passed the great castle of Windsor, its towers and battlements soaring over the Thames. It had always looked large to Philippa but from her vantage on the river it looked huge and almost forbidding. She thought of the autumn hunting parties she had joined as the queen's maid of honor. Their barge left Windsor behind, and to the east she could see the Chiltern Hills of Berkshire. They reached the King's Head Inn shortly after sunset, but the sky would be light for several more hours to come with the spring twilight. Lucy and the earl's valet, Peter, were awaiting them. Lord Cambridge had engaged an entire wing of the inn for the newlyweds. There was a large bedchamber for the earl and his bride, two small chambers for their servants, and a private dining room. The two oarsmen would be fed in the inn's kitchens, and housed in the stables for the night.

"The dinner was pre-ordered by Lord Cambridge, milord," Peter told his master.

"Have the innkeeper serve it then," the earl said. "It has been a long day, and I can see her ladyship is anxious for her bed."

"Yes, milord," the valet answered politely.

Lucy had taken her mistress into the bedchamber, where she had a basin of water waiting so Philippa might wash herself. "The trip weren't half bad," she told her mistress. "That Peter of his lordship's is a good fellow, and pleasant company. Was your river voyage a nice one, my lady?"

"You should have seen Windsor from the water," Philippa told her. "It looked twice the size it looks riding up to it. I felt very tiny in our little barge. Everything is so different when you travel upon the river. How clever of Uncle Thomas to arrange it." She bathed her face and hands, telling Lucy when she finished, "Go and get your supper now, lass. But come back to prepare me for bed."

"Thank you, my lady," Lucy replied, curtseying. And when she had escorted Philippa back into the dining chamber she hurried off, Peter in her wake.

The innkeeper himself arrived with three serving wenches struggling beneath the weight of three large trays. "Good evening, my lord, my lady. I am Master Summers, and I shall serve you myself." He beamed effusively at them as the earl seated his bride.

He offered the earl a dish of cold fresh oysters, and Crispin St. Claire grinned to himself. Tom Bolton was hardly being subtle, he thought. Oysters for himself, and gazing across the table he watched his young wife eating fresh green asparagus in a lemony sauce, sucking the meat from the stalks and licking her lips enthusiastically.

"I adore asparagus!" Philippa enthused. "How kind of Lord Cambridge to remember it." She had no idea how her innocent consumption was affecting her husband.

The trays now revealed a roast of beef from which the innkeeper carved several slices; a well-browned duck, its skin crisp and golden, in a sauce of orange and raisins; individual little pastries filled with minced venison and sweet onions cooked in butter; a platter of little lamb chops; a bowl of tiny carrots, and another bowl of small onions swimming in butter and cream that had been sprinkled with fresh dill. The innkeeper filled their plates. He poured a fragrant wine into their goblets. Lastly he took a fresh cottage loaf, still hot from the oven, and placed it between them with a large crock of butter.

"Your lordship will find an apple tartlet and clotted cream on the sideboard," he told the earl as he bowed himself out of the room, shooing his serving girls before him. He shut the door with a firm click.

Crispin and Philippa burst out laughing.

"I see Uncle Thomas's hand in this," she giggled. "Poor Master Summers has been given most specific and careful instructions by him. I expect he visited in person to deliver his orders to this innkeeper."

"Well, I shall not fault him, little one. The menu is perfect, and the food delicious," the earl told her. "I can only hope each inn in which we stay is as good."

"It will be," Philippa replied. She knew Thomas Bolton well, and with each passing moment she realized she owed him a greater debt than she could ever repay him. And she was certainly enjoying the bedsport she and her husband shared. The earl was a kind man. She had to give him an heir as soon as she might. But first they would go to France for the glorious summer progress. In the autumn they would visit her mother, and then it would be back to court for the Christmas revels. They would spend the winter in Oxfordshire, but then it would be back to court for the month of May, a year from now. There simply wasn't time for her to give Crispin an heir until the end of next year. She hoped he would understand.

Philippa Meredith did not have an important family, although she did now possess a title. But she had Queen Katherine's friendship, a fact she knew drew the envy of other women and girls from families of greater significance. Philippa's loyalty to the queen was as great as her mother's had been. She would serve Katherine of Aragon as long as the queen asked it of her. This was something she was not certain her husband fully comprehended yet. She prayed silently that she could make him understand. Women, after all, possessed their own personal honor too.

It was still light when they had finished their meal. Outside their windows they heard music, flutes, and drums and cymbals. Going to the window they saw a Maypole had been set up on the village green, and the dancers were even now assembling. Philippa looked at her husband questioningly, and he nodded. There was a door leading to the outside in the corridor outside their apartments. Hand in hand they strolled out to watch the girls and boys dancing around the Maypole, weaving the colored ribbons about the tall pole as they pranced and capered. It was a perfect ending to the day.

He made love to her again that night, cajoling her with the fact their rooms were at the far end of the inn. He was tender and gentle, as he had previously been. In the morning after breakfast they once again embarked, traveling as far as Henley that afternoon. The Queen's Arms was as fine an establishment as the King's Head had been. They were housed in another large and private apartment. The food was excellent. They made love in the night as they had the previous night. And in the morning they left the barge to ride across the countryside to the village of Cholsey. The day was sunny, and all around them the woods and fields were burgeoning with new green growth.

The next day the earl gifted Lord Cambridge's two bargemen and sent them back down the river. They had so enjoyed the ride the day before that they decided to go on to Oxford by horseback rather than spending another day on the river. Philippa had been to Oxford once before, with the queen when they had traveled to Woodstock. She found the hustle and bustle of the town invigorating, and preferred it to London. The inn that Lord Cambridge had chosen was on the edge of the city on the road they would take tomorrow to Brierewode.

"We can reach it if we leave just at first light," the earl told Philippa.

"I can be ready," she promised. "I can see how anxious you are to be there, my lord. And I am curious to see my new home."

"You will love it," he promised her.

She smiled, but she thought it is just another country house. It is not court. I shall be quickly bored, but then in just a few weeks we will rejoin the king and queen.

The following morning was gray and cloudy, the first dull day since their wedding on April thirtieth. But it was not raining. They departed Oxford in a dim half-light. They had been met at Henley by a troupe of hired men-at-arms who had accompanied them ever since. Behind them Lucy and Peter followed upon their own mounts, riding next to the vehicle carrying the bride's possessions. The innkeeper at the Saracen's Head in Oxford had seen them off with a hamper of food for their ride. They stopped only briefly, more to rest the horses than themselves, and quickly ate. Then they were on the road again.

In late afternoon the earl called to Philippa over the noise of the horses' hooves. "We are almost there, little one. Look up ahead. It is my village of Wittonsby. You can see the church steeple."

"What is the river we ride along?" she asked him.

"The Windrush," he answered. "You can see it from the house, and around the next bend you will see Brierewode up there on the hillside." He was smiling.

As they rounded the curve in the road Philippa gazed up, and there was a beautiful gabled gray stone house with several tall chimneys. It did not look at all grand, and she found she was very relieved. She was not certain she could have managed a sumptuous dwelling. "It's lovely," she told him, smiling back.

In the meadows along the river there were cattle grazing. The fields they passed were newly tilled, the rich brown earth smooth and ready for planting. The workers in the fields looked up as they passed by. Recognizing their master a shout went up, and they waved enthusiastically as he rode on. Crispin St. Claire waved back. Philippa could see right away that her husband was well liked by his people.

The village was set along the riverbank, which was lined with ancient willows. The stone cottages were neatly kept, from their thatched roofs to their little front door gardens. There was a fountain in the village square across from the steepled stone church, and it was here they stopped. The earl's tenants came from their houses and from their fields to greet him. The priest, alerted by one of the children, came forth from the church.

The earl held up his hand for silence, and was obeyed. "I have brought you a new countess," he said. "Greet Lady Philippa, countess of Witton, who became my wife in Queen Katherine's own chapel six days ago."

The priest stepped forward and bowed. He was not a young man, but neither was he an old man. "Welcome home, my lord, and welcome to Wittonsby, my lady. May God bless your union with many children. I am Father Paul."

A stocky ruddy-faced man stepped forward next. "Welcome home, milord," he said with a small awkward bow. "I am relieved you were not gone for too long a time. Milady." He pulled politely at his forelock in greeting. Then he turned to the crowd of villagers, and called out, "Let's have three cheers for his lordship and his bride! Huzzah! Huzzah! Huzzah!" And the others in the small square joined him.

"This is my bailiff, Bartholomew, little one," the earl told Philippa. "He's a good man is Barto. My countess and I thank you all for your kind greetings," he said to the crowd. Then with a wave of his hand the earl led his party from the village square, and up the treed hill to the house known as Brierewode.

The earl's majordomo was awaiting them as they rode up to the house, and there were stable boys to take their horses as they dismounted. "Welcome home, milord, my lady," the majordomo said, bowing. "Shall I see to the men-at-arms?"

"Aye," the earl responded. "Feed them, house them, and in the morning have Robert pay them for their service." He turned to Philippa, and surprised her by picking her up in his strong arms and carrying her across the open threshold of the house, depositing her gently in the hallway. "Old custom," he said with a grin.

"I know," she said, laughing. "But I had forgotten." She looked about her. "Show me everything, Crispin. I cannot rest until I see it all."

Now he laughed. "Are you not tired with all our traveling, little one?"

"Aye, but this is to be my home, and my curiosity is outweighing my exhaustion," she told him. "First, the hall!" And she took him by the hand, looking questioningly.

The hall of Brierewode was paneled in a dark wood. Its ceiling soared, and from the carved and gilded beams hung colorful flags which, the earl explained to his wife, were the banners that his ancestors had carried into battle in England, Scotland, and the Holy Land. It was the oldest part of the house.

"We have always fought for God, king, and country, Philippa," he told her.

There was a very large stone fireplace on one side of the hall. It was ablaze now, warming the room. Across from it were three tall arched glass windows that looked out over the river Windrush, which flowed through the valley below the hill upon which the house was situated. At the far end of the room was the high board, and behind it two high-backed chairs. There were several bed spaces in the walls of the chamber.

"It is a very old hall," Philippa said, seeing them.

"The house has been here in one form or another for over three hundred years," he replied. "We have made certain improvements over the years. The kitchens are now below us, and not in a separate building. There is an open shaft over there by the fire. Inside it is a platform that can be drawn up and down from kitchens to hall by means of a rope and pulley. That way the food arrives hot at table."

"That is a most modern arrangement," she said, surprised. Then, "What else is on this floor of the house, my lord?"

"There is a room where the bailiff, Robert, my secretary, and I discuss the business of Brierewode between us. And I have a library of books. Can you read?"

"Of course," she told him proudly. "And I can write and do accounts, for it was expected that one day I would manage Friarsgate. My mother does not believe in allowing others to have so great a control over her fortune. My sisters and I can do all of these things, and we speak foreign languages as well. I came to court knowing French, and both church and spoken Latin as well as Greek. I have learned a little Italian and German at court. The Venetians are so charming, I have found. My mother's portrait was painted by a Venetian once. It hangs in the hall at Friarsgate."

The earl looked momentarily startled. There had been a portrait of a nymph in diaphanous garments with a single bared breast in the hall of the duke of San Lorenzo. He had admired it when he had gone to attempt to repair the damage Lord Howard, the king's ambassador, had done. He had seen it only once, for he had been received by the duke only once. Thinking back, he realized it bore a startling resemblance to his wife. He would have to learn one day why that was. It was not Philippa, he knew. She had not that sensual look about her yet. It had been the look of a woman well loved, and in love. He must remember to ask Thomas Bolton about it when they next met.

"May I use your library?" Philippa asked him.

"Of course!"

"Show me more now," she demanded.

"There is little more to see other than the bedchambers, and the attics where the servants sleep, little one. Would you not enjoy exploring them yourself one day when I am about my business in the fields?"

"Aye, I suppose I should. It will keep me from being bored," she told him.

"Milord, welcome home." A tall, large-boned woman had entered the hall. She curtseyed to them politely, and then she said, "Your ladyship, I am Marian. I have the honor to be the housekeeper here at

Brierewode, and I am at your service." She handed a ring of keys to Philippa. "You will want these," she said.

"Keep them for me, Marian," Philippa said warmly. "I am the stranger here, and I will need you to guide my steps until I am more comfortable. And I shall be at court much of the time, for I am in the service of our good queen."

The housekeeper's head nodded. "Thank you for your trust in me, my lady."

"If my husband trusts you then so do I," Philippa responded. "I have brought my tiring woman with me. She is to have her own chamber, a small one, but hers nonetheless, and it should be near mine. Her name is Lucy, and she is no London slut, but a lass from my own home in Cumbria."

"I will see to it, my lady," Marian said. "May I show you your apartment now?"

"Go along," the earl encouraged his wife. "I must speak with Barto and Robert before the day ends." He kissed Philippa on her lips, and then went off.

"You are in service to Queen Katherine?" Marian sounded impressed by this knowledge. She led Philippa from the hall and up a wide flight of stairs.

Philippa noticed that the banisters were beautifully carved, even on the edges of the handrails. "My mother was a friend of the queen from the days before she wed with King Henry. I have been in her service since I was twelve years of age. I am now sixteen. The earl and I are invited to join the summer progress to France when our king and the French king will meet. I will remain with my mistress until she no longer requires my services. It is an honor to serve her. She is the kindest of ladies."

"We are fortunate in our queen, yet the king has no heir," Marian said.

"Princess Mary will rule us one day," Philippa replied.

"Mayhap the queen will yet bear a living son," Marian responded hopefully.

Philippa shook her head. "Alas, there is no hope of that now, I fear, unless God grants England a miracle."

Marian stopped before a pair of double doors, and flung them open. "These are your apartments, my lady," she said, ushering the young countess inside.

Lucy was already there, and she hurried forward, stopping to curtsey to her mistress. "It's lovely, my lady!" she burst out. "We will be so happy here, I know."

Philippa laughed. "When we are not at court, Lucy, I'm sure we will. Have you been properly presented to Mistress Marian, the housekeeper, yet?"

Lucy nodded politely. "Mistress," she said.

The older woman smiled. "Lucy," she replied, "if you feel you can leave your lady for a brief time, I shall take you and introduce you to the rest of the staff. You have traveled with Peter, my lord's valet. He is my brother. He has already said you are a mannerly lass, with no high London ways about you."

"My lady?" Lucy looked to Philippa.

"Go along," Philippa said with a nod. "I shall explore while you are gone."

"I realize you will not have had time for a proper meal today, my lady, but we did not know when to expect the earl home. The supper will be simple," Marian told her new mistress.

"We are both tired from our travels, Marian, and more anxious for rest. Whatever you have prepared will do us tonight. Tomorrow we will discuss food. You will tell me what pleases the earl, and I will tell you what I like best."

"Very good, my lady," Marion said with a bow, and then together she and Lucy departed Philippa's company.

The new countess of Witton looked about her. She was in a paneled dayroom. There was a single fireplace even now blazing to take the damp off the May afternoon. The floors were almost black with age, but they were clean. There were three casement windows that overlooked part of the gardens. The furniture was oak. A rectangular table with twisted legs stood before the window. Upon it was an earthenware bowl of potpourri. There was a matching table in the center of the room with a second bowl of fragrance, and two heavy silver candlesticks. Before the fire were two high-backed chairs with woven cane backs and upholstered cushions. There was a small woven rug between the chairs before the fire. To Philippa's surprise there was a gray tabby curled up directly in the center of the rug. She laughed softly, but the beastie never even twitched an ear.

Philippa now opened a door on one side of the fireplace and stepped into the adjoining room. There was another fireplace that backed up on the one in the dayroom. The walls in this chamber were also paneled in light wood. The windows here, however, looked out over the river as well as the garden. They were hung with natural-colored linen and deep green velvet brocade draperies. There was a wooden settle to one side of the fireplace. It had a tapestried cushion. A table was set before the windows. A large wooden chest stood at the foot of the bed, which was draped with deep green velvet curtains hung from old brass rings. The bed was more than spacious. Indeed it was a very large bed. It had a linenfold headboard, and heavy twisted bedposts that held up its wood-paneled canopy. There was a small table on one side of the bed.

The furnishings in both rooms were old-fashioned, Philippa thought. Much like the furnishings at Friarsgate and Claven's Carn. It was a country house, and country people did not concern themselves with the latest styles in furniture. Any item in a household that remained sturdy and serviceable stayed in its place forever. She smiled to herself. Had she but traded one country house for another? Nay. At least Brierewode was within easy traveling distance of the court. They had spent several days drifting on the river, but Philippa suspected that if they had ridden straight through they would have cut their travel time by half. She opened another door on one side of the room. It was obviously a garderobe where her clothing could be stored, for she saw her husband's clothing there.

With Mistress Marian in her place as the longtime housekeeper it would be an easy establishment to run when they were here. She wondered if her husband would come to court with her all the time, or if he would choose to spend his time in Oxfordshire. She had decided that she liked Crispin St. Claire. He was intelligent, and he was witty. And she certainly enjoyed their bedsport. It did not matter that he was plain of face. She wondered what their children would look like. Philippa knew she was a very pretty girl. At least if their daughters resembled her, she thought.

Daughters. Sons. Just how many children did he want? Would she have? Her mother had borne eight babes, of which seven had lived. Would she have any more? She knew her mother well enough to know that it would be Rosamund who made that decision, and not her stepfather, Logan Hepburn. How did a woman make decisions like that? This was the disadvantage of marrying without her mother. But come the autumn when they met again she would ask Rosamund what to do. And Philippa knew that her mother would offer her knowledge to her eldest child.

She sat down on the settle by the warm fire, and before she knew it Philippa had fallen asleep. Lucy awakened her gently when she returned. Philippa yawned and stretched.

"I do not think I can even eat my supper," she told her tiring woman.

Lucy nodded. "I'm fair worn out myself, my lady. Let me get you out of your gown and into a fresh night chemise." She began to unlace Philippa's bodice. " 'Tis a very nice house into which we have come, my lady. The other servants are friendly and pleasant. Much like our Friarsgate folk. We won't be unhappy here." She worked briskly, divesting her mistress of her garments. "You have to eat something," she counseled Philippa. "There's a nice rabbit stew bubbling down in the kitchens. I'll bring you some water to wash the dust of the road off of you, and then go and fetch a nice bowl of it for you."

"In the morning I want a proper bath," Philippa said, yawning again.

"Of course you do," Lucy said. "I found the tub before you arrived. It's most satisfactory, my lady. Now you sit down while I get your basin of water."

Philippa sat down in her chemise upon the bed. Then unable to help herself she lay back upon the coverlet. Her eyes closed, snapped open as she attempted to keep herself awake, and then closed again. Finding her dozing, Lucy set the brass washbasin in the warm ashes of the fireplace, and tiptoed out to go down to the kitchens. Passing the hall she saw the earl in conversation with the bailiff. She stopped, and walking up to her master, caught his eye.

"Yes, Lucy?" he asked her.

"Your pardon, my lord, but I thought you should know that her ladyship is exhausted from your travels, and will be having a bowl of stew in her chamber." She curtseyed politely to him. "She cannot remain awake, poor lass."

"I will go to her as soon as I can," he said.

Lucy hurried off to get her mistress her supper. When she returned with a tray containing the stew, bread and butter, and a mug of cider, the earl was already there watching his wife sleep. Why, bless me! Lucy thought. He cares for her, or I am a gypsy whore. The look in his eye is tender. She set the tray down upon the table. Then going to Philippa's side she gently shook her shoulder. "My lady, come and eat. You will feel better for it, I promise, and here is your good lord waiting for you."

"Ummm," Philippa said, and then she opened her eyes. "Crispin," she said.

He smiled down at her. "Lucy is right, little one. A bit of food before you go to sleep again. Come," and he took her hand. "I will sit with you. Lucy, bring the tray here, and your mistress will eat in bed." He helped Philippa to sit up, propping pillows behind her back.

Lucy set the tray on her mistress's lap, and then stepped back.

Philippa looked sleepily at the bowl of stew, and shook her head. It smelled delicious, but she did not think she could eat.

The earl took up the spoon from the bowl and began to feed his wife. She opened her mouth, accepted the food, and swallowed. He repeated his actions until the bowl was empty. At that point Philippa took up the piece of buttered bread and mopped the gravy from the bowl with it before popping it into her mouth. She sighed, and reached for the cider which she drank as if parched.

"I cannot believe how exhausted I am," she told them.

"Your duties at court are tiring," the earl said quietly. "I hope that once we have children you will consider foregoing the pleasures you seem to enjoy there."

"I cannot simply dismiss my duties to the queen," she told him. "I owe her my loyalty."

"Lucy, remove the tray. I will call you when you are needed," the earl said. Then when the tiring woman had left the room he said to Philippa, "You have been a maid of honor for four years, madame. You are now a married woman. Your place will be assigned to another very shortly."

"We were invited to accompany the court to France," she reminded him.

"The queen knew how much you wanted to go, little one, and she has rewarded your loyalty. But once the summer progress is over you must take up your role as the countess of Witton first. I want an heir, and it is your duty to give me one. No one knows the obligations of a wife better than Queen Katherine, and should you ask her she would counsel you thusly, Philippa."

"You said you would let me remain with the court," Philippa replied.

"I said we would go to court. If you are not with child, then we shall go twice a year. For the Christmas revels, and for the month of May. I did not marry you because you were a maid of honor, little one."

"Nay, you did not!" she snapped at him. "You married me for Melville's lands."

"Aye, your dowry was of consequence in the matter," he agreed sanguinely.

Philippa glared angrily at him. "I could hate you!" she told him fiercely.

"Aye, I expect you could," he admitted, "but I hope you will not, little one. I find I am becoming used to your company. I should be lonely without it now. Is it really so terrible, not being at court?" He took her hand and kissed the palm, and then each finger.

"From the time I was ten years old and first went to court it has been all I have ever wanted," she told him.

"A girl's dream," he responded, "but you are now a woman, Philippa. Did you not dream of marriage and children, like other girls?"

"With Giles FitzHugh," she said, "aye, but then he deserted me for the church."

"And Lord Cambridge sought another husband for you, and by coincidence found me," the earl reminded her. "You said you were willing, little one, and you have hardly been reticent in my arms at night, or in a willow glade by the Thames."

"Should I not like our coupling then?" she demanded of him.

He chuckled. "Aye, you should like it, and I am well pleased that you do, Philippa, but part of the purpose of our bedsport is that you give me children. You cannot do that if you spend all your time at court, for I will not be with you. I will be here at Brierewode looking after my lands as I should."

"You are beginning to sound like my mother," she huffed at him.

"And you are beginning to sound like a spoiled child who will not accept the responsibilities that belong to her," he said seriously.

"If you feel that way, then why don't you just stay home while I go to France with the court?" she snapped. "You can husband your precious land then by yourself, for you surely do not need me for that."

"Because you are my wife now, and you will not go to France if I am not accompanying you, Philippa," he told her.

"Are you forbidding me to go?" she demanded, and he saw the light of battle in her hazel eyes.

"Nay, I am not, for I know how much it means to you, and I believe this meeting between King Henry and King Francois will be an amazing event that we will want to recount to our children one day." He kissed her little hand again. "Come, little one, release your anger, and make peace with me now. We have many years ahead in which we can fight with one another."

Philippa laughed in spite of herself. Her husband had great charm, and there was no denying it. "I will forgive you for upsetting me, Crispin," she told him wickedly.

He chuckled. She would always want the upper hand, he realized in that moment, and it would be up to him to let her think she had it most of the time. "I will send Lucy back to you so you may prepare yourself for bed, little one," he said. "I shall go down to the hall to eat now. You shall rest undisturbed tonight." Then he arose from his place at her bedside and, bowing, left her.

Lucy came back a few moments afterwards, and fetching the brass basin from the warm ashes of the fire helped her mistress bathe, and then don a clean night chemise. The tiring woman tucked the countess of Witton into her bed, and bidding her good night, left her. Philippa was quickly asleep, but she did awaken briefly once in the night to feel her husband's comfortable bulk against her back. It was, she decided before she fell back asleep, a very good sensation.

Chapter 15

﹏﹏﹏✦﹏﹏﹏

heir brief time at Brierewode was a revelation to Philippa. Her mother's lands were vast in comparison with her husband's, even with the addition of the Melville properties that she had brought Crispin as part of her dowry. Brierewode was far more civilized as well. Where Friarsgate had huge meadows and fields, Brierewode's small fields were neatly tilled and planted. The meadows where the earl's cattle grazed were enclosed by low hedges as a means of keeping the beasts from roaming. This new enclosure of pastures was raising a number of eyebrows, and in some cases causing outright disagreements between landowners, but the earl seemed to have no difficulty with any of his neighbors over it.

And the area was far more civilized than she had anticipated a country estate would be. Philippa was pleased. Any time she had to spend at Brierewode would not be dull. They had near neighbors, Crispin told her. It would be a fine place to raise the children that they would have. And there was the difficulty, for Philippa could find no way to explain to Crispin that her service to Queen Katherine came before all else in her life. The Merediths had a history of service to the Tudors. It was just that simple.

To her surprise Philippa had found a letter from her mother awaiting her at Brierewode. In it her mother included a recipe for preventing conception should she wish it. Enclosed had been a packet of wild carrot seeds, the brew's main ingredient.

"I don't know if the priest here would approve what you're doing," Lucy fretted. "It's your duty to give the earl an heir, my lady, and I know I'm bold to say it, but it is!"

"Mama takes the brew," Philippa said.

"Your mama has done her duty by both your da and the laird," Lucy shot back.

"It's only until we get back from France," Philippa replied.

"Oh, you plan on giving up the Christmas revels, and your position at court?" Lucy inquired innocently.

Philippa's eyes narrowed. "Are you unhappy in my service, Lucy?" she asked sweetly. "Would you like to return to the wilds of Cumbria perhaps?"

But Lucy had served her mistress long enough to know the threat was an idle one, and so she countered, "You would ask me to endanger my immortal soul, my lady?"

Philippa stamped her foot. "If my mother sent this to me, then she wants me to use it. Would you question the lady of Friarsgate? Annie would never question mama."

"Well, I ain't my sister!" Lucy said. Then she sighed. "Alright then, until we get back from France, my lady. You're fortunate he ain't got you with child by now. He's a vigorous husband, I can see."

Philippa blushed. "How can you see?" she demanded.

"You sleep side by side, and I'm the one that straightens your bed every morning," Lucy replied with a grin. "Those bedclothes are well rumpled more nights than not."

"Your eyes are too sharp, and your nose too long," Philippa answered sharply.

"I'll make the brew for you," Lucy promised. "You won't need it, however, until your monthly courses are run now, my lady. That's what the letter says."

"Sometimes I regret ever teaching you to read," Philippa muttered.

Then she added, "And not a word to my husband, or anyone else. Agreed?"

Lucy nodded. "If the earl knew, he'd pack me off to Cumbria himself," she said. "I like the south even as you do, my lady. If I went home they'd marry me off to some farmer's son, and I'd live in the north forever. Like I said. I ain't my sister, and content to look after a man and her bairns. Ever since that first trip we took together to Edinburgh when you was just a little girl I've had an itchy foot like you."

"But when I have children, Lucy, we will be stuck here at Brierewode," Philippa said wickedly, but Lucy was not in the least disquieted by her mistress's words.

"Now, my lady, you and I both know that once you have given the earl an heir or two you will cajole him into letting you go right back to court. So go to France, come home and do your duty, and all will be well," Lucy said sensibly.

Philippa nodded. "Did you know that Uncle Thomas has hired us a ship to go to France? We'll sail with the royal fleet, and the queen has asked me to take along several of her maids of honor. And we will have our own pavilion and not have to beg for sleeping space."

"Well, at least we'll be comfortable in that foreign place," Lucy said dubiously. "I ain't never been in a sailing ship, my lady. Will we be out of sight of the land?"

"I don't know," Philippa said. "I've never been to France myself."

"Well, I suppose if Annie, my sister, can cross the water in a sailing ship I can too," Lucy finally decided. "I ain't going to like it, but I'll do it."

Philippa rode across her husband's estates, and found herself relaxing with each passing day. It had been a long time since she had been away from the court. Crispin was diligent in his duties to both his lands and his wife. Philippa had to admit that she enjoyed the time spent in his arms. She had never really considered what this side of marriage would be like, but she was learning that she liked it. She liked it very much. She was almost sorry to realize their time at Brierewode was coming to an end, but they had to get to Dover to join the court.

The queen's nephew, who was both king of Spain and the new Holy Roman Emperor, would be coming just before they departed for France. Those of the court invited on the summer progress to France would be expected to be at Dover in time to greet Charles V. The emperor was just twenty, the son of Queen Katherine's deceased sister, and he had never met his aunt. He and the French king did not get on at all, for Francois, like Henry, had hoped to be elected Holy Roman Emperor. The honor, however, had gone to Charles of Spain.

They departed Brierewode on a rainy May morning. Philippa was more rested than she had been in years, and she was very excited. "We shall see you in the late autumn," she told Mistress Marian, her housekeeper, "before we return to court for the Christmas revels. I know Brierewode is safe in your capable hands."

The housekeeper nodded and smiled. It was difficult to be annoyed with Philippa. She was charming and mannerly. But all this traveling about! When was the lady going to remain home and do what was expected of her? "God speed you, my lady, my lord," she murmured politely.

They traveled directly down to London, stopping at Bolton House where Lucy, who had gone before them, was waiting with Philippa's trunks packed and ready.

"Wait until you see the gowns Lord Cambridge had made for you," she whispered excitedly to her mistress. "And suits for his lordship as well. I've packed them in a separate trunk. And I've taken your jewels from the secret place. 'Tis going to be such a grand event. Everyone is talking about it. Supper will be simple, for it's me doing the cooking. Everyone else has gone with his lordship back to Otterly, and the extras were paid and sent on their way."

"Serve the supper then in our apartments," Philippa said to her tiring woman. Then she sighed. "I suppose with none to haul water I can have no bath. I'm already filthy with our travel."

"I can do a little tub in the kitchens, my lady," Lucy said.

"And Peter and I will carry the water from the kitchen well," the earl said, coming upon them and hearing his wife's conversation.

"Oh, thank you, my lord!" Lucy dimpled.

Crispin St. Claire slid an arm about his new wife. "I shall remain to scrub your back, madame," he told her with a leer.

"And I will scrub yours, for you shall share the water with me, my lord," she replied. "We have been wed long enough for me to recognize that look in your eye, and I'll not lie with a man stinking of horses and the road."

"How fastidious you are, madame," he teased her. "I have never known such a woman for bathing, but I will admit you smell better than any woman I have ever known." He kissed the top of her head. "We may not be so fortunate in France."

"Wherever I am, Crispin, I will have my bath," she told him. "I know how many of my companions use scent to cover up their stink, but my nose is sharp. When we first were introduced I knew you bathed more than twice a year with water and soap."

He grinned. "I'll begin fetching the water," he told her, letting her go. "Peter!"

Lucy directed them to fill two large cauldrons which she then swung over the fire. "It will be a while before the water is hot enough for you," she said.

"Then let us eat here," Philippa decided. "It will save you the trouble of bringing it upstairs to us. We'll eat now before we bathe. What of the men-at-arms and the coachman? They must be fed too."

" 'Tis done. Peter and I took their meal out to the stables just a while ago," Lucy responded. "We're all eating the same tonight. Venison stew. I made two pots with what was left in the larder. Arranged it with his lordship's cook before we went to Oxfordshire at the beginning of the month." She bustled about, putting pewter plates and mugs upon the big kitchen table. She pulled a large loaf of bread from the warming oven and put it, with a board, a knife, and a crock of sweet butter, on the table. Then looking to the earl's manservant she snapped, "Peter! Get that jug of cider from the larder, and fill the gob-lets." Taking up a small cauldron she ladled stew into the two dishes. It was rich with a winy gravy that embraced the chunks of venison, the leeks, and the carrots in it.

"Sit down, sit down," the earl invited the two servants. "There's no sense in you waiting. The food will get cold, and cold venison stew is not pleasant to eat."

"Thank you, my lord," Peter said as Lucy added two more plates and mugs to the far end of the table, and filled the plates with stew.

They ate, and Philippa could hear the water for their baths begin-ning to boil up in their cauldrons. She mopped the remaining gravy from her plate and waited patiently for the others to finish. When they had, Peter stood up.

"I'll fill the tub for you, my lady," he told her.

"And I'll make certain the temperature is just right," Lucy said as she gathered up the plates and mugs and took them to the stone sink to be washed. "My lord, if you do not mind, a bucket of cool water from the well would be appreciated. Peter, when you've got the water in the tub, go to the stables and get the stew pot back from the men."

Finally all was ready for the bath. Peter had gone, returned, and gone again to the stables where he would keep company with the men-at-arms. Philippa was in her little tub, pleased she was able to wash. It was unlikely she would be able to do so again until they reached France. The earl had sent Lucy away, and now sat watching his wife as she bathed. Philippa had a beautiful young body, and it gave him pleasure just to look at it.

"Ply your brush, my lord," she suddenly spoke, breaking into his train of thought. "Did you not say you would scrub my back?"

Kneeling next to the tub, he picked up the brush, soaped it, and began to scour her back. "I am sorry this little oak tub is not big enough for us both," he murmured in her ear, kissing the little curl of flesh. "I like it when we bathe together, Philippa."

She giggled. "When you bathe with me, Crispin, we seem to become entangled in each other," Philippa teased him.

"I am going to make love to you tonight," he said low.

"We must make an early start," she protested.

"And when will I have the time again once we get to Dover?" he asked her. "And I know how you feel about passion in a public inn."

"I shall have Lucy bring us an extra pitcher of water tonight," she said softly. "Now stop, Crispin, or you will have all the skin off of my back."

He gently laved water over her, rinsing away the heavy lather he had built up. Philippa stood up, and the droplets from her tub sluiced down her lithe body. Reaching out, she wrapped herself in one of the two large towels Lucy had placed on a drying rack by the fire. She stepped from the tub, and his arms wrapped themselves about her.

"Crispin," she murmured warningly, seeing the bulge between his thighs.

"I don't choose to wait, little one," he told her, pulling his shirt off and loosening his other garments. He backed her with his body to the large table where they had just eaten, his hands imprisoning her heart-shaped face between them, kissing her hungrily.

"Crispin!" she protested again. "Lucy and Peter!"

"Peter dices with the men-at-arms, and will sleep in the stables. Lucy is above stairs, and will not return unless called," the earl told his wife. His manhood was freed now from its constraints, and it was ready to play. He pushed her down, and her legs came up to fasten themselves about his waist. He drove into her in a single smooth motion as her arms went about him, and she sighed. "Ah, countess," he told her, "you consume me, I fear. No woman has ever entranced me as do you, Philippa."

She sighed again. "Then it is fortunate I am your wife, Crispin," she told him. Sweet Mother of God, how he filled her. His bare skin crushing her breasts was almost hot. Her nipples had tightened into hard points, and she arched herself into him. She loved the possession he took of her. It thrilled and overwhelmed her. Philippa's head fell back, and his mouth began almost at once to press wet, hot kisses on her vulnerable throat. His tongue lapped from the pulse at the base of her neck up beneath her chin. She unlocked her grip about his neck, her hands smoothing down his long back, scoring him with her nails, lightly at first, and then with more vigor as her own ardor increased.

He felt her nails digging into his flesh. Reaching back, he took her hands and pulled her arms over her head, pinioning them there. "Would you mark me, little one?" he growled in her ear, and then his tongue teased the delicate flesh. His hips did all the work now, thrusting forwards and backwards, driving himself deep into her, enjoying the little mewling cries that had begun to issue forth from her throat. He could feel the very faint trembling beginning from within her, but he wasn't ready yet. He drew back slowly, and held himself still.

"Oh, Crispin, don't!" she pleaded. "I need it! I need it!"

"In a moment, little one," he promised her, and his mouth found her sweet lips, brushing them gently at first, and then kissing her with a fierce and demanding yearning. He began to move within her once more, feeling himself so swollen that he actually ached with the pleasure being inside of her gave him.

Philippa had thought she would die of the unfulfilled longing that had swept over her when he had briefly stopped. Then he had kissed her, and she was quickly lost in her own desire for him. The storm began to once more brew. It burgeoned and swelled until it finally burst over them both, and he collapsed breathless atop her. Suddenly she could feel the hard wood of the table beneath her shoulders, her back, and her buttocks. Philippa began to laugh. "Get off me, you great beastie!" she told him. "Your wicked games have made it necessary for me to get back in the tub again." She pushed at him.

Crispin groaned. He was drained. His limbs felt like jellies. She pushed at him again, and he managed to pull himself up. "God's boots, woman," he complained at her, "you weaken me to the point of exhaustion with your constant demands."

"My demands?" Philippa sat up, and then she slid from the table. "My lord, you are mistaken, I fear. 'Tis your demands that are so insatiable!"

"Nay," he insisted. "Now, countess, just look at those adorable little breasts of yours. They plead with me to be caressed." He bent his ash brown head and kissed one of her nipples. "Do you not see? It is pointing at me, for I see no other here it points to, do you, madame?" He was grinning at her.

"You are a wicked man, my lord earl," she scolded him, but she was smiling. Then she pushed past him, and climbing back into the small tub she sat down and washed herself free of any residue of their shared passions. Then standing up again she instructed him, "Bring that smaller cauldron of water, for the bath is too cool to be comfortable for you." She stepped from the tub and began to dry herself off again.

He reheated the little tub and then, pulling the remainder of his clothing off, he climbed in and began to wash himself. When he had finished she helped him dry himself. He donned his shirt, and she was already in her chemise. Gathering up their clothing they walked upstairs past the lovely hall, and climbed a second flight of steps up to their bedchamber.

"Call Lucy, and tell her to go to bed," he whispered to her.

She nodded. "But remember we must leave at the very hour of dawn," Philippa said. She drew back the coverlet for him, taking the shirt before he entered their bed. Then she called Lucy, and bid her go to bed. "We depart early," she reminded her tiring woman. "But put the tub away before you sleep," she concluded.

Lucy nodded. "I'll see to it, and then lock the kitchen door. Peter is in the stables with the others for the night, my lady. Good night. Good night, my lord." Then she was gone, and Philippa could hear her footsteps hurrying off down the corridor.

"Come to bed," Crispin called sleepily.

Philippa drew off her chemise and laid it aside before climbing in with her husband. She smiled when he wrapped his arms about her.

He was already sleepy, she knew, and sure enough the earl was shortly snoring. But in the dark hours of the night he awoke, and made passionate love to her before falling asleep again.

"Won't be able to do that again until we reach France," he murmured in her ear.

"The king and the queen would be shocked by your lust, my lord," she teased him, but Philippa had thought it too. In the past few weeks she had become less prudish about their coupling. It had been from the very beginning a pleasurable experience lying with her husband. Obviously the queen did not find it so, although she had certainly never said it. How sad, Philippa considered. She wondered if every woman had such delight in bedsport with her husband.

The next day dawned fair, and they saw the sunrise on the road to Canterbury. It was the twenty-fourth day of May. The closer they came to the town, the more crowded the roads they traveled became. Finally reaching Canterbury where they would meet up with the court, they found their way to a small inn, the Swan, where Lord Cambridge had thoughtfully arranged for them to stay. But the inn was so crowded that Peter was housed in the stable loft with several other men, and Lucy slept on a trundle bed in her lord and lady's room.

The emperor had not yet arrived but was expected any day. Philippa reported to the queen, who was pleased to see her.

"You are happy, my child?" she inquired solicitously.

"Very," Philippa admitted, "but I am ready to serve you, madame."

"When we return," the queen said, "I am releasing you from my service. I have women aplenty around me, and you have been as your sire before you, most faithful to the house of Tudor. Now, however, your first duty must be to supply your husband with an heir. No one knows this requirement of a successful marriage better than I do, child."

"But, madame," Philippa protested, "I am willing to serve you forever!"

The queen reached out and touched the young woman's face gently. "I know that, my dear," she said. "If I have been fortunate in anything, it is the love that both you and your good mother have borne me. But like Rosamund you must now live your own life, not live that life through me. I have allowed you and your husband to come to France with us on this glorious progress as a reward for your faithfulness. But when we return, Philippa, I shall bid you adieu. You will always be welcome at court, but I know that you know your first duty is to provide children for your husband's family."

"Ohh, madame, my heart is broken," Philippa said, and her eyes filled with tears. "I should have never wed if I knew I could no longer serve you."

"Nonsense!" The queen laughed softly. "You are not the proper material for the church, despite your passionate declarations last year. Like your mother before you, you are meant to be a wife and a mother yourself. There is nothing else for a woman, Philippa. Now dry your eyes. You are among my prettiest ladies, and I want you to be with us when we greet my nephew's arrival."

"Very well, madame," Philippa replied. When she managed to see her husband later that evening she told him, half angrily, of the queen's decision.

"I am sorry," he said, "but the queen does what she thinks is best for you. We are very fortunate to have her friendship, Philippa. If we have a daughter she may one day serve the queen, or Princess Mary."

"We are still welcome at court," Philippa answered him. "We will come for the Christmas revels, won't we?"

"Let us see when we return from France, and from visiting your family in the north, how we feel about it. You could be with child, Philippa, and all that traveling might not be good for you. I could not bear it if anything happened to you."

"Why?" she said cruelly. "You have the lands you sought."

"Because I find you are of equal value to me as the lands," he told her quietly.

She was surprised by his words. "Are you falling in love with me?" she asked him frankly.

"I don't know," he said. "Our acquaintance is still new. Do you think you could ever love me, Philippa?"

She thought a long moment, and then replied, "I am not certain yet. I have seen what love looks like, how it can raise you to the heights, yet pain you deeply. I thought that I loved Giles FitzHugh but obviously I did not, for his loss is long gone from my memory and my heart. I think if I had really loved him it would not be."

"But can you love me one day, Philippa?" he repeated.

"I don't know," she teased him. "Our acquaintance is still new, Crispin."

He laughed. "You are not an easy woman," he told her.

Philippa had wondered if the princess Mary would travel to France with her parents to meet the Dauphin, her betrothed, but learned she would not. The little princess would remain in England keeping royal state at Richmond Palace under the eye of the duke of Norfolk and Bishop Foxe, who would share responsibility for the government as well. She had bid her parents good-bye at Greenwich, going from there to Richmond while her parents had moved towards the coast, staying at Leeds Castle on the twenty-second of May. The king and queen reached Canterbury late in the afternoon of the twenty-fourth of May. Two days later Emperor Charles V arrived with his fleet to a welcoming cannon-ade from the English fleet awaiting his arrival in the straits of Dover.

Crispin and Philippa had ridden to Dover upon learning that Car-dinal Wolsey had been informed of the emperor's impending arrival. They stood in the crowds on the waterfront watching as Charles V came ashore beneath a cloth of gold canopy that had his badge, a black eagle, upon it. The plump and haughty cardinal in his scarlet robes came forward to meet the emperor, bowing obsequiously, a smile on his lips. They could not hear his words for the noise of the crowds. They knew that Cardinal Wolsey would escort the emperor to Dover Castle where he was to spend the night.

The next day was Whitsunday. The king, having not been informed of his nephew's arrival as quickly as the cardinal, made a hasty and very early departure for Dover. He was there to greet Charles V as the young emperor descended the staircase that morning. Henry then escorted him back to Canterbury. All along their route the English gathered to cheer both the emperor and their king. They did not like the French.

Upon their arrival in Canterbury the two men entered the cathedral for a high mass of thanksgiving celebrating not simply the church holiday itself, but the emperor's safe arrival as well. Afterwards Henry showed Charles the shrine of St. Thomas à Becket. The holy relics were displayed: the hair shirt; the saintly archbishop's cracked skull; the weapon that had done the damage. These, along with several other relics, the king and the emperor kissed devoutly. Then they moved on to Archbishop Warham's palace where the royal party was staying so that Charles V might at last meet his aunt.

The earl of Witton moved discreetly among the cardinal's party. His wife was among the queen's ladies. They made a pretty show hurrying from the hallway to greet the king and the emperor at the palace door. It had, of course, all been planned that way. The ladies then escorted the gentlemen inside and back down the corridor, which was lined with twenty of the queen's pages garbed in gold brocade and crimson satin. Finally reaching a wide marble staircase, the emperor looked up. There the queen sat, halfway up the marble steps upon a landing, waiting to greet him. She was gowned in ermine-lined cloth of gold robes, and about her neck were several strands of fat pearls. Katherine smiled in welcome. She had not his mother, Joanna's, beauty. Indeed at this point in her life Katherine of Aragon was plump, matronly. But she was his nearest blood relation next to his mother and his sisters. Reaching her, he took the outstretched hands in his and kissed them lovingly. Katherine wept openly with her joy even as she took him to her heart, and he reciprocated.

The young emperor was not an attractive man by any stretch of the imagination. Philippa overheard several of the woman remarking on it, and hoped the queen did not. Charles V was twenty. He had a large misshapen jaw that was the most prominent feature of his face. His eyes were a watery blue, and his skin the white of a fish's belly. His teeth were irregular in a large mouth, and it affected his speech somewhat. But he had grown a handsome beard to help disguise some of his deficiencies. He was nonetheless an intelligent and amusing man. As the lord of the Low Countries he was important to English trade, and while England had always been his firm and fast ally, this sudden attempt at harmony with France concerned the emperor enough that he felt a visit to England, however brief, was necessary. He did not think for one moment that he could change Henry Tudor's plans, but he knew the French would be very annoyed by his meeting with the English king, even as he knew that Henry was extremely pleased by his visit. The royals and their immediate family adjourned for a private dinner, leaving the members of the court to wander about and find their own meal and entertainment.

Later that day the beautiful dowager queen of Aragon, Germaine de Foix, widow of Katherine's father, Ferdinand, arrived with sixty of her ladies. That evening there was a large banquet for the court. The king, the emperor, and the three queens, Katherine, Germaine, and Mary Tudor, who had been France's queen and was now the wife of Charles Brandon, the duke of Suffolk, sat at the high board. The food was lavish, the wine never stopped flowing, and a merry time was had by all in attendance.

One Spanish count became enamored of one of the queen's ladies, and wooed her so vigorously with poetry and song that he at last fainted away and was carried from the room. The old duke of Alba, a charming gentleman, demonstrated with others in his party some Spanish dancing. The king, who loved to dance, now led his sister, Mary, onto the floor, and of course the others followed. Philippa defied convention by dancing with her husband first, but the king saw her, and having enjoyed dancing with her previously, took her for his partner for one of the dances.

"My dear countess," he said with a grin. "Are you used to being called that yet, Philippa?" He lifted her high, and she laughed down into his handsome face.

"Nay, sire, I am not, but I expect in time it will become familiar," she told him as he placed her back on the floor, and lifting her skirts she pranced by his side.

"How is your mother?" He twirled her about.

"I have heard naught since I learned she birthed twin sons, your majesty," Philippa answered, dipping and then pirouetting.

"How many lads is that now?" He lifted her up again and swung her about.

"Four, sire," Philippa replied, dancing gracefully by his side.

"May God grant your husband that you prove as good a breeder," the king said, and she saw his eyes were troubled.

When the dance was over the king led Philippa to where the queen sat with her nephew. "Kate, my dear, perhaps you will introduce the countess to the emperor." He kissed Philippa's hand and moved off to dance again with his sister.

Philippa curtseyed low, her deep blue and silver skirts belling out as she did so.

"I have written to you of the kindness of Rosamund Bolton, Carlos," the queen began. "This is her eldest daughter, Philippa, countess of Witton. She has served me loyally for the past four years but will retire after the summer progress, for she is newly married, and her duty now is to give her husband's family heirs. Philippa, my child, may I present the emperor to you."

Philippa curtseyed once again. "Your majesty," she said softly.

"Your madre is well, countess?" the emperor asked politely.

"She is, your majesty, and will be honored that you asked," Philippa responded.

"She is from the north of this country?" the emperor queried.

"Aye, your majesty. She is a landowner and along with Lord Cambridge, a relation, involved in the merchant trade with the Low Countries. Perhaps you have heard of our Friarsgate Blue wool. It is the finest cloth," Philippa found herself saying.

"It is a very difficult commodity to obtain," the emperor surprised her by saying. "I have had complaints about that, for it is much in demand, countess."

"Aye, they control its distribution in order to keep the price high," Philippa returned. He knew of her mother's wool. Wait until she told them that at Friarsgate come the autumn!

"Your mother, it would appear, is a clever woman," the emperor said.

"She is indeed, Carlos," the queen agreed. Then she said to Philippa in a gentle gesture of dismissal, "I think I see the earl, your husband, seeking for you, my child."

Philippa curtseyed once more. "Thank you, your highness. Your majesty." And then she backed away, finally turning about to look for Crispin. She was suddenly aware of her new status. She was no longer plain Mistress Meredith, the queen's maid of honor. She was the countess of Witton, worthy of being introduced to an emperor. It was quite a revelation.

And then Crispin was at her elbow. "You met the emperor," he said, and she heard the pride in his voice.

"Aye," she said, looking up at him. "He knew about my mother's famous wool. He said he had had complaints from the merchants in the Low Countries of its scarcity. Imagine, Crispin! The Holy Roman Emperor and king of Spain knew about Friarsgate Blue wool. I am astounded."

"He is young," the earl answered her, "but I suspect he will be a great man one day, little one. Nothing, it would seem, escapes his notice. Not even Friarsgate Blue." He chuckled. "It has been quite an evening for you. You danced with the king, and you were introduced to and held a conversation with an emperor."

"I have danced with the king before," she said. "He is very demanding, and will only dance with the best dancers."

"If he dances with you in France you will certainly catch the eye of King Francois," her husband told her. "Then I shall have to be jealous."

"Would you? Would you really be jealous?" Philippa demanded, eyes sparkling.

"Aye!" he replied without hesitation. "I should be insanely jealous."

"Then I shall have to arrange it," she teased him.

"Be careful, little one," he warned her. "No lady, it is said, remains chaste at the French court. Tom Boleyn's daughter, Mary, has been there for several years, and is said to have become a most accomplished whore. King Francois calls her his English Mare, and claims to have ridden her innumerable times to his pleasure."

"What a terrible thing to claim of the earl of Wiltshire's daughter!" Philippa cried.

"It would not be said of her were it not so, little one. So be cautious in your dealings with the noblemen of France," he cautioned her. "I should not like to have to fight a duel over your honor. Not, at least, until you have given me a son or two."

"Do you think you would not win?" she asked innocently, but her mouth was twitching with amusement.

"Vixen! Would you put some poor Frenchman in danger simply to amuse yourself? I see I may have to correct your behavior one of these days soon."

"Correct my behavior?" She looked surprised. "How?"

"Have you never been spanked, madame?" he murmured.

"Crispin, you would not dare!" she exclaimed.

"You do not want to try my patience, madame," he warned her.

"Not today at least," she teased him.

"Unless you have a good reason for remaining here," he told her, "we should return to the inn. Did you get enough to eat? It seemed to me that those of us not at the high board or the tables directly below it tonight were stinted."

Philippa nodded. "The presentation of the dishes was splendid, but

I scarce saw a thing upon my plate," she admitted. "Do you think the innkeeper will have a crust of bread and a rind of cheese he might spare us?" She was smiling.

"Now I can see how you survived at court as a maid of honor," he said, smiling back. "I think we can do better than a crust and a rind. I was considering a fat capon, strawberries, fresh bread, butter, and a lovely runny Brie cheese, madame." He escorted her from the hall, and from the bishop's palace.

She sighed. "It sounds wonderful!" she agreed as they came out onto the streets of the town.

They had walked from the inn earlier, and now they returned the same way. Because of the king's visit the streets were well lit and patrolled tonight. And they had not far to go. He held her hand, and walking along in the spring night Philippa considered that never before had she strolled hand in hand with a gentleman. Her marriage to Crispin St. Claire was bringing her many new adventures, and she had earlier decided that she liked it. And after tonight she knew that she liked being the countess of Witton. It was much more fun being a countess than just an ordinary girl. Her sisters would simply be pea green with envy when she saw them again and told them. And Banon was only marrying a second son, even if she did love him. And as for Bessie, what could poor Bessie expect with nothing to recommend her but a small dowry? No, it was definitely better to be the countess of Witton.

Chapter 16

⟨decorative flourish⟩

The king would make no treaty excluding France with his wife's nephew. Henry Tudor preferred to keep all his options open. He did agree to meet again with Charles at Gravelines, which was imperial territory, after his meeting with King Francois. The young emperor left for Sandwich on Tuesday evening, the twenty-ninth of May. The following morning, the king and the court departed for Dover where they embarked in a fleet of twenty-seven vessels led by his majesty's own personal ship, *Henri Grace à Dieu*, more familiarly known as the *Great Harry*. It took nine hundred sailors to manage the huge vessel, which had been built seven years earlier to the king's exact specifications by over a hundred carpenters and shipwrights.

Newly refitted for this summer progress, the *Great Harry* had magnificent cloth of gold sails that billowed perfectly in the summer breezes. There was not a mast that did not fly a beautiful banner or exquisite pennant. The king knew the French had nothing like this incredible ship. And while he was sorry his rival king would not be at Calais to see it, he knew that everything about the vessel would be reported in minute detail to Francois. Only his late brother-in-law's the *Great Michael* could have come close to the sumptuousness of the *Great Harry*. But James IV of Scotland was dead, and his ship lost but to memory.

Three thousand nine hundred and ninety-seven persons made up the king's retinue. There were peers and bishops; the king's personal secretary, Richard Pace; twelve chaplains; and the entire staff of the Chapel Royal. There were heralds, two hundred guards, seventy grooms of the chamber, and two hundred sixty-six household officers, each with their own servants. The queen's party totaled eleven hundred and seventy-five persons, all of whom traveled with their servants. Philippa and Lucy were counted among them. Cardinal Wolsey had a train of gentlemen, among them the earl of Witton, chaplains, and two hundred thirty-seven servants. The duke of Buckingham and Archbishop Warham were not allowed as many retainers as was Wolsey. All in all, five thousand one hundred seventy-two people and two thousand eight hundred sixty-five horses traveled to France.

The great royal summer progress departed Dover just before dawn on the morning of May thirty-first. By noon they had sailed across the gentle seas to arrive at Calais. The earl and countess of Witton had taken with them in their private ship six of the queen's ladies and their servants. Among them was Thomas Boleyn's eldest daughter, Mary, who had spent time at the French court when Mary Tudor had been France's queen. She seemed pleasant enough to Philippa, but Crispin was not pleased to have her aboard his transport.

"She has a bad reputation," he told his wife.

"The queen asked me to take her," Philippa answered her husband. "I could not refuse her, could I? She seems a quiet girl, my lord. What do you hear of her?"

"That she whores easily," he replied.

"I would assume most whores do so easily, else they would not be whores," Philippa responded. "Was she ever your whore?"

"Damn it, Philippa!" he swore softly. "No! I have never been eager to travel a road so well used."

"Is the king traveling that road now?" Philippa asked. "Perhaps that is why the queen wanted me to take her. She must put up with much, but even a queen is entitled to a respite now and again. This is a hard trip for her. She prefers her summers at Woodstock these days. She says the quiet there reminds her of a convent, and allows her to concentrate on her prayers."

"There are rumors, aye," the earl said. "Now that Bessie Blount is gone, and the queen pronounced barren of future children, he is restless. Mary Boleyn is of easy virtue, and not apt to seek to outshine or insult the queen."

"How tragic that the king's only son should be bastard-born," Philippa remarked.

"The king is young, and can marry again," the earl said.

"He is married," Philippa said sharply.

"He will eventually find a way to dispose of his old queen, and take a new, fecund one," the earl answered quietly. "There is precedent for this, Philippa, and Henry Tudor will have his son. He does not mean the Tudor dynasty his father sought to build to end with him. Any husband Princess Mary takes one day will have to be equal to her in rank. This means a king to her queen. England will not want a foreign-born king ruling them."

"Such a thing will never happen," Philippa said firmly.

They remained upon their vessel until June third, when the great train began its departure for Guisnes, where the summit was to be held. Philippa was awestruck by the small city that had been constructed to house the two kings and their retinues. Bishop Fisher, however, was appalled by the abundance of extravagance. He shook his head at the excess, among the few to notice the gathering of beggars surrounding the encampment in hopes of receiving alms.

The French had put up four hundred tents by the side of a river bordering the village of Ardres, while the English pitched two thousand eight hundred tents by the village of Guisnes. The French king had a tent made from cloth of gold. Its canvas roof was painted with astrological signs and stars. Its interior entrance was filled with young trees and pots of ivy. A great gilt statue of Saint Michael sat in the entry's center, reflecting the sunlight that touched it through the wide opening of the pavilion.

The English king, however, more than equaled his fellow monarch. Six thousand carpenters, masons, bricklayers, and others had spent months building an Italianate palace for Henry Tudor and his guests. It had been fashioned of stone and brick, and was embellished with battlements and crenellations. There was much ornamental tile work, fan-shaped stone and ironwork ornamentations, and life-size statues of famous heroes filling every niche. From the corners of the roofs sprang heraldic animals of stone. From the center of the palace sprang a six-sided cupola topped with more fantastic beasts, and a life-size gilt angel. Long arched windows of glass lined the upper floor of Henry Tudor's temporary summer palace.

Inside, all the windows were edged in gold inlay. The most precious rugs, tapestries, silk hangings, furniture, and ornaments had been transported to France from Greenwich and Richmond palaces in order to furnish this fairy-tale castle. There was a little chapel with altar cloths of gold tissue embroidered with pearls and other gemstones. The candlesticks and the chalices had been brought from Westminster Abbey for the occasion. There were gold statues of the twelve apostles half the size of a grown man. But most amazing of all were the two fountains in the open planted courtyard of this castle. One poured forth claret, or hippocras, and the other ran with beer or ale for any and all who cared to drink.

The earl and countess of Witton were rather relieved to find their tent set up on the edge of the English area between the queen's and the cardinal's sections. Lord Cambridge had arranged a fine canvas tent, with an awning before it where the horses might be sheltered. Inside, the tent was divided into two sections, one for sleeping and the other for eating or entertaining. Lucy would sleep in the main section. Peter would bed with the horses outside so they would not be stolen. The earl's man had made a small fire outside their pavilion, and set braziers with burning coals in each of the tent's two rooms to take the dampness and chill from the air inside. There was a table and several chairs in the front of their accommodation, and a pallet for Lucy in the far corner. In the back chamber of the tent their trunks had been set out along with a bed, a chair, and a small table. Peter had cleverly strung a line in this back room, and Lucy was already laying out her mistress's gowns across it.

They had barely gotten themselves settled when they had a visitor. A gentleman of medium height, dressed in splendid garments, and just faintly resembling Crispin St. Claire, entered their pavilion. He looked about and then, spotting the earl, cried, "Mon chou! It is you! I was not certain you were still in service to Monsieur le Cardinal!"

"Guy-Paul," the earl said, coming to greet their guest. "And I am no longer in the cardinal's service, but my wife is one of the queen's women."

"Wife? You have taken a wife, Crispin?"

"Do you not think it was about time, Guy-Paul? Philippa, this is my cousin, Guy-Paul St. Claire, the comte de Renard. Cousin, my wife."

Philippa held out her hand to the count. "Monsieur le comte," she said politely.

"Madame la comtesse," he said, his blue eyes sweeping over her. He kissed her hand and then, taking her by the shoulders, kissed both of her cheeks. Then setting her back he said admiringly, "Mon cher Crispin, you have a most beautiful wife."

"How charming of you to say it, though it be not true, monsieur le comte," Philippa quickly spoke up for herself. "I will admit to being a pretty woman, but nothing more." She smiled at him, moving back just slightly. "However, you will find among our court several great beauties."

Guy-Paul St. Claire looked slightly surprised by her words, but then he grinned. "I can see, madame la comtesse, that I shall not win you over with my charm."

"Only a little bit," Philippa returned. "Please, will you not sit?" She turned to her husband. "I will fetch wine, my lord." She moved away to a table along the side of the tent where a tray with decanters and goblets had been set up.

The two men sat, and the Frenchman asked, "How long have you had this wife, cousin? I do not remember you having a wife the last time we met."

"We were wed the last day of April," came the answer.

"She is rich?" The question was blunt, but fair.

"She had a piece of property I desired, and came with a good-sized dowry as well," the earl replied.

"But not of a noble family," the comte said.

The earl shook his head. "She was an excellent bargain nonetheless, and her connections cannot be faulted. Her mother is a friend of the queen, and Philippa has been in service to Katherine for four years. The queen is most fond of my wife."

Guy-Paul St. Claire nodded. "It is good every few generations to wed a woman from a slightly lower class. It strengthens the blood," he observed. "I must consider it myself one of these days. The family is becoming most demanding, I fear. My sister says I shall have no seed for sons left if I keep having bastards." He chuckled.

"How many now?" his cousin inquired.

The comte considered thoughtfully. "I think it is eight sons, and four daughters."

"You have always been a man to do things in the grand manner," the earl responded. "But it is time, Guy-Paul, to take a wife. I recommend it. And you are two years older than I am, after all."

"Wine, my lords," Philippa said, holding out a tray. She had listened carefully, and overheard everything the two men had said.

"Sit down and join us, *cherie*," the comte invited her, and she did.

"I was not aware my husband had relations in France," she murmured, and sipped at her own wine. There was so much she didn't know about Crispin, other than the fact they had a great deal of enjoyment from each other in their bedsport.

"The common ancestor had two sons," the comte told her. "The eldest, of course, was his heir. The younger went with Duke William of Normandy when he claimed England. He was rewarded for his service with lands there."

"But," the earl took up the tale, "the two branches of the family have never grown apart. We have fought on opposite sides against one another in the service of our kings. We have fought side by side on crusade. I spent two summers as a boy here in France with the St. Claires, and Guy-Paul spent two summers in England with me. Our women have married their cousins now and again. Each generation corresponds."

Philippa nodded. "I like that your families have always kept in contact with each other. Once my mother's family had a similar situation, but they did not remain close. Only a fortunate coincidence brought us back together again."

"You are one of the queen's women, Crispin tells me," the comte said.

"I have been a maid of honor for four years," Philippa responded. "When we return to England, however, the queen has said she is dismissing me so I may do my duty as my husband's wife, and give him heirs. She did not do so sooner because she knows how very much I wanted to come to France with her, and how I will miss my service."

"Then you like this court of your King Henry," he replied.

"It is the finest court in all the world!" Philippa said enthusiastically.

"How shall you bear not being a part of it?" he asked slyly.

"I cannot, but I will," Philippa responded. "My father was in service to the Tudors from the time he was six years of age. My mother has husbanded a large estate, and made it more profitable since she was three years of age. Duty, monsieur le comte, has been bred into me. While I shall miss being with the queen, my duty now is to my husband, and I have never failed in my duty."

Guy-Paul St. Claire was slightly taken aback by Philippa's statement. She looked so young. So delicious. So female. To learn she was of far sterner stuff than she appeared was quite surprising. More interesting, his cousin looked happy and pleased by his young wife's words. "Madame, I salute you," he said, "and Crispin, I believe I shall envy you, which I have certainly never done before."

Philippa arose from her chair. "My lords," she said, "I shall leave you to renew your acquaintance. I am quite fatigued with all our travels. Lucy, attend me," she called to her tiring woman. Then she curtseyed to the two men and moved through the brocade curtain that separated the two halves of the pavilion.

"She is so young, but so fierce," the Frenchman noted. "Is she as fierce in your bed, cousin? If you answer *oui* I shall indeed be envious." He grinned.

"*Oui*," the earl said, returning the grin.

The comte de Renard looked pained. "It is intolerable," he said. "Tell me how you gained such a lovely little treasure, cousin."

The earl explained, and when he had finished his relative shook his head, but Crispin St. Claire only chuckled. "If you would seek among the wealthy bourgeois you could probably find just such a wife, Guy-Paul, but I suspect you are too lazy to even try. Still you will have to eventually, mon cousin."

"Perhaps after this spectacle has run its course, *mon chou*," the comte replied. "I have no duties other than to be amusing, which is why I am here. Francois has brought half the people your king has. I suppose being the superior, he feels he need not try as hard as your king Henry."

The earl laughed. "Do not say such a thing aloud again, Guy-Paul. Any other Englishman hearing you would take umbrage and challenge you to a duel, which you would, of course, win, and then there would be merry hell to pay. All my king has done he has done in order to impress upon your king and the French that he is the superior one. Remember that one day his daughter will be France's queen."

The comte de Renard shrugged. "I wonder if that will indeed happen, or if the English queen will get her way to see her daughter wed to Spain. These betrothals are but pieces on a game board, cousin, and you know it as well as I do."

"Indeed, but for now the princess Mary and the young Dauphin are matched," the earl noted. "England and France are lovers."

"With Spain waiting eagerly in the wings," the comte said.

"Charles must wed long before our little princess is ready for marriage," the earl responded. "His responsibilities are great."

The two men continued to speak back and forth for some time before they finally parted, agreeing to meet again. The meeting of the two kings, which was the summer's first great event, would not occur for another two days. It was a choreographed event that had been carefully planned. The two kings spoke through their messengers. Cardinal Wolsey was the king's emissary. Each time he rode out he was accompanied by fifty mounted gentlemen in crimson velvet with fifty ushers bearing gold maces. His gold cross with its bejeweled crucifix went ahead of Cardinal Wolsey, who rode upon a magnificently caparisoned mule, surrounded by his priests. One hundred mounted archers brought up the rear of his train. The cardinal's great entourage was much talked about.

Though the French had attempted to prevent and discourage it, many spectators came to drink the English king's wine and to gawk at the great assemblage of royalty and its two courts. Beggars and peddlers appeared at the tents of the courtiers. The earl's Peter had to hire two young men from the nearby village to guard his master's belongings. He was not pleased, for he could not be certain that they would not steal from the earl and his wife in the end.

Finally the day of the first meeting came. It was June seventh, the feast of Corpus Christi. Artificial hills had been erected at either end of the entrances to the *val d'ore*, or golden valley, as it was called. In late afternoon the trumpets sounded. The English rode out from their encampment, the French from theirs. Each king was accompanied by a party of his courtiers. Henry wore cloth of gold and silver. It was heavily bejeweled. He had a black feathered bonnet and his Order of the Garter collar. His bay stallion was hung with golden bells that tinkled, and he was attended by his Yeomen of the Guard. The French king, not to be outdone, was as splendid in jewel-encrusted cloth of gold and silver. He wore white boots on his large feet, and a black cap. The French monarch was escorted by his Swiss Guards.

Reaching the top of their respective hillocks at the entrance to the valley, each king stopped. At the sound of trumpets and sackbuts they galloped down the mounts and into the valley towards each other. Taking their caps off with a grand flourish, Henry and Francois embraced each other, still a-horse, although the English bay danced nervously, bringing the embrace to a quick close. Then, dismounting, arm in arm they entered a small pavilion that had been set up for their meeting, thus avoiding the sticky issue of which king should go first. Inside there were chairs, cushions, and refreshments. Once inside, the two kings were joined by Cardinal Wolsey and the French admiral Bonnivet. The articles of the meeting were read out, as were Henry's titles, including King of France.

Henry Tudor laughed. "I fear that the presence of *mon frère* Francois would invalidate that particular title," he said, clapping his French counterpart on the back jovially. "And one day our children will make this ancient argument between England and France a moot point, eh?" And he laughed heartily once again.

The two men sat for some time drinking and talking. Finally they arose, went outside once again to the cheers of both parties of onlookers, embraced several more times, and parted, each to return to his own encampment. The sounds of the English oboes and sackbuts and the French flutes and drums filled the air as they went. And for the next few weeks there was feasting and jousting such as few had ever seen.

Philippa barely saw her husband during this time, for her place was with the queen. She hardly slept in their own comfortable pavilion, as she was expected to remain in the queen's great tent at her mistress's command. She returned to change her clothes, and among all the

English ladies she was the best dressed, according to Guy-Paul St. Claire.

She would have been considered well dressed among the French, he declared gallantly. The English thought the French ladies' gowns, with their open, low necklines, immodest. The ambassadors from Venice and Mantua thought the French more elegant with few exceptions, but much admired the beautiful gold chains that all of the English ladies seemed to possess. They also remarked that the English ladies drank too much.

On the tenth day of June, the king of France came to pay his respects to Queen Katherine. A banquet was given in his honor, and the choir from the Chapel Royal entertained the guests. Philippa had chosen to wear a gown of green and gold brocade with full sleeves of gold tissue that ended at the wrists in tight bejeweled bands. Her neckline was as fashionable as any French woman's, and caused some whispering among the other women. The countess of Witton smiled to herself, well pleased. Her hair had been fashioned into a chignon at the nape of her neck, and was decorated with fresh flowers. Not even the French could match her daring style. Upon her head she wore a small gold tissue cap that was sewn with pearls.

The French king had spotted Philippa immediately, and asked among his attendants who she was.

"She is the countess of Witton," Guy-Paul St. Claire told his master. "She is my English cousin's new wife, sire."

"Is she French-born?" Francois asked.

"Non. Indeed she is from the far north of England," the comte de Renard said.

"*Mon Dieu!*" Francois exclaimed. "How did such a lovely girl gain such style?"

"I could not tell you, sire," the comte answered. "I have only just met her myself."

"I should like to meet her," the king said, his black eyes narrowing speculatively.

"I think I could arrange it," Guy-Paul St. Claire murmured. "I am certain that madame la comtesse would be honored, sire." Now here was a stroke of good fortune, he thought to himself. He did not believe that Crispin's wife was foolish enough to allow herself to be seduced by his king, but he could certainly gain a small social credit with the king by introducing them. What happened afterward would happen. And Francois was known to be very persuasive where the ladies were concerned. Mayhap he could seduce her. Whatever transpired, it was unlikely the lady would escape totally unscathed. There were many women eager to be seduced by the king of France. One who refused his king would present a challenge, and the comte de Renard knew Francois loved a challenge. But either way, the king would enjoy himself.

"Do so then," his master replied; then he turned away to smile at his hostess who was even now saying she should like to present her ladies to him. Francois nodded pleasantly, and greeted each of the one hundred and thirty women brought before him with the traditional French dual kiss. Among those ladies was the lovely countess of Witton who curtseyed deeply, revealing a pair of quite magnificent breasts to his eye as she did so. His hands on her shoulders as he kissed her lingered perhaps just a trifle too long. But he also considered that Anne Chambers, another of the queen's ladies, was quite lovely.

Philippa moved away and found herself in the company of her husband's cousin once more.

"*Cousine*." He smiled toothily at her. "How lovely you are today. My master the king was even now remarking upon it. Would you like to be introduced to him, *cherie*?"

"I have already been presented by the queen," Philippa said. She was considering if she liked Crispin's cousin or not.

"*Non, non*," the comte de Renard replied. "My master indeed remarked upon your beauty to me, wondering who you were. Fortunately I was able to enlighten him since you are my cousin's wife. He has expressed his interest in spending a private moment with you."

"Amid all this hubbub?" Philippa looked disbelieving. "What you mean, *mon cher* Guy-Paul, is that your king would like to seduce me. His reputation precedes him, I fear, and I have been a courtier far too long not to know when a man is bent upon seduction. Were I still a maid the answer would be no. However, even though I be a married woman, the answer is still no." And she laughed. "Do not look so disappointed, *mon brave*. Did you really believe I should accept such an invitation?" No, she decided, she did not like Guy-Paul St. Claire, but she would be polite to him for Crispin's sake.

He looked downcast for a moment, but then he said, "Since you are more than aware of my king's behavior, *cherie*, you should be in no danger. Crispin tells me that your mama is a good friend of both your king and your queen. Would it not be of value to you to make a friend of France's king?"

Philippa laughed. "To what purpose, Guy-Paul? If I do not allow myself to be seduced I shall offend King Francois. And I most certainly would not allow myself to be tempted by any man other than my husband, who is your cousin. Do you think that Crispin would approve of your pandering his wife to the king of France?"

The comte de Renard looked deeply offended at her words. "One never knows, madame," he said, "when one will need a friend in high places. If not for yourself, then for your family. You will have children one day. And Crispin tells me that your mother is involved quite successfully in the merchant trade. Are not your friends her friends? Could having a king of France as an acquaintance not be of help to you one day?"

"I would say you speak wisdom, were I not suspicious of your motives, Guy-Paul. Why on earth would the king of France want to meet me except for the purpose of seduction? And why would you offer up your cousin's wife to him?" Yet, Philippa thought, if she could make a friend of this king without compromising her virtue it might be of value to her family one day. Would it really hurt to attempt such a thing? She didn't have to succumb to a seduction, after all.

"Madame, you are far too suspicious of me, and I am hurt that you would be. I offer you, an English country girl if the truth be known, the opportunity to meet a king of great renown. What stories you will have to tell your children and your grandchildren one day. That a king of France admired you. That he sought to seduce you, and you resisted, yet kept his friendship. And yes, my king will owe me a small debt for bringing him the beautiful woman he admired. But he would never put your refusal at my door. He is not that kind of man. And you, I believe, are clever enough to keep his amity and goodwill, which cannot do harm to Crispin."

Philippa was forced to laugh. "You are, I think, a very bad man, Guy-Paul St. Claire. You reason as well as Thomas More, although he is far more godly than you are or will ever be. If I agreed to meet King Francois, when and where would it be?"

The comte de Renard struggled to contain his glee. He had believed that by appealing to her intellect and her devotion to her family he would eventually bring her around to his way of thinking. Yet there was a moment he thought she might refuse him.

"I will not meet him at night," Philippa quickly said. "And it must be sometime when Crispin is otherwise occupied. He would forbid me, as you are well aware. Then I would be angry, and probably do something foolish," she finished with a small smile. "Better I tell him after the fact than before it that I have met your king. And he might be angry at you, Guy-Paul. Have you considered that?"

"Perhaps one afternoon after the jousting, and before the evening's entertainment," the comte suggested helpfully. He ignored her other words.

"Aye, that would be a good time," Philippa answered him. "Crispin is usually with his gentlemen friends then."

"I shall arrange everything," Guy-Paul said smoothly. He quickly took her hand and kissed it. "Be as charming with him as you have been with me, and King Francois will be enchanted by you, *ma chere cousine*."

"I do not wish him to be enchanted," Philippa said. "I shall meet your king privately, say the right things, and then remove myself from his presence lest he gain the wrong idea of why I am with him. Now go away, for the queen, I can see, is curious as to why we have been in conversation so long. I can hardly repeat our words, now can I?"

While the French king had been visiting Queen Katherine, King Henry had gone to visit the French queen, Claude. He was equally amused, diverted, and dined. Returning home, he met Francois along the way. The two kings stopped for a few moments, each praising the other's wife, and saying how well they had been treated during their visit. Then, embracing, they continued on their way.

More banquets followed, with Henry celebrating the French knights and Francois entertaining the English knights. One night the two kings dined together in a hall lined in rose pink silk brocade. On another night Cardinal Wolsey hosted a great feast in honor of the French queen dowager, Louise of Savoy. She was actually far more powerful at the French court than her quiet daughter-in-law, Queen Claude. When the French king was not jousting, or feasting, or flirting with other beautiful women, he was with his mother. He greatly valued her judgment. She considered him a Caesar for this age in which they were now living, and spurred him on in all his ambitions.

The banquets were lavish, with a huge variety of fresh foods and excellent French and Italian wines. The Venetian ambassador was quite shocked by the great capacity that the English women seemed to have for wine. The royal cooks on both sides of the valley worked hard to outdo one another in their menus. Those at the high board, however, usually dined before arriving at these banquets in order that they might talk among themselves during the meal while their courtiers feasted.

Each day was filled with jousting upon a great field that had been created for just this event. It measured nine hundred feet by three hundred and twenty feet in size. On either side of the field grandstands for the royalty and their guests had been built. Two trees of honor, one bearing the hawthorn emblem of King Henry and the other the raspberry leaf emblem of King Francois, were set up. Each of these delu-sory trees stood thirty-four feet high. Each day the knights entering the lists hung their shields upon these trees, with each king's shield hung at exactly the same level to show their equality. The rules of pro-tocol had been agreed upon by a council of French and English knights. Swords and lances would be blunted. Even the style of armor was agreed to beforehand.

Stablemen, armorers, and blacksmiths were in the employ of both sides of combatants. They were kept busy repairing the damaged swords and broken lances of the knights who tilted and jousted each day. And in between these jousts, the knights and their squires en-gaged in all manner of games. By some miracle there was no violence between the English and the French except on the playing field.

It was agreed that the two kings would run the same number of courses and break the same number of lances, although it was decided before the games began that Henry and Francois would not compete against each other. The jousting was so wild and turbulent that at one point sparks flew off of King Henry's armor. He sprained his hand, and a horse died under him. King Francois managed to get a black eye in his own fray.

Diplomacy was almost lost on the afternoon of June thirteenth when, at a wrestling match between men from the Yeoman of the Guard and some Bretons, Henry challenged Francois to a similar bout. He was thrown by the French king, and while honor demanded that Francois offer Henry another round, his own courtiers wisely pre-vented it. Henry, however, regained his dignity that afternoon, best-ing his French rival several times during an archery contest. Francois was no archer, but Henry was quite expert at the sport. Still Francois was aware that Henry, while smiling and charming, was not placated quite yet. Accompanied by two of his own gentlemen, he arrived at the king's tent several days later before Henry arose, and offered to serve his fellow monarch as valet.

The English king was well pleased by this seeming mark of respect.

He complimented Francois, saying the Frenchman had shown him the kind of trust that they should both have in each other. He gifted his fellow monarch with a great collar of bloodred rubies, and received in return a bracelet of diamonds worth at least double. Everyone's feelings were now well and properly soothed.

The weather had turned unusually hot for mid-June, and on several days the winds blew fiercely. The uninvited were beginning to cause problems, wandering drunkenly about the English encampment, vomiting their surfeit of wine, and collapsing by the fountain from which it poured. The crowds coming to watch the jousting every day grew huge, numbering over ten thousand at one point. It was a dangerous situation, but the provost marshal of the field was unable to control it.

It was on one of those fearsome hot afternoons that Guy-Paul St. Claire greeted Philippa as she stepped from the grandstand where the English sat. "Are you free to walk with me?" he asked her cordially.

"Your highness, this is my husband's cousin, Monsieur le Comte de Renard," Philippa said to the queen. "If you do not need me I would stroll with him."

"Of course, my child," the queen replied. Her eyes briefly touched the Frenchman, and she barely nodded. "I will see you at the banquet tonight."

Philippa curtseyed. "Thank you, your highness," she replied, and then taking Guy-Paul's arm, she moved off with him.

"I wonder if the earl of Witton knows he has a French cousin," one of the queen's women said meanly. "He is well named, for he looks like a fox."

The other women laughed.

"He is indeed the earl's cousin," the queen said quietly. "Philippa has told me of him. She was not aware of her husband's French relations until they arrived here. I think, Alice, that you need to spend more time at prayer asking God and his blessed Mother to help you in curbing your wicked tongue. Of all the ladies who have ever served in my household, only two can be said to be truly virtuous, and one of them is Philippa Meredith. Confess your sin to one of the priests, and do penance, Alice, before you come into my presence again." Then the queen turned her back on the woman.

Philippa meanwhile found herself escorted through the crowds that had come to watch today's contests. Her companion discreetly ushered her into the tent the French king used to prepare for the jousts. There Francois, bare-chested and in his *haut-de-chausses*, was being sponged down by a servant as he sat upon a three-legged stool. He looked up as they entered, smiling somewhat toothily, Philippa thought.

"Madame la comtesse, it is kind of you to come and visit me," he said. He stood up, and the water sluiced down his broad chest. He was very, very tall. Very masculine.

Philippa took a step back. *"Monseigneur le roi."* She curtseyed. "You fought well today, and I see the eye is healing nicely." Out of the corner of her own eye she could see that Guy-Paul had disappeared, and she knew that she had been foolish to allow him to goad her into coming. What had she been thinking? She knew better than to expect that a brief rendezvous with anyone could be of value to her or her family. Now she stood in danger of doing damage to herself and her husband. She had allowed Guy-Paul to taunt her into this foolishness, and now she must find a way out of the situation.

The French king waved his servant away and took Philippa's hand in his, raising it slowly to his lips, kissing it, but not releasing it. "I singled you out that day at the queen's banquet. Of all the English ladies you were the most elegant. Why do your countrywomen dress so dowdily? Do they not wish to be admired?" His black eyes plunged into the shadowed valley between her breasts.

Philippa felt almost violated by the look. She could feel the heat in it, but she knew better than to disclose her feelings. "I have been fortunate in having a relation who has a great flair for style. He has taught me how to dress, although he says I have the proper instincts for garb and for color. I do not know what I should do without the good counsel of my uncle Thomas. Few women could wear this particular shade of yellow."

"And this *oncle* has also taught you about jewelry?" He touched the pearls she was wearing. "These are most fine, madame la comtesse." And his fingers casually brushed the tops of her breasts, lingering just a moment too long.

"Uncle Thomas says I have an instinct for good jewels as well," she said with charming understatement, fighting back a shudder of distaste. This king repelled her.

The French king laughed. "And what other instincts do you have, madame?" he purred at her, as his arm snaked out to draw her against him.

His body was damp. His male scent filled her nostrils. His dark eyes were mesmerizing, and her own eyes widened at his quick attempt at seduction. Philippa suddenly felt like a little rabbit cornered by a rather large hound. She swallowed hard and then, putting her palms against the king of France's bare chest, she pushed him gently but firmly away. "Oh, monseigneur," she said, "you are so strong, and I am but a weak woman. Yet I am newly wed, and I would not shame my husband. Forgive me!" She quickly fell to her knees and looked up at him, her hands held out imploringly. "I should not have come, but the honor of having been noticed by your majesty rendered me, I fear, foolish. I am really just a country girl, monseigneur. And I am ashamed that I shall have to confess my wicked behavior to my mistress, the queen's, priest." Her head drooped, and she managed to squeeze a tear from her eyes.

"But not to your husband?" Francois murmured, amused.

"Ohh, I dare not!" Philippa cried. "He would surely beat me."

"If you were mine, madame la comtesse, and looked at another man, I think I should beat you too," the king remarked. Then he raised her. "Go back to your husband, madame, but rest easy that your unfortunate inclination towards chastity has kept you from any real sin. I have never found it necessary to force a woman." He kissed her lips quickly, chuckling at her surprise. "I could not resist, *cherie*, and I shall claim a dance from you tonight as compensation for my great disappointment." He bowed to her.

Philippa curtseyed prettily and fled the tent, silently thanking her lucky stars that she had been able to escape him unscathed. What a little fool she had been to even consider a tête à tête with the French king. The man's reputation as a lover more than preceded him. But Guy-Paul had been correct. She was clever, and her little performance had indeed fooled the king. She had escaped with her virtue still intact. And then she stopped. Where was she? She hadn't paid a great deal of attention to where they were going when Guy-Paul brought her from the spectator's seat. She was lost. And although it was late afternoon and the sun would not set for several more hours, the light between the tents was not strong. And the wind was blowing the dust up again, making it nearly impossible to see where she was going.

Well, she thought, if she walked to the end of the row of tents surely she would be able to see the field, and then she might find her way back to the English side. The line of tents seemed to go on forever. She came to the end of the row only to find another row before her, and the path straight before her ended. Should she go right? Or should she go left? She tried to remember in which direction the camps had been placed. The English camp was set to the west. She turned left, and continued walking. When she came to the end of this corridor of tents she was faced once again with the decision of which way to turn. She stopped to consider it very carefully. This was worse than any garden maze. Right! She should turn to the right. She could hear the noise of the crowds still milling about the field, and all she wanted to do was reach that field. These damned tents couldn't go on forever even if it seemed they did. She was a woman alone, in the opposite camp. Damn Guy-Paul! He should have waited for her, but then he had thought his master would be successful in his seduction. She would never speak to him again! But she would have to, if she was to keep this unfortunate incident she had created from her husband's knowledge. But should she? God's bloody wounds! Where was the jousting field? What if it got dark? How would she find her way then?

Finally she saw the field ahead of her, and relief poured through her veins. But there was a group of knights standing talking to one another. Caution bade her move over just one row in order to avoid passing them. They were French, and she didn't choose to place herself in the position of being accosted by a group of ordinary knights. Especially when she had just turned down their king, Philippa considered with a small chuckle. Then she saw a smaller group of men ahead of her. They were clustered in a small knot, but they were not knights. She wondered if she should consider them dangerous. She thought she should be safe, especially with the knights just a row over. The wind was higher now, and the dust began to blow. Philippa had to stop, for she could see nothing ahead of her now in the yellow brown haze. She knew she was practically upon the men ahead, yet she was suddenly fearful of moving forward under the circumstances.

And then her brain focused, shocked at the conversation she overheard. They were planning to kill someone. They were planning to kill Henry Tudor! She froze, terrified, for a long moment. What had she stumbled upon, and what could she do about it? And then Philippa realized that she was in the gravest danger of being killed herself. She would have to be extremely clever to extricate herself from this dangerous situation.

Her throat was so tight she didn't think she could swallow. She was in fact barely breathing. Her legs felt like jelly beneath her. Philippa forced herself to be perfectly still, and then she drew a long, deep breath. And another. And another. Her aching throat eased and opened, allowing her to swallow. She had to be brave if she was to get through this and warn the king. Pressing herself back into the shadows of the tent, Philippa listened carefully.

Chapter 17

$\mathscr{S}$he could not see the men who spoke so easily of murdering King Henry. And fortunately they could not see her. But when the dust storm subsided and they did see her, would they realize she had overheard them? She listened more closely. Her French was excellent, but these men spoke it with some sort of local dialect. She could understand them, but only barely.

"It is agreed then?" a rough voice said.

"It is agreed. They will all be there in the same place at the same time. It is too good an opportunity for us to pass by, *mes amis*. We shall never again have such a chance. Instead of the cursed English always troubling us with their claims on France, we shall claim England. With the upstart Tudor, his pious Spanish wife, and the fat cardinal out of the way, our king will take custody of the princess Marie who is betrothed to our own Dauphin, and England will be ours in the chaos that follows these deaths. When the king learns what we have done for him we will all be well rewarded."

"Will the emperor not object?" the second voice said. "The English queen is his aunt after all, and blood is valued among the Spanish. And are you certain we will be rewarded? Or will we be executed for what we have done?"

"Of course the emperor will be annoyed, you fool! But we have people in England who will grab the little princess from her keepers and bring her quickly to France. Our king may be angry at first, but he will see the advantages in what we have done. And the queen dowager will protect us, for we are her servants, are we not? Once King Francois has the English princess in his possession the marriage can be performed. Even the emperor would dare not defy the church. The threat the English have always been to us will be removed. France will govern England. And their noble families will come around quickly enough. They always do, don't they? When push comes to shove they will think of themselves before anyone else." And then there was laughter.

"The king's salamander will be the signal, eh?"

"*Oui!*"

The wind was beginning to die down, and with it the dust storm. There was no place for her to hide. Philippa gritted her teeth. "Coming through!" she shouted, and pushed through the gloom towards the men whom she could now just make out. "Coming through! Make way for the countess of Witton! Make way!" She was almost upon them.

"What the devil . . ." one of the men, a rough-looking fellow, exclaimed, and he stepped forward to block Philippa's path.

"Get out of my way, you French baboon!" Philippa said in English, her tone decidedly haughty. She glared at the man.

"Did she hear us?" the second man asked.

"Move aside for the countess of Witton!" Philippa said boldly. And she shoved at the large man before her.

"How long have you been here, madame?" he asked her, grasping her wrists. "How long?"

"How dare you put your hands on me, sirrah!" Philippa shrieked, outraged. "Release me at once! I shall have you punished for this!" Her heart was hammering wildly. Could she get away with this? Could she convince them she didn't understand them, or their language? She kicked the man holding her, hard.

He released her at once, leaping backwards and cursing, rubbing his shins. "The bitch kicked me," he said to his two companions, who were now laughing at his antics.

"Madame," one of the other men said, *"parlez-vous français?"*

"What?" Philippa replied. "What is it you say? Why do you not speak English? Damned French bandits! Let me pass at once. I shall have you arrested! Help! Help!" she began to shout. "Bandits! Thieves! I am being attacked!"

The three men looked horrified at her shrieks.

"She does not speak French," one of them said. "She could not have understood what we said, and her cries will bring those who should not see us together. Let her go, Pierre, before she brings knights upon us. Look at her garments. She is a lady."

The large man who had been blocking Philippa's way snarled angrily. "I think we should strangle the bitch, and have done with it! I thought all these fine court ladies spoke French, but then they are English, Michel, aren't they." He stepped aside, opening the way for Philippa, and picking up her skirts she ran down the path between the tents, emerging with relief onto the jousting field once again.

The area was still crowded with spectators, and she felt safer. She slowed her pace and looked about for someone she knew, giving a cry of surprise when a hand clamped firmly about her elbow. Whirling, she found herself facing her husband, and Crispin did not look very pleased at all.

"Where have you been, madame?" he demanded of her. "And just what have you been doing?" His gaze was stern, and perhaps angry, perhaps worried.

"There is a plot, my lord," she managed to gasp out. "A plot to kill the king!"

"Which king?" he snapped, suddenly looking alert.

"Our king!" Philippa hissed at him. "Do you think I give a bloody damn about the French king? It is Henry Tudor who matters!"

"When?" he said.

"I don't know," she replied.

"Where?" he asked.

"I don't know," she answered.

"Who are the assassins?" He was looking very exasperated.

"I don't know," she told him for the third time.

"God's blood, woman!" he roared, causing those about them to stare. He lowered his voice. "There is a plot against the king, but you don't know who, or where, or when, or even why. Are you mad then, Philippa? Has the heat of this dusty and damnable French countryside finally affected your wits?" He appeared even more irritable now.

"Please, Crispin, not here," Philippa pleaded with her husband. "Let us go back to our own pavilion, and I will tell you what I heard."

Almost dragging his wife by her arm, the earl of Witton made his way to where their horses were waiting. He boosted Philippa into her saddle and climbed aboard his own mount. Together they made their way back to the English encampment. The wind was rising again, and the sky was growing darker with the dust swirling up into the atmosphere. Some of the smaller tents were beginning to pull loose from their pegs and collapse onto the ground. They could hear the shouts of the French, frantic to keep their camp from blowing away entirely. Ahead of them they could see Queen Katherine's open litter with its gilt columns. Its cloth of gold curtains with their red satin trim were blowing wildly in the winds. The queen was huddled inside, a scarf drawn about her face to protect herself from the fine stinging dust.

Crispin and Philippa finally reached the comparative safety of their own tent. While it was swaying in the wind, the earl could see the pegs holding it to the earth were planted firmly. They dismounted, and he said to Peter, his serving man, "Bring the horses inside the tent. This is a nasty blow, and I don't think it will end soon."

Peter nodded. "Aye, milord. I agree."

Inside, the earl led his wife past the partition that served to divide the tent, waving Lucy away for the moment. He sat in one of the two chairs and pointed to the other. "Sit down," he said to Philippa, "and explain yourself to me, madame. I go to find you among the queen's ladies, only to be told you have gone off with my cousin. Surely you realize that Guy-Paul is not a man to be trusted. He was a sly boy, and I saw immediately upon our renewing our acquaintance that he had not changed. What the hell were you doing with him, Philippa?"

"You're jealous!" she said, astounded to hear herself voicing the words. Why on earth would he be jealous? She was his wife, of course, but certainly he understood that she had an honorable nature, that she would never betray him. Why should he feel so strongly about her being with his cousin?

"Answer the question, madame," the earl said.

"King Francois saw me at the queen's banquet. He admired me. He wished to meet me. I saw no harm in it," Philippa explained.

"You saw no harm in being served up like a lamb to that great lecher?" the earl shouted at her. "What happened between you two?" he demanded. His eyes were cold.

"Nothing happened!" Philippa shouted back, enraged that he should doubt her. "How dare you impugn my honor, Crispin? I am your wife and not some court whore!"

"A woman alone with that king stands in danger of losing her good name, madame. And it is my name, damnit! Where was my cousin while you met Francois de Valois? And who else was there, or were you alone with that seducer of women?"

"Your cousin left me with the French king," Philippa said coldly. "The little turd scuttled away like the dung beetle he is. Were it not for the king's servant, I should have had my good name compromised, Crispin. I hope you will speak to Guy-Paul about his less than chivalrous behavior. I know that I shall never acknowledge his existence again. Now if you are through making certain that your possession was not damaged or used by another, I shall tell you what I overheard as I was attempting to make my way through the French camp and back here."

God's blood! the earl thought irritably. Was that what she thought? That he considered her only his possession? Did she think he could make love to her the way he did and have no feelings for her? He gritted his teeth. "My concern was only for you, little one. I could not find you, nor could I find that bastard with whom I share blood. I . . . I . . . never mind! Tell me about this alleged plot you think you overheard."

"There is nothing wrong with my hearing, Crispin," Philippa snapped. "As I was desperately attempting to find my way back to the jousting field I was caught in one of these dust storms that we have been having recently. It was then I heard them, and what I heard froze my blood in my veins. There were three of them. From what they said I believe them to be in the service of the dowager queen Louise of Savoy. The largest of the trio is Pierre. Another is Michel. The third was not named, and he remained silent. They spoke of murdering King Henry, the queen, and the cardinal."

"To what purpose?" he wondered aloud.

"They said they had compatriots in England who would steal Princess Mary away from her keepers and bring her to France. Once here her marriage to the Dauphin would be celebrated."

"And England would be France's," the earl finished.

"They said not even the pope would stop it," Philippa continued.

"Nay, he would have no grounds, the betrothal having been agreed upon by both Henry Tudor and Francois de Valois," the earl remarked.

"And they said our great families would not oppose them," she told him.

"Some would, and look for another English heir. Others would side with France because they had the princess. It would be civil war, Philippa." He shook his head. "I thought we were past that when the differences between Lancaster and York were settled. The question of England's throne has been raised before. When Duke William of Normandy overcame the last of the Saxon rulers, Harold. When Stephen and Matilda fought each other for years. The wars between the roses of Lancaster and York." He sighed. Then he said, "What else did you overhear?"

"They mean to do it sometime when they are all together, and they said that the salamander would be the sign," Philippa replied.

"The salamander is the French king's personal sign, but from what you have said he is innocent of any involvement in this plot. His mother, however, is another matter altogether. The woman is fiercely ambitious, and I would put nothing past her. She would do anything for her son, but murdering a king of England, his queen, and the cardinal is quite a grand scheme. I wonder if she knows, or if these men are acting on their own? Still, I shall have to speak to the cardinal, and he may want to talk to you, Philippa. How fortunate it is that you overheard this intrigue. You are certain that these conspirators did not see you."

"Of course they saw me when the dust died down, and they accosted me for they were afraid, but I pretended not to understand them. I spoke English to them, and was quite imperious. Make way for the countess of Witton!" She giggled. "The one called Pierre wanted to strangle me, but the one called Michel said my clothing indicated I was of some importance, and there would be questions. He thought since I didn't speak French it would be safe to let me go, and so they did. I was frightened to death, but I never showed it. And I was quite rude, as they expected an English lady to be when dealing with mere French minions," she finished with a grin.

"You could have been killed," he said softly. He felt his heart ache at the thought of losing her. Not once had he ever told her he loved her, but he realized now that he did. What if she had died never knowing that he loved her?

Outside there came a great shouting, and Peter ran out to see what it was. He came back several minutes later to tell them that the French king's huge pavilion had just blown away in the windstorm. "Their tents were flimsily affixed, my lord. There has been but slight damage among our tents."

Taking Philippa by the shoulders, the earl looked down into her face. "Promise me that you will remain here, little one. I must go and speak with Wolsey. It is up to him to decide what to do about this matter." He kissed her forehead. "I will come for you if the cardinal wants to see you. Go with no one else. Do you understand?"

She nodded, and watched as he left her. There had been an odd look in his eye when he had spoken to her that she did not understand. Philippa stood up, and then sat down again. The realization of the danger she had been in was now beginning to sink in. She looked after Crispin, but he had quickly gone. He had been very angry when he had first found her. She had accused him of being jealous. Was he jealous? And if he was, why was he jealous? He had to know she would do nothing to bring shame upon his good name. She knew he knew that. So why was he jealous?

A tiny curl of possibility began to awaken in her brain. Was it possible, just possible, that Crispin St. Claire actually cared for his wife? Liked her? Loved her? She had no knowledge other than that he had given her, but surely a man did not make love to his wife the way her husband did if there was not something pleasing about the lady. Philippa sighed. The queen would not know such things. Royalty were different from ordinary folk. Lucy would not know. Her practical serving woman had never been in love in her life. Only her mother would have such answers. But she was in France, and Rosamund was in the north of England. Philippa sat quietly waiting. She had no other choice in the matter.

"Is there another banquet tonight?" Lucy was at her side.

Philippa nodded. "Go to one of the queen's women, and say I ask to be excused. That the wind and the dust have given me a terrible aching in my head. That I will wait upon her highness in the morning before the mass."

"Are you alright?" Lucy wanted to know.

"I am not certain," Philippa responded. "Go now!"

"I'll come right back," Lucy promised, and hurried off.

Now that the storm had passed, Peter led their horses back outside and tied them to the railing set up for that purpose. Returning, he shoveled up the manure and removed it. Lucy returned, and Philippa gathered the two servants to her side and told them what she had overheard, and that the earl had gone to inform the cardinal.

"You can say nothing," she warned them. "I do not know what the cardinal will do, but I expect he will want to catch the conspirators if he can. We must give them no advantage over us," Philippa finished.

"What a terrible thing!" Lucy said, genuinely shocked.

"I'll keep me ears open, and me mouth shut," Peter offered.

Philippa smiled. "It will all be resolved to the good," she assured them.

"You might have been killed," Lucy said. "And what would I have told your mother then? And Annie would have killed me."

The remark made Philippa laugh. "I fear life back in England is going to be intolerably dull for us, Lucy," she teased her serving woman.

Both Lucy and Peter chortled.

"It has surely been more interesting for me since you married my master," Peter admitted with a small grin. "If your ladyship doesn't mind me saying so."

Crispin returned with the news that the cardinal wanted to see Philippa, but that he would come under cover of darkness to their pavilion, for it would seem odd if she appeared in his quarters. There were too many people around the cardinal, and that would lead to too many questions. He would come after the evening's banquet.

"I have sent word to the queen that I am ill," Philippa said. "I did not think I could face a large gathering tonight so soon after learning what I did this afternoon."

The earl nodded. "I will go, and I will bring Wolsey back here myself with only one servant. No one will think it odd that we are together given my previous service." He smiled a small smile. "Here I was supposed to be the one listening for information that might be of use to the king, and I have heard nothing that everyone else does not know, until today when my wife stumbled upon a scheme that could change the face of our world as we know it. Thank God you did overhear these men, Philippa, but I am even more grateful that you escaped them unscathed." His previous anger over her foolish visit to King Francois seemed now to be forgotten.

"I have told Peter and Lucy," Philippa said. Why did his eyes warm so when he looked at her?

"Aye, they should know, and they are wise enough to keep silent," he replied. Then he put his arms about her and tipped her face up to his. "Promise me you will go nowhere alone until this matter is settled," he said.

"I promise," she said breathlessly, and then he kissed her tenderly, and Philippa melted against him. If only he would love her, she thought, and then wondered why such an idea had come into her head. She was his wife. It didn't matter if he loved her or not. But it did, she suddenly realized. But why did it matter? She didn't understand why it mattered so much to her. Yet it did. She wanted to go home to England. She wanted to see her mother, who could surely explain all these puzzlements to her.

"You must not think when I kiss you," he gently teased her.

"I was thinking how much I like it when you kiss me," she flattered him. "I believe that I like being married to you, my lord husband."

His heart leapt beneath his doublet. "I am glad that you do, Philippa, for I find that I enjoy being your husband. Far more than I ever anticipated." He kissed her again. "I miss our bedsport," he murmured in her ear. "Do you?"

She nodded, blushing. "I was also thinking I cannot wait to get home to England, my lord. I think perhaps that I have had enough of the court for now. I want to see my family in the north. I want you to meet them, and know them. My stepfather will want to take you grouse hunting. He does love the sport muchly. I want you to see Friarsgate."

"Have you changed your mind about it, little one?" he asked her.

"Nay, it is not for me. Your Brierewode suits me far better," she said. "It is peaceful, and would appear to be a good place to raise children," and she blushed again.

He drew away from her. "I must get ready for tonight's banquet. Holding you in my arms like this is difficult, Philippa, especially when I want to take you to bed, and make love to you, and create that first of our children."

Reaching up, Philippa caressed his face with delicate fingers. "There is time, my lord, for all of that. We will depart this Field of the Cloth of Gold, as it has come to be known, in just a few more days. England and the rest of this summer await us."

"I want to go to Brierewode first," he said. "Before we go north."

"My sister is to be wed in late summer," she reminded him. "We shall know the date when we reach Oxfordshire. We will stay at Brierewode as long as we may, but I must see Banon wed to her Neville."

"Agreed, as long as you and I may spend the winter in our own little nest," he replied. "I picture us by ourselves before a warm fire on a snowy winter's night."

"Agreed," she responded with a small smile. "But you must let me sit in your lap, husband, and you must promise to caress my breasts so I may have pleasure of you."

He groaned. "Madame, the picture you paint makes me want to wish away the months until we may be together in so intimate a conjunction."

"Peter," Philippa called. "Come and help your master prepare for the banquet this evening. Lucy, go to the cook tents, and fetch me some supper." She slipped from his embrace easily with a small smile. I love him, she thought to herself, surprised.

The earl washed himself in a basin, and then with his serving man's aid dressed for the banquet being held this evening, given by the French admiral for the two royal couples. "I don't know when I'll be back," he told her before he left. "You know how these things can go, and each side has been striving to outdo the other." He kissed her lips lingeringly, and then with a sigh drew away.

"If I fall asleep, Lucy will awaken me when you return," she said. "I want to be helpful to the cardinal. It cannot hurt to have him in our debt."

"Thomas Wolsey only takes, little one," her husband said. "And he will not remain in power forever. He has made many enemies over the years. No matter his value to the king, there will come a day when he makes one mistake too many, offends the absolute wrong person one time too many, and poof! The king will dismiss him without a thought, and even take revenge on him for disappointing him."

"King Henry would never be unkind," Philippa said innocently.

"May you never see that side of him, little one," the earl told her, and then, turning on his heel, he went off to the banquet being held this night.

Lucy was returning with food for them as he left. She was practically bowed down by the weight of the tray she carried. Mistress and servants sat down at the table to eat. There was a fat capon roasted to a golden brown, three meat pastries, fresh bread, butter, a soft French cheese, and some fresh peaches. To her surprise Philippa found, despite all that had happened today, she had a large appetite. She ate heartily, and drank two cups of a sweet rich wine. But having eaten, she found that she grew quickly sleepy.

"I can't sleep," she said.

"You can't remain awake either, my lady," Lucy said. "Come along. When the earl returns I will awaken you." She escorted Philippa into the smaller half of the tent, helped her to undress, leaving her mistress in her chemise, brushed her long hair, and put her to bed. Philippa was instantly asleep. "Poor lady," Lucy said to Peter when she had returned into the other room, "she was so brave today, but surely she must have been very frightened. I know I should have been."

"Aye," Peter agreed. "I've seen those before who have taken a fright. Afterwards they sleep, and it helps to heal them. She was a brave young woman standing up to those French ruffians, pretending she didn't understand their garbled tongue."

The earl returned close to midnight, bringing Cardinal Wolsey and his servant with him. He instructed Lucy to awaken Philippa, and then the three servants waited outside beneath the awning while their masters met in secret. Philippa came from the makeshift bedchamber in her long silk chemise. It was tied at the neck with white silk ribbons, and had long sleeves. Her garb was as modest as it could be under the circumstances. Her unbound long hair gave her a particularly young and innocent look.

"Your grace," she said, curtseying, and kissing the outstretched hand. The cardinal, she noted, had a large hand with well-shaped, graceful fingers and neatly pared, clean fingernails.

The cardinal was seated, but he did not invite his host and hostess to sit. "Your husband has told me, madame, of your adventure this afternoon. Now I would have you tell me. Begin where you left the French king's tent."

Philippa blushed, but then she began. "My husband's cousin had departed, and left me to find my own way. And the tent, your grace, was where the king changed after the jousts. It was not that great thing that blew away this afternoon. As you may know, the tents in that area are small, and lined up one after the other. It was like being in the midst of a garden maze. I had no idea where I was, or how to proceed. Then I recalled that our encampment was to the west. I looked to see if I might ascertain the position of the sun, and once I had I went in that direction, turning twice. I finally saw the jousting field ahead of me, but there was also a party of rather rough-looking knights near the exit, and so I moved one row over in order to avoid them. Frankly I did not wish to be seen. At that point another of those nasty little dust storms came up, and I could see nothing ahead of me. I was afraid to proceed lest I be lost again, and so I stopped, waiting for the storm to subside. It was then I overhead two men talking."

"Your husband said there were three," the cardinal interrupted.

"There were, but only two spoke. And when I first heard them I could not see them through the dust," Philippa replied. She looked directly at the cardinal. He was a fat man with a long nose. He was dressed in his red cardinal's robes, but the sleeves that showed from beneath his robes were black.

He looked back at her from beneath his hooded eyelids. "Continue, madame."

She did, reciting her tale once more, and when she had finished he nodded at her.

"You are certain they are in the service of the dowager of France?" he asked.

"Aye, and they said she would protect them if they were caught. Your grace, I somehow believe this plot is of their own making in an effort to ingratiate themselves with their mistress. Although she could have said something in an unguarded moment that they misunderstood, or mistook, I cannot believe a great lady like Louise of Savoy would devise such a conspiracy."

"For a girl at court for four years, madame, you remain singularly innocent of the evils that men do. I suppose it is the queen's influence upon you," the cardinal noted dryly. "Frankly it matters not to me if the French dowager is personally involved. What is important is that we find a way to foil this plot. Except for these three fools, anyone else implicated will escape retribution, especially the higher one looks up the ladder. But when will they attempt this perfidy? That is the puzzle we must solve."

"They said it was a time when you would all be together," Philippa said.

The cardinal appeared to be deep in thought. His elegant fingers drummed softly upon the wooden arm of the chair in which he sat. His mouth was pursed. His eyes closed. And then they opened. "Of course!" he exclaimed. "It is the perfect time!"

"My lord?" the earl said.

"The last event of this great flummery is a mass at which I will personally preside," the cardinal said. "Everyone will be there. Both royal houses, both courts, and as many of their servants as can crowd into the chapel that will be erected over the tiltyard. What better place for an assassination to take place? King Henry and his queen will be up front, as will the dowager of France, King Francois, and his queen. And I will be there." He fixed his gaze upon Philippa. "Would you recognize these three men, madame, if you saw them again? Did you get a good enough look at their faces in your fright?"

"I was frightened, your grace, but I was not blinded by that fear," Philippa told him. "I can recognize those three without any difficulty."

"Excellent, madame," the cardinal said.

"What of the salamander that is to be the signal?" Philippa boldly queried him.

The cardinal shrugged. "I have no idea what it might mean, but the important thing is that you are able to identify these men among the queen dowager's servants."

"Surely you cannot demand that Louise of Savoy make her servants line themselves up for your inspection," the earl said.

The cardinal barked a small laugh. "Nay, my dear Crispin, it would be too easy for our conspirators to avoid such an event, and frankly I doubt the dowager could identify the faces of all of her servants. How often do we actually observe those who serve us, my lord? They matter not. Only that they do their duty to us."

"Then you plan to wait until the mass itself," the earl said. "Is that not dangerous, your grace? Will there be time at that moment to stop these assassinations?"

"There is no other way," the cardinal said calmly. "God will protect us." Then he arose from the chair where he had been ensconced. "I must return to my own quarters before it is realized that I have not yet come back from the banquet. Madame, I thank you for your cleverness, and your sharp ears. I did not know your father personally, but I do know from what has been said of him that he would be proud of you this day." He held out his hand to her once again, and Philippa kissed it. The cardinal then looked to the earl. "You are to be commended in your choice of a wife, Crispin." The hand was once more extended, and the earl kissed it. "Good night to you both," the powerful cleric said, and then sweeping past them, he departed the pavilion of the earl and countess of Witton.

"In all my time at court I never before met him," Philippa said softly. "I find him both compelling and frightening."

The earl laughed. "He is indeed both, little one."

"Will he indeed make no effort to find the assassins before the mass?" Philippa asked her husband. "If we walked about the French camp, especially near the dowager's pavilion, we might spot them."

"Or they might spot us, and realize that you had indeed understood every foul word that they had uttered," the earl said. "Nay, little one. While the cardinal's plan may seem simple, perhaps even dangerous, he always seems to know just what to do." He put an arm about her and kissed the top of her head.

Unable to help herself, Philippa leaned against her husband as a feeling of total happiness seemed to sweep over her. I love him, she thought once again. If only he could love me, but then as kind as he has been since our wedding, he only wed me for the lands he wanted. It is unlikely to ever be anything more. And yet . . . She sighed.

On the following day gifts were exchanged between England and France. They were lavish to the point of excess, but illustrated the amity that seemed to exist between the two sovereigns. But even though Henry and Francois had exhibited great cordiality towards one another, it was not genuine. Beneath the civilized veneer the old enmity still existed. Yet there had been no breaches of etiquette between any of the participants at the Field of the Cloth of Gold as the courtiers and their servants followed in the footsteps of their masters.

The French king presented his English counterpart with two magnificent horses. One was a sorrel mare named Mantellino who was prized for her great ability on the jousting field. The other, the dappled Mozaurcha, was equally famed. Henry gave the French king a jeweled collar with an enormous ruby pendant in the shape of a heart, as well as several horses. The Mantuan ambassador, however, was heard to remark that the French horses were the better bargain.

Queen Claude gifted Queen Katherine with a beautiful litter complete with mules to pull it, and several pages. Queen Katherine gave Queen Claude four splendidly trapped riding horses. The cardinal received from the French king two gold vases. In return he offered Francois an illuminated Book of the Hours that had been made for King Louis who was called saint. Louise of Savoy gave Wolsey a jeweled crucifix. He gave her a relic of the true cross that had been placed in a jeweled setting.

After almost a month of feasting and jousting and general sociability, the Field of the Cloth of Gold was drawing to a close. On the day of the gifts the jousting field was empty of combatants. Instead it was filled with carpenters and joiners, glaziers and tilers, all busily erecting a temporary chapel. The two kings swore that a church, Our Lady of Friendship, would one day rise on the spot, and that they would return to pray and socialize in the years to come. It was planned that Cardinal Wolsey lay the foundation stone of the new church after the final mass.

The court crowded into the chapel, Philippa making certain she was near the queen with her husband. The choir from the Chapel Royal would sing the mass. The candlesticks from Westminster Abbey adorned the altar, sitting upon an altar cloth brought from the Notre Dame cathedral in Paris. The chalices came from both cathedrals. The cardinal in his scarlet robes was attended by both English and French priests.

And then Philippa saw him. The man who had remained silent the day she had heard the conspirators. For a moment she could not believe her eyes, but then she leaned over and whispered softly to her husband. "Crispin, one of the three is on the altar with the cardinal. My God! Is he a priest? This is terrible!"

"Which one?" the earl whispered back, signaling discreetly to one of the English priests he knew who stood with the queen even as he asked the question.

"The red-haired man. He wore a cap that day, and the dust obscured his hair color, but it is he. There are just two elderly priests between him and the cardinal," Philippa said nervously.

"My lord?" The priest was at his side.

"The red-haired man near Wolsey is an assassin, father. Wolsey was expecting it, but did not know the identity of the man. We have only just identified him. Can you reach the cardinal?" the earl of Witton asked.

The priest nodded. He recognized the earl as a man once in the king's service who took his orders through the cardinal. He recognized his pale-faced young wife as a devoted servant of the queen. Quietly he slipped into the choir, moving past the choristers in the rear row until he was at the far end on the altar. He murmured to another priest, and together the two men eased themselves nearer the red-haired priest until they were on either side of him.

"You will come with us, father," the queen's man said softly. "Your plot has been discovered, and the cardinal will want to speak with you after the mass."

The French priest looked startled, but then allowed himself to be escorted off without making any disturbance. They took him through a side door out into the field. The earl was already there, and a quick search of the prisoner revealed a rather nasty-looking dagger. Its tip was darker than the rest of the blade.

"Beware!" the earl cried. "The tip is poison!"

"You may have saved your cardinal, but shortly your king and your queen will be dead. There is nothing you can do to save them," the priest snarled.

The earl of Witton grasped the French priest about the neck, the tip of the poisoned dagger close, but not yet touching his throat. "I want the location and names of the other two in this nefarious plot," he said.

"Go to the devil!" the priest replied venomously.

"Are you really ready to give up your life in this ridiculous hope that having murdered England's monarchs in order to steal their child, France will rule England? There are still men in England whose blood makes them legitimate heirs to its throne. The duke of Buckingham for one. Only their acquiescence to the Tudors has allowed that family to rule, but if the Tudors were gone these men would rise up to claim what is their right." He moved the dagger closer to the priest's skin.

The priest was silent, but they could see he was considering the earl's words very carefully. "What will become of us?" he finally asked nervously.

"Give me the names of the others, and where they stand. I will return you all to your mistress. What she does with you is her business. We do not want to destroy the amity that has existed in this month between our nations. Tell me now, or as God is my witness I will prick you with this blade, and leave you to die unshriven! Will you go to your maker, priest, with this sin on your soul?"

"Pierre and Michel, serving men of the dowager queen. They stand with her now in the chapel. Pierre is taller than any other there but your own king. Michel stands to his right," the priest cried. "Take the blade from my neck, I beg you!"

The earl shoved the man to the ground and handed the dagger to the queen's priest. "Watch him carefully, and do not permit him off his knees until the Swiss Guard come for him, good fathers. If he attempts to escape you, blood him with the dagger."

Then the earl hurried back into the chapel, quickly speaking with the captain of the king's own Yeomen. Quietly the men-at-arms moved to where the two men they sought stood among the French dowager queen's servants. Discreetly they hustled the two from the chapel even before they might protest. Few noticed, for the courtiers were caught up in the sumptuous beauty and magnificence of the mass. Most there recognized that this was the close of a most historic event. They wanted to absorb it all so they might tell their children and their grandchildren one day. Even Louise of Savoy ignored the small to-do.

Outside, the three conspirators were now on their knees, their arms bound behind them, the yeomen watching over them. The two English priests had disappeared back into the chapel.

"Take them somewhere where they will not be seen by the kings or the courts," the earl said to the captain of the guard. "I will speak with his grace after the mass, and he will decide what is to be done with them."

"Aye, my lord," came the response.

Suddenly down the field there came a shouting. "The Salamander! The Salamander!" There was the smell of gunpowder and a whine in the sky.

"What is it?" the captain of the yeomen asked.

"It would appear," the earl said, "that one of the fireworks for the festivities later was exploded prematurely. I will go and check." And when he did, the earl learned that he was correct in his assumption. The Salamander, which was the French king's own personal sign, had been accidentally lit by a young boy, those in charge of the fireworks told the earl. A local lad hired to help.

"Clumsy brat!" the fireworks artisan said angrily. "Any other piece I could have tolerated, but the king's own symbol! There will be no time to make another."

"Where is the boy?"

"I beat him, and sent him off," the man said.

"Do you know who he is?" the earl asked patiently.

"My sister's worthless son," came the answer.

"I need to speak with the lad," the earl told the artisan.

"Piers, you miserable little turd, where are you?" the man shouted. "Get back here or when I catch you I'll flay the very flesh from your skinny bottom!"

They waited a long moment, and then a boy crept from the shadows of the artisan's wagon. He was dirty, and looked hungry.

"Come here, brat!" the artisan shouted. "This fine gentleman wishes to speak with you, though why I have no idea."

"Stay," the earl said quietly. "Come, lad." He beckoned the boy in kindly tones.

"Yes, milord?" the boy whispered. He looked frightened.

"Now, lad, you must tell me the truth, and if you do I will reward you. But I will know if you are lying to me. Do you understand?"

"Yes, milord." The answer was subdued.

"Did someone pay you to fire the king's Salamander when the sun reached its zenith this morning? The truth now, lad."

The boy looked very frightened. "Did I do something wrong, milord?"

"Perhaps you did, but I will not punish you for it nor will anyone else. But I need the truth from you. Did someone pay you to fire the Salamander?"

"Aye, milord." The boy nodded his head. " 'Twas a priest, and he gave me a silver penny to do it. He said the king's mother wished to play a jest upon him."

"A silver penny?" the artisan exclaimed. "Where is it, you little turd? The penny should be mine for all the trouble you've caused me." He glowered menacingly at his nephew, and thrust his hand in the boy's face. "Give it to me!"

"I gave it to my mother," the boy shouted back at his uncle. "You have paid me nothing since you took me as your apprentice. My mother needs to feed her children."

The artisan cuffed the boy angrily, but the earl put a hand on the man's arm.

"Leave the boy alone," he said. "I may need him to identify this priest, and if he can there is something in it for you."

"What is this about?" the artisan suddenly asked, now nervous of this tall Englishman.

"There has been a plot against someone in a high place, and your nephew was duped into lighting the Salamander which was to be the signal for the assassins," the earl answered.

The fireworks artisan crossed himself nervously, murmuring, "Mother of God!"

"The boy is innocent of any wrongdoing," the earl told the artisan quietly. "He was offered a chance to gain a silver penny, and he took it. No one was harmed, because the conspiracy was discovered in time. But I will want the boy to identify the priest for the proper authorities. You must both come with me."

"Who are you?" the artisan asked.

"My name would mean naught to you, but you should know I am in the service of Cardinal Wolsey. You will be rewarded for your cooperation, I promise you."

The artisan shook his head. "Very well, we will come with you," he said. He might be French, but everyone knew of the great cardinal who some said was the real ruler of England and the English. He reached out and grabbed his nephew by the collar of his shirt. "Come along, Piers, and tell the truth, you worthless piece of merde!"

The earl led the way from the field where the fireworks display was set up, through the English encampment to the cardinal's pavilion. Recognized by the guard at the entrance, he was allowed to pass into the tent with his companions. Inside he saw the trio of miscreants on their knees before Wolsey, now returned from the mass.

"That's him!" the boy burst out without even being asked. " 'Tis yon priest who paid me a silver penny to light the Salamander before I should."

Cardinal Wolsey beckoned them forward. "Explain, Witton," he said.

"Remember that Philippa said 'the salamander' was to be the sign for the assassination. The lad is the fireworks artisan's apprentice. He was paid a silver penny to light the Salamander when the sun reached its zenith this morning. The fireworks, of course, are not until this evening. The Salamander was to be the signal for the assassination to commence. The boy knew nothing of that, of course. He said a priest paid him, and said that the king's mother wished to play a jest on her son."

"And you see that same priest here in my pavilion, lad?" the cardinal said.

"Aye, your grace. He kneels before you there." The boy pointed directly at the guilty man.

Cardinal Wolsey nodded. "Thank you, lad. Kneel, both of you, and I will give you my blessing." The cardinal was known to be parsimonious. When he had blessed the pair he surprised the earl by reaching deep into a pocket hidden in his robes and drawing forth two coins. The larger of the two he gave to the artisan, the smaller to the boy.

The earl saw the glint of silver, and almost smiled. This information must have meant a great deal to the cardinal that he would part with silver.

"You," Wolsey said to the artisan, "will return to your fireworks, for the display tonight must be a fine one. I will send the boy to you before evening. I need him to remain for now. He will have to tell his story to another." The cardinal turned to one of his servants. "Have my litter prepared and brought forth. I am going to pay a visit upon the dowager queen herself, and see what she has to say about this plot." Now he focused his gaze upon the earl of Witton. "You have done well, as you have always been wont to do, Crispin. Now go and find your wife, and enjoy the rest of this spectacle. One more interminable banquet filled with over-rich foods, a show of fireworks, and we may all finally go home again to our perfect English summer. Provided, of course, that it does not rain for weeks on end, but then after this unbearable heat and all this dust I think I will welcome the rain. Go! Go!" He waved his beringed hand at the earl.

Crispin St. Claire bowed to the cardinal. "Thank you, your grace," he said. "I am glad to have once again been of service, but it is really my wife to whom the glory should go. If she had not overheard these three, their wicked plot might have succeeded."

Philippa

Comprehension dawned upon the face of the largest prisoner. He looked to the man called Michel and said, "I told you we should have strangled the bitch. She understood every word we said that day."

"Aye, she did," the earl told them. And then, laughing, he left the cardinal's pavilion to find Philippa and tell her all that had transpired.

Chapter 18

꧁꧂

They came home to Brierewode on a warm summer's day. A bluish haze hung over the hills, and the greenery had that lush, perfect summer fullness about it. When the Field of the Cloth of Gold had ended, the king and the court had retired to Calais where Henry dismissed most of his entourage, sending them home. He and the queen then rode to Gravelines to meet with the Emperor Charles and the Regent Margaret. The four returned to Calais where a treaty was signed between Charles and Henry in which England agreed not to sign any new treaties with France for the next two years. King Francois was not pleased, but there was nothing he could do. Crispin and Philippa had arrived home even before these events had transpired.

They had made the brief voyage from Calais to Dover in the vessel Lord Cambridge had hired for them, along with a dozen minor courtiers who had begged passage in order to return to England quickly. Most were Oxford men that Crispin knew, and he was glad to aid his neighbors. Their trip was even swifter than the last one, for the summer winds blew briskly. Philippa and Lucy sat out upon the deck, for being in the small cabin seemed to encourage seasickness. Crispin and their fellow passengers played at cards and diced to pass the time.

They had departed before dawn, and watched the sun rise over the receding French coast. In Dover their horses were unloaded from the ship, and they began their ride home to Oxfordshire. Something was happening, Philippa realized almost at once. The careful friendly and mannerly relationship she had built up these past two months with her husband seemed to be changing. It had begun in France when he had come upon her after she had heard the assassins. She didn't understand it. He was more attentive. She caught him gazing at her more times than not now with a tender look in those silvery gray eyes of his that could turn so cold at a moment's notice. What was happening? Did he love her? Was such a thing even possible between them? And did she love him? She thought she did, but she wasn't really certain just what being in love with someone entailed. And she could not tell him. If there was one lesson she had learned well at the court, it was that a woman never declared her affections until a gentleman did first.

He made no move to touch her when they went to bed at their roadside inns. When she asked him why, he said it was because he preferred to wait until they were at home. Philippa understood, for their accommodations had not been arranged by Lord Cambridge as he had not known when they would return. Yet she was anxious to see if their bedsport was still as pleasurable as it had previously been. They rode each day until dark, staying at whatever respectable accommodation they found. And then they were at Brierewode once more, and Mistress Marian was surprised, for she had not thought to see them again until the autumn.

Philippa ordered up her bath. She could scarcely wait to bathe, not having been able to do so for many days. And her hair was filthy with the dusty summer roads. Even brushing could not help it. While Lucy was busy preparing the tub out in the dayroom, and the serving men were busy filling it with the hot water, Philippa flung open the casement windows in the bedchamber and leaned out. The air was sweet and fresh with the smells of summer, but the haze on the hills was heavier now. There would be rain by evening. She sighed with the realization that she was glad to be home. She had spent very little time at Brierewode, but aye, it was home. She could feel it in her bones.

This was where she would live out her life but for yearly court visits. This would be where her children would be born.

Her children. His children. Their children. But it was not likely there would be any children if she continued to take her mother's secret draught to prevent conception. Philippa felt a deep stab of guilt. What she was doing was against the church. The queen would be horrified. And yet Philippa had not confessed her sin to a priest. She had continued to claim little sins of this and that, and then open her mouth for the host. It was a wonder it had not choked her, she considered remorsefully. But was she really sorry? She didn't think she was. Nor did she believe she would ever share her knowledge with the church. She had seen enough women in her time die from too many offspring in too short a time. Nay. Her guilt stemmed not from what she was doing, but from the fact she was not doing her duty by Crispin, who was so good to her and who badly wanted an heir.

There had been a message from Otterly when they had arrived. Lord Cambridge had written that Banon's wedding was set for September twentieth. He would expect to see them there, and at Friarsgate beforehand. Rosamund was most anxious to meet her new son-in-law. "Your mother has not yet given up the hope that you will have Friarsgate as she has always planned," Thomas Bolton wrote to the countess of Witton.

If you and Crispin have not changed your minds I am certain that he shall convince Rosamund otherwise, but what she will do then I do not know. Still, she is young enough yet, and there is time for a new heir to be chosen.

It would probably be one of her Hepburn half brothers, Philippa considered. She almost laughed to think what the late Henry Bolton would think of such a thing. Had he not already died, such a plan was more than likely to kill him. She chuckled aloud.

"Bath's ready," Lucy said, coming into the bedchamber. "What makes you laugh? It's a most wicked sound that you made."

"I was imagining great-uncle Henry's reaction to one of my Hepburn kinsmen inheriting Friarsgate one day," Philippa replied.

"So you're certain, are you, that you really don't want it," Lucy said. Her supple fingers unlaced her mistress's bodice.

Philippa nodded. "Just now gazing out the windows I realized that I had come home at last," she told her serving woman. "Brierewode is where we belong, Lucy."

"Aye, and you'll have no argument from me, my lady. This Oxfordshire is a fair land." She undid the tabs holding the bodice to the skirt, and untied the skirt.

The skirt and its petticoats slid to the carpet, and Philippa stepped out of them even as Lucy drew the bodice off of her mistress. "Wash what can be washed, but those skirts, I think, have seen better days," Philippa noted with a wry smile.

"I'll have them cleaned up nonetheless, and you can wear them to travel north rather than waste another garment," Lucy responded in practical tones.

Philippa sat down, and Lucy drew off the heavy leather shoes her mistress used for riding. "These will need repair, and a good polishing," she noted as she pulled the stockings from Philippa's feet. "And these can be burned, for they are worn out from your travels, I can see. There's a hole in one heel, and another starting in the toe of the other."

Philippa stood up again and, untying the ribbons of her chemise, shrugged it off. She was quite naked now. She walked from her bedchamber into the dayroom where the tub was set up before the fireplace. Even on a summer's day a fire burned, taking the damp off of the chamber. Lucy had set towels to warming on a towel rack in front of the hearth. She stooped to gather up her lady's garments and followed her into the dayroom.

"I'll take these to the laundress now," she said, "and be back to help you."

"Nay," Philippa said, "wash my hair first. I would make certain there are no fleas or bedbugs in it, for the inns we stayed at coming home were only the ones we could find when it grew dark. I far prefer it when Uncle Thomas makes our arrangements. I intend to write him so our trip north will be a pleasant one." She climbed up the steps and down into her tub. "Ahhh, the water is deliciously hot, Lucy."

Lucy dropped her bundle of garments on the floor of the dayroom, and climbing up the steps to the tub she said, "Duck under now, my lady, and I'll give your head a good scrubbing." She dipped her hand into the soap jar, scooping out a handful, and placing it on Philippa's head she began to wash the young woman's hair. Twice she lathered, and twice she rinsed. Finishing, she wrapped Philippa's head in a warmed towel. "There, my lady, and not a flea, nit, or bedbug did I find." Then climbing down she gathered up the clothing on the floor and hurried out.

Philippa closed her eyes. Just having her head washed so thoroughly made her feel good. She heard a faint rumble of thunder and, opening her eyes, looked through the open windows of the dayroom. The skies were darkening now, and it would rain soon. She didn't care. She was home. Her hair was clean, and her bed tonight would be fresh. The door to the dayroom opened again, and Crispin entered.

Seeing her, he grinned. "I'm going to join you," he told her, and began stripping off his garments.

"What if Lucy comes back, and sees you naked?" Philippa protested.

"Lucy won't be back until we call her. I ran into her out in the corridor. And when I pull that bellpull by our bed, madame, she will come with supper for us. I am not of a mind to go into the hall tonight. You are to be my appetizer, wife." The last of his clothing hit the floor, and he walked towards the tub.

"We'll overflow the water," she protested weakly.

"Nay, we won't," he replied. "I told the men just how much water to fill." He climbed up the steps, and then stepped into the water.

Yanking Philippa to him he kissed her, a deep and passionate kiss. "We have been too long apart, little one."

"We have not been apart at all," she exclaimed breathlessly.

He pulled the towel from her head, and his fingers dug into her scalp. "Aye, we have been apart, madame, but we will not be apart any longer." He released her head, and his hands dove beneath the water to cup the twin halves of her bottom, lifting her up to impale her upon his love rod. "Now, wife, we are no longer apart," he growled as her eyes widened with surprise, and he pressed her back against the wooden sides of the tub.

"Oh, my lord!" she exclaimed as he slipped into her love channel. She had not forgotten how marvelous his passion was these last few weeks, but she had forgotten how big he was. He plumbed her to the very depths of her soul, his lean hips moving faster and faster until to her surprise they both cried out.

"God's wounds, I am a beast!" he groaned. "I had not a damned thought for you. Only my own pleasure. Forgive me, Philippa!"

She laughed weakly. "Crispin, I do not know how ladylike it is of me to admit that despite the swiftness of it all I gained pleasure too."

"You wanted this too?" he asked.

"Very much, my lord," she answered him with a small smile. "I have missed our couplings, husband. But we must wash each other first so we may get into bed, and continue this delightful interlude. Then I shall want to eat, and possibly make love again, unless, of course, you are too tired from all our travels," she concluded teasingly. She unlocked her grip about his neck, her feet touching the bottom of the tub once more.

"Madame, you truly amaze me," he told her, approval in his eyes.

"I shall wash your hair, for though Lucy found no bugs in mine that does not mean you have escaped unscathed, my lord." Then Philippa set about to slosh water on his ash brown hair and wash it. When she had finished, she took up the bathing brush and scrubbed his back, his shoulders, and his arms. She took up the soft flannel cloth and, soaping it, wiped it across his broad chest and over his dear face. She washed and she rinsed until she declared him clean. "Now get out, and let me conclude my ablutions, my lord. The towels are warm."

He obeyed, climbing from the tub, taking up a towel with which to dry himself, and then watching with pleasure as the tips of her breasts bobbed above the water while she scrubbed her back. His mouth yearned to close over those tempting little bits of flesh. He toweled off his head, and then wrapped the fabric about his loins, but it did nothing to disguise the burgeoning lust that was beginning to consume him. He had never wanted any woman in the way that he desired Philippa. Philippa, his adorable little wife! Philippa, who not only burned a fire in his body, but in his heart as well. But how could he tell her, when she gave no evidence that her heart was engaged by his. She was sweet, and biddable. She was faithful to the church, and passionate in their bed. But she gave nothing of her emotions even as she gave so generously of her body. "I will wait for you in our bedchamber," he said, and disappeared through the door into the other room.

"I will not be long," she called after him. Holy Mary! she thought. He was so very passionate. Were all men like this? Another question among the many for her mother to answer. And suddenly Philippa knew that she had to go to Friarsgate as soon as possible. If he was passionate, then why did he not love her, and if he did, why did he not declare it? Her mother would surely have the solutions to all her queries. She climbed from her tub, and slowly, carefully, dried herself off. Then sitting by the fire, she rubbed her hair with the toweling until it was dry too. Dropping the towel upon the floor, she walked into their bedchamber.

"Stop!" he said as she stepped across the threshold. "I want to look at you, little one. You are so outrageously fair, Philippa." His gaze warmed her flesh, and then he held out his hand to her, and she came forward to take it. He drew her into their bed, pulling her down to kiss him.

Outside there was a crack of lightning, and Philippa felt as if it were the joining of their lips that had caused it. Their mouths seemed fused together in a hot and wet kiss that deepened in intensity as her naked breasts pressed against his smooth broad chest. She lay atop him, and her hands tangled themselves into his hair even as his ensnared themselves in her thick auburn hair, his fingers kneading her scalp. His body was warm against hers. She could feel his need for her once again, sense his restraint as they sought to savor this heated moment building between them. Finally she drew her head away from his, her lips bruised and actually aching.

He lifted her up so that she sat upon his torso, her legs on either side of him. She held down his lust with her sweet small bottom, and for now he wanted it that way. Reaching up, he fondled her breasts. They were perfect little spheres of delight. He cupped one breast in the palm of his hand. The fingers from his other hand brushed the tender flesh lightly. He put those fingers in his mouth, and then encircled her nipple with the wetness. She shivered slightly. He took that nipple between his thumb and his forefinger, rubbing it until it had become a very hard little nub. He pinched it, and she made a sound. Looking up at her face he saw that her eyes were closed as she experienced each new pleasure that he offered. He played with the first breast for a time, and then moved on to the second.

She sighed, but was silent. He knew what he would do next. It was time. After a month of celibacy for them both she would be ready for what he wanted from her next. "Lie back now, little one," he said low. "Lie back for me, and I will give you a wonderful new experience. You must not be fearful, Philippa. I would never harm you."

Her heart beat faster at his words. The unknown frightened her, but every unknown she had unveiled with him had brought her nothing but pleasure. Obediently she lay back. He pushed her legs up halfway, and she felt him press a pillow beneath her buttocks. What was he doing? Her eyes remained closed. She didn't know if she was ready yet to view him as he made love to her. Then he raised her legs higher, and over her shoulders. She felt his hands holding her firmly in that position. His head? Was that his head between her thighs? Holy Mary, it was! And then she felt his tongue beginning to push between her nether lips and forage in her most secret place. Philippa gasped, shocked. "Crispin!" she managed to cry out, and her eyes flew open.

He lifted his head to meet her gaze. "Trust me, little one," was all he said, and then his head fell again, and she felt his tongue on her.

The tongue was the most exquisite torment she had ever known before. It licked, and it lapped her silken flesh. Her juices were flowing faster and more copiously than they ever had. And he was eagerly drinking them down from the sound that his busy tongue was making. Then the tongue touched a place that heretofore only his finger had touched. And that tongue worked back and forth over the sensitive jewel of her womanhood until Philippa was moaning. It was too sweet. She would die of it, but she didn't. The wave simply rose, and rose, and rose before falling. Twice he pleasured her in this new way, and then he was mounting her. His lover's lance was pushing into her love sheath. He was moving on her. Her body responded, rising up to meet him again and again until she was whimpering with her need to be satisfied. And then their mutual hunger was met. He exploded his juices into her and, shuddering, fell away from her with a deep groan of satisfaction.

They lay side by side gasping with the wonder of what had just transpired between them. Reaching out, he took her hand in his, but he said nothing. Why could she not say she cared for him, the earl wondered? Surely what had just happened to them could not have happened did she not love him.

Philippa felt several tears slip down her cheeks, but she too remained silent. Why would he not say he loved her? But perhaps he didn't.

Finally Crispin St. Claire spoke in low tones. "Is it possible that we have made a child this night?" he wondered aloud.

"I do not know, my lord," Philippa whispered back, knowing that they had not because of the brew she took each day.

"I think we have," he said with certainty. "Such passion between a man and his wife should not go for naught."

"I have never considered the passion between us for naught, my lord," she replied.

"Indeed, madame?" How interesting, he thought. Her responses to their lovemaking was everything a man could want of a woman, but she rarely spoke on it. "Are you hungry?" he asked her. "Shall I call Lucy to bring us our supper?"

"Hmmm." She nodded. "Wake me when it comes," and her eyes closed.

He reached out and yanked the bellpull. He had already ordered their supper from the kitchens and so he knew what the tray would contain. Putting his arm around Philippa, he lay quietly listening to her sleep. She was very tired from their travels, and he almost wished they did not have to go north in another few weeks, but he had promised her the visit. Her sister's wedding was important to her, and he needed to meet his in-laws. He considered Philippa's birthright, and wondered if he was wise in refusing it, in allowing her to refuse it. Aye, he was. The St. Claires of Wittonsby were no great family, nor were they likely to be a great family. The days in which a man might draw his family higher were gone. Hearing Lucy outside in the dayroom, the earl rose from his bed, wrapping the discarded toweling about him, and went to speak with her.

"Empty the tub out, and then get Peter to help you put it away. Her ladyship will not need you again tonight, Lucy. Was your chamber ready for you?"

"Oh, yes, my lord," Lucy said. "Everything was just as I left it, and Mistress Marian is most kind. She has asked me to have supper with her and Peter."

"Do the tub then, and you are both dismissed," he told the young servant, and returned into the bedchamber, shutting the door behind him.

Lucy quickly went to the cupboard and pulled out a length of hose.

Attaching it to a spout on the side of the tub, she brought the hose over to the window. Drawing back the drapery, she lifted a copper flap on the outside wall and pushed the hose through the opening into a drain that ran down the outside wall of the house. Then hurrying back to the tub she turned a spigot, and the water in the tub began to drain out. The door from the corridor outside opened, and Peter entered.

"Ah," he said, "you have it going already. I came to help you so we might go and have supper with my sister. She wants to know more about you."

"You can help me get the tub back into its cupboard," Lucy said. "Why does your sister want to know more about me? What is there to know? I was raised at Friarsgate. My sister is the Lady Rosamund's tiring woman. I have been with my lady since she was ten years old. There is no mystery about me. I am what you see."

"My sister thinks we should marry," Peter said quietly.

"What?" Lucy looked very surprised. "Why would she think that?"

"She says it is a good thing for the earl's valet and the countess's tiring woman to be wed. That way each is not distracted in their duty by others," Peter replied.

"Your sister is a bossy woman if you were to ask me," Lucy said sharply. "I'm not of a mind to wed right now. Besides, I think you are probably too old for me."

"I am forty," he answered her.

"And I am twenty," Lucy said. "Still, if one day we were to become fond of one another I might consider marriage. But not now, and I will tell your sister so if she presses the issue. Come on now, and help me tip the tub to get the last of the water out. The supper on the table will be cold if we do not complete our duty, and depart. Our master and mistress will not thank us if it is."

"I think they are more interested in their bedsport right now than food," Peter said with a twinkle in his eye.

"Why, bless me," Lucy chuckled, "you are not all stiff and starch, are you?"

"We shall not tell Mistress Marian that, however, shall we?" he responded.

"Nay, we won't, Master Slyboots," Lucy said with a grin.

The tub emptied, together they wrestled it back into the large cupboard in the wall and departed the apartment, Lucy giving the door a little slam on the way out to alert her master that they were gone.

The door to the bedchamber opened, and the earl came out to inspect the covered dishes on the tray. There was a small dish of oysters that had come up the river today, and he swallowed six down, pouring himself a goblet of red wine and drinking it along with the oysters. Philippa came sleepily from the bedchamber. She was naked. She said nothing, but inspected the tray, and picking up a meat pastry began to eat it hungrily. He poured another goblet of wine and handed it to her.

"Thank you," she murmured, reaching for a second pastry, which she devoured as quickly as the first. She peered at the dishes, and seeing a long dish she began picking asparagus in a lemony sauce from it, sucking the meat from the stalks, and licking her lips as she finished each stem of the vegetable.

He felt his member tingling as he watched her and quickly looked away, taking up next a small haunch of venison, tearing the meat from the bone with his strong white teeth. The venison was flavorful and chewy. He drank more wine. He could never recall in all his life eating with a naked woman. Well, why not? They were man and wife in the privacy of their own chambers. And then, unable to restrain himself, he casually pulled off the toweling around his loins.

The sound of the toweling hitting the floor caused Philippa to look up. Her eyes met his, sliding slowly down his long and lean body. Then she shrugged, and reached for a piece of capon. They were both still standing at the sideboard, not having bothered to sit in their hunger. Having satisfied themselves somewhat with the oysters, the meat, and the asparagus, they tore the warm cottage loaf apart. Philippa scooped some butter from the crock, smearing it over the bread with her thumb. Then to her surprise he took it from her, and pulling little pieces from the chunk he began to feed her. She reciprocated, putting bits of the cheddar cheese into his mouth. He sucked on her fingers, and she then sucked on his.

He took the bowl of strawberries, the bowl of clotted cream, and a small jug of honey and set them on the floor before the fire. Then reaching up he drew her down, and kissed her slowly before laying her on her back. Philippa watched him silently as he placed a dab of the clotted cream on each of her nipples, and topped it with a strawberry. He then smeared her torso with the cream and strawberries, and began to eat them one by one from her belly, licking her completely free of the cream. The two little fruits on her nipples he saved for last, sucking on her flesh until she was squirming.

Finally he spoke. "Did you like what I did to you earlier?" His hot breath tickled her ear.

She knew exactly to what he referred. "Aye," she said low. "But I am certain it is very wicked, Crispin."

"Aye," he drawled softly, "it is very wicked." He nibbled at her lips. "I can show you another way to be wicked, little one. Do you want to be wicked with me?"

She nodded eagerly, and then watched wide-eyed as he took the small jug of honey and dipped his partly swollen manhood into it. Drawing it out, he sat lightly atop her and pressed himself against her lips. They opened, and her pink tongue began to lick the honey from it, but because the thick sweet was beginning to drizzle with the warmth of his body he pushed himself into her mouth. For a moment Philippa looked startled, but then she began to suck on him until she had removed every vestige of the honey, and he had grown hard in the cavern of her mouth. She released him finally, and sliding down and between her legs he began to pump her fiercely.

Philippa's nails raked down his long back. She whimpered, and her whimpers grew into a moan which grew into a scream of total pleasure as he thrust himself back and forth, back and forth, back and forth, until her head was spinning wildly, and she was dizzy and weak with the hot pleasure coursing through her. I love him! I love him! she thought, but she would not say it, for he had not said it.

Their bodies were wet with the passion of their efforts. He ground himself deep into her love channel. He felt her shuddering as she reached the apex of her delight, and yet she did not cry her love for him. Was she incapable of that tender emotion, or had she just a whore's nature? He didn't know, and right now he didn't care. His juices burst forth again, leaving him weak and helpless to his love for her.

They remained before the fire for some time. Outside the dusk faded into evening. The birds ceased their calls, and the rain pattered gently down with only an occasional rumble of thunder or brief flash of lightning now. The earl of Witton finally got to his feet, and reaching down, pulled Philippa up. Together they walked into their bedchamber and fell into bed where they slept until well after dawn the next day.

Philippa awoke first, and heard the sounds of morning outside of their window. She lay quietly pondering the events of the previous evening. I have to go back to Friarsgate, she thought. I cannot bear not understanding all of this. I need my mother. She smiled to herself, thinking that she had never thought to hear herself say such a thing, but this love was totally confusing. She slipped from the bed, and walking across the chamber brought forth from the warm coals of the hearth the pitcher of water that Lucy had left them. Pouring some into the silver ewer, she washed herself free of the residue of their shared passion. Then she disposed of the water, throwing it out the window.

He stirred slowly, watching her as she opened her trunk and pulled on a clean chemise. Watched her as she sat down at the little table that held her female fripperies, and taking up her brush began to brush her long auburn hair, carefully working through the knots and tangles until her hair was a shining silken swath. "Good morrow, countess," he finally said.

Philippa turned, smiling. "Good morning, my lord. There is water for bathing." She gestured gracefully towards the other table.

"Did you not bathe me well last night, little one?" he said low.

She actually blushed. "My lord," she remonstrated with him.

He laughed. "The next time I shall drizzle honey on you, and lick it off."

"Crispin, you really are wicked," she said, but she was smiling with the hot memories of honey, and strawberries and cream.

The next few weeks were wonderful. They traveled his estate together on horseback. He made love to her in a pile of hay in a distant meadow, and almost had his bottom bee-stung for his trouble. Philippa had laughed so hard that she had wept. He explained the workings of his estates to her. They walked the three streets of Wittonsby, stopping at each cottage to greet their tenants and speak with them. The nights were filled with pleasure and passion. And then the world intruded upon them.

A messenger arrived at Brierewode. He wore the badge of Cardinal Wolsey. The earl of Witton was ordered to attend upon the cardinal at Hampton Court. The king was now on his summer progress in Wiltshire and Berkshire. The queen had gone to her favorite Woodstock. The king would come to Oxford in September to fetch the queen.

"It is almost mid-August," Philippa protested. "We must leave for the north if I am to be there for my sister's wedding. Why does he want you? Are you not finished with that part of your life?"

"I am," Crispin said, "but I cannot refuse the cardinal. He speaks with the king's voice, little one. I must go. We shall travel north as soon as I return."

"When will that be?" she demanded to know.

He shook his head. "I don't know. Why do you not prepare for our travels while I am away? Peter will pack for me."

"He is not coming with you?" she asked.

"The cardinal has some scheme or business he wishes to discuss with me, Philippa. I do not need a valet with me. I will ride quickly with my men, and return as quickly. The cardinal knows I cannot serve him any longer. If the truth be known I am not certain how long he will remain in favor. He has been the king's own man for many years now, little one," the earl told his wife. "No one retains a king's favor forever."

"If you are not back in seven days I shall travel north without you," Philippa said.

"You will remain here at Brierewode until I return, little one," he replied. "I have told you that you will go to your sister's wedding, and I always keep my promises. But if you disobey me, so much the worse for you, Philippa. I will be the master in my own house, madame. Do you understand me?"

The earl departed the following morning with the cardinal's messenger and a small troupe of his own men-at-arms for protection. Reaching Hampton Court, he was kept waiting for two days until the cardinal could see him. Wolsey was very busy in his master's service even as the king was on progress. Ushered into the cardinal's presence at last, the earl of Witton bowed and was waved to a chair. He sat, and waited.

"I need your eyes and ears again, my lord," the cardinal began.

"I can be of no help to your grace in the country," the earl replied, "and my estates are where I intend remaining. At least until my wife and I have heirs. I apologize, your grace, but I am past thirty, and I cannot get an heir on Philippa if I am not at Brierewode. The king would understand, I know."

"It is the king's business I am about, Witton," the cardinal said sharply. "What I say to you this day must not be repeated. Buckingham and Suffolk and several others are under suspicion. Some of those involved with them, men of lesser rank, are your neighbors. Henry Tudor has no male heir. There are some who would attempt to overthrow the Tudor throne and put another in its place. Buckingham descends from Edward III. He and his ilk have always been ambitious. And it is said by some that his claim is stronger than the king's."

"It would be foolish to voice such a thought aloud, your grace," the earl replied.

"Aye, but then the court is peopled by foolish men. You must be my eyes and ears in Oxford, my lord. I need a man I can be certain of, Crispin."

"Suffolk? But he is the king's friend. His brother-in-law," the earl mused.

The cardinal laughed a harsh laugh. "He married Mary Tudor without the king's permission, didn't he? And remained in France until his wife had gained her brother's forgiveness, didn't he? Suffolk has no loyalties except to himself."

"So all you seek of me is to report anything I hear which might cause the king difficulty, your grace?"

"That is all," the cardinal replied. "I did not dare trust my wishes to parchment lest it be read by the wrong people. Even I have spies in my household, although I do try to have them weeded out regularly. You are not the only one recalled to my secret service, my lord." Then he engaged the earl's gaze and said, "And how is your fair wife? Is she proving satisfactory? Was Melville worth the wench?"

The earl of Witton smiled, and nodded. "Aye, it was, and she is proving most satisfactory as a mate. Her mother and the queen taught her well."

The cardinal nodded. "Then go home, Witton, and my thanks for coming," he finished. "I know I can trust in you."

Crispin St. Claire stood up, bowed, and left the cardinal's privy chamber immediately. It was not yet the noon hour. There was no need to remain. He gathered his men up, and they took the road to Oxford. Arriving home several days later, however, the earl of Witton learned that his wife had departed two days previously for her mother's home at Friarsgate. He swore angrily, and Mistress Marian looked askance.

"My lord!" she exclaimed, having never heard him utter such foul words before. She waved to one of the servants in the hall to bring their master a goblet of wine.

The earl snatched it from the servant and drank it down. "How did she go?" he asked his housekeeper. "Who was with her?"

"Lucy and my brother among others, my lord, but they did ride with six men-at-arms. It was all she would take, and Peter had to insist at that. I do not know what possessed her ladyship, but from the moment you departed she grew more and more agitated. She told me that she had to see her mother. That she needed her mother, my lord. I think she would have gone the day after you left but that Lucy dissuaded her."

"What did she take with her?" the earl asked Mistress Marian, growing a little calmer now.

"She took nothing but a small saddlebag, my lord. She said that Friarsgate was not a place for fancy gowns, and she needed to get there quickly. She could not be kept by a baggage cart trailing behind her. What will she wear to her sister's wedding, my lord? I cannot believe the wedding will not be a grand one," Mistress Marian fretted.

"Lord Cambridge will supply her with a gown, I have not a doubt. His family, especially my wife, seem to rely upon him for such things."

"You have ridden long, my lord. Come to the board, and I will see that you are fed," the housekeeper coaxed her master.

"I must ride north," he said grimly.

"Aye, my lord, you must, but it will soon be dark. The days are shorter now than a few weeks ago," Mistress Marian said. "A good supper, and a good night's sleep in your own bed, my lord, and you will be ready to go in the morning." She gently drew him to the high board, signaling the servants to hurry to the kitchens for food.

"Ah, Marian, though she drives me to distraction I love her," the earl said softly.

"I know, my lord, and she loves you too," the housekeeper replied, seating him.

"She has never said it," the earl said mournfully.

"Have you told her that you love her, my lord?" Mistress Marian asked. "A woman will never say those words to a man unless he has said them to her first."

The earl put his head in his hands. "I am a fool," he groaned.

"Most men are, my lord," the housekeeper replied low, with the familiarity of a trusted and well-loved servant. "But she has not left you, my lord. And there is time to correct your omission."

"But why would she not wait?" the earl asked.

"I do not know," Mistress Marian responded, "but it was suddenly very necessary for her ladyship to leave Brierewode and go back to her mother. Now here is a nice hot rabbit pie for you. It's just come from the ovens. I want to see every bit of it eaten, my lord. And there is bread, and butter and cheese. And I think there might be an apple tart to finish the meal."

He looked up gratefully at her. "Tell the men we ride tomorrow for Cumbria."

"Yes, my lord," the housekeeper said with a small smile, and she bustled off.

She was right, of course. He felt better after a good meal. And even better in the morning after a sound sleep in his own bed. With Peter gone he had one of the other men pack for him, and he took one pack animal with them. Perhaps they might even catch up with his headstrong wife before she reached Friarsgate.

Philippa, however, was determined to reach her mother as quickly as possible. She rode hard, surprising the men with her, who had not thought such a dainty lady could manage such a trip without all the fripperies necessary to a woman's existence. One day the night caught up with them before they could reach the shelter of an inn or a religious house. They bedded down in a hayfield, sleeping in the haystacks, and there was no complaint from their mistress. At last they crossed into Cumbria, heading even further north. And then late one morning they topped a rise, and the lake lay below them while in the meadows below the vast flocks of Friarsgate browsed contentedly.

"Thank Gawd I can die in my own bed," Lucy sighed.

"You'll have to get down the hill first," Philippa laughed. It was just like she remembered it. Beautiful and peaceful. She pushed her horse forward.

"Your mother may be up at Claven's Carn," Lucy said.

"They can fetch her easily if she is," Philippa said in a determined voice.

But Rosamund was not in Scotland. She was at her own holding, and very surprised to see her eldest child so soon. "It's almost a month until Banon's wedding," she remarked, and then she said, "Welcome home, my darling! Where is this husband of yours of whom Tom speaks so highly? Indeed he gushes so about him that Logan is determined to dislike him." She hugged her daughter.

Nothing had changed, Philippa thought. Except for the two cradles by the hearth. She walked over to them and looked in. "My new brothers?"

"Aye. Are they not beautiful? Praise God, though they came from my womb at the same time they do not look much alike. There is a woman in our village with sons born as Tommy and Edmund were, but they are as alike as two peas in a pod." Her eye went past her daughter. "Lucy, you look exhausted. Welcome home. And who is this fine fellow with you?"

Peter stepped forward. "I am Peter, my lady, the earl's valet."

Rosamund nodded. "And just why are you here, Peter, but not your master?" she asked.

"I believe that is a question that her ladyship should answer, madame," the valet said politely, stepping back.

"Philippa?" Rosamund's face was serious with her concern.

"I warned him if he was not back in seven days that I should start north without him, mama. There is nothing more to it than that," Philippa answered her mother.

"And just where had your husband gone?" Rosamund persisted.

"To Hampton Court. The cardinal wished to see him," Philippa said. "Mama, I am tired, and I am filthy. I want my bath, and my bed."

"You have still not explained to me why you departed Brierewode without your husband. Why did you not wait for him?"

"And miss my sister's wedding?" Philippa cried. "Please do not treat me like a child, mama. I am a married woman, and the countess of Witton."

"Banon and Robbie will not be wed for several weeks, Philippa. You might have waited for the earl," Rosamund murmured calmly. "There was no need to come rushing. When did you get home from France?"

"Over a month ago," Philippa said.

Her mother nodded. "Go along then, my daughter, and the servants will bring your bath. Lucy, introduce Peter to the other servants, and show him where he may lay his head. Ah, here is Annie. Annie, run and find Maybel. Tell her Philippa is home." Rosamund looked and saw her daughter was already gone from the hall. "Lucy, attend me. Annie, find Maybel, and take Peter with you. He is the earl's servant."

When Annie had gone from the hall with Peter, Rosamund motioned to Lucy to sit down. "Now tell me," she said, "just what is this all about?"

"I am not certain, my lady. The marriage is a good one. The earl is the kindest of masters, and a good husband to my lady. But no sooner had he departed for Hampton Court than my lady began to fret. She said she was afraid if the cardinal kept the earl too long she would not be with her sister on her wedding day. She fussed, and she fumed, and then nothing would do but that we leave and ride posthaste for Friarsgate. We have no clothing but what we wore, my lady Rosamund. But I do not believe my mistress tells the truth. She thinks she does, but she does not."

Rosamund nodded. "She has been taking the draught each morning but for the days of her monthly flow?"

Lucy flushed. "Nay, my lady."

"Then she wants a child sooner than later? Well, I cannot disagree, for it is her duty to provide her husband with an heir. I know I was eager to when I married her father, may God assoil his good soul." Rosamund crossed herself.

"Nay, my lady, she wanted to wait so she could go back to court," Lucy said. "There was no opportunity for my mistress and her husband to cohabit in France. Our quarters were very close, and there was no privacy at all. She had to bathe in a chemise just like the queen. I didn't think it was necessary to give her your potion while we were there, but I gave her a drink of water mixed with celery seeds each morning so she would believe she had had the draught. And then when we returned from France my mistress began talking about perhaps having a child, and not going back to court since the queen had dismissed her from her service. I thought that there would be no need for the preventative then."

"But you continued to feed her the celery seed and water," Rosamund said softly.

"Yes, my lady Rosamund," Lucy responded. "When my mistress makes up her mind to something there is no reasoning with her. She is very stubborn. I thought, let God decide the matter, and I will not have to argue with her, or be a disobedient servant."

Rosamund laughed softly. "When did my daughter have her last bloody flux, Lucy? I will wager she has not had one since her return from France."

Lucy thought a moment, and then her eyes widened. "Oh, my lady, you are correct! She had her flow in Calais, but none since. Oh, my lady, what have I done?"

Rosamund nodded. "I will wager that Philippa is with child, Lucy, and the charming little fool is so wrapped up in herself and her husband that it has not occurred to her yet." She shook her head. "Tell me how angry the earl will be when he gets here?"

"You would have to ask Peter that," Lucy said. "All I've ever seen of him is goodness to my mistress, although she has sorely tried him at times."

Rosamund laughed again. "Do not tell her what I suspect, Lucy, nor anyone else either." She arose from her seat. "Watch my two bairns. I must go upstairs and deal with my oldest."

"Mama!" A young girl had come into the hall. She was tall and willowy, with long dark blond hair. "I am told Philippa is back."

"Aye, Bessie, she is. Come, and Lucy will tell you all. I must go upstairs and see your sister." She hurried from the hall.

"Well, she's home early for Banie's wedding," Elizabeth Meredith said. "What's her husband like, Lucy? Is he handsome and gallant? Is he rich?"

"How old are you now?" Lucy asked.

"I'll be thirteen my next birthday," Bessie said. "Now tell me everything, Lucy!"

"I thought you wasn't interested in all the goings-on of the fine ladies and gentlemen," Lucy teased.

"Well, I don't want to be one of them," Bessie said, "but it cannot harm me to learn about them. I'm not like my older sisters. I have no need to go to court and kneel to the high and the mighty. But hearing about them is like listening to a fairy tale."

"Going to court ain't no easy life, I can tell you," Lucy began.

Upstairs, Rosamund had gone to Philippa's bedchamber. Her daughter had finished her bath and was drying herself off as Rosamund entered the room. "I always felt better getting the dirt of the road off of me," she said. "Where is your hairbrush? I'll brush you dry, darling child."

"Here it is." Philippa handed the requested item to her mother. "Just let me get into a clean chemise. I left some from my last visit." She pulled out a silky garment from the chest at the foot of her bed, and drew it on. Then sitting next to her mother she let Rosamund brush and towel her long hair dry.

"Now tell me, Philippa," her mother said quietly as she brushed. "What is troubling you? And do not say naught. You did not dash pellmell to Friarsgate because of Banon's wedding."

"What is love?" Philippa burst out. "And how do you know you are in love? And why will he not say it to me after all these months?" She began to cry. "Oh, mama, I cannot explain it in a way which I understand, but I love him! Yet he does not love me! He is passionate, and tender, but he says nothing to me that would indicate that he loves me. Yet how can he make love to me the way he does, and not love me?"

"I don't believe he can," Rosamund responded calmly. "What is love, Philippa? It is the most elusive emotion in the world. It defies a rational explanation, but the very fact that you don't understand it, yet know in your heart that you love him, is your answer. As for your husband, I suspect if he is gentle and tender with you that he does indeed love you. But men are most reticent to say it aloud. More often than not it is up to the woman, but she must be very certain before she voices her emotions that they will be reciprocated. Consequently a woman is loath to cry love, and a man is no better. It is an age-old conundrum, Philippa."

"When we were in France I overheard a plot against the king, and I told Crispin. At first he was angry, and then I realized that his anger wasn't directed at me, but at himself. He was afraid for me, and that he had not been with me when I escaped the assassins," Philippa said.

Rosamund smiled, and put her daughter's hairbrush aside. "Aye, he loves you," she said.

"He must say it without my prompting or I shall never be certain," Philippa cried, and then she flung herself in Rosamund's arms and sobbed.

Rosamund held her daughter and caressed her tenderly. She was going to be a grandmother. There was absolutely no doubt in her mind that Philippa was with child. The wild emotional outbursts made her certain. Her elegant and sophisticated Philippa had fallen in love, and was going to have a baby. "Are you hungry?" she asked her daughter. "We're having rabbit stew for supper tonight."

"Nay, mama, I am just so tired. I needed to get here, find you, and now I feel better, but I am exhausted. I want to go to bed."

"Then you shall," her mother answered her soothingly. Standing, she helped Philippa into the bed and drew the coverlet over her. "Sleep well, my darling. You are safe home now. And your earl will be here soon, I am quite certain."

Two days later the earl of Witton arrived at Friarsgate. Lord Cambridge had been summoned from Otterly the day of Philippa's arrival, and Logan Hepburn had come over the border from Claven's Carn. Rosamund had decided that she would need every bit of help her family could give her to bring Philippa and Crispin to an understanding. At her first sight of her son-in-law Rosamund knew she was going to like him. And she could also see he was perfect for Philippa.

"How did you know, you old dear?" she whispered to Thomas Bolton.

"It's an instinct," he murmured softly, and then he moved forward, his hands outstretched to greet the earl of Witton. "My dear boy, how delightful to see you once again. May I present your mother-in-law, the lady of Friarsgate. Cousin, this is Philippa's husband."

The earl took Rosamund's hand, and bowing, kissed it. "Madame," he said.

"You are most welcome to Friarsgate, my lord," Rosamund told him.

"And Rosamund's husband, Logan Hepburn, the laird of Claven's Carn," Lord Cambridge continued smoothly.

The two men eyed each other warily, and shook hands.

"Come into the hall," Rosamund invited Crispin St. Claire, and she took his arm to lead him into the house.

"Where is my wife?" he asked her.

"In her chamber," Rosamund said with a hint of laughter in her voice. "Please don't be too angry with her, my lord. She had a sudden urge to see her mother. Young wives can be like that. I sent her sister up to fetch her when we saw you coming."

"I returned to Brierewode just two days after she had gone," he said. "I forbade her to travel without me. Yet she deliberately disobeyed me."

Rosamund shook her head. "You have not a great deal of experience with women, my lord, do you? You must never forbid a woman, for if you do, she is certain to do exactly what you told her not to do." She laughed softly. "You love her very much, don't you? Sit down. Sit down."

"How is it that you can see that but your daughter cannot, madame?" he asked her despairingly. "And I question if she is even capable of love herself."

"She loves you very much," Rosamund told him quietly, and handed him a goblet of sweet red wine. "We have spoken more these past two days, Philippa and I, than we have in many years."

"Then why will she not say it?" he asked her.

"Why will you not say it?" Rosamund countered, smiling.

"Why, madame, I am a man," he replied with all seriousness.

"And she a courtier who has been taught never to admit to her emotions unless the gentleman in question does first," Rosamund explained to him.

"God's bloody wounds!" the earl swore.

"I could not say it better myself, my lord," Rosamund told him.

"Mama." Elizabeth Meredith was by her mother's side. "Philippa says she will not come down. As usual she is being a mutton-headed little fool. My stepfather has gone to fetch her for you," the young girl finished with a grin.

"Oh, Bessie, you bad thing!" Maybel, who had joined them, said laughing.

"What is it?" asked Lord Cambridge.

"Bessie sent Logan up to fetch Philippa down, for she will not come," Rosamund told him.

"Oh lord!" Thomas Bolton said, but he was grinning.

A shriek pierced the hall, and then another, and another.

"It sounds like a murder is being committed," the earl said.

"Nay, 'tis just Philippa's stepfather bringing her down into the hall," Rosamund said, still laughing.

The laird of Claven's Carn entered the room, Philippa slung over his shoulder. Walking up to the earl he dumped the girl down into Crispin's lap. With a yelp like that of a scalded cat Philippa was on her feet. She swung on the laird, her fist making contact with his shoulder. Logan Hepburn burst out laughing, and Philippa turned, raging at her husband.

"Are you going to permit this damned Scots savage to treat me so, my lord?" she demanded furiously. Her usually neat hair was loose and swirling about with her movements.

"Good morrow, madame. As I recall, the last time we spoke I told you to wait until I returned from Hampton Court to make this journey," he said.

"Was I to miss my sister's wedding because of the cardinal's politicking?" Philippa said.

"The wedding is not for another few weeks, madame," he remarked.

"Very well then, my lord, I needed to see my mother," Philippa said.

"Why?" he asked her. "What was so important that you could not wait for me?"

"I needed to ask her about love," Philippa said, "and why you do not love me." Her hazel eyes were wet with unshed tears.

"What in the name of all that is holy makes you think that I don't love you?" the earl said, outraged.

"You have never said it!" Philippa wailed, the tears now flowing.

"God's bloody wounds, wench, do you think I came galloping up to Cumbria from Oxfordshire because I don't love you? Of course I love you! I adore you! You are so lovely that to look at you hurts my heart. You are braver than any woman I have ever known. The thought of losing you is the darkest thought I could think, Philippa. I love you! Never doubt it, little one."

"Oh, Crispin, and I love you!" Philippa sobbed, and flung herself into his arms.

"Jesu, Mary!" Elizabeth Meredith groaned, rolling her eyes.

The earl and his wife were kissing, and the others smiled, pleased that the matter was now settled.

"Do not swear, Bessie," Rosamund said. "It is not ladylike. Now let us all gather around the hearth, for I have something to say." She looked directly at her eldest child. "I am, it seems, going to become a grandmother in the spring. You are with child, Philippa. Did you not realize it?"

Philippa's mouth fell open. She made to speak, and then seeing a warning in her mother's eye she closed her mouth.

"Of course it is your first child, and you would be less apt to pay attention to the little signs than a woman of experience, Philippa," Rosamund continued. "I shall explain all to you in the privacy of my chambers later. Well, son-in-law, what say you? Your bride is doing her duty, and you are to have an heir."

"Madame," he replied, "I am delighted, and astounded in turn," and he kissed his wife a long slow kiss. "I told you we made a child that night," he murmured against her mouth, and Philippa blushed.

"Now we must speak on the matter of the Friarsgate inheritance. Philippa, it is yours and your husband's by right. Now you are to have a child. Will you not accept your rightful place here, my daughter?"

"Madame, I speak for both my wife and myself when I tell you that we are grateful for your generosity, but we do not want Friarsgate," the earl said.

"You must accept this, mama," Philippa said. "I'm sorry, for I know how much you love your home, but I do not. Brierewode is where I belong."

"But a second son could have these lands," Rosamund persisted.

"Nay," Philippa responded. "My second son when he is born will be for the court one day. He shall begin his career as a page, and who knows to what heights he may aspire."

"And you agree with her, my lord?" Rosamund asked the earl.

He nodded. "I do, madame. Both Philippa and I have served the royal household in our own capacities. We are creatures of the court as our children will undoubtedly be one day. Cumbria and this vast estate of yours is not for us. We could not give it the time needed to hus-band it, and it is much too far from London."

Rosamund sighed deeply. "Then what has it all been for?" she said as if she were speaking to herself. "I have watched over Friarsgate my whole lifetime. When I lost Owein Meredith's son and then he died, I pinned all my hopes on you, Philippa. Banon has Otterly, and does not want Friarsgate either. What am I going to do? I am more at Claven's Carn these days, for that is where my Hepburn sons must be raised. What am I to do, and who will care for Friarsgate now?"

"I will," Elizabeth Meredith said in a strong voice, and they all turned to look at her, surprised. She was the youngest of Owein Meredith's daughters. The baby. The little girl who tagged along, and ran barefooted through the meadows chasing the sheep. But looking at her they all realized that she was no longer a child. She was a young girl on the brink of womanhood. "I will look after Friarsgate, mama, for I love it every bit as much as you do. I have never wanted to go to court, or be anywhere else except here. This is my home. These are my lands. Friarsgate should be mine. You cannot give it to the Hepburns. Friarsgate must remain English."

Rosamund was astounded. For the first time in a long while she ac-tually looked at her youngest daughter, and when she did she saw Owein Meredith. Owein who had been so dutiful in his service to the Tudors. Owein who had loved Friarsgate from the moment he had laid eyes upon it.

"Aye, Friarsgate must be English," Logan Hepburn agreed. "My boys would not know what to do with the sheep anyway. The lass is right, Rosamund."

"Aye, she is right," Lord Cambridge said. "If Philippa and Banon do not want Friarsgate it should be Bessie's, and no one else's." He put his arm about the girl. "What say you, Bessie? Will you be the heiress of Friarsgate as your mother was before you?"

The girl nodded, and then she added, "And do not call me Bessie. It is a child's name, and I am not a child. I am Elizabeth Meredith, the future lady of Friarsgate, and I will not answer to Bessie ever again."

"Then let us have three cheers for the heiress of Friarsgate," Philippa said, smiling, and the hall echoed thrice. "Hip Hip Hoorah! Hip Hip Hoorah! Hip Hip Hoorah!"

Epilogue

$\mathcal{T}$he wedding of Banon Meredith to Robert Neville took place on a warm late September day. As Banon was Thomas Bolton's heiress to Otterly the celebration took place there. Helping her sister to dress, Philippa had difficulty drawing the laces on Banon's pale blue satin bodice closed.

"Are you gaining weight already?" she teased her sibling.

Banon turned her head and grinned at her senior. "I am with child," she said proudly.

"But you aren't wed!" Philippa gasped, shocked.

"I will be in another hour," Banon laughed. "It was a lovely summer here, sister. Rob and I enjoyed ourselves immensely. And Uncle Thomas was kind enough to turn a blind eye, bless him."

"What if your Neville had cried off?" Philippa said primly. "Remember the cow and the cream?"

Banon laughed again. "Rob loves me, and his family loves the fact that I am wealthy, and likely to grow wealthier as the years go by. No one will be surprised by an early spring bairn, Philippa. Just pray I deliver a son, for I want a son for Otterly, and I know Uncle Thomas would be as pleased as anyone should that bairn be a lad."

Philippa shook her head. "You are too wild a girl, sister. I hope you will temper your ways now that you are to be first a wife, and then a mother. You want no gossip."

"Always the perfect courtier," Banon replied, and then to Philippa's surprise she kissed her sister's cheek. "Who know, sister, I may have a child who falls in love with the court even as you did. And if I do I shall send that child to my sister, the countess of Witton, who will introduce her nephew or niece into the exalted ranks of the aristocracy."

Philippa smiled, and then she grew wistful. "I cannot believe that we are both wed, and you to be a mother. Our girlhood is indeed over."

"Ah, but we still have Bessie, don't we?" Banon said. "Or I should say our younger sister, Elizabeth, the heiress of Friarsgate."

"Who would have thought it would all end up like this," Philippa noted. "Me a countess, you the heiress to Otterly, and Bessie the next heiress of Friarsgate. She is a wild child, I fear, but as you are nearer to her than I, Banon, you must see she learns some manners and graces, or God only knows who will have her as a wife. Certainly no gentleman, and mama would not like to see Friarsgate in the hands of the wrong man one day."

"Shows how little you know or understand about B— Elizabeth," Banon replied. "She'll never allow any husband to tell her how to manage Friarsgate. She'd sooner go to her grave a maiden. And her manners and graces are everything you would expect of a lady, sister. She just doesn't choose to display them regularly. And she particularly enjoys annoying you, for she thinks you are too high and mighty for a lass reared in Cumbria. Watch her today. You'll see. Now get those laces as best you can. I'll not keep my Neville waiting at the altar. When is your bairn due?"

"The middle of March, mama says. Crispin says once we get home we must remain home," Philippa told her sister.

"And my bairn will come at the end of March or the beginning of April," she said. "Does that mean you won't go to court for the Christmas revels?" Her hand touched her auburn hair, which was unbound. Then she set a circlet of Michaelmas daisies upon her head.

"Nay," Philippa replied. "We will remain home at Brierewode, but I am not unhappy. The thought of spending the autumn and the winter with Crispin makes me happier than I ever thought to be. I will return to court one day. But not right away."

"You do love him," Banon said softly.

"Aye, I do," Philippa admitted with a small smile. Then she said, "Shall I call Uncle Thomas now? Are you ready?"

Banon nodded. "I'm ready," she responded.

And Lord Cambridge came, and proudly led his heiress from his house to the little church at Otterburn, his village. The villagers lined the road waving and cheering as the bride made her way to the church where she was united in holy matrimony to her Neville. And afterwards at the wedding feast Banon's stepfather, the laird of Claven's Carn, danced a sensuous Scottish dance with his wife, and seeing the intensity between them Philippa wondered if, despite her mother's good intentions, there would be another Hepburn son born sooner than later.

Crispin, seated next to her, took her hand in his. "A few more days, little one, and then we go home," he told her.

"Aye," Philippa agreed. "I look forward to the months to come."

"I look forward to the years to come," he said with a slow smile. Reaching out he put his hand on her belly. "Is it a lad, little one?"

"Only God knows the answer to that, but if it is not, we shall make another, and another, until we get it right, my lord," Philippa told him with a mischievous smile. "And if it is, he will need brothers and sisters. Our duty is clear, my lord."

"I can see you have our life together well planned," the earl told his countess. "But what of the court, Philippa? Will you go back?"

"One day," Philippa said, "but the queen was right when she told me that my duty was to make a family. Family is the greatest gift God gives us, Crispin."

And in the spring of 1521 the countess of Witton presented her husband with their first son who was called Henry Thomas St. Claire.

And three weeks afterwards Banon Meredith Neville bore a daughter who was christened Katherine Rose. And at Friarsgate Elizabeth Meredith celebrated her thirteenth birthday on the twenty-third of May knowing that when she turned fourteen her mother would formally turn Friarsgate over to her. She wanted no husband, no man to tell her what to do. She had already made Friarsgate her own domain, and it was all she ever wanted. But Elizabeth Meredith was yet young, and though she knew it not, fate had already planned her future.

ABOUT THE AUTHOR

Bertrice Small is a *New York Times* bestselling author and the recipient of numerous writing awards. In keeping with her profession, she lives in the oldest English-speaking town in the state of New York, founded in 1640, and works in a light-filled studio surrounded by the paintings of her favorite cover artist, Elaine Duillo. Because she believes in happy endings, Bertrice Small has been married to the same man, her hero, George, for forty-one years. They have a son, a daughter-in-law, and three adorable grandchildren. Longtime readers will be happy to know that Nicki the Cockatiel flourishes along with his fellow housemates, Pookie, the long-haired greige and white feline, Honeybun, the petite orange lady cat with the cream-colored paws, and Finnegan, the naughty black kitty.